Born in Peru and raised in Chile, **Isabel Allende** is the author of numerous bestselling and critically acclaimed books, including *The House of the Spirits*, *Daughter of Fortune*, *Paula*, and *My Invented Country*. Her books have been translated into more than 35 languages and have sold more than 65 million copies worldwide. *The Japanese Lover* was an international and *New York Times* hardback bestseller. Isabel Allende lives in California.

Praise for *The Japanese Lover*

'Isabel Allende is a master storyteller. *The Japanese Lover* is Allende at the top of her game. When it comes to love Isabel writes from the heart to the heart and I feel all the richer for having been touched by her'
Santa Montefiore, bestselling author of
The Beekeeper's Daughter

'Themes of ageing and identity dominate this highly entertaining tale of a great passion kept secret for decades ... A gripping and tender tribute to the human heart'　　　　*Mail on Sunday*, Best Books of 2015

'Masterfully constructed and beautifully written, Allende's tale of thwarted but unquenched passion is both heart-breaking and heart-warming'
Daily Mail

'Isabel Allende is the most romantic of writers and this is a novel of high romance and lush sensuality, unashamedly about the enduring power of love and ending on a note of grace'　　　　　　　　　*The Times*

'Gloriously romantic, funny, intelligent and wise. Allende's characters find happiness and solace in friendship, botany, the strokes of a *sumi-e* painting, and above all in every kind of love'
Rosamund Lupton, bestselling author of *Sister*

'A fiercely intelligent and deeply moving story that is a tender examination of love, morality and mortality. It is spellbinding. No other word for it. I turned the pages hungrily. A luminous love story that is haunting and resonates in the heart'　　　Kate Furnivall, author of *The Russian Concubine*

'Allende's poetic prose balances the dark themes of war, xenophobia and inner conflict. It is a novel that sweeps through time, spanning generations and continents, to explore questions of identity, abandonment, redemption and fate. A tale of family secrets, human frailty and resilience, it is an uplifting masterpiece'

The Lady

'Allende skilfully weaves a tapestry of stories ... An enlightening and moving reflection on the ageing process ... For me, the best barometer of a book is how I feel when I turn the final page. If, like me, you like to finish with a lump in your throat and a head full of characters you care about, then this is for you'

Stylist

'An against-the-odds love story that spans cultures and decades but shies away from sentimentality'

Red

'Bittersweet'

Sunday Mirror

'The vivid description of passion and loss that maps out Alma's life is so heart-warming that I couldn't hold back the tears'

Essentials

'Over the course of this spare but intricately plotted novel, Allende reveals a love affair that's been hidden for years'

Sunday Express

'Allende highlights a dark chapter in America's history and juggles her saga's different elements with a great deal of skill'

Sunday Times

'Allende's magical and sweeping tale focuses on two survivors of separation and loss'

Publisher's Weekly

'Allende is a dazzling storyteller, with a wry, sometimes dark wit and a great eye for society's changing fashions'

National, UAE

'Believable and affecting'

Boston Globe

'There's nothing cloying about this unabashedly sweet story – and nothing unambitious about it, either. Allende sweeps across the second half of the twentieth century ... *The Japanese Lover* is, despite its fearless engagement with horrors both national and personal, a story of genuine and refreshing generosity'

Washington Post

ISABEL ALLENDE

The Japanese Lover

Translated by Nick Caistor and Amanda Hopkinson

SCRIBNER

LONDON NEW YORK TORONTO SYDNEY NEW DELHI

Originally published as *El Amante Japonés* in 2015 in Spain by
Penguin Random House Grupo Editorial, SAU
First published in the USA by Atria Books, an imprint of Simon & Schuster Inc., 2015
First published in Great Britain by Scribner, an imprint of Simon & Schuster UK Ltd, 2015
First paperback edition published by Scribner, 2016
This paperback edition published 2018
A CBS COMPANY

3 5 7 9 10 8 6 4 2

Simon & Schuster UK Ltd
1st Floor
222 Gray's Inn Road
London WC1X 8HB

www.simonandschuster.co.uk

Simon & Schuster Australia, Sydney
Simon & Schuster India, New Delhi

A CIP catalogue record for this book
is available from the British Library

ISBN 978-1-4711-8152-8

Printed and bound by CPI Group (UK) Ltd, Croydon, CR0 4YY

MIX
Paper from
responsible sources
FSC® C020471

To my parents, Panchita and Ramón

Pause, shadow of my elusive love,
image of my most dear enchanter,
Beautiful illusion for whom I die gladly
Sweet fiction for whom I live sadly.

—SOR JUANA INÉS DE LA CRUZ

The
Japanese
Lover

LARK HOUSE

When Irina Bazili began working at Lark House in 2010, she was twenty-three years old but already had few illusions about life. Since the age of fifteen she had drifted from one job, one town, to another. She could not have imagined she would find a perfect niche for herself in that senior residence, or that over the next three years she would come to be as happy as in her childhood, before fate took a hand. Founded in the mid-twentieth century to offer shelter with dignity to elderly persons of slender means, for some unknown reason from the beginning it had attracted left-wing intellectuals, oddballs, and second-rate artists. Lark House had undergone many changes over the years but still charged fees in line with each resident's income, the idea being to create a certain economic and racial diversity. In practice, all the residents were white and middle class, and the only diversity was between freethinkers, spiritual searchers, social and ecological activists, nihilists, and some of the few hippies still alive in the San Francisco Bay Area.

At Irina's first interview, the director of the community, Hans Voigt, pointed out that she was too young for a job with such responsibility, but since they had a vacancy they needed to fill urgently, she could stay until they found someone more suitable. Irina thought the same could be said of him: he looked like a chubby little boy going prematurely bald, someone who was out of his depth running an establishment of this sort. As time went by, she realized that the initial impression of Voigt could be deceiving, at a certain distance and in poor light: in fact, he was fifty-four years old and had proved himself to be an excellent administrator. Irina assured him that her lack of qualifications was more than compensated for by the experience she had of dealing with old people in her native Moldova.

Her shy smile softened the director's heart. He forgot to ask her for a reference and instead began outlining her duties, which could be quickly summarized: to make life easier for the second- and third-level residents. Irina would not be working with anyone on the first level, because they lived independently as tenants in an apartment building. Nor would she be working with those on level four—the aptly named Paradise—because they were awaiting their transfer to heaven and spent most of the time dozing, and thus did not require the kind of assistance she was there to provide. Irina's duties were to accompany the residents on their visits to doctors, lawyers, and accountants; to help them with their medical and tax forms; to take them on shopping expeditions; and to perform various other tasks. Her only link with the clients in Paradise, Voigt told her, would be to plan their funerals, but for that she would receive specific instructions, because the wishes of the dying did not always coincide with those of their families. Lark House residents tended to have myriad religious beliefs, which made their funerals rather complicated ecumenical affairs.

Voigt explained that only the domestic staff, the care and health assistants, were obliged to wear a uniform. There was however a tacit dress code for the rest of the employees; respect and good taste were the order of the day when it came to clothes. For example, he said emphatically, the T-shirt printed with Malcolm X's face that Irina was wearing was definitely inappropriate. In fact it wasn't Malcolm X but Che Guevara, but Irina didn't tell him this because she assumed that Hans Voigt would never have heard of the guerrilla leader who fifty years after his heroic exploits was still worshipped in Cuba and by a handful of radical followers in Berkeley, where she was living. The T-shirt had cost two dollars in a used clothing store, and was almost new.

"No smoking on the premises," the director warned her.

"I don't smoke or drink, sir."

"Is your health good? That's important when you're dealing with old people."

"Yes."

"Anything special I ought to know about you?"

"Well, I'm addicted to fantasy videos and novels. You know, like Tolkien, Neil Gaiman, Philip Pullman."

"What you do in your free time is your business, young lady, just as long as you stay focused at work."

"Of course. Listen, sir, if you give me a chance you'll see I know how to get along with elderly people. You won't regret it," the young woman said with feigned self-assurance.

Once the formal interview in his office was concluded, Voigt showed her around the premises, which housed some two hundred and fifty people, with an average age of eighty-five. Lark House had once been the magnificent property of a chocolate magnate, who not only bequeathed it to the city but left a generous donation to finance its upkeep. It consisted of the main house, a pretentious mansion where the offices, communal areas, library, dining room, and workshops were situated, and a row of pleasant redwood tile buildings that fitted in well with the ten acres of grounds, which looked wild but were in fact carefully tended by a host of gardeners. The independent apartments and the buildings housing the second- and third-level residents were linked by wide, enclosed walkways, which allowed wheelchairs to circulate sheltered from the extremes of climate, but were glassed in on both sides to provide a view of nature, the best solace for the troubles of all ages. Paradise, a detached concrete building, would have looked out of place were it not for the fact it was completely overgrown with ivy. The library and games room were open day and night, the beauty salon kept flexible hours, and the workshops provided a variety of classes from painting to astrology for those who still longed for pleasant surprises in their future. The Shop of Forgotten Objects, staffed by volunteer ladies, offered for sale clothing, furniture, jewelry, and other treasures cast off by the residents, or left behind by the deceased.

"We have an excellent cinema club and show films three times a week in the library," Voigt told her.

"What kind of films?" asked Irina, hoping they might contain vampires or science fiction.

"A committee chooses them, and they prefer crime movies, especially Tarantino. There's a certain fascination with violence in here, but don't worry, they're well aware it's fiction and that the actors will reappear safe and sound in other films. Let's call it a safety valve. Several of our guests fantasize about killing somebody, usually a family member."

"Me too," said Irina without hesitation.

Thinking she must be joking, Voigt laughed indulgently. He appreciated a sense of humor almost as much as he did patience among his staff.

Squirrels and an unusually large number of deer roamed freely among the ancient trees of the grounds, Voigt explained, adding that the does gave birth to and raised their young until they could fend for themselves. The grounds also served as a bird sanctuary, above all for skylarks, whose presence there had given the facility its name: Lark House. There were several cameras strategically placed to monitor the animals in their habitat and also any residents who might wander off or suffer an accident, but Lark House had no strict security measures. By day the main gates remained open, with only a couple of unarmed guards patrolling the grounds. These two retired policemen, aged seventy and seventy-four, offered more than adequate protection, since no thief in his right mind would waste time on penniless old folks.

Voigt and Irina passed a pair of women in wheelchairs, a group carrying easels and paint boxes to an open-air art class, and several residents out exercising dogs as careworn as them. The property adjoined the bay, and when the tide came in it was possible to go kayaking, which some of the residents not yet disabled by their infirmities were happy to do. This is how I would like to live, thought Irina, taking deep breaths of the sweet aroma of pines and laurels. She couldn't help comparing these pleasant surroundings to the sordid dives she had drifted through since the age of fifteen.

"Last but not least, Miss Bazili, I should mention the two

ghosts, because I'm sure that will be the first thing our Haitian staff will tell you about."

"I don't believe in ghosts, Mr. Voigt."

"Congratulations. Neither do I. The ones in Lark House are a young woman wearing a pink gauze dress, and a three-year-old child. The woman is Emily, the chocolate magnate's daughter. Poor Emily died of grief after her son drowned in the pool at the end of the 1940s. It was then that the magnate abandoned the house and created the Lark House Foundation."

"Did the boy drown in the pool you showed me?"

"Yes, but no one else has died there that I know of."

Irina soon changed her mind about ghosts, realizing that Emily and her son weren't the only resident spirits. She was to discover that many of the old folk were permanently accompanied by their dead.

Early the next morning, Irina arrived at work in her best pair of jeans and a discreet T-shirt. She quickly confirmed that the atmosphere at Lark House was relaxed without being negligent. It was more like a college than an old people's home. The food was as good as that of any reasonable Californian restaurant, and organic as far as possible. The cleaning staff did a thorough job, and the health aides and nurses were as cheerful as could be expected under the circumstances. It took her only a few days to learn the names and quirks of her colleagues and the residents in her care. The handful of Spanish and French phrases she memorized helped win over the staff, who came almost exclusively from Mexico, Guatemala, and Haiti. Although what they earned did not correspond to the hard work they put in, very few of them went around with long faces.

"You have to spoil the grannies a bit, but always treat them with respect. The same goes for the grandpas, but you need to watch out for them, because some of them get up to mischief," she was told by Lupita Farias, a stocky woman with the features of an Olmec statue who was head of the cleaning staff. Having worked at Lark House for thirty-two years and having access to every room, Lupita knew all the inhabitants intimately. She had learned about their lives, could see at a glance what was wrong with them, and accompanied them in their sorrows.

"Watch out for depression, Irina. That's very common here. If you notice that somebody seems isolated or very sad, if they stay in bed or stop eating, come and find me right away, okay?"

"What do you do in those cases, Lupita?"

"It depends. I stroke them, and they always like that, because old people don't have anyone who touches them, and I get them hooked on a TV series, because nobody wants to die before the final episode. Some of them find comfort in prayer, but there are lots of atheists here, and they don't pray. What's most important is not to leave them on their own. If I'm not around, go and see Cathy. She knows what to do."

Dr. Catherine Hope, a second-level resident, had been the first person to welcome Irina on behalf of the community. At sixty-eight, she was the youngest resident. Ever since being confined to a wheelchair she had opted for the help and company that Lark House offered. She had been living there a couple of years and during that time had become the life and soul of the place.

"The elderly are the most entertaining people in the world," she eventually told Irina. "They have lived a lot, say whatever they like, and couldn't care less about other people's opinion. You'll never get bored here. Our residents are well educated, and if they're in good health they keep on learning and experimenting. This community stimulates them and they can avoid the worst scourge of old age: loneliness."

Irina knew from newspaper reports about the progressive spirit of the Lark House residents. There was a waiting list of several years for admission, which would have been much longer if many of the candidates had not passed away before it was their turn. The old folks in the home were conclusive proof that age, despite all its limitations, does not stop one from having fun and taking part in the hubbub of life. Several of the residents who were active members of Seniors for Peace spent their Friday mornings in street protests at the aberrations and injustices in the world, especially those committed by the American empire, for which they felt responsible. These activists, among whom was an old lady aged a hundred and one, met up in the northern corner of the square opposite the police station with their canes, walkers, and wheelchairs. They held up banners against war or global warming, while the public showed their support by honking their car horns or signing petitions that these furious elders stuck under their noses. The protesters had appeared on television on more than one occasion, while the police were made to look ridiculous as they tried to disperse them with threats of tear gas that never materialized. Clearly moved, Voigt had shown Irina a plaque in the park in honor of a ninety-six-year-old musician, who had died of a seizure with his boots on in broad daylight during a 2006 protest against the war in Iraq.

Irina had grown up in a Moldovan village that was inhabited only by old people and children. She thought of her own grandparents and, as so often in recent years, regretted having abandoned them. Lark House gave her the opportunity to give to others what she hadn't been able to give them, and she kept this in mind as she began looking after those in her care. She soon won the residents over, including several on the first level, the independent ones.

From the start, Alma Belasco had caught her attention. She stood out from the other women thanks not only to her aristocratic bearing but to the magnetic force field that seemed to separate her from the rest of humanity. Lupita insisted that the Belasco woman did not fit in at Lark House and would not last long: any day now the same chauffeur who had brought her in a Mercedes-Benz would come and take her away again. And yet the months went by and this didn't happen. Irina did no more than observe Alma Belasco from a distance, because Hans Voigt had instructed her to focus on people from the second and third levels, and not to get distracted by the independents. Besides, Irina had more than enough to do in looking after her own clients—they were not to be called patients—and learning the ins and outs of her new job. As part of her training, she had to study the videos of recent funerals: a Buddhist Jewish woman and a repentant agnostic. For her part, Alma Belasco would not have paid any attention to Irina if circumstances had not briefly turned the young woman into the most noteworthy member of the community.

FRENCHIE

*I*n Lark House, where there was a depressing majority of women, Jacques Devine was considered the star attraction, the only heartthrob among the twenty-eight male residents. He was known as Frenchie, not because he had been born in France, but because of his exquisite manners—he held the door open for the ladies, pulled their chairs back for them, and never went around with his fly unzipped—and because he could dance, despite his fossilized spine. At the age of ninety he walked with a straight back thanks to the rods and screws that had been surgically attached to it. He still sported some of his curly head of hair and knew how to play cards, at which he cheated shamelessly. He was sound in body, apart from the usual arthritis, high blood pressure, and deafness inevitable in the winter of life, and quite lucid, although not sufficiently to recall whether he had had lunch or not. That was why he was on the second level, where he received all the help he needed. He had arrived in Lark House with his third wife, but she had only survived for a few weeks before being run over in the street by an absentminded cyclist.

Frenchie's day began early. He took a shower, shaved, and got dressed with the help of Jean Daniel, his Haitian aide. He would make his way across the parking lot leaning on his cane, keeping an eye out for cyclists, and continue to the corner Starbucks for the first of his five daily cups of coffee. Divorced once and twice a widower, he had never lacked lady admirers, whom he seduced with his magical charms. On one recent occasion he had calculated he had fallen in love sixty-seven times. He wrote the number down in his notebook so that he wouldn't forget it, as the faces and names of these lucky ladies were fading fast in his memory. He had several legitimate children, as well as one from a clandestine romance with someone whose name he couldn't remember, and any number of nephews and nieces, all of them ungrateful wretches who were only counting the days for him to depart this world so that they could inherit. There was talk of a small fortune amassed boldly and with few scruples. He himself admitted without the slightest hint of remorse that he had spent time in prison, where he had obtained the pirate tattoos adorning his arms, although flabby muscles, age spots, and wrinkles had blurred the images. He had also won considerable amounts speculating with the guards' savings.

Although the attentions of several Lark House ladies left him little room for any amorous adventures, Jacques was fascinated by Irina from the first moment he saw her going around with her clipboard and pert behind. She had not a drop of Caribbean blood, which made her voluptuous backside even more of a feat of nature, he would tell everyone after his first martini of the evening, astonished that no one else had noticed it. He had spent his prime doing business between Puerto Rico and Venezuela, and it was then that he had become so keen on appreciating women from the rear. The epic buttocks of those distant days had become fixed forever in his mind's eye. He dreamed of them, and saw them everywhere, even in such an unlikely spot as Lark House and in someone as skinny as Irina. His aimless final days were suddenly filled with this belated, all-encompassing love that wreaked havoc with his tranquil routines. Soon after they met, he showed how besotted he was with the gift of a topaz and diamond scarab, one of the few of his dead wives' jewels that had escaped his descendants' clutches. Irina refused to accept it, but her refusal sent his blood pressure shooting sky-high, so that she was forced to spend the whole night with him in the emergency ward. Hooked up to an IV drip, Jacques declared his undemanding, platonic love for her. Sighing and lamenting, he said he only wanted her company so that he could regale his eyes with her youth and beauty, hear her enchanting voice, and imagine that she loved him too, even if it was only like a father. Or even a great-grandfather.

The following evening, back at Lark House, while Jacques was enjoying his ritual martini, Irina, her eyes red rimmed and with dark circles beneath them from lack of sleep, went to find Lupita to confide the mess she was in.

"There's nothing new about that, child. We're always discovering the residents in someone else's bed. And not just the grandpas; the old women too. With so few men around, they have to make do with whatever they can find. Everybody needs company."

"With Mr. Devine it's platonic love, Lupita."

"I have no idea what that is, but if it's what I think, then don't you believe it. Frenchie has a penis implant, a plastic sausage that inflates with a pump hidden between his balls."

"What on earth are you saying, Lupita?" said Irina, laughing out loud.

"You heard me. I swear it's true. I haven't seen it, but Frenchie demonstrated how it works to Jean Daniel. It's amazing."

The good woman told Irina what she had observed during the many years she had worked at Lark House: that in itself age doesn't make anyone better or wiser, but only accentuates what they have always been.

"A person who is tightfisted won't become generous with age, Irina; they only become more miserly. I'm sure Devine was a rake, and that's why he's a dirty old man now."

Since she could not return the scarab brooch to her suitor, Irina took it to Hans Voigt. The director told her it was strictly forbidden to accept tips and gifts. This rule did not apply to the possessions Lark House received from dying residents, or to the donations accepted under the counter so as to allow a family member to jump the queue, but these matters were not discussed. The director took the hideous topaz insect, promising to return it to its rightful owner. In the meantime he would keep it in a drawer in his office.

A week later, Jacques presented Irina with a hundred and sixty dollars in twenty-dollar bills. This time she went straight to Lupita, who was in favor of simple solutions: she restored it to the cigar box where the beau kept his cash, certain he wouldn't remember having taken the money out or how much was in there. This allowed Irina to solve the problem of his tips, but she could not prevent Jacques sending her passionate love letters, inviting her to dine in expensive restaurants, or using a string of pretexts to summon her to his room, where he boasted about conquests that had never happened, and finally proposed marriage. Normally so skilled in the arts of seduction, Frenchie had lapsed back into a painful adolescent bashfulness, so that instead of making his declaration in person, he gave her a perfectly comprehensible letter, written on his computer. The envelope contained two pages full of circumlocutions, metaphors, and repetitions, which all amounted to: Irina had restored his energy and his will to live; he could offer her a wonderful lifestyle, in Florida for example, where the sun was always warm; and that when she became a widow she would have no money problems. Whichever way she looked at it, he wrote, it would be to her advantage, especially since the difference in their ages was so much in her favor. His signature looked like a scrawl made by mosquitoes. Fearing she would be sacked, Irina did not tell Voigt. Nor did she reply to the letter, hoping that it would soon slip her suitor's mind, but for once Jacques's short-term memory did not fail him. Rejuvenated by passion, he kept sending her increasingly urgent missives, while she did her best to avoid him, and prayed to Saint Parascheva for the old man to turn his attention to the dozen or so octogenarian women chasing him.

The situation grew so tense it would have been impossible to hide, had an unexpected event not put an end both to Jacques and with him to Irina's dilemma. That week Frenchie had left Lark House twice in a taxi. This was very unusual for him, as he used to become very confused out in the street. One of Irina's duties was to accompany him, but on these occasions he sneaked out without saying a word about what he was doing. The second trip must have exhausted him, because when he returned to the home he was so lost and frail that the taxi driver almost had to carry him out and hand him over to the receptionist like a package.

"Whatever happened to Mr. Devine?" she asked.

"I don't know, I wasn't there," came the reply.

After checking him and finding that his blood pressure was within normal limits, the duty doctor advised there was no point sending him back to the hospital, but recommended bed rest for a couple of days. However, he also told Hans Voigt that Jacques Devine was no longer in a fit mental state to remain on the second level. The time had come to transfer him to the third, where he would receive twenty-four-hour care. The next day, the director was gearing himself up to tell the old man of the change, something that always left a bitter taste in his mouth, as everyone knew that the third level was the waiting room for Paradise, from which there was no return. He was interrupted by a grief-stricken Jean Daniel, who informed him that when he went to help him get dressed he had found Jacques's body stiff and cold on the floor. The doctor suggested an autopsy, because when he had examined him the previous day there had been nothing to suggest such a dramatic outcome, but Voigt was against the idea. Why arouse suspicions over something as natural as the death of a ninety-year-old man? An autopsy could sully Lark House's impeccable reputation. When she heard the news, Irina could not help weeping, because in spite of herself she had come to feel affection for her pathetic Romeo. At the same time, she felt both a sense of relief that she was free of him, and shame at feeling so relieved.

Frenchie's death united the club of his admirers in an outpouring of widows' mourning, but they were robbed of the comfort of planning a memorial service, because his family members opted for a quick cremation. He would have soon been forgotten, even by his admirers, had his family not raised a storm. Shortly after his ashes were scattered without any great show of emotion, the would-be heirs learned that all the old man's possessions had been bequeathed to a certain Irina Bazili. According to the brief codicil attached to the will, Irina had brought tenderness to the final days of his long life, and therefore deserved the inheritance. Jacques's lawyer explained that his client had dictated the changes by telephone, and then had come to his office on two occasions, the first to check the documents, the second to sign them and have them notarized. He had seemed quite clear about what he was doing. His descendants accused the Lark House administration of negligence regarding the old man's state of mind, and Irina Bazili, whoever she was, of willfully stealing from him. They announced their intention to contest the will, to sue the lawyer for incompetence and Lark House for damages and compensation. Hans Voigt received the horde of frustrated relatives with the outward calm and courtesy he had acquired over many years of being in charge of the institution, yet inside he was fuming. He had not expected such treachery from Irina Bazili, whom he had thought incapable of hurting a fly, but you never learn, you can never trust anyone. He took the lawyer aside and asked how much money was involved: it turned out to be a few parcels of desert in New Mexico, as well as some stocks and shares whose value had yet to be assessed. The amount of available cash was insignificant.

The director asked for twenty-four hours to find a less costly solution than going to court and summoned Irina to his office at once. He had intended to treat the matter with kid gloves, as there was no point making an enemy of this vixen, but as soon as she came in, he lost control.

"I want to know how on earth you managed to bamboozle the old man like that," he accused her.

"Who do you mean, Mr. Voigt?"

"Who do I mean? Frenchie, of course. How could this have happened right under my nose?"

"I'm sorry, I didn't mention it because I thought the problem would sort itself out."

"Oh boy, it did sort itself out, didn't it? How am I going to explain it to his family?"

"They don't need to know, Mr. Voigt. You know very well that old people fall in love, even if it shocks people outside."

"Did you sleep with Devine?"

"No! How could you suggest that!"

"Then I don't understand. Why did he name you as his sole heir?"

"What?"

To his astonishment, Voigt realized that Irina had no idea what Frenchie was planning to do, and was more surprised than anyone at the contents of the will. He was about to warn her she would find it extremely difficult to lay her hands on any of it, because his legitimate heirs would fight down to the last cent, when she announced point-blank that she didn't want a thing, because they would be ill-gotten gains and would be bound to bring her misfortune. Everybody at Lark House knew Jacques was not in his right mind, and so it would be best to sort things out quietly: surely a diagnosis of senile dementia from the doctor would be enough. Irina had to repeat this twice before the dumbfounded director could take it in.

Their attempts to keep the situation quiet soon came to

naught. Everybody in Lark House heard about it, and Irina became an overnight sensation, admired by the residents but criticized by the Latino and Haitian staff, for whom it was a sin to refuse money. "Don't spit into the sky, it'll only fall on your face," Lupita warned her. Irina couldn't figure out how to translate such a cryptic proverb into her native Romanian. Impressed by the lack of self-interest of this humble immigrant from a country hard to find on a map, Voigt offered her a full-time contract with a higher salary. He also convinced Jacques's descendants to give Irina two thousand dollars as a token of their gratitude. In the end, she never received the promised reward, but as she could not even imagine such a large sum, she soon forgot about it.

ALMA BELASCO

*T*he intrigue and commotion surrounding Jacques Devine's inheritance brought Irina to the attention of Alma Belasco, and once all the fuss had died down, she asked to see the young woman. She received Irina in her spartan apartment, seated with imperial dignity in a small apricot-colored armchair, with Neko, her tabby cat, curled in her lap.

"I need a secretary. I want you to work for me," she announced.

This was not so much an offer as an order. Since Alma barely acknowledged her whenever they passed by each other in the corridor, Irina was completely taken aback. Besides, half the residents lived modestly on their pensions, occasionally augmented thanks to help from their families, and had to strictly make do with the services provided, because even an extra meal could ruin their meager budgets. None of them could afford the luxury of a personal assistant. The specter of poverty, like that of loneliness, always hovered around them. So Irina explained that she had little free time, because after finishing her day at Lark House, she worked in a café and also went to people's houses to wash and groom their pet dogs.

"How does this dog thing work?" asked Alma.

"I've got a partner. His name is Tim. He works at the same café as me. He's also a neighbor in Berkeley. He owns a van equipped with two tubs and a long hosepipe; we go to the houses where the dogs live—I mean where the dogs' owners live; we connect the hose and wash the clients—I mean the dogs—in the yard or out on the street. We also clean their ears and trim their nails."

"The dogs' nails?" asked Alma, hiding her smile.

"Yes."

"How much do you earn an hour?"

"Nine dollars in the café, and twenty-five per dog, but I split that with Tim, so I get twelve and a half dollars."

"I'll take you on trial at thirteen dollars an hour, for three months. If I like the way you work, I'll raise it to fifteen. You are to work for me in the evenings, as soon as you finish your duties at Lark House, two hours a day to start with. The hours can be flexible, depending on my needs and your availability. Do we have a deal?"

"I could quit the café, Mrs. Belasco, but I can't leave the dogs. They already know me and are expecting me."

This was how things were left, and how a business relationship that was soon to become a friendship began.

During the first few weeks in her new job, Irina went around on tiptoe and was often at a loss, because Alma Belasco turned out to be bossy and demanding about details but vague about instructions. Soon, however, Irina lost her fear and became as indispensable to Alma as she was to Lark House in general. Irina observed Alma with the fascination of a zoologist, as if she were some kind of immortal salamander. This woman was unlike anyone she had ever known, and very different from the old people on the second and third levels. Jealous of her independence, she was not in the least sentimental or attached to material possessions, and seemed aloof toward everyone but her grandson, Seth. She appeared so self-assured that she did not look for support either from God or in the sickly-sweet religiosity of some of the Lark House residents, who flaunted their spirituality and went around preaching ways of reaching a higher state of awareness. Alma had her feet firmly on the ground. Irina assumed her haughty attitude was a defense against other people's curiosity, and her simplicity a kind of elegance that few women could copy without appearing to have let themselves go. She wore her white, wiry hair short, and combed it through with her fingers. Her sole concessions to vanity were bright red lipstick, and a masculine fragrance of bergamot and orange blossom; wherever she went, its fresh smell covered the faint odor of disinfectant, old age, and—occasionally—marijuana that was typical of Lark House. She had a prominent nose, a proud mouth, big bones, and hands worn rough by hard work; brown eyes with heavy, dark eyebrows and violet rings beneath them gave her the look of a night owl, which even the black-framed glasses she wore failed to disguise. Her enigmatic demeanor created a sense of distance: none of the staff addressed her in the patronizing way they did the other residents, and none could boast that they really knew her, at least not until Irina Bazili managed to penetrate her private fortress.

Alma lived with her cat in one of the independent apartments, with a minimum of furniture and personal belongings. She drove around in a tiny car, completely ignoring all traffic regulations, which she chose to regard as optional. One of Irina's duties was to pay the parking fines that regularly arrived. Alma's upbringing meant that she was polite, but the only friends she had made at Lark House were Victor, the gardener, with whom she spent many long hours working on the raised beds where they planted vegetables and flowers, and Dr. Catherine Hope, against whom all resistance failed. Alma rented a studio in a warehouse space divided by wooden partitions that she shared with other artisans. She continued with her silk-screening, as she had done for sixty years, although she no longer sought artistic inspiration in her work, but simply to avoid dying of boredom before her time. She spent several hours a week there, assisted by Kirsten, who despite her Down syndrome was able to fulfill all her tasks. Kirsten knew the color combinations and tools that Alma used. She prepared the fabrics, kept the studio neat and tidy, and cleaned the brushes. The two women worked harmoniously together, without the need for words, intuiting each other's intentions. When Alma's hands began to shake and she could no longer grip a brush, she hired a couple of students to copy onto silk the designs she drew on paper, while her faithful helper watched them as keenly as a prison guard. Kirsten was the only person who allowed herself to greet Alma with a hug, or to interrupt her with wet kisses whenever she felt a sudden wave of tenderness.

Without ever seriously intending to, Alma had become famous for her original, brightly colored kimonos, tunics, kerchiefs, and scarves. She herself never wore them: she preferred black, white, or gray loose-fitting trousers and linen blouses that Lupita dismissed as the rags of a tramp, never once suspecting how much those rags cost. Alma's silk screens were sold in art galleries at exorbitant prices to raise funds for the Belasco Foundation. Her collections were inspired by her journeys around the world—animals from the Serengeti National Park, Ottoman ceramics, Ethiopian lettering, Inca hieroglyphics, Greek bas-reliefs—which she quickly renewed as soon as her rivals began to copy them. She had refused to sell her brand or to work with fashion designers; each of her original creations was reproduced in a limited edition that she closely supervised and then signed. In her heyday she'd had around fifty people working for her and had produced a considerable volume of work in a big industrial warehouse south of Market Street in San Francisco. Since she had no need to sell anything to earn her living, she had never advertised, but her name had become a watchword for exclusivity and excellence. When she turned seventy she decided to cut back on production, to the severe detriment of the Belasco Foundation, which had counted on this income.

Established in 1955 by her father-in-law, the legendary Isaac Belasco, the foundation created green spaces in at-risk neighborhoods. Although the goals of this initiative had primarily been aesthetic, ecological, and recreational, it also produced unexpected social benefits. Wherever a garden, park, or square sprang up, delinquency rates declined, as gang members and addicts who had been previously ready to kill each other for a packet of heroin or a few more inches of turf now found a common interest in looking after this corner of the city that belonged to them. In some they had painted murals, in others built sculptures and children's playground equipment; in all of them, artists and musicians gathered to entertain the public. In every generation, the Belasco Foundation had been headed by the firstborn male member of the family. This tacit rule did not change with female liberation, because none of the daughters bothered to question it. One day the responsibility would fall on Seth, the founder's great-grandson, who could not refuse it even though he had no wish whatsoever to receive such an honor.

Alma Belasco was so accustomed to giving orders and keeping her distance, and Irina so accustomed to receiving orders and being discreet, that they would never have come to appreciate each other were it not for Seth Belasco, Alma's favorite grandson, who made it his job to pull down the barriers between them. Seth met Irina shortly after his grandmother moved to Lark House. The young woman fascinated him from the start, although he could not have said why. Despite her name, she had little in common with the East European beauties who in the previous decade had taken the men's clubs and model agencies by storm; in fact, from a distance Irina could be taken for a scruffy-looking young boy. She was so inclined to remain invisible that it took a good pair of eyes to even notice her. Her baggy clothes and knitted hat pulled down low did not exactly make her stand out. Seth was attracted by her mysterious intelligence, her impish, heart-shaped face with a deep dimple in the chin, her startled greenish eyes, her slender neck that emphasized her vulnerability, and her skin, so white it seemed to glow in the darkness. Even her childlike hands and chewed nails moved him. He felt a previously unknown and disturbing desire to protect her and shower her with affection. In the winter, Irina wore so many layers of clothes that it was impossible to judge the rest of her appearance, but several months later, when summer forced her to abandon the protective coverings, she turned out to be well proportioned and attractive, in her own raggedy way. The knitted cap was replaced by gypsy head scarves that could not completely cover her head, so that a few locks of almost albino blond hair constantly framed her face.

At first, the only link Seth could establish with her was thanks to his grandmother, since none of his usual seduction techniques appeared to work. Later on, he discovered the irresistible power of writing. He told her that with his grandmother's aid he was compiling a century and a half of the history not only of the Belasco family but of San Francisco itself, from its foundation to the present day. He had been mulling over this vast saga for fifteen years: a raucous torrent of images, anecdotes, and ideas. If he could not get it all down on paper it would drown him. This was something of an exaggeration—the torrent was little more than a tiny trickle—but his description so caught Irina's imagination that Seth had no choice but to set to work. In addition to visiting his grandmother, who contributed her oral history, he began to collect information from books and the Internet, and to collect photographs and letters written at different time periods. This won him Irina's admiration, but not Alma's. She accused him of having grandiose ideas and sloppy habits, a fatal combination for a writer. If Seth had paused to reflect, he would have admitted that both the book and his grandmother were nothing more than pretexts to see Irina, this creature straight out of a Nordic saga who had materialized where least expected: in an old people's home. But however long and hard he reflected, he would have been at a loss to explain the irresistible attraction she exerted on him: her tiny orphan's bone structure and consumptive pallor were the exact opposite of his ideal woman. He usually went for the healthy, tanned, cheerful girls who were so common in California and in his past. Irina showed no sign of being aware of the effect she had on him; she treated him with the casual kindness usually reserved for other people's pets. Her polite indifference, which he would once have seen as a challenge, left him in a constant state of shy paralysis.

Seth's grandmother began to dig among her memories to help her grandson with a book that, by his own admission, he had already spent ten years writing in fits and starts. No one was better qualified to aid him in this way than Alma, who had the spare time and was not yet afflicted with any signs of senile dementia. Alma took Irina with her to visit the ancestral Belasco residence at Sea Cliff, to go through her boxes that no one had touched since she had left. Her old bedroom remained under lock and key, entered only for cleaning purposes. Alma had disposed of almost all her possessions: she gave her jewelry to her daughter-in-law and granddaughter, with the exception of a diamond wedding ring reserved for Seth's future wife; her books to hospitals and schools; clothes and furs, which no one dared wear anymore in California for fear of animal-rights protesters who might launch a knife attack, to charity shops; she distributed other things to whoever wanted them, keeping only what mattered to her: letters, diaries, press cuttings, documents, and photographs. "I have to sort out all this stuff, Irina, I don't want anyone rummaging in my private life when I am really old." To begin with she tried to do it all on her own, but as she began to trust Irina she began to delegate to her. The young woman ended up in charge of everything, apart from the letters in yellow envelopes that arrived from time to time, which Alma always made vanish immediately. Irina was under strict instructions not to touch them.

Alma doled out her memories to her grandson in a sparing manner, one by one, to keep him hanging on for as long as possible, because she was afraid that if he became bored of fluttering around Irina, the famous manuscript would be returned to a bottom drawer and she would see far less of the young man. Irina's presence was essential to the sessions with Seth, otherwise he became distracted waiting for her to appear. Alma laughed to herself when she thought how the family would react if Seth, the heir to the Belasco dynasty, were to get together with an immigrant who lived by caring for old people and washing dogs. She herself did not consider it such a bad idea, as Irina was far more intelligent than Seth's previous athletic but short-lived girlfriends; yet Irina was a rough diamond, and required polishing. Alma set herself the task of providing her with a veneer of culture, taking her to concerts and museums, lending her grown-up books to read instead of those absurdly lengthy novels about fantasy worlds and supernatural creatures that she so enjoyed, and teaching her proper manners, including how to handle cutlery at table. Irina had learned none of this from her peasant grandparents in Moldova or from her alcoholic mother in Texas, but she was quick-witted and grateful. It would be easy to refine her, and it would be a subtle way of paying her back for attracting Seth to Lark House.

THE INVISIBLE MAN

A year after she started to work for Alma Belasco, Irina began
to suspect the older woman had a lover. She did not admit her
suspicions to Seth until much later. At first, before Seth had lured
her into the intrigue, she had never dreamed of spying on Alma.
She had been drawn into Alma's private world gradually, without
either of them realizing it. The idea of a lover started to take shape
when Irina was sorting out the boxes Alma had brought from the
house at Sea Cliff and when she examined the silver-framed photograph of a man that Alma kept in her bedroom, which she polished regularly. Apart from a smaller one of her family in the living
room, there were no other photos in the apartment. This caught
Irina's attention, because all the other residents at Lark House surrounded themselves with photographs to keep them company.
All Alma said was that the man in the portrait was a childhood
friend. On the rare occasion that Irina plucked up the courage to
ask something more, Alma changed the subject. Still, Irina managed to drag out of her that his name was Ichimei Fukuda, and that
he had painted the strange canvas that hung in the living room, a
desolate snowy landscape beneath a gray sky, with dark one-story

buildings, electricity posts and wires, and the only sign of life a black bird in flight. Irina couldn't understand why, from among the wealth of artworks the Belasco family owned, Alma had chosen such a depressing picture to decorate her home with. The portrait of Ichimei Fukuda showed a man of uncertain age, his head quizzically tilted to one side, eyes half-closed because he was squinting into the sun; even so, his look was candid and direct. He had a fine head of straight hair, and the hint of a smile on his thick, sensual lips. Irina felt herself irresistibly drawn to his face, which seemed to be either entreating her or trying to convey something of vital importance. When she was on her own in the apartment she studied the portrait so avidly that she began to imagine a full-length version of Ichimei Fukuda, endowing him with physical attributes as well as inventing a life for him: broad shoulders, a lonely character, someone whom suffering had taught to keep his emotions in check. Alma's refusal to talk about him only further aroused Irina's desire to meet him. In one of the boxes she found another photo of the same man on a beach with Alma. Both of them had their pants rolled up, sandals in hand, and were wading in the water, laughing and splashing each other. The couple's attitude suggested love and sexual intimacy. Irina guessed they were alone there and had asked a passing stranger to take this snapshot of them. If Ichimei was more or less the same age as Alma, Irina calculated he must be in his eighties now, but she was certain that she would recognize him if ever she saw him. Ichimei had to be the reason behind Alma's erratic behavior.

Irina could predict Alma's disappearances from her melancholy, self-absorbed silences in the days leading up to them. These gave way to a sudden, barely controlled euphoria once she had made up her mind to leave. She was waiting for something to happen, and when it arrived, she was overjoyed. She threw a few clothes into a small overnight bag, told Kirsten not to go to the workshop, and left Neko for Irina to look after. The cat was old, and suffered from a series of quirks and ailments. The long list of recommendations and medicines for his care was stuck to the refrigerator door. Neko was the fourth in a line of similar cats, all with the same name, that had kept Alma company at different stages in her life.

Alma would leave with a lover's haste, without saying where she was going or when she thought she'd be back. Two or three days would go by with no news from her, and then all at once, as unexpectedly as she had left, she would reappear, with a beaming smile on her face and her toy car's gas tank nearly empty. Irina was in charge of her accounts and had seen the hotel receipts. She had also discovered that on these adventures Alma took the only two silk nightgowns she possessed, instead of her usual flannel pajamas. She wondered why Alma slipped away as though she were committing a sin; after all, she was a free woman and could receive whomever she liked in her Lark House apartment.

Inevitably, Irina's suspicions about the man in the photograph infected Seth. Even though Irina had been careful not to mention her doubts, Seth's frequent visits led him to notice his grandmother's repeated absences. Whenever he raised the subject, Alma said she was going to train with terrorists, or experiment with the hallucinatory drug ayahuasca, or gave some equally absurd explanation, in the mock-sarcastic tone they employed with each other. Seth decided to enlist Irina's help to solve the mystery, although this was not easy to obtain, as the young woman's loyalty to Alma was absolute. He had to convince Irina that his grandmother was in peril. Alma appeared strong for her age, he told her, but the truth was she was delicate, had high blood pressure and a weak heart, and was in the early stages of Parkinson's disease, which was why her hands shook. He couldn't give her any further details, because Alma had refused to undergo the required medical examinations, but the two of them needed to keep an eye on her and avoid her running any risks.

"We want our loved ones to be safe, Seth. But what they want for themselves is autonomy. Your grandmother would never accept us poking our noses into her private life, even if it is to protect her."

"That's why we have to do it without her realizing it," Seth asserted.

According to Seth, early in 2010 his grandmother's personality underwent a complete change in the space of two hours. Although she had been a successful artist and someone who always fulfilled her obligations, she suddenly cut herself off from the world, family, and friends, shutting herself away in an old people's home that was beneath her and deciding, in her daughter-in-law Doris's opinion, to dress like a Tibetan refugee. She must have had some kind of short circuit in the brain, Doris said. The last they saw of the former Alma was when she announced, after a perfectly normal lunch, that she was going to take a nap. When at five o'clock Doris knocked on her bedroom door to remind her about that evening's reception, she found her standing at the window staring out into the mist. She was barefoot, and in her underwear. Her splendid formal gown lay abandoned on a chair. "Tell Larry I'm not going to the reception, and that he can't count on me for anything for the rest of my life." Her emphatic tone brooked no argument. Her daughter-in-law closed the door silently and went to give her husband the message. The gala was to raise funds for the Belasco Foundation and was the most important event of the year, putting the family's ability to attract donors to the test. The waiters were putting the finishing touches to the tables, the cooks were busy with the banquet, and the chamber orchestra musicians were tuning their instruments. Each year, Alma gave a short speech that was always more or less the same. Afterward she posed for photographs with the most important benefactors and spoke to the press. That was all that was asked of her: the rest was handled by Larry, her son. That night they had to make do without her.

The dramatic changes started the next day. Alma began to pack her bags and decided that very little of what she had would be of any use to her in her new life. She had to simplify. First she went shopping, and then got together with her accountant and her lawyer. She allotted herself a modest pension, handed the rest of her wealth over to Larry without instructions as to how he should spend it, and announced she would be going to live at Lark House. In order to avoid the waiting list she purchased the right to become a resident from an anthropologist, who for the right price was willing to wait a few more years. No one in the Belasco family had ever heard of the place.

"It's a rest home," said Alma vaguely.

"A nursing home?" asked Larry with alarm.

"More or less. I want to live the time I have left without complications or burdens."

"Burdens! I hope you don't mean us!"

"And what are we going to tell people?" exclaimed Doris.

"That I'm old and crazy. That wouldn't be far off the mark," Alma replied.

The chauffeur drove her there with her cat and two suitcases. A week later, Alma renewed a driving license that she hadn't needed in decades and bought a lime-green Smart car. It was so tiny and light that once, when it was parked on the street, three mischievous youths tipped it on its roof and left it with its wheels in the air like an upended tortoise. Her reason for choosing it was that the garish color made it visible for other drivers, and its small size meant that if by some misfortune she ran someone over, she would most likely not kill them. It was like driving a cross between a bicycle and a wheelchair.

"I think my grandmother has serious health problems, Irina," Seth told her. "And she shut herself up in Lark House out of a sense of pride, so that no one would find out."

"If that were the case, she'd be dead by now. Besides, no one shuts themselves up in Lark House, it's an open community where people come and go as they like. That's why we don't admit people suffering from Alzheimer's, who might get out and wander off."

"That's exactly what scares me. My grandmother could get lost on one of her excursions."

"She always comes back. She knows where she's going, and I don't think she goes there alone."

"Then who does she go with? A boyfriend? You can't possibly think my grandmother stays at hotels with a lover!" Seth said mockingly, but Irina's serious expression cut his laughter short.

"Why not?"

"She's ancient!"

"It's all relative. She's old, not ancient. In Lark House, Alma is considered young. Besides, love can strike at any age. Voigt thinks it's good to fall in love when you're old: it keeps you healthy and wards off depression."

"How do old people do it? In bed, I mean?" asked Seth.

"Taking their time, I suppose. You'd have to ask your grandmother that," Irina responded.

Seth soon succeeded in winning Irina over, and the two of them began trying to solve the puzzle. Once a week, Alma received a box containing three gardenias that was left at the reception desk by a delivery boy. The box never included the sender's name or the florist's, but Alma displayed neither surprise nor curiosity. She also regularly received yellow envelopes, again with no indication as to who had sent them. Alma would throw these away after extracting from them a smaller envelope, with her name and old address at Sea Cliff handwritten on it. None of the Belasco family or their staff had either seen these envelopes or forwarded them on to Lark House in the bigger yellow ones. They knew nothing about the yellow envelopes until Seth mentioned them. He and Irina were unable to discover the identity of the sender, or why two envelopes and two addresses were necessary for the same letter, much less where this unusual correspondence ended up. Since Irina found no trace of the letters in the apartment and Seth nothing at Sea Cliff, they assumed Alma must have stored them in a safe-deposit box at her bank.

April 12, 1996

Yet another unforgettable honeymoon with you, Alma! It's been a long time since I saw you so relaxed and happy. And for us to be greeted like that, in Washington, with the magical sight of one thousand seven hundred cherry trees in bloom! I saw something similar in Kyoto many years ago. Does the cherry tree my father planted at Sea Cliff still bloom each year?

I remember how you stroked the names inscribed in the dark stone of the Vietnam Memorial and told me that stones speak, that you can hear their voices, that the dead are trapped inside the wall and cry out to us, outraged at their sacrifice. I've been thinking about that. There are spirits all around us, Alma, but I believe they are free and do not harbor any resentment.

Ichi

THE POLISH GIRL

*T*o satisfy Irina and Seth's curiosity, Alma began by telling them, with the lucidity that preserves crucial moments for us, of the first time she saw Ichimei Fukuda. She met him in the splendid garden at the Sea Cliff mansion in the spring of 1939. In those days she was a girl with less appetite than a canary, who went around silent by day and tearful by night, hiding in the depths of the three-mirrored wardrobe in the bedroom her aunt and uncle had prepared for her. The room was a symphony in blue: the drapes were blue, and so too the curtains around the four-poster bed, the Flemish carpet, the birds on the wallpaper, and the Renoir reproductions in their gilt frames; blue also were the sky and the sea she could view from her window whenever the fog lifted. Alma Mendel was weeping for everything she had lost forever, even though her aunt and uncle insisted so vehemently that the separation from her parents and brother was only temporary that they would have convinced any girl less intuitive than her. The very last image she had of her parents was that of a man of mature years, bearded and stern looking, dressed entirely in black with a heavy overcoat and hat, standing next to a much younger woman, who was sobbing disconsolately. They were on the quay at the port of Danzig, waving good-bye to her with white handkerchiefs. They grew smaller and smaller, more and more indistinct, as the boat set out on its journey toward London with a mournful blast from its foghorn and she, clutching the railing, found it impossible to return their farewell wave. Shivering in her travel clothes, lost among the crowd of passengers gathered at the stern to watch their native land disappear in the distance, Alma tried to maintain the composure her parents had instilled in her from birth. As the ship moved off, she could sense their despair, and this reinforced her premonition that she would never see them again. With a gesture that was rare in him, her father had put his arm around her mother's shoulders, as if to prevent her from throwing herself into the water. She meanwhile was holding down her hat with one hand to prevent the wind from blowing it off as she frantically waved the handkerchief with her other.

Three months earlier, Alma had been with them on this same quay to wave good-bye to her brother, Samuel, who was ten years older than her. Her mother shed many tears before accepting her husband's decision to send him to England as a precaution just in case the rumors of war became real. He would be safe there from being recruited into the army or being tempted to volunteer. The Mendel family could never have imagined that two years later Samuel would be in the Royal Air Force fighting against Germany. When she saw her brother embark with the swagger of someone off on his first adventure, Alma had a foretaste of the threat hanging over her family. Her brother had been like a beacon to her: shedding light on her darkest moments and driving off her fears with his triumphant laugh, his friendly teasing, and the songs he sang at the piano. For his part, Samuel had been delighted with Alma from the moment he held her as a newborn baby, a pink bundle smelling of talcum powder and mewling like a kitten. This passion for his sister had done nothing but grow over the following seven years, until they were forced apart. When she learned that Samuel was leaving, Alma had her first ever tantrum. It began with crying and screaming, followed by her writhing in agony on the floor, and only ended when her mother and governess plunged her ruthlessly into a tub of icy water. Samuel's departure left her both sad and on edge, as she suspected it was the prologue to even more drastic changes. Alma had heard her parents talk about Lillian, one of her mother's sisters who lived in the United States and was married to Isaac Belasco—someone important, as they never failed to add whenever they mentioned his name. Before this, she had been unaware of the existence of this distant aunt and the important man, and so she was very surprised when her parents obliged her to write them postcards in her best handwriting. She also saw it as an ill omen that her governess suddenly incorporated the orange-colored blotch of California into her history and geography lessons. Her parents waited until after the end-of-year celebrations before announcing that she too would be going to study abroad for a while. Unlike her brother, however, she would remain within the family, and go to live in San Francisco with her aunt Lillian, her uncle Isaac, and her three cousins.

The entire journey from Danzig to London, and then to Southampton, where they boarded a transatlantic liner to San Francisco, took seventeen days. The Mendels had given Miss Honeycomb, her English governess, the responsibility of delivering Alma safe and sound to the Belasco home. Miss Honeycomb was a spinster

with a pretentious accent, prim manners, and a snooty expression.
She treated those she regarded as her social inferiors with disdain,
while displaying a cloying servility toward her superiors, and yet
in the eighteen months she had worked for the Mendels she had
won their trust. No one liked her, least of all Alma, but the girl's
opinion counted for nothing in the choice of the governesses and
tutors who educated her at home in her early years. To sweeten
Miss Honeycomb, her employers had promised her a substantial
bonus in San Francisco, once Alma was safely installed with her
relatives. The two of them traveled in one of the best cabins on
the ship; initially they were seasick, and then bored. The Englishwoman did not fit in with the first-class passengers and would
rather have thrown herself overboard than mingle with people of
her own social class. As a result, she spent more than a fortnight
without speaking to anyone apart from her young ward. Although
there were other children on board, Alma wasn't interested in any
of the planned children's activities and made no friends. She was
in a sulk with her governess and sobbed in secret because this was
the first time she had been away from her mother. She spent the
voyage reading fairy tales and writing melodramatic letters she
handed directly to the captain for him to post in some port or
other, because she was scared that if she gave them to Miss Honeycomb they would end up being fed to the fishes. The only memorable moments of the slow crossing were the passage through the
Panama Canal and a fancy-dress party when someone costumed
as an Apache Indian pushed her governess, dressed up in a sheet
to represent a Grecian vestal virgin, into the swimming pool.

The Belasco uncle, aunt, and cousins were all waiting for
Alma on the dock at San Francisco, which was teeming with such

a dense throng of Asian stevedores that Miss Honeycomb feared they had docked at Shanghai by mistake. Aunt Lillian, dressed in a gray Persian lamb coat and Turkish turban, clasped her niece in a suffocating embrace, while Isaac Belasco and the chauffeur tried to gather up the travelers' fourteen trunks and bundles. The two female cousins, Martha and Sarah, greeted the new arrival with a cold peck on the cheek, then forgot she existed—not out of malice, but because they were of an age to be looking for boyfriends, and this blinded them to the rest of the world. Despite the Belasco family's wealth and prestige, it wasn't going to be easy for them to land these much-sought-after husbands, as the two girls had inherited their father's nose and their mother's ample outline, but little of the former's intelligence or the latter's kindliness. Her cousin Nathaniel, the only male, born six years after his sister Sarah, was edging into puberty with the gawkiness of a heron. He was pale, skinny, lanky, ill at ease in a body that seemed to have too many elbows and knees, but with the sad, thoughtful eyes of a big dog. He kept his eyes fixed firmly on the ground when he held out his hand and muttered the welcome his parents had insisted on. Alma clung so steadfastly to his hand like a life vest that his efforts to free himself proved fruitless.

So began Alma's stay in the grand house at Sea Cliff, where she was to spend seventy largely uninterrupted years. She almost completely exhausted her stock of tears in her first months there in 1939, and from then on wept only rarely. She learned to bear her troubles alone and with dignity, convinced no one was interested in other people's problems, and that pain borne in silence eventually evaporated. She had assimilated her father's philosophy: he was a man of rigid and unshakable principles, proud of having done everything for himself and owing nothing to anyone, which was not exactly true. The simple recipe for success that Mendel had instilled in his children from the cradle on consisted in never complaining, never asking for anything, striving to be the best in everything you do, and never trusting anyone. Alma had to carry this heavy weight on her back for several decades, until love helped her shed some of it. Her stoic attitude contributed to the air of mystery surrounding her, long before she had any secrets to keep.

During the Great Depression, Isaac Belasco not only had managed to avoid the worst effects of the crisis but had increased his fortune. While others were losing everything, he worked eighteen hours a day at his law firm and invested in commercial ventures that seemed risky at the time but in the long run turned out to have been extremely shrewd. He was formal, a man of few words, but with a soft heart. He saw this softness as a character weakness and tried to give an impression of harsh authority, but one had only to deal with him once or twice to become aware of his underlying generosity. He acquired a reputation for compassion that eventually became a drawback to his legal career. Later on, when he ran for judge in the Californian supreme court, he lost the election because his adversaries accused him of showing too much clemency, to the detriment of justice and public safety.

Although Isaac gave Alma a warm welcome, he was soon unnerved by the little girl's nocturnal crying. Her sobs were muffled and barely audible through the thick carved mahogany doors of her wardrobe, but they still reached his bedroom on the far side of the hallway, where he would be trying to read. He assumed that, like animals, children possess a natural ability to adapt, and that the girl would soon get used to the separation from her parents, or that they would immigrate to America. He felt incapable of help-ing her, restrained by the awkwardness he felt whenever it came to female matters. He found it hard to understand his wife and daughters' usual reactions, so what chance did he have with this Polish girl who was not yet eight? Gradually he found himself over-taken by the superstitious feeling that his niece's tears were her-alding some great catastrophe. The scars of the Great War were still visible in Europe: the land disfigured by trenches, the millions of dead, the widows and orphans, the rotting corpses of mutilated horses, the lethal gases, the flies and hunger were all still fresh in the memory. Nobody wanted another conflict like that, but Hitler had already annexed Austria and was in control of part of Czecho-slovakia, and his inflammatory calls for the establishment of the empire of the super race could not be dismissed as the ravings of a madman. At the end of that January, Hitler had spoken of his intention to rid the world of the Jewish menace. Some children possess psychic powers, thought Isaac, and so it would not be so odd if Alma glimpsed something dreadful in her nightmares and was suffering from a terrible premonitory grief. Why were his in-laws waiting to leave Poland? For a year now he had been unsuc-cessfully pressing them to flee Europe, as so many other Jews were doing. He had offered them his hospitality, although the Mendels had ample means and did not need financial help from him. Baruj Mendel responded that Poland's sovereignty was guaranteed by England and France. He thought he was safe, protected by his money and his business connections, so the only concession he made to the relentless assault of Nazi propaganda was to send his children abroad to weather the storm. Isaac Belasco did not know Mendel, but it was obvious from his letters and cables that his sister-in-law's husband was as arrogant and unlikable as he was stubborn.

Almost a month was to go by before Isaac finally decided to intervene in Alma's drama, and even then he could not bring himself to do so personally, as he felt the problem lay within his wife's domain. At night, only a constantly half-open door separated the spouses, but Lillian was hard of hearing and took tincture of opium to get to sleep, and so would have never learned of the sobbing in the wardrobe had her husband not pointed it out to her. By this time, Miss Honeycomb was no longer with them. On reaching San Francisco she had been paid the promised bonus, and twelve days later she returned to her native land, disgusted she said by the rude manners, incomprehensible accent, and democracy of the Americans, without considering how offensive these remarks were to the Belascos, a refined family who had treated her with great consideration. When Lillian, alerted by a delayed letter from her sister, unpicked the lining of Alma's travel coat, she found that the diamonds spoken of in the letter were missing. The Mendels had put them in this classic hiding place more out of a sense of tradition than to protect their daughter against the vicissitudes of fortune, because the stones were not particularly valuable. Suspicion immediately fell on Miss Honeycomb, and Lillian suggested sending one of the investigators from her husband's practice after the Englishwoman so that they could confront her wherever she was and recoup what she had stolen. Isaac however determined that it was not worth the trouble. The world and their family were already in enough turmoil as it was to have to go chasing governesses across seas and continents; a few diamonds more or less did not weigh much in the balance of Alma's life.

"My bridge companions tell me there's a wonderful child psychologist in San Francisco," Lillian said to her husband when she learned of her niece's suffering.

"And what might that be?" asked the patriarch, raising his eyes from his newspaper for an instant.

"The name says it all, Isaac, don't pretend you don't understand."

"Do any of your friends know anyone with a child so disturbed they've had to turn to a psychologist?"

"No doubt they do, Isaac, but they'd never in their lives admit it."

"Childhood is a naturally unhappy period of our existence, Lillian. It was Walt Disney who invented the notion that it has to be happy, simply to make money."

"You're so stubborn! We can't let Alma sob her heart out forever. We have to do something."

"All right, Lillian. We'll resort to that extreme if all else fails. For now, you could give Alma a few drops of your mixture at night."

"I'm not sure, Isaac. That's a double-edged sword. We don't want to turn the girl into an opium addict so early in her life."

They were still debating the relative merits of the psychologist and the opium when they realized that for three nights now there had been no sound from the wardrobe. They listened for another couple of nights and were able to confirm that for some unknown reason the girl had calmed down, and not only slept the whole night but had begun to eat like any normal child. Alma had not forgotten her parents or her brother, and still wanted the family to be reunited as soon as possible, but she was running out of tears and was starting to enjoy her burgeoning friendship with the two people who were to become her life's only loves: Nathaniel Belasco and Ichimei Fukuda. Nathaniel was about to turn thirteen and was the Belascos' youngest child. Like her, Ichimei was almost eight, and he was the gardener's youngest son.

The Belascos' two daughters, Martha and Sarah, lived in such a different world from Alma, concerned only with fashion, parties, and potential boyfriends, that whenever they bumped into her in the nooks and crannies of the Sea Cliff mansion or during the rare formal dinners in the dining room, they were startled, as if unable to recall who this little girl was or what she was doing there. Nathaniel on the other hand could not ignore her, because Alma followed him around from the very first day, determined to replace her beloved brother, Samuel, with this shy cousin. Even though he was five years older, he was the closest to her in age of the Belasco clan, and the most approachable due to his gentle disposition. In Nathaniel she aroused a mixture of fascination and dread. To him she seemed to have stepped out of an old-fashioned photograph, with her grave demeanor and the pretentious British accent she had learned from her devious governess. She was as stiff and angular as a board, smelled of the mothballs from her traveling trunks, and had a defiant white lock that fell over her forehead and contrasted strongly with the rest of her black hair and her olive complexion. At first, Nathaniel tried to escape, but when nothing managed to deter Alma's clumsy attempts to become friends, he surrendered. He had inherited his father's kind heart and could intuit his cousin's secret pain, which she proudly concealed. Still, he found a variety of excuses to avoid helping her. She was a little brat, she wasn't a close relative, she was only in San Francisco for a while, and it would be a waste of time to become friends with her. After three weeks had gone by with no sign that his cousin's visit might be coming to an end, his excuses were wearing thin, and so Nathaniel went to ask his mother if they were thinking of adopting her. "I hope it doesn't come to that," Lillian replied with a shudder. The news from Europe was very disturbing, and the possibility that her niece might become an orphan was gradually taking shape in her mind. From the tone of his mother's reply, Nathaniel concluded that Alma would be there indefinitely, and so he yielded to his instinct to care for her. He slept in another wing of the mansion and no one had told him that Alma was whimpering in the wardrobe, but he somehow found this out and on many nights tiptoed there to be with her.

It was Nathaniel who introduced the Fukuda family to Alma. She had seen them through the windows but didn't go out to explore the garden until later in the spring, when the weather improved. One Saturday, Nathaniel blindfolded her and told her he had a surprise for her. Then he led her through the kitchen and laundry and out into the garden. When he removed the blindfold and she looked up, she found she was standing beneath a cherry tree in blossom, a cloud of pink cotton. Next to the tree was a short, broad-shouldered Asian man in overalls and a straw hat, leaning on a spade. His face was weathered, and in a halting English difficult to follow, he told Alma that this moment was beautiful, but that it would last only a few days before the blooms fell like rain to the ground; much better was the memory of the cherry tree in bloom, because that would last all year, until the following spring. He was Takao Fukuda, the Japanese gardener who had worked at Sea Cliff for years, and the only person Isaac Belasco doffed his hat to as a mark of respect.

Nathaniel went back inside, leaving his cousin with Takao, who showed her around the rest of the garden. He took her to the different terraces built into the side of the hill, from the summit where the house stood all the way down to the beach. He walked with her along narrow paths between classical statues stained green with damp and among fountains, exotic trees, and succulents, explaining where each one came from and the kind of care it needed, until they reached a pergola covered in climbing roses with a panoramic view of the ocean, the entrance to the bay on the left, and the Golden Gate Bridge, inaugurated a couple of years earlier, on the right. Colonies of sea lions were visible resting on the rocks, and scanning the horizon, he told her that with patience and luck you could sometimes see whales coming from the north to have their young in Californian waters. Then Takao showed her the greenhouse, a miniature replica of a classic Victorian railway station, all wrought iron and glass. Inside, thanks to the filtered light, the moist warmth of the heating, and the humidifiers, the delicate plants began their lives on trays, each one labeled by name and the date when it was to be transplanted. Between two long rough wooden tables, Alma saw a boy bent over some seedlings. When he heard them come in, he dropped his pair of pruning shears and stood stiffly to attention. Going over to him, Takao whispered something in a language Alma could not understand and ruffled his hair. "My youngest son," he said. Alma stared wide-eyed at father and son as if they were from another species: they were nothing like the Chinese she had seen in the illustrations in the *Encyclopaedia Britannica*.

The boy greeted her with a bow and kept his head down while he introduced himself.

"I am Ichimei, the fourth child of Takao and Heideko Fukuda. It is an honor to meet you, miss."

"I am Alma, the niece of Isaac and Lillian Belasco. An honor to meet you, sir," she replied, taken aback but amused.

This initial formality, which as time went on became tinged with humor, set the tone for their lifelong relation. Alma was taller and more robust, and so looked older than him. Ichimei's slender frame was deceptive, because he could pick up heavy bags of soil effortlessly and push a laden wheelbarrow uphill. His head was large compared to his body; he had a honey-colored complexion, black eyes set wide apart, and thick, unruly hair. His adult teeth were still emerging, and when he smiled his eyes seemed to disappear.

For the rest of that morning, Alma followed Ichimei around as he planted the seedlings in the holes his father had dug and pointed out the secret life of the garden to her, the roots beneath the surface, the near-invisible insects, the tiny shoots that in a week would be several inches tall. He explained about the chrysanthemums he was taking out of the greenhouse, and how they were transplanted in spring to flower at the start of autumn so that they could provide color and life to the garden after all the summer flowers had withered. He showed her some rosebushes still in bud and revealed how you had to remove most of them so that the remaining ones gave big, healthy blooms. He told her about the difference between plants coming from seed and those growing from bulbs, the ones that preferred sun or shade, the native ones and those brought from elsewhere. Takao Fukuda, who was keeping his eye on them, came up and proudly announced that it was Ichimei who carried out the most delicate tasks, because he had been born with a green thumb. The boy blushed at this praise.

From that day on, Alma waited impatiently for the gardeners to arrive, as they did punctually each weekend. Takao Fukuda always brought Ichimei and occasionally, if there was extra work to do, he was also accompanied by Charles and James, his older boys, or by Megumi, his only daughter. Several years older than Ichimei, she was only interested in science and detested getting her hands dirty with soil. Ichimei remained patient and disciplined, carrying out his tasks without being distracted by Alma, trusting his father to give him half an hour off at the end of the day to play with her.

ALMA, NATHANIEL, AND ICHIMEI

*T*he house at Sea Cliff was so vast, and its inhabitants always so busy, that the children's games went unnoticed. If one of the adults suddenly noticed that Nathaniel was spending hours with a much younger girl, the interest soon passed, because there was always something else to attend to. Alma had grown out of what little devotion she felt for dolls, and instead learned to play Scrabble with a dictionary and chess out of pure determination, since strategy was never her strong point. For his part, Nathaniel had grown bored of collecting stamps and going camping with Boy Scouts. Both became absorbed in the plays for two or three characters that he wrote and then they put on together in the attic. The lack of an audience never bothered them, because the process was far more interesting than the outcome, and they were not seeking applause: the pleasure resided in fighting over the script and rehearsing. Old clothes, discarded curtains, battered furniture, and odds and ends in various stages of decay were the raw material for their disguises, props, and special effects; their imagination supplied everything else. Ichimei, who often came to the house because he had no need of an invitation, was only allowed to take on minor roles in their theater company because he was such a lousy actor. This lack of talent was compensated for by his prodigious memory and his skill at drawing. He could recite verbatim lengthy monologues inspired by Nathaniel's favorite characters, from Dracula to the Count of Monte Cristo. He was also in charge of painting the backdrops. But this camaraderie, which helped rescue Alma from her initial sense of being an abandoned orphan, was not to last long.

The following year Nathaniel began his secondary education at a boys' school based on the British model. His life changed overnight. As well as starting to wear long trousers, he had to face the endless brutality of youths learning to be grown-ups. He was not ready for this: he looked more like a ten-year-old than the fourteen he actually was. He was not yet suffering from the merciless bombardment of hormones; he was introverted, wary, and unfortunately for him loved books and hated sports. He would never be boastful, cruel, or vulgar like the other boys, and since none of this came naturally, he tried in vain to copy them; his sweat smelled of fear. On the first Wednesday of classes he came home with a black eye and his shirt stained from a nosebleed. He refused to answer his mother's questions and told Alma he had bumped into the flagpole. That night, for the first time he could remember, he wet his bed. In his horror, he stuffed the soaking sheets up the chimney, where they were only discovered at the end of September, when the fire was lit and the house immediately filled with smoke. Lillian could not get her son to explain what had happened to the sheets either, but she guessed the reason and decided to intervene. She went to see the headmaster, a red-haired Scotsman with a drinker's nose, who received her behind a regimental desk in a dark-paneled room presided over by a portrait of King George VI. He told Lillian that a proper dose of violence was seen as an essential part of the school's educational methods. That was why they encouraged tough sports, quarrels between students were resolved in a ring with boxing gloves, and discipline infractions were punished by caning on the backside, which he himself administered. Blows made men. That was how it had always been, and the sooner Nathaniel learned how to gain respect, the better for him. He added that Lillian's intervention made her son look ridiculous, but since Nathaniel was a new pupil, he would make an exception and not mention it.

Furious, Lillian rushed off to her husband's office on Montgomery Street but got no support there either.

"Don't get involved in this, Lillian. All boys have to go through these initiation rites, and almost all of them survive," Isaac told her.

"Did you get roughed up as well?"

"Of course. And as you can see, it didn't turn out so bad."

The four years of secondary school would have been endless torment for Nathaniel without help from a wholly unexpected quarter. The weekend following the beating, when he saw Nathaniel covered in scratches and bruises, Ichimei took him to the garden pergola and gave him a useful demonstration of the martial arts, which he had practiced since he could stand upright. He handed Nathaniel a spade and told him to come at him as if he wanted to slice his head in two. Nathaniel assumed he was joking and raised the spade in the air like an umbrella. Ichimei had to insist before he finally understood and made to attack him for real. Nathaniel never knew how he lost control of the spade, flew through the air, and landed on his back on the pergola's Italian tiles, all of this witnessed by an astonished Alma, who was looking on closely. This was how Nathaniel found out that the imperturbable Takao Fukuda taught a combination of judo and karate to his children as well as other youngsters from the Japanese community, in a rented garage on Pine Street. Nathaniel told his father, who had vaguely heard of these sports, which were gaining popularity in California at the time. And so Isaac visited Pine Street. He did not really think Fukuda could help his son, but the gardener explained that the beauty of the martial arts was that they did not require physical strength as much as concentration and the ability to use the adversary's weight and thrust to topple him. Nathaniel began the classes. The chauffeur drove him to the garage three times a week, and there he first took on Ichimei and the younger boys, and later Charles, James, and other older opponents. For several months it felt as if his body were being crushed to pieces, until he finally learned to fall without hurting himself. He lost his fear of getting into a fight. He never got beyond the beginners' level, but that was more than the school bullies knew. They soon stopped picking on him because if any of them came looking for a fight he would put them off with four guttural cries and an exaggerated choreography of martial poses. Just as he had never admitted he was aware of his son's beatings, Isaac never inquired about the outcome of the classes, and yet he must have checked up, because one day he arrived at Pine Street in a truck with four workmen to lay a wooden floor in the garage. Takao Fukuda gave several formal bows but made no comment either.

Nathaniel's entry into the boys' school put an end to the performances in the attic theater. Together with his studies and the sustained effort to defend himself, his time was devoted to meta-physical anguish and a studied gloominess that his mother sought to remedy with spoonfuls of cod liver oil. There was barely time for a few games of Scrabble or chess, if Alma managed to catch him before he shut himself in his bedroom to hammer away at his guitar. He was discovering jazz and the blues but looked down on fashionable dances: he would have been paralyzed with embarrassment on a dance floor, where his inability to follow a rhythm, a long-standing Belasco family trait, would have immediately become evident. He looked on with a mixture of sarcasm and envy when Alma and Ichimei demonstrated the Lindy Hop to arouse his interest. The two of them had practiced with two scratched records and a broken phonograph Lillian had thrown away but Alma had rescued from the garbage. Ichimei had then used his nimble fingers and patient intuition to dismantle it and restore it to working order.

Secondary school, which began so badly for Nathaniel, continued to be an ordeal for him throughout the following years. Although his classmates grew tired of ambushing him to beat him up, they subjected him to four years of taunts and ostracism; they couldn't forgive his intellectual curiosity, his good grades, and his physical awkwardness. He never overcame the feeling that he had been born in the wrong place at the wrong time. He had to participate in sports, because they were a central part of this English-style education, and so he suffered the repeated humiliation of coming in last and not being wanted on anyone's team. At fifteen he shot up in size: his mother had to buy him new pairs of shoes and to get his trousers lengthened every couple of months. After starting out as the smallest in his class, he finally reached a normal height. His legs, arms, and nose all grew; the outline of his ribs was visible beneath his shirt, and the Adam's apple in his scrawny neck became so prominent that he took to wearing a scarf even in summer. He knew his profile made him look like a plucked buzzard, and so he tended to sit in corners, where people had to look at him face on. He was spared the acne that plagued his enemies, but not the typical teenage complexes. He could never have imagined that in less than three years his body would be well proportioned, his features would have settled down, and he would become as handsome as a movie star. He felt ugly, unhappy, and alone; he began to toy with the idea of suicide, something he admitted to Alma in one of his harshest moments of self-criticism. "That would be a waste, Nat. Better complete your schooling, study medicine, and then go out to India and take care of lepers. I'll go with you," she replied without much sympathy, because compared to her family's situation, her cousin's existential crises seemed laughable.

The age difference between the two of them was barely noticeable, because Alma had developed early, and her tendency toward solitude had made her very mature for her age. Whereas Nathaniel swam in what seemed like an insurmountable adolescence, the seriousness and strength that her father had instilled in Alma and that she saw as essential virtues only became more pronounced. She felt abandoned by her cousin and by life. She could imagine the intense self-loathing Nathaniel had experienced when he entered high school, because she felt something similar, if less acutely, but she did not allow herself the luxury of studying herself in the mirror to spot her defects, or of complaining about her fate. She had other worries.

With apocalyptic hurricane force, war had descended on Europe. Alma only caught blurred black-and-white images of it in cinema newsreels: jumbled battle scenes, faces of soldiers covered with the stubborn soot of gunpowder and death, planes dropping bombs that fell through the sky with absurd elegance, explosions of fire and smoke, crowds baying their devotion to Hitler in Germany. She no longer had a clear memory of her country, the house she grew up in, or the language she spoke as a child, but her family was constantly present in her yearnings. On her bedside table she kept photographs of her brother and the last one of her parents on the quayside at Danzig, and kissed them every night before going to sleep. The war images pursued her by day, popped up in her dreams, and never allowed her to behave truly like the girl she was. When Nathaniel gave in to the illusion that he was a misunderstood genius, Ichimei was left as her only confidant. He had not grown much, so that she was now a half a head taller than him, but he was intelligent, and always found a way to distract her when she was overcome by ghastly visions of war. Ichimei would make arrangements to reach the Belascos' mansion by trolley bus, by bicycle, or in the gardening van, if he could persuade his father or a brother to give him a lift; Lillian would send him home later with her driver. If two or three days went by without their meeting, he and Alma would find some time at night to whisper to each other on the phone. Even the most trivial comments took on transcendental importance during these furtive calls. It never occurred to either of them to ask permission, since they thought telephones eventually could be used up, and thus would never be at their disposal.

The Belasco family followed the alarming news from Europe with increasing dread. The Germans had occupied Warsaw, and four hundred thousand Jews were crammed into a ghetto of 1.3 square miles. They had learned from Samuel Mendel in London, where he was an RAF pilot, that their relatives were among them. The Mendels' wealth could not save them; early on in the occupation they lost all their possessions in Poland, as well as access to their Swiss bank accounts. They had to quit the family mansion, requisitioned and turned into offices by the Nazis and their collaborators, and found themselves reduced to the same level of unimaginable misery as the other inhabitants of the ghetto. It was then that they discovered they did not have a single friend among their own people. That was all that Isaac managed to establish. It was impossible to get in touch with them, and none of his attempts to rescue them was successful. He used his connections with influential politicians, including a couple of senators in Washington and the secretary of war, who had been a fellow law student at Harvard, but they all replied with vague promises that they never kept, because they had to deal with far more urgent matters than a rescue mission in the hell of Warsaw. The Americans were watching and waiting, still believing that the war on the far side of the Atlantic had nothing to do with them, despite the Roosevelt government's subtle propaganda to turn the public against the Germans. Behind the high wall marking the boundary of the Warsaw ghetto, the Jews survived in extremes of hunger and terror. There was talk of large-scale deportations; of men, women, and children being dragged off to cargo trains that vanished into the night; of the Nazis' determination to wipe out not only the entire Jewish race but other undesirables as well; of gas chambers, cremation ovens, and other atrocities that were impossible to confirm and therefore hard for the Americans to give credence to.

IRINA BAZILI

*I*n 2013, Irina privately celebrated her third anniversary of working for Alma Belasco by gorging on cream cakes and drinking two cups of hot cocoa. Over that period she had come to know Alma very well, although there were secrets in the old woman's life that neither she nor Seth had managed to uncover, partly because they had not yet seriously set about doing so. As she sorted through Alma's boxes, Irina had been gradually discovering the Belasco family. She became acquainted with Isaac, with his stern prominent nose and kindly eyes; Lillian, who was short, ample bosomed, and had a beautiful face; their daughters, Sarah and Martha, homely but extremely well dressed; Nathaniel as a boy, skinny and lost looking, and then as a young man, slender and very handsome, and at the end of his life, his features ravaged by illness. She saw Alma as a child, newly arrived in America; as a twenty-one-year-old, studying art in Boston; in a black beret and a detective's trench coat, a masculine fashion she adopted after liberating herself from her aunt Lillian's choice of wardrobe, which she had never liked; Alma as a mother, seated in the pergola of the garden at Sea Cliff, with her three-month-old son, Larry, on her lap and her husband standing behind her with one hand on her shoulder, posing as if for a royal portrait. Even as a girl, there were telltale signs of the woman she would grow up to become: she looked imposing, with the white stripe of hair across her brow, her slightly crooked mouth, and the dark circles under her eyes. Irina was supposed to arrange the photographs in chronological order in the albums following Alma's instructions, but she didn't always remember where or when they had been taken. Apart from Ichimei Fukuda's portrait, there was only one other framed photograph in her apartment: the family in the main room at Sea Cliff when Alma was celebrating her fiftieth birthday. The men were in tuxedos, and the women wore long dresses. Alma was in black satin, as haughty as a dowager empress; her daughter-in-law, Doris, looked pale and tired in a gray silk dress pleated at the front to conceal her second pregnancy: she was expecting her daughter, Pauline. Seth, eighteen months old, was standing, clutching his grandmother's dress with one hand and the ear of a cocker spaniel with the other.

As time went by, the relationship between Alma and Irina became increasingly like that of aunt and niece. Their routines were so settled that they could spend hours together in the cramped apartment without talking or even glancing each other's way, both of them caught up in their own activity. They needed each other. Besides sorting through the boxes from Sea Cliff, Irina was also responsible for filing Alma's papers, taking dictation, going to the shops or the laundry, accompanying Alma on her errands, taking care of her cat, and organizing her minimal social life. Irina considered it a privilege to be able to count on Alma's trust and support, whereas the older woman was thankful for the young woman's loyalty. She was flattered by Irina's interest in her past, and she depended on her for practical matters as well as for maintaining her independence and autonomy. Seth had told Alma that when the time came that she needed more help, she ought to either return to the family home at Sea Cliff or take on someone to assist her full-time in her apartment, since money would be no problem. Alma, who was about to turn eighty-two, planned to live another ten years before she needed that kind of support: she did not want anybody to feel they had the right to decide on her behalf.

"I was terrified of being dependent too, Alma," Dr. Catherine Hope told her one day. "But I've realized it's not such a big deal. You get used to it, and are grateful for the assistance. I can't dress or take a shower on my own, I have problems brushing my teeth and cutting the chicken on my plate, but I've never been more contented than I am now."

"Why's that?" Alma asked her friend.

"Because I have time to spare, and for the first time in my life nobody expects anything of me. I don't have to prove anything, I'm not rushing everywhere; each day is a gift I enjoy to the fullest."

Catherine Hope was still in this world thanks only to her fierce determination and the marvels of modern surgery; she knew what it meant to be incapacitated and to feel constant pain. For her, becoming dependent on others had not come gradually, as is usually the case, but overnight, after an unfortunate accident. While mountain climbing, she had fallen down a crevasse and gotten trapped between two rocks, with her arms, legs, and pelvis smashed. Her rescue was a heroic effort that was reported live on the TV news as it was filmed from the air by helicopter. This showed the dramatic scenes from a distance but was unable to get close to the deep chasm where she was lying, in a state of shock and hemorrhaging. It was only a day and a night later that two mountain rescuers succeeded in climbing down to her, in a daring maneuver that almost cost them their lives, and hoisted her up in a harness. Cathy was taken to a hospital that specialized in war traumas, where they began the task of resetting her numerous broken bones. Two months later, she woke up from her coma and, after asking after her daughter, announced she was glad to be alive. That same day, from India the Dalai Lama had sent her a *kata*, a white scarf he had blessed. Following fourteen complicated operations and years of brave rehabilitation, Cathy was forced to accept that she would never walk again.

"My first life is over, this is the start of the second one. If you see me depressed or exasperated, don't pay any attention, because it won't last," she told her daughter.

Zen Buddhism and her lifelong habit of meditation gave her a great advantage in this situation, since she could bear being immobile in a way that would have driven any other person as athletic and energetic as her crazy. She was also able calmly to accept the loss of her companion of many years, who was less able to come to terms with the tragedy and left her. She discovered that she could practice medicine as a surgery consultant from a studio equipped with TV cameras hooked up with the operating room, but her ambition was to work with patients face-to-face, as she had always done. When she decided to live at the second level in

Lark House, she visited a couple of times to talk to the residents who would be her new family and soon saw that there were more than enough opportunities for her to work as she wished.

Barely a week after her arrival she was already planning a free pain clinic for residents with chronic illnesses, and an office where she could attend to lesser complaints. Lark House had doctors on standby, but Catherine Hope convinced them that she was not competing with them, but would complement their work. Hans Voigt offered her a room for the clinic and suggested to the trustees that they pay her a salary; however, she preferred to offer her services as a volunteer and not to have to pay the home's monthly charges. This agreement suited both parties. Cathy, as everyone called her, quickly became the mother who greeted the new arrivals, listened to their secrets, comforted those who were sad, guided the dying, and handed out the marijuana. Half of the residents had medical prescriptions for its use, and Cathy, who doled it out at her clinic, was generous toward those who had neither permits nor enough money to buy it under the counter. It was not uncommon to see a line of clients waiting outside her door to get the grass in many different forms, including delicious biscuits and sweets. Voigt did not intervene—why deprive them of innocuous relief?—and only demanded they refrain from smoking in the corridors or common spaces, because smoking tobacco was forbidden, and it would be unfair if the same did not apply to marijuana. Even so, some of the smoke escaped through the heating or air-conditioning systems, and occasionally even the residents' pets were as high as kites.

———

After her three years at Lark House, Irina had finally begun to feel safe. She had not spent so long in one place since her arrival in the United States fourteen years earlier; she knew this tranquility could not last and savored every moment of this truce in her life. Not everything was idyllic, but compared to her past problems, those of the present were trivial. She had to have her wisdom teeth out, but her medical insurance did not cover dental treatment. She knew Seth Belasco was in love with her and that it would be increasingly difficult to keep him in check without losing his valuable friendship. Voigt, who had always been relaxed and friendly, had in recent months become so bad tempered that some of the residents were meeting secretly to find a tactful way to get rid of him, although Catherine Hope thought he should be given time, and for the moment her opinion prevailed. The director had twice been operated on for hemorrhoids, only partially successfully, and this had embittered him.

Irina's most urgent problem was an invasion of mice in the old Berkeley house where she rented a room. She could hear them scratching behind the cracked walls and underneath the wooden floorboards. At her neighbor Tim's insistence, the other tenants decided to lay traps, because it seemed inhumane to poison the creatures. Irina argued that the traps were just as cruel, and had the added disadvantage that somebody had to dispose of the corpses, but no one listened to her. Once, one of the tiny animals survived in a trap and was rescued by Tim, who passed it on to Irina, tears in his eyes. He was someone who ate only vegetables and nuts, because he could not bear the idea of harming any living thing, much less cooking it. Irina had to bandage up the mouse's broken foot, keep it in a cage with cotton wool, and take care of it until it had recovered from the shock and could walk properly and be released back with the others.

Some of Irina's duties at Lark House irritated her, such as the bureaucratic paperwork for the insurance companies or fighting with residents' relatives, who would complain over anything in order to assuage their sense of guilt at having abandoned their loved ones. Worst of all for Irina were the compulsory computer lessons, because no sooner had she learned something than the technology made another leap forward and she was left behind yet again. She had no complaints about the residents in her care. As Cathy had predicted on her first day at Lark House, she was never bored.

"There's a difference between being old and being ancient. It doesn't have to do with age, but physical and mental health," Cathy explained. "Those who are old can remain independent, but those who are ancient need help and supervision; there comes a moment when they're like children again."

Irina learned a lot from both the elderly and the ancient. Nearly all of them were sentimental, amusing, and had no fear of seeming ridiculous; Irina laughed with them and sometimes cried for them. Many had led interesting lives, or invented them. In general if they seemed very lost it was because they were hard of hearing. Irina made sure their hearing-aid batteries never ran out.

"What's the worst thing about growing old?" she would ask them.

They never thought about their age, was a common reply; they had once been adolescents, then they were thirty, fifty, sixty, and never gave it a thought, so why should they do so now? Some of them were very restricted, finding it hard to walk or move, and yet there was nowhere they wanted to go. Others were absentminded, confused, or forgetful, but this worried their carers and relatives more than it did them. Catherine Hope insisted that the residents of the second and third levels remain active, and it was Irina's job to keep them interested, entertained, and connected.

"However old one is, we need a goal in our lives. It's the best cure for many ills," Cathy insisted. In her case, the goal had always been to help others, and her accident had not altered this in the slightest.

On Friday mornings, Irina used to accompany the most active residents on their street protests, to make sure things didn't get out of hand. She also took part in the vigils for noble causes and in the knitting club; all the women who could wield a pair of needles (apart from Alma Belasco) were knitting cardigans for Syrian refugees. The recurring theme was peace; there was argument about everything apart from that. In Lark House there were 244 disillusioned Democrats who had voted to reelect Barack Obama but criticized him for being indecisive, for not having closed the Guantánamo facility, for deporting Latino immigrants, for the use of drones; there were more than enough reasons to send letters to the president and Congress. The half-dozen Republicans were careful not to voice their opinions out loud.

Irina was also responsible for helping with the spiritual needs of the residents. Many of them who were from a religious tradition sought refuge in it, even if they had spent sixty years denying God, while others sought comfort in esoteric and psychological alternatives typical of the Age of Aquarius. Irina brought in guides and masters for transcendental meditation, courses in miracles, the I Ching, the development of intuition, Kabbalah, the mystic tarot, animism, reincarnation, psychic perception, universal energy, and extraterrestrial life. She was the organizer of religious festivals, a potpourri of rituals drawn from several beliefs, so that no one could possibly feel excluded. At the summer solstice, she took a group of the women to the local woods, where they danced barefoot in circles to the sound of tambourines, with flowers in their hair. The rangers knew them and were happy to take photos of them hugging trees and talking to Gaia, Mother Earth, and with their own dead. Irina stopped mocking them inwardly the day she heard her grandparents in the trunk of a sequoia, one of those millenarian giants that unite our world to that of the spirits, as the octogenarian dancers had been quick to remind her. Costea and Petruta did not have much to say when they were alive, and nor did they from within the tree, but what little they did convey convinced their granddaughter that they were watching over her. At the winter solstice, Irina improvised ceremonies inside Lark House, as Cathy had warned her of a possible outbreak of pneumonia if they celebrated in the damp, windy woods at that time of year.

Irina's salary would barely have been enough for a normal person to live on, but her ambitions were so humble and her needs so modest that sometimes she could even save money. Her income from her dog-grooming business and as an assistant to Alma, who always looked for reasons to pay her more than they had agreed, made her feel rich. Lark House had become her home, and the residents, whose lives she shared every day, replaced her grandparents. She was touched by these slow, pallid old people with all their ailments. Faced with their problems she was infinitely good-humored; she didn't mind repeating the same answer to the same question a thousand times, and she enjoyed pushing their wheelchairs, encouraging, aiding, consoling them. She learned to deflect the violent impulses that occasionally swept over them like fleeting storms and wasn't frightened by the avarice or persecution complexes some of them suffered from out of loneliness. She tried to understand what it meant to carry winter on your back, to hesitate over every step, to confuse words you don't hear properly, to have the impression that the rest of the world is going about in a great rush; the emptiness, frailty, fatigue, and indifference toward everything not directly related to you, even children and grandchildren, whose absence was not felt as it once had been, and whose names you had to struggle to remember. She felt tender toward their wrinkles, arthritic fingers, and poor sight. She imagined how she herself would be as an elderly and then ancient woman.

But Alma Belasco never fit into that category; she didn't need looking after. On the contrary, Irina felt taken care of by her and enjoyed the role of helpless niece that had been allotted to her. Alma, who was pragmatic, agnostic, and fundamentally skeptical, wanted nothing to do with crystals, zodiacs, or talking trees; keeping her company, Irina found relief from her own uncertainties. She wanted to be like Alma and live in a manageable reality, where problems had definite causes and solutions, where there were no dreadful creatures lurking in her dreams, no lecherous enemies spying from every street corner. Hours with her were precious and Irina would willingly have worked for free. Once she had gone so far as to suggest it.

"I have more than enough money, and you don't have enough. Don't ever mention it again," said Alma in that imperious tone she almost never used with her.

SETH BELASCO

Alma Belasco enjoyed a leisurely breakfast, watched the news on TV, and then went to her yoga class or for an hour's walk. On her return, she showered, got dressed, and at the time when she calculated a cleaner sent by Lupita was due to arrive, she would escape to the clinic to help her friend Cathy. The best treatment for pain was to keep the patients busy and mobile. Cathy always needed volunteers in the clinic and had asked Alma to give silk-screen classes, but that required space and materials that no one there could afford. Cathy refused to have Alma pay for everything, because as she said, it would not be good for the participants' morale, as nobody wants to be the object of charity. As a result, Alma reached back to her former experience in the Sea Cliff attic with Nathaniel and Ichimei and improvised theatrical skits that were not only free but provoked gales of laughter. She went to her workshop three times a week to paint with Kirsten. She rarely frequented the Lark House dining room, preferring to eat out at local restaurants where the owners knew her, or in her apartment, when her daughter-in-law sent the chauffeur around with one of her favorite dishes. Irina kept only basic necessities in her kitchen: fresh fruit, oatmeal, whole-grain bread, honey.

Alma and Seth often invited Irina to their ritual Sunday lunch at Sea Cliff, where the family paid the matriarch homage. To Seth, who had previously used any pretext not to arrive before dessert—for even he was unable to consider not putting in an appearance at all—Irina's presence made the occasion infinitely more appealing. He was still stubbornly pursuing her, but since he was meeting with little success he also went out with previous girlfriends willing to put up with his fickleness. He was bored with them and did not succeed in making Irina jealous. As his grandmother often said and the family often repeated, why waste ammunition on vultures? It was yet another enigmatic saying often used by the Belascos. To Alma, these family reunions began with a pleasant sense of anticipation at seeing her loved ones, particularly her granddaughter, Pauline (she saw Seth frequently enough), but often ended up being a bore, since every topic of conversation became a pretext for getting angry, not from any lack of affection, but out of the bad habit of arguing over trivialities. Seth always looked for ways to challenge or scandalize his parents; Pauline brought to the table yet another cause she had embraced, which she explained in great detail, from genital mutilation to animal slaughterhouses; Doris took great pains to offer her most exquisite culinary experiments, which were veritable banquets, yet regularly ended up weeping in her room because nobody appreciated them; good old Larry meanwhile performed a constant balancing act to avoid quarrels. The grandmother took advantage of Irina to dissipate tension, because the Belascos always behaved in a civilized fashion in front of strangers, even if it was only a humble employee from Lark House.

To Irina, the Sea Cliff mansion seemed an extravagant luxury, with its six bedrooms, two living rooms, book-lined library, twin marble staircase, and garden fit for a palace. She was oblivious to the slow deterioration that almost a century's existence had wrought, which Doris's determined vigilance barely managed to keep at bay: the rust on the ornamental railings, the uneven floors and walls as a result of two earthquakes, the cracks in the floor tiles, and the termites' trails in the woodwork. The house stood in a privileged position on top of a promontory between the Pacific Ocean and San Francisco Bay. At first light, the thick mist rolling in from the sea like an avalanche of cotton wool often obscured the Golden Gate Bridge altogether, but in the course of the morning it would lift and the elegant red iron structure would gradually emerge against a sky dotted with gulls, so close to the Belascos' garden that it seemed possible to reach out and touch it.

Just as Alma became Irina's adoptive aunt, so Seth played the role of cousin, since he was having no success in that of lover. Over the three years of their acquaintance, the relationship between the two young people, born of Irina's solitude, Seth's poorly disguised passion, and the curiosity they both felt for Alma, grew increasingly close. Any man less stubborn and infatuated than Seth would have thrown in the towel long ago, but he learned to control his impetuosity and adapted to the tortoiselike progress imposed by Irina. It was no use trying to hasten things along, because at the slightest sign of intrusion she withdrew into her shell, and it took weeks for him to make up the lost ground. If they happened to touch each other, she pulled away at once; and if he did it on purpose, she grew alarmed. Seth searched in vain for something that might justify this mistrust, but her past remained a closed book. On the surface, no one would have suspected Irina's true nature, because she had already won the title of Lark House's most popular employee thanks to her open, friendly attitude, and yet Seth knew that this façade hid a wary squirrel.

In those three years, Seth's book began to come to life without any great effort on his part, thanks to the material his grandmother provided and Irina's insistence. Alma took it on herself to compile the Belasco family history, as they were the only family she had left after the war had swept away the Mendels in Poland and before her brother, Samuel, was resurrected. The Belascos were not part of the San Francisco aristocracy, simply among the most well-off, but they could trace their origins back to the Gold Rush. Isaac Belasco liked to say that there was only one aristocracy, that of decency, and that this was not inherited or bought with money or titles, but was only gained through good deeds. Their most famous ancestor was David Belasco, a theatrical director and producer, an impresario and author of more than a hundred works, who left the city in 1882 to go and triumph on Broadway. Seth's great-grandfather Isaac belonged to the branch of the family that stayed on in San Francisco, put down roots, and made a fortune thanks to a prosperous law firm and a good eye for investment.

Like all the Belasco males, Seth was expected to become a partner in the firm, even though he lacked the adversarial instinct of previous generations. He got a law degree out of a sense of duty and practiced because he felt sorry for his clients, not because he had any confidence in the legal system, still less out of an appetite for money. His sister, Pauline, two years younger, was better suited to such a thankless profession, but that did not exempt him from his responsibilities. He had reached the age of thirty-two without settling down, something for which his father reproached him. He continued to pass difficult cases on to his sister, preferring to enjoy life without caring about the cost, as he flitted between half a dozen short-lived love affairs. He boasted of his poetic vocation and his prowess at racing motorcycles in order to impress his girlfriends and scare his parents, but never considered renouncing the secure income he obtained from the family law firm. He was not cynical, merely lazy with regard to work, and much more excited by just about anything else. He was the first to be surprised at discovering that the pages of a manuscript were mounting up in the briefcase where he was supposed to keep court documents. In this digital era, the heavy caramel-colored case inscribed with his grandfather's gold initials was an anachronism, but Seth treasured it, convinced it contained supernatural powers: that was the only possible explanation for his manuscript's spontaneous growth. The words sprang forth unaided within the fertile womb of the briefcase and strolled tranquilly through the panorama of the imagination: two hundred and fifteen pages that came gushing out and that he never bothered to correct, as his plan consisted in setting down what he could elicit from his grandmother, adding what contributions he himself could muster, and then paying a ghostwriter and a conscientious editor to shape and polish the resulting book. Even so, the pages would never have existed without Irina's insistence on reading them, and her boldness in making criticisms, which obliged him to produce regular batches of ten or twelve for her perusal. In this way the pages began to mount up, and without intending to, he gradually became a novelist.

Seth was the only member of her family that Alma missed, although she would never have admitted it. If several days passed without his calling or visiting her, she grew irritable and soon invented an excuse to summon him. Her grandson scarcely needed any encouragement. He would arrive like a whirlwind, bike helmet under his arm, hair disheveled, red cheeked, and always with a small gift for her and another for Irina: sweet *dulce de leche alfajores*, almond soap, sketching paper, a zombie video. He was visibly upset if Irina wasn't there, but Alma pretended not to notice. He greeted his grandmother with a pat on the shoulder; she responded with her usual grunt; they were frank and trusting in their dealings with each other, like companions on an adventure, but they avoided all demonstration of affection, which they considered corny. They talked at length like old fishwives: first they would briefly discuss the news, including what the family was up to, and then soon immersed themselves in what really interested them. They were endlessly caught up in a mythical past full of improbable anecdotes and people from before Seth's birth. As she reminisced with her grandson, Alma showed herself to be an imaginative storyteller: she would recall in precise detail the Warsaw mansion where she had spent her early years, with its dark rooms and massive pieces of furniture, the uniformed servants gliding along the walls without raising their eyes—but she would add an imaginary wheat-colored pony with a long mane, which, according to her, was turned into stew during the years of hunger. She could resuscitate her Mendel great-grandparents and restore to them everything the Nazis had looted. She would picture them sitting at table for Passover with their silver candelabra and cutlery, French crystal, Bavarian porcelain, and tablecloths embroidered by Spanish nuns.

She was so eloquent in her description of the most tragic episodes that Seth and Irina felt they were accompanying the Mendel family on its way to Treblinka; they traveled with them inside the boxcar amidst hundreds of other desperate hungry people, without air or light, vomiting, defecating, dying before their eyes; they went naked with them into the chamber of horrors, vanished with them in the chimney smoke. Alma also told them about Seth's great-grandfather Isaac Belasco, and how although he died one month in the spring, that night there was an ice storm that completely destroyed his garden, and how he had two funerals, because there wasn't enough room in the first for all the people who wanted to pay their respects: hundreds of whites, blacks, Asians, Latinos, and others who felt indebted to him filed past his grave, so many that the rabbi had to repeat the ceremony. And she described Seth's great-grandmother Lillian, eternally in love with her husband, who on the day he died went blind and spent her remaining years in darkness, as no doctors could trace a cause for it. She also mentioned the Fukuda family and the evacuation of the Japanese in the Second World War, which had blighted her childhood—although she did not give any special emphasis to her relationship with Ichimei Fukuda.

THE FUKUDA FAMILY

*T*akao Fukuda had lived in the United States from the age of twenty without feeling any desire to integrate. Like many *issei*, the first generation of Japanese immigrants, he had no wish to dissolve in the American melting pot in the way that other races from all four corners of the world did. Proud of his culture and his language, he kept them intact and tried in vain to transmit them to his descendants, who were seduced by the grandeur of America. He admired many aspects of this immense land where the horizon blended with the sky but could not help feeling superior, although he never allowed this to show outside his home as this would have been an unforgivable lack of courtesy toward the country that had received him. As the years went by, he inevitably fell into the trap of nostalgia; the reasons why he left Japan became blurred, and he ended up idealizing those same stuffy traditions that had led him to emigrate in the first place. He was shocked by the Americans' self-confidence and materialism, which he saw not as character building and pragmatic, but as vulgarity; he suffered to see his children adopt the individualistic values and brash behavior of the local population. His four children may have been born in

California, but they were Japanese on both sides of their family, and so there was no justification for their lack of interest in their ancestors or lack of respect for their elders. They were unaware of the position destiny had allotted each of them; they had become infected by the foolish ambition of the Americans, to whom nothing seemed impossible. Takao knew that his children were betraying him even over small things: they drank beer until their heads were spinning, they chewed gum like cattle and danced to the frenetic rhythms that were fashionable, with greased hair and two-tone shoes. He was sure Charles and James sought out dark corners where they could fondle girls of dubious virtue, but at least he trusted that Megumi didn't do such things. His daughter copied the ridiculous fashions of American girls and in secret read the magazines full of love stories and gossip about movie idols that he had prohibited, but she was a good student and on the surface at least was respectful. The only one Takao could still control was Ichimei, but soon his youngest too would slip through his fingers and become a stranger like his brothers. That was the price to pay for living in America.

In 1912, Takao Fukuda had left his family and emigrated for metaphysical reasons, but this fact had gradually lost its importance in his memories of Japan, and he often wondered why he had taken such a drastic step. Japan had opened up to foreign influences, and many young men had been leaving to seek opportunities elsewhere, but for a member of the Fukuda family to leave their native country was regarded as an unpardonable betrayal. They came from a military line and for centuries had shed their blood for the emperor. Being the only male of the four children who survived the diseases and accidents of infancy, Takao was destined to be the guardian of the family's honor, responsible for his parents and sisters. It was he who would later lead the ancestor worship at the domestic altar and every religious festival. However, at fifteen he discovered Oomoto, the way of the gods, a new religion derived from Shintoism that was taking off in Japan at the time, and felt that at last he had discovered a map that could guide his steps through life. According to its spiritual leaders, nearly all of whom were women, there may be many gods, but they are all essentially the same, and it did not matter by what name or ritual they were worshipped. Throughout history, gods, religions, prophets, and messengers have all come from the same source: the Universe's Supreme God, the One Spirit, which impregnates all that exists. With the help of human beings, God tries to purify and rebuild the harmony of the universe, and when this task is complete, God, mankind, and nature will coexist in friendship on earth and in the spiritual realm. Takao threw himself into this new faith. Oomoto preached peace, which could be reached only through personal virtue, and Takao therefore realized that he could not follow a military career as those of his lineage were meant to. The only way out he could see was to get as far away as possible, because to stay in Japan and renounce warfare would be seen as unforgivable cowardice and the worst affront he could inflict on his family. When he tried to explain this to his father, he only managed to break his heart, but he expressed his reasons with such fervor that the old man finally accepted he would have to lose his son. Young people who left never returned. Dishonor can only be washed away by blood. His father told him that death at his own hand would be preferable, but this alternative went against the principles of Oomoto.

Takao reached the coast of California with two changes of clothes, a hand-tinted portrait of his mother and father, and the *samurai* sword that had been in his family for seven generations. His father handed it to him when they bade farewell, because he could not give it to any of his daughters. Even if his son were never to use it, the sword belonged to him by right. This *katana* was the Fukudas' sole treasure. It was made of the finest steel folded and refolded sixteen times by ancient craftsmen; its hilt was of wrought silver and bronze, and its wooden scabbard was decorated with red lacquer and gold leaf. Takao traveled with it wrapped in sacks for protection, but its long, curved shape was unmistakable. The men who shared the ship's hold with him during the tedious crossing treated him with due deference, as the weapon proved he was from a distinguished family.

After disembarking, he immediately received help from the tiny Oomoto community in San Francisco, and a few days later he found a job as a gardener for a compatriot. Far from the reproving gaze of his father, who thought a soldier should never dirty his hands with soil, only with blood, Takao devoted himself to learning this new skill, and it was not long before he established a reputation among the *issei* who made a living from agriculture. He worked tirelessly and lived frugally and virtuously as his religion required, so that in less than ten years he had saved the necessary eight hundred dollars to bring a wife over from Japan. The marriage broker offered him three candidates and he selected the first, because he liked her name, Heideko. Takao went down to await her arrival at the dock in his one and only suit, bought thirdhand and worn shiny at the elbows and on the backside, but well made; his shoes were polished and he wore a Panama hat he had bought in Chinatown. The fiancée he had sent for turned out to be a peasant girl ten years younger than him. She was stockily built, with a placid expression but a resolute temperament, and she was always ready to speak her mind. As he could tell from the very first moment, she was much less submissive than the marriage broker had suggested. Once he had recovered from the initial shock, Takao decided that this strength of character was a definite advantage.

Heideko arrived in California with few illusions. On board ship, where she had shared the narrow space allotted her with a dozen other girls in a similar situation, she had heard terrible stories of innocent virgins like her who had faced the dangers of the ocean in order to marry well-off young men in America, only to discover that waiting on the quayside to receive them were impecunious old men, or in the worst cases, pimps who sold them into prostitution or as slaves in clandestine workshops. This did not happen to her, as Takao Fukuda had sent her a recent photograph and did not lie to her about his situation, telling her he could only offer a life of effort and hard work, but one that was honorable and less backbreaking than that of her village in Japan. They had four children: first Charles, Megumi, and James, and then years later, in 1932, when Heideko thought she was no longer fertile, Ichimei arrived. He was premature and so puny that they thought he would not survive, and so did not give him a name for the first few months. His mother built up his strength as best she could with herbal infusions, acupuncture sessions, and cold water, until by some miracle it began to seem as though he would pull through. It was then that they gave him a Japanese name, unlike his brothers, who had been given English first names that were easy to pronounce in America. They called him Ichimei, meaning

"life," "light," "brilliance," or "star," according to the *kanji*, or ideo-
gram, used to represent it. From the age of three, he could swim
like an eel, at first in local pools and then in the freezing waters of
San Francisco Bay. His father molded his character through hard
physical work, a love of plants, and martial arts.

At the time Ichimei was born, the Fukuda family was struggling to
deal with the worst years of the Great Depression. They rented a
plot of land on the edge of San Francisco, where they grew vegetables and fruit trees to supply local markets. Takao supplemented
his income by working for the Belascos, the first family to employ him when he set up independently from the Japanese colleague who introduced him to gardening. His reputation was such
that Isaac Belasco invited him to create the garden for a property
he had recently acquired at Sea Cliff, where he wanted to build
a house that would stay in the family for at least a century, as he
joked to his architect, little thinking that his joke might come true.
His law firm was not short of funds, as he now represented the
California Western Railroad and Navigation Company; Isaac was
one of the few businessmen who did not suffer during the crisis.
He kept his money in gold and invested it in fishing boats, a saw-
mill, mechanics' workshops, a laundry, and other such businesses.
In doing so his intention was to employ some of the desperate folk
who lined up outside the charity soup kitchens, so that he could
help alleviate their misery, but this altruistic goal brought him unexpected benefits. While the house was being built according to
his wife's extravagant whims, Isaac shared with Takao his dream
of reproducing the plant life of other latitudes on a steep hillside

exposed to fog and wind. As they began the process of turning this crazy dream into reality, Isaac Belasco and Takao Fukuda established a respectful relationship. Together they read the catalogs, selected and ordered the trees and plants from other continents, which arrived wrapped in damp sacks with the original soil still sticking to their roots; together they pored over the instruction manual and assembled the glass greenhouse shipped piece by piece from London like a jigsaw puzzle; and together they kept this eclectic Garden of Eden alive.

Isaac's lack of interest in social life and the majority of his family affairs, which he delegated entirely to Lillian, was compensated for by an unbridled passion for botany. He neither smoked nor drank, and did not succumb to any known vices or irresistible temptations; he was wholly unable to appreciate either fine music or fine cuisine, and if Lillian had allowed it, he would have dined on the same coarse bread and poor man's soup eaten by the unemployed, standing up in the kitchen. A man like him was immune to corruption and vanity. Instead, he showed great intellectual curiosity, a passion for defending his clients with artful legal subterfuges, and a secret weakness for helping the needy. But none of these pleasures could compare to that of gardening. A third of his library was dedicated to botany. His ceremonious friendship with Takao, based on a mutual admiration and respect for nature, became fundamental to his peace of mind, an essential balm for his frustrations with the law. In his garden, Isaac became the humble apprentice of his Japanese master, who revealed secrets of the vegetable kingdom to him that his botanical treatises so often failed to clarify. Lillian adored her husband and looked after him with a young lover's care, but she never desired him so much as when she caught sight of him from her balcony, working side by side with the gardener. In his overalls, boots, and straw hat, sweating under the glare of the sun or soaked by fine rain, Isaac was rejuvenated, and in Lillian's eyes once more became the passionate lover who had seduced her at the age of nineteen, or the newlywed who possessed her on the stairs, before they could get as far as their bed.

Two years after Alma came to live at Sea Cliff, Isaac Belasco and Takao Fukuda formed a partnership to set up a nursery for flowers and decorative plants. Their dream was to make it the best in California. The first step was to purchase some parcels of land in Isaac's name, as a way of getting around the 1913 law that prohibited *issei* from becoming American citizens, owning land, or buying property. For Fukuda this was a unique opportunity; for Belasco it was a wise investment similar to others he had made at the height of the Depression. He had never been interested in the vagaries of the stock exchange, always preferring to invest in creating jobs. The two men became partners on the understanding that when Charles, Takao's eldest son, came of age, the Fukudas could buy out Isaac's share at the then prevailing prices, the nursery would be put into Charles's name, and their partnership would be dissolved. Because he was born in the United States, Charles was an American citizen. All this was a gentleman's agreement, sealed with a simple handshake.

The Belascos' garden remained deaf to the defamatory propaganda campaign against the Japanese, who were accused of unfair competition against American farmers and fishermen, threatening white women's virtue with their insatiable lust, and corrupting American society by their Oriental, anti-Christian ways. Alma only found out about these slurs two years after she had arrived in San Francisco, when from one day to the next the Fukuda family became the "yellow peril." By that time she and Ichimei were inseparable friends.

Imperial Japan's surprise attack on Pearl Harbor in December 1941 severely damaged twenty-one ships of the US fleet, leaving a tally of twenty-three hundred dead and more than a thousand wounded, and in less than twenty-four hours completely changed the Americans' isolationist mentality. President Roosevelt declared war on Japan, and a few days later Hitler and Mussolini, Japan's allies, declared war on the United States. The entire country was mobilized to fight the war that had been soaking Europe in blood for the past eighteen months. The reaction of widespread terror provoked by Japan's attack was whipped up by a hysterical media campaign that warned of an imminent invasion on the Pacific Coast by the "yellows." Hatred toward East Asians, which had already existed for a century, was exacerbated. Japanese who had lived in the country for years, as well as their children and grandchildren, suddenly became suspected of spying and collaborating with the enemy. The roundups and arrests began soon afterward. It was enough for a boat to have a shortwave radio—the only way for fishermen to communicate with the land—for the owner to be taken in. The dynamite used by small farmers to remove trunks and rocks from their crop fields was seen as proof of terrorism. Shotguns, and even kitchen knives and other tools, were impounded; so too were binoculars, cameras, small religious statues, ceremonial kimonos, and documents in another tongue.

Two months later, Roosevelt signed the order to evacuate for reasons of military security all persons of Japanese origin from the Pacific coast states—California, Oregon, and Washington, where the "yellow" troops might carry out the feared invasion. Arizona, Idaho, Montana, Nevada, and Utah were also declared military zones. The US Army was given three weeks to build the necessary shelters.

In March of 1942, San Francisco awoke plastered with warnings that announced the evacuation of the Japanese population. Takao and Heideko did not understand them, but their son Charles explained. First of all, the Japanese could not go outside a radius of five miles from their homes without a special permit and had to obey a nighttime curfew from eight p.m. to six a.m. The authorities began to raid houses and confiscate possessions; they arrested influential men who might incite treason, community leaders, company directors, teachers, pastors, and took them away to undisclosed destinations; their terrified wives and children were left behind. The Japanese had to quickly sell off whatever they owned at knockdown prices, and to close their businesses. They soon discovered that their bank accounts had been frozen; they were ruined. The plant nursery Takao Fukuda and Isaac Belasco had planned together never saw the light of day.

By August, more than a hundred and twenty thousand men, women, and children would be evacuated, old people snatched from hospitals, babies from orphanages, and mental patients from asylums. They would be interned in ten concentration camps in isolated areas of the interior, while cities would be left with phantom neighborhoods full of empty homes and desolate streets, where abandoned pets and the confused spirits of the ancestors who had arrived in America with the immigrants wandered aim-lessly. The evacuation order was aimed at protecting not only the Pacific coast but also the Japanese themselves, as they could be-come the victims of misunderstanding by the rest of the popu-lation; it was a temporary solution and would be carried out in a humane fashion. This was the official line, but meanwhile the hate speech spread. "A snake is always a snake, wherever it lays its eggs. A Japanese-American born of Japanese parents, brought up in a Japanese tradition, living in an atmosphere transplanted from Japan, inevitably and with only rare exceptions grows up as Japa-nese and not American. They are all enemies." It was enough to have a great-grandfather born in Japan to be seen as a snake.

As soon as Isaac Belasco learned of the imminent evacuation, he went to see Takao to offer help and reassure him that his ab-sence would be a short one because the evacuation was uncon-stitutional, violating the principles of American democracy. His Japanese partner replied with a deep bow. He was profoundly moved by this man's friendship, because in recent weeks his family had suffered insults, snubs, and even aggression from other whites. *Shikata ga nai*, what can we do, Takao told him. That was his peo-ple's slogan in times of adversity. When Isaac insisted, Takao asked a special favor of him: to allow him to bury the Fukuda sword in the garden at Sea Cliff. He had managed to hide it from the agents who raided his house, but it wasn't safe. The sword represented the courage of his forebears and the blood shed for the emperor; it could not run the risk of being dishonored.

That same night the entire Fukuda family, dressed in the white kimonos of the Oomoto religion, went to Sea Cliff, where Isaac and his son, Nathaniel, received them in dark suits and wearing the yarmulkes they used on the rare occasions they attended a synagogue. Ichimei brought his cat in a basket covered in a cloth and handed him to Alma to look after for a while.

"What's his name?" she asked him.

"Neko. It's Japanese for 'cat.'"

Accompanied by her daughters, Lillian served Heideko and Megumi tea in one of the first-floor living rooms, while Alma, who did not understand what was going on but was aware of the solemnity of the occasion, slipped through the shadows beneath the trees and followed the men, clutching the basket. They filed downhill through the terraces, lighting their way with oil lamps, until they reached the spot overlooking the sea where they had dug a small trench. In the lead was Takao, carrying the *katana* wrapped in white silk; after him came his eldest son, Charles, with the metal box they had had made to protect the sword; James and Ichimei followed him; and Isaac and Nathaniel Belasco brought up the rear. Not bothering to hide his tears, Takao prayed for several minutes, then placed the sword in the box his eldest son held out and fell to his knees, forehead pressed against the ground, while Charles and James lowered the *katana* into the hole and Ichimei scattered handfuls of soil onto it. Then they filled the hole in and flattened the earth with spades. "Tomorrow I will plant white chrysanthemums here to mark the spot," said Isaac, his voice hoarse with emotion, as he helped Takao to his feet.

Alma did not dare run over to Ichimei, because she guessed there must be an overriding reason why women were excluded from the ceremony. She waited until they had returned to the house to catch Ichimei and drag him off to a corner out of sight. The boy explained he would not be returning the following Saturday or any other day for the time being, possibly for several weeks or months, and that they would not be able to talk on the telephone either. "Why? Why?" shouted Alma, shaking him, but Ichimei could not explain. He himself had no idea why they had to leave or where they were going.

THE YELLOW PERIL

*T*he Fukudas covered their windows and put a padlock on the street door. It was March, and they had paid a year's rent, as well as a deposit to buy the house just as soon as they could put it in Charles's name. They gave away what they could not or would not sell, because the opportunist buyers were offering two or three dollars for things that were worth twenty times that. They had only a few days to dispose of their possessions, pack one suitcase each and what they could carry, and present themselves at the "buses of shame." They were forced to accept internment, otherwise they would be arrested and face the consequences of spying and treason in wartime. Joining hundreds of other families shuffling along in their best clothes, the women wearing hats, the men with neckties, the children in patent leather bootees, they went to the Civil Control Center. The families gave themselves up because there was no alternative and because by so doing they thought they were demonstrating their loyalty toward the United States and their repudiation of Japan's attack on Pearl Harbor. This was their contribution to the war effort, the leaders of the Japanese community said, and very few voices were raised against them.

The Fukudas were destined for the camp at Topaz, in a desert area of Utah, but were unaware of this until September; in the meantime they were housed six months at a racetrack.

Accustomed as they were to being discreet, the *issei* obeyed without protest, but they could not prevent some young people, second-generation *nisei*, from openly rebelling. These youngsters were separated from their families and dispatched to Tule Lake, the strictest concentration camp, where they were treated like criminals for the duration of the war. In San Francisco, the local white population observed the harrowing procession along the streets of people they knew well: the owners of stores where they shopped every day; the fishermen, gardeners, and carpenters they often dealt with; their sons' and daughters' schoolmates; their neighbors. Most of them looked on in troubled silence, although there was no shortage of racist insults and malicious jeers. Two-thirds of those evacuated at that time had been born in the United States and were American citizens. Standing in long lines, the Japanese had to wait for hours in front of the desks of the officials, who took down their names and handed out labels for them to wear around their necks with their identity number, the same as for their luggage. A group of Quakers, who were opposed to this measure because they considered it racist and anti-Christian, offered them water, sandwiches, and fruit.

Takao Fukuda was about to climb on board the bus with his family when Isaac Belasco appeared, dragging Alma along with him. He had used the weight of his authority to intimidate the officials and soldiers who tried to stop him. He was deeply disturbed, as he could not help but compare what was taking place only a few blocks from his home with what had probably happened to his in-laws in Warsaw. He pushed his way through to hug his friend and hand him an envelope stuffed with cash, which Takao tried in vain to refuse, while Alma bade farewell to Ichimei. Write to me, write to me, was the last thing both children could say to each other before the disconsolate line of buses pulled away.

At the end of what seemed to them an interminable journey, although in reality it lasted little more than an hour, the Fukuda family reached the racetrack at Tanforan, in the city of San Bruno. The authorities had enclosed the stadium in a barbed-wire fence, hurriedly cleared out the stables, and constructed makeshift barracks to house eight thousand people. The evacuation order had been so rushed, there had been no time to finish the installations or to equip the camps with the essentials. The buses' engines were switched off, and the prisoners began to disembark, carrying children and bundles, helping the old folk. They moved forward without a word in huddled, uncertain groups, unable to understand the squawking of the blaring loudspeakers. Rain had turned the ground into a quagmire, and was soaking them and their belongings.

Armed guards separated men and women for an initial medical examination; later on they were to be inoculated against typhus and measles. Over the next few hours the Fukudas tried to recover their things from the jumbled mountains of luggage and then moved into the empty stable stall assigned to them. Cobwebs hung from the roof; there were cockroaches and mice, and several inches of dust and straw on the floor. The smell of horses still lingered in the air, as well as that of the creosote used to little effect as a disinfectant. They were given a cot, a sack, and two army blankets each. Takao was so weary and humiliated to the depths of his being that he sat down on the floor with his elbows on his knees and buried his head in his hands. Heideko took off her hat, put on her sandals, rolled her sleeves up, and prepared to make the best of their misfortune. She didn't give the children time to feel sorry for themselves, but immediately got them to make up the beds and sweep the floor. Then she sent Charles and James to fetch bits of board and sticks, left over from the hasty construction work, that she had seen when they arrived, in order to make shelves where she could put the few kitchen utensils she had brought with her. She told Megumi and Ichimei to fill the sacks with straw to make mattresses, as they had been instructed to do, while she set out to explore the installations, say hello to the other women, and size up the camp guards and officials, who were as bewildered as the detainees they were in charge of, wondering how long they were going to have to stay there. The only obvious enemies Heideko could identify on her first tour of inspection were the Korean interpreters, whom she saw as odious toward the evacuees and fawning toward the American officials. She saw that there were not enough latrines or showers, and that they had no doors; the women had four baths between them, and insufficient hot water. The right to privacy had been abolished. But she thought they wouldn't be short of food, because she saw the provision trucks and learned that they would be serving three meals a day in the mess halls, starting that evening.

Supper consisted of potatoes, sausages, and bread, but the sausages ran out before it was the Fukuda family's turn. "Come back later," one of the Japanese servers whispered. Heideko and Megumi waited for the canteen to empty and were given a tin of minced meat and more potatoes, which they took back to the family room. That night, Heideko went through a mental list of the steps to be taken to make their stay at the racetrack more bearable. The first item was their diet, and the last, in parentheses because she seriously doubted she could achieve it, was to change the interpreters. She didn't shut her eyes all that night, and as the first rays of sunlight filtered through the bars of the stable window, she shook her husband, who had not slept either and was lying there motionless.

"There's a lot to do here, Takao. We need representatives to negotiate with the authorities. Put your jacket on and go and gather the men together."

Problems arose at once at Tanforan, but before the week was out the evacuees had organized themselves. After taking a democratic vote to elect their representatives, among whom Heideko Fukuda was the only woman, they registered the adults according to their professions and skills—teachers, farmers, carpenters, blacksmiths, accountants, doctors. Then they started a school without either pencils or notebooks, and put sports and other activities on the schedule to keep the young people busy so as to combat their frustration and boredom. The evacuees spent much of the day and night lining up, for the shower, hospital, religious services, mail, and three meals in the canteens; they had to show a great deal of patience to avoid disturbances and fights. There was a daily curfew, and a twice-daily roll call. Speaking in Japanese was prohibited, which made life impossible for the *issei*. To prevent the guards from intervening, the internees themselves took charge of keeping order and controlling any troublemakers, but no one could stop the rumors from swirling around, which frequently caused panic.

People tried to stay polite, so that the hardship, the crowded living conditions, and the humiliation were more tolerable.

Six months later, on the eleventh of September, the detainees began to be transferred by train. Nobody knew where they were headed. After a day and two nights of travel on dilapidated, suffocating trains with few toilets and no lights in the dark hours, crossing desolate landscapes they did not recognize and that many confused with Mexico, they came to a halt at Delta station in Utah. From there they continued the journey in trucks and buses to Topaz, the Jewel of the Desert, as the concentration camp had been called, possibly without any ironic intent. The filthy evacuees were trembling and half-dead from exhaustion but had not been hungry or thirsty, because sandwiches had been handed out in each carriage, and there were baskets full of oranges.

At an altitude of more than four thousand feet, Topaz was a ghastly makeshift city of identical low buildings like a military base. It was ringed by barbed wire, tall watchtowers, and armed soldiers, and was set in an arid, godforsaken landscape that was lashed by the wind and whirling dust storms. The other Japanese concentration camps in the West were similar, and placed in desert areas to discourage any attempt at escape. There was not a single tree or bush to be seen, nothing green in any direction, only rows of gloomy huts stretching to the horizon. Families huddled together, holding hands to avoid getting lost in the confusion. They all needed to use the latrines but had no idea where they were. It took the guards several hours to organize the new arrivals, because they did not understand the instructions either, but they finally assigned all the accommodations.

The Fukuda family defied the dust clouding the air and making it hard to breathe, and found their allotted lodging. Each hut was divided into six units measuring roughly twelve by twenty feet per family, separated by thin partitions of tar paper. There were twelve huts per block, forty-two blocks in total; each of them had a canteen, laundry, showers, and latrines. The camp occupied a vast area, but the eight thousand evacuees had to live in little more than seven thousand square feet. The detainees were soon to discover that the temperature varied between an infernal heat in the summer and several degrees below zero in the winter. In the summer months, as well as the terrible heat, they had to endure the constant onslaught of mosquitoes and dust storms that darkened the sky and scorched their lungs. The wind blew all year round, bringing with it the stench of the sewage that formed a swamp a half mile from the camp.

Just as they had done at the Tanforan racetrack, the Japanese organized quickly at Topaz. Within a few weeks there were schools, nurseries, sports areas, and a newspaper. They created art from bits of wood, stones, and other material left over from the construction of the camp. They made jewelry from fossilized shells and peach stones, stuffed dolls with rags, and toys with sticks. They started a library with donated books, as well as theater companies and music groups. Ichimei convinced his father that they could grow vegetables in boxes despite the harsh climate and alkaline soil. This encouraged Takao, and soon others were copying him. Several *issei* decided to start a decorative garden. They dug a hole, filled it with water, and so made a pond that was the delight of the children. With his magic fingers, Ichimei built a wooden yacht that he sailed across the pond; less than four days later there were races of dozens of these small boats. The kitchens in each block were run by the detainees, who performed marvels with dry and canned goods that were brought in from the nearest towns. The following year they would also use the vegetables they managed to harvest, watering them by the spoonful. As Heideko had foreseen, the unusual amounts of fat and sugar they consumed soon led to problems. The lines for the latrines stretched for several blocks; the need was so desperate and anguished that no one waited for darkness to compensate for the lack of privacy. The latrines became blocked with the diarrhea of thousands of patients, and the rudimentary hospital staffed by white personnel and Japanese doctors and nurses could not cope.

Once the pieces of wood for making furniture had run out, and tasks had been assigned to all those who felt impatience gnawing at their entrails, most of the evacuees succumbed to boredom. Days seemed endless in this nightmare city supervised by disinterested guards in their nearby towers and in the distance by the magnificent mountains of Utah. Every day was the same, nothing to do, lines and more lines, waiting for the mail, passing the idle hours playing cards, inventing pointless jobs, repeating the exact same conversations that gradually lost all meaning as the words became threadbare. Ancestral traditions began to disappear, parents and grandparents saw their authority diminish, couples were trapped in a proximity without intimacy, families began to disintegrate. They could not even sit down together for meals, but were forced to eat in the din of the communal mess halls. However much Takao insisted the Fukuda family sit together, his boys preferred to go with others of the same age, and it was hard to restrain Megumi, who had turned into a real beauty, with pink cheeks and flashing eyes. The only ones free from the torments of despair were the little children, who roamed the camp in packs, getting up to mischief and imagining adventures, and saw all this as one long vacation.

Winter arrived early. When the snow began to fall, each family was given a coal-burning stove, which soon became the center of social life, and discarded military clothing was distributed. These faded green uniforms were too large, and were as depressing as the frozen countryside and black huts. The women began to make paper flowers for their dwellings. At night there was no way to prevent the wind, which brought slivers of ice with it, from whistling through the cracks in the huts and lifting the roofs. Like everyone else, the Fukuda family slept in all their clothes, wrapped in the pair of blankets they had been given, curled up together on the camp beds to lend each other warmth and comfort. Months later, when summer came, they would sleep almost naked and wake up covered in a layer of ash-colored sand as fine as talcum powder. Despite all this, they considered themselves fortunate, because they were together. Other families had been split up; first the men had been taken off to what were known as relocation camps, then the women and children sent to another one. In some cases it was two or three years before they were reunited.

The correspondence between Alma and Ichimei suffered right from the start. The letters took weeks to arrive, although the postal service was not to blame so much as the slowness of the Topaz officials, overwhelmed by having to read the hundreds of letters that piled up on their desks every day. Alma's letters, which in no way put the safety of the United States in danger, were allowed through without a problem, but Ichimei's were so mutilated by the censorship that she had to guess at the meaning of his sentences between the lines of black ink. His descriptions of barracks, food, latrines, the guards' behavior, even comments about the weather, were all regarded as suspicious. Advised by others more practiced in the art of deception, Ichimei sprinkled his letters with praise for the Americans and patriotic outbursts until he felt so nauseous he had to stop. Instead he decided to draw. It had been more than usually difficult for him to learn to read and write, and at ten he was still not sure of all the alphabet, which he mixed up without proper regard for spelling, but he had always had a good eye and a steady hand for drawing. His illustrations passed through censorship without a hitch, and so Alma was able to learn about the details of his life at Topaz as if she were looking at photographs.

Yesterday when we talked about Topaz I didn't mention the most important thing, Alma: not everything was negative. We had parties, sports, art. We ate turkey at Thanksgiving and decorated the barracks for Christmas. People sent us parcels with candy, toys, and books. My mother was always busy with new plans; everyone respected her, even the whites. Megumi was in love and overjoyed with her work at the hospital. I painted, planted the vegetable garden, mended broken things. The classes were so short and easy that even I got good grades. I used to play almost all day long; there were lots of children and hundreds of stray dogs, all of them the same, short legged and with wiry hair. The ones who suffered most were my father and James.

After the war, the people from the camps spread throughout the country. The youngsters became independent; the idea of living isolated in a poor imitation of Japan was finished. We integrated into America.

I think of you. When we meet I'll make you tea and we'll talk again.

Ichi

IRINA, ALMA, AND LENNY

*T*he two women were having lunch under the historic stained-glass cupola in Neiman Marcus on Union Square. More than anything, they went there for the popovers, served warm straight from the oven, and the pink champagne, which was Alma's favorite. Irina ordered lemonade and both raised their glasses to the good life. In silence, so as not to offend Alma, Irina also toasted the Belascos' wealth, which allowed her the luxury of this moment, with its soft music, elegant shoppers, willowy models parading in high-fashion dresses to tempt purchasers, and obsequious waiters wearing green ties. This refined world was infinitely removed from her Moldovan village and all the hardships she had suffered in her childhood, let alone the terrors of her adolescence.

The two women ate peacefully, savoring Asian dishes and ordering more popovers. A second glass of champagne loosened Alma's tongue, and on this occasion she talked about Nathaniel, her husband, who was nearly always part of her reminiscences; she had managed to keep him alive in her memory for three decades now. Seth had vague memories of his grandfather as an exhausted skeleton with burning eyes propped up on downy pillows. He was barely four years old when his grandfather's painful expression was gone forever, but he had never forgotten the smell of medicines and eucalyptus vapor in his bedroom. Alma told Irina that Nathaniel was as generous as his father, Isaac Belasco, and that when he died, among his papers she had found hundreds of IOUs for loans he never called in, and precise instructions to pardon his many debtors. She found herself unprepared to take charge of all the matters he had left unfinished during his devastating final illness.

"I've never in all my life worried about money matters. Strange, isn't it?"

"You were lucky. Almost everyone I know has money worries. The residents at Lark House all scrape by, and some of them can't even buy the medicines they need."

"Don't they have health insurance?" asked Alma in astonishment.

"The insurance covers part of the expense, but not all. If their families don't help them, Mr. Voigt has to draw on Lark House's special reserves."

"I'll go and talk to him. Why did you never tell me this before, Irina?"

"You can't solve every case, Alma."

"No, but the Belasco Foundation could maintain the park at Lark House. Then Voigt would save a stack of money he could use to help the neediest residents."

"Mr. Voigt would faint in your arms if you suggested such a thing, Alma."

"What an appalling thought! I sincerely hope not."

"But tell me more about what happened to you after your husband died."

"I was drowning in all the paperwork, when it finally occurred to me to ask Larry. My son had lived quietly in the shadows and had grown up to become a cautious and responsible gentleman without anyone really noticing."

Larry Belasco had married young, in a rush and without fuss, both because of his father's illness and because his fiancée, Doris, was visibly pregnant. Alma admitted that at the time she was so preoccupied looking after her husband that she had few opportunities to get to know her daughter-in-law, even though they lived under the same roof. Yet she ended up loving her dearly because, quite apart from her virtues, Doris adored Larry and was a good mother both to Seth, the little mischief maker, who soon was bounding around the house like a kangaroo, driving out the lugubrious atmosphere, and later to Pauline, a placid little girl, who kept herself amused and seemed to have no further needs.

"Just as I never had to worry about money, so I never had the bother of domestic chores. In spite of being blind, my mother-in-law looked after the Sea Cliff house until her dying breath, and after her we had a butler, who seemed to have come straight out of one of those English films. He was so mannered that in the family we always thought he was making fun of us."

She told Irina that the butler was at Sea Cliff for eleven years and left when Doris dared to suggest how he should do his job. "It's her or me," the butler told Nathaniel, who by this time no longer left his bed and had little strength to struggle with this kind of problem, despite his having hired all the staff. Faced with this ultimatum, Nathaniel chose his brand-new daughter-in-law, who, despite her youth and her belly rounded by seven months of pregnancy, had already proved herself a compulsive lady of the house. During Lillian's lifetime the mansion had been run with goodwill and spontaneity; as for the butler, the only noticeable changes were the length of time it took to serve each dish at table and the cook's sour expression, because he could not stand him. With Doris's strict regime, the house became a model of precision where no one felt completely at ease. Irina had observed the results of her efficiency: the kitchen was a spotless laboratory, no children were allowed in the living rooms, the wardrobes were scented with lavender, the sheets were starched, daily meals consisted of minuscule portions of fancy dishes, and the flower displays were renewed weekly by a florist. All of this however did not lend the house a festive atmosphere, but made it as solemn as a funeral parlor. The only thing that the magic wand of domesticity had spared was Alma's empty bedroom, as Doris held her in reverential awe.

"When Nathaniel fell ill, Larry took charge of the Belasco law firm," Alma went on. "He ran it very well from day one. So when Nathaniel died I could delegate the family finances to him and devote myself to resurrecting the moribund Belasco Foundation. The public parks were drying out and were filled with garbage, needles, and used condoms. Beggars had moved in, with shopping carts crammed full of filthy bags and their cardboard shelters. I know nothing about plants, but I threw myself into gardening out of love for my father-in-law and my husband. To them it was a sacred mission."

"It seems as if all the men in your family have been kindhearted, Alma. There aren't many people like them in this world of ours."

"There are a lot of good people, Irina, but they keep quiet

about it. It's the bad ones who make a lot of noise, and that's why they get noticed. You don't know Larry very well, but if you need something at any time and I'm not around, don't hesitate to turn to him. My son is a good man, he won't let you down."

"He seems very serious, I wouldn't dare disturb him."

"He's always been serious. When he was twenty he looked fifty, but he got stuck like that and has stayed the same as he's aged. Just look, in every photograph he has that same worried expression and drooping shoulders."

Hans Voigt had established a simple system for the Lark House residents to judge the performance of each member of staff, and he was intrigued by the fact that Irina always obtained an excellent report. He guessed her secret must be her ability to listen to the same story a thousand times over as if she were hearing it for the first time, all those tales the old folks keep repeating to accommodate the past and create an acceptable self-portrait, erasing remorse and extolling their real or imagined virtues. Nobody wants to end their life with a banal past. However, Irina's secret was in fact more complicated: to her each one of the Lark House residents was a replica of her grandparents Costea and Petruta, to whom she prayed every night before going to sleep, asking them to accompany her through the darkness, as they had done throughout her childhood. They had raised her, toiling on a thankless patch of ground in their remote Moldovan village, where not even the slightest breeze of progress blew. Most of the locals still lived in the country and continued working the land just as their ancestors had done a century earlier. Irina was two years old in

1989 when the Berlin wall came down, and four when the Soviet Union collapsed and her country became an independent republic. Neither of these events meant anything to her, but her grandparents lamented them, as did their neighbors. They all agreed that under communism they had been just as poor, but at least there was food and security, whereas independence had brought them only ruin and abandonment. Anyone who could leave did so, including Irina's mother, Radmila, so that the only ones left behind were the old and children whose parents could not take them with them. Irina remembered her grandparents bent double from the effort of growing potatoes, faces lined by the August sun and freezing Januarys, with little strength left and no hope. She concluded that the countryside was fatal to health. She was the reason her grandparents kept on struggling, their one joy—with the exception of homemade red wine, a drink as rough as paint stripper that gave them the chance to escape their loneliness and boredom for a while.

At first light, before she walked to school, Irina used to carry buckets from the well, and in the evening, before soup and bread for supper, she would chop wood for the stove. In California she weighed 110 pounds in her winter clothes and boots but was strong as an ox and could lift Cathy, her favorite client, like a newborn babe to transfer her from her wheelchair to a sofa or the bed. If she owed her muscles to the buckets of water and the ax, she owed the good luck that she was alive to Saint Parascheva, the patron saint of Moldova and the intermediary between the earth and the kindly beings in the heavens. At night as a child she would kneel with her grandparents before the saint's icon to pray for the potato harvest and the health of their chickens; for protection against evildoers and soldiers; for their fragile republic; and for Radmila. To Irina as a child, the haloed saint in the blue cloak who was holding a cross seemed far more human than the silhouette of her mother in a faded photograph. Irina did not miss her but enjoyed imagining that one day Radmila would return with a bag full of gifts for her. She heard nothing from her mother until she was eight years old, when her grandparents received a little money from their distant daughter. They spent it cautiously so as not to make their neighbors jealous. Irina felt cheated, because her mother did not send anything special for her, not even a note. The envelope contained nothing more than the money and a couple of photographs of a stranger with peroxide-blond hair and a harsh expression who looked very different from the young woman in the photo the old couple kept next to the icon. After that they received money from her two or three times a year, which helped alleviate their poverty.

Radmila's drama was similar to that of thousands of other young Moldovan women. She had become pregnant at sixteen by a Russian soldier passing through with his regiment and from whom she heard nothing more. She had Irina because her attempts at abortion failed, and she escaped far away as soon as she could. Years later, in order to warn her about the world's perils, Radmila told her daughter the details of her odyssey, with a glass of vodka in her hand and two more already down the hatch.

One day a woman from the city had come to the village to recruit young girls to work as waitresses in another country. She offered Radmila an amazing once-in-a-lifetime opportunity: passport and ticket, easy work and a good wage. She assured her that just from the tips she would be able to save enough to buy herself a house in less than three years. Ignoring her parents' desperate pleas, Radmila boarded the train with the procurer, little suspecting she would end up in the claws of Turkish pimps in a brothel in the Aksaray neighborhood of Istanbul. She was kept prisoner there for two years, servicing between thirty and forty men daily to pay off her ticket, although the debt was never reduced because she was charged for her lodging, food, shower, and condoms. Any girls who resisted were beaten up, marked with knives, burned, or even found dead in an alleyway. Without money or documents escape was impossible; they were locked in, did not know the language, the neighborhood, or the wider city. If they did manage to evade the pimps, they came up against the police, who were also their most assiduous clients and whom they had to pleasure for free.

"One girl threw herself out of a third-floor window and was left half paralyzed, but she still had to keep working," Radmila told Irina in the half-melodramatic, half-didactic tone she used to refer to this wretched episode in her life. "As she couldn't control her sphincter and constantly soiled herself, men could go with her for half price. Another girl became pregnant and performed on a mattress with a hole in it to fit her belly into; in her case, the clients paid more, because they thought that fucking a pregnant woman cured gonorrhea. When the pimps wanted new faces, they sold us to other brothels, and so we went down and down until we reached the depths of hell. I was saved by fire and a man who took pity on me. One night there was a blaze that spread to several houses in the neighborhood. Journalists arrived with their cameras, and so the police couldn't turn a blind eye; they arrested us girls shivering in the street, but not one of the damned pimps or clients. We appeared on TV, where we were accused of being depraved and responsible for all the filth that occurred in Aksaray. They were going to deport us, but a cop I knew helped me escape and got me a passport." Eventually, Radmila reached Italy, where she worked as an office cleaner and then in a factory. She had kidney problems, and was worn out from her experiences, drugs, and alcohol, yet she was still young and her skin had some of the translucent quality of her youth, similar to her daughter's. An American technician fell for her, they got married, and he took her with him to Texas, where some years later her daughter also arrived.

The last time Irina saw her grandparents, one morning in 1999 when they left her at the train that was to take her to Chisinau on the first stage of her long journey to Texas, Costea was sixty-two and Petruta a year younger. They were much more decrepit than any of the residents of over ninety at Lark House, who aged slowly and with dignity, with full sets of their own teeth or proper dentures. Irina had discovered that the process was the same: they advanced step by step toward the end, some more quickly than others, and lost everything along the way, for we cannot take anything with us to the other side of death. A few months after Irina left, Petruta's head slumped over a plate of potatoes and onion and she didn't wake up again. Costea had lived with her for forty years and concluded there was no point going on alone. He hanged himself from the beam in the barn, where the neighbors found him three days later, drawn by his barking dog and the bleating of the goat, which had not been milked. Irina learned this years later from a judge at the juvenile court in Dallas. But she never talked about it.

Early that autumn, Lenny Beal came to live in one of the independent apartments at Lark House. The new guest came with Sophia, his white dog with a black patch over one eye that gave her the air of a pirate. His arrival was a memorable event, as none of the few other male residents could compare to him. Some of them were married, others were in diapers on the third level, about to pass on to Paradise, and the rare available widowers held no interest for any of the women. Lenny was eighty years old, but nobody would have said he was more than sixty. He was the most desirable specimen seen at Lark House in decades, with a mane of white hair that ended in a small ponytail, his astonishing lapis lazuli eyes, his youthfully cut crumpled linen trousers, and the rope-soled sandals he wore without socks. He almost caused a riot among the ladies; he filled all the empty space, as if someone had let a tiger loose in this world of female longing.

Even Voigt, with all his years as an administrator, wondered what Lenny was doing there. Mature, well-preserved men like him always had a much younger woman—their second or third wife— to look after them. He greeted Lenny with all the enthusiasm he could muster between spasms from his hemorrhoids which were still torturing him. Despite the fact that Catherine Hope had been trying to help him at her clinic, where a Chinese doctor came three times a week to perform acupuncture, his progress was slow. The director calculated that even the most damaged ladies, the ones who sat staring into space as they delved into their past because the present was slipping away from them, would stand a chance of coming back to life thanks to Lenny Beal. He wasn't wrong. Overnight blue-rinse wigs appeared, together with strings of pearls and varnished nails—all of which were a novelty for these ladies who despised artifice and had a tendency toward Buddhism and ecology.

"Good grief! It looks like a geriatric home in Miami," Voigt told Cathy.

Bets were laid as to what the newcomer had been in his previous life: actor, fashion designer, an importer of Oriental art, professional tennis player. Alma put a stop to all this speculation when she told Irina to pass on the news that Lenny had actually been a dentist, although none of the residents could quite believe he had earned a living poking around other people's teeth.

Lenny Beal and Alma Belasco had met thirty years earlier. When they saw each other again in Lark House, they gave each other a long hug in the middle of the reception hall, and when they finally stepped back, both of them had tears in their eyes. Irina had never seen such a show of emotion from Alma, and if she had not been so convinced about the Japanese lover, she would have thought Lenny was the reason for all those clandestine meetings. She called Seth at once to tell him the news.

"You say he's a friend of my grandmother's? I've never heard of him. I'll check him out."

"How?"

"That's why I employ investigators."

Seth's investigators were two former criminals, one white and the other black, both of them fearsome looking, who spent their time gathering information on cases before they were presented at court. Seth explained the most recent case to Irina. This involved a seaman who was suing a shipping company for a work accident that he claimed had left him paralyzed, but Seth did not believe him. His toughs invited the invalid to a shady nightclub, where they got him drunk and then videoed him dancing with a hostess. Armed with this proof, Seth was able to silence the other man's lawyer; they made a settlement and were spared the trouble of a court case. Seth confessed to Irina that this had been one of the more honorable tasks that his investigators performed; others had been far more questionable.

Two days later, Seth called Irina for them to meet in the usual pizzeria, but she had bathed five dogs that weekend and was feeling generous. She proposed that this once they go to a decent restaurant: Alma had put the obsession for white tablecloths into her head.

"This time I'm paying," she told him.

Seth picked her up on his motorcycle and zigzagged with her through the traffic well beyond the speed limit until they reached the Italian district. They arrived with their hair plastered down from their helmets and their noses dripping. Irina realized she was not properly dressed for the restaurant—she never was—and the waiter's disdainful look only served to confirm it. When she saw the prices on the menu she almost fainted.

"Don't worry, my firm will pay," Seth reassured her.

"This is going to cost more than a wheelchair!"

"Why do you want a wheelchair?"

"It's just a comparison, Seth. There are a couple of old ladies in Lark House who can't afford the wheelchairs they need."

"That's very sad, Irina. I can recommend the scallops with truffles. And a good white wine, of course."

"Coca-Cola for me."

"To go with scallops it has to be Chablis. They don't serve Coca-Cola here."

"Then I'll have mineral water with a twist of lemon."

"Are you an alcoholic in rehab, Irina? You can tell me, there's no reason to be ashamed. It's an illness, like diabetes."

"No, I'm not an alcoholic, but wine gives me a headache," replied Irina, who had no intention of sharing her worst memories with him.

Before the first course they were served, courtesy of the chef, a spoonful of a blackish foam that seemed to her like it had been vomited by a dragon. Irina tasted it suspiciously, while Seth was explaining that Lenny was a bachelor, had no children, and had specialized in root canal treatment at a dental clinic in Santa Barbara. There was nothing noteworthy about his life, except that he was a great sportsman who had done the Ironman challenge several times—a crazy combination of swimming, cycling, and running that frankly did not sound very appealing. Seth had mentioned Lenny to his father, who had the impression he had been a friend of Alma and Nathaniel, although he couldn't be sure. He vaguely recalled having seen him at Sea Cliff during Nathaniel's final illness. Many loyal friends passed through to keep his father company in those days, and Lenny might have been one of them. For the moment, Seth had no more information about him, but he had discovered something about Ichimei.

"The Fukuda family spent three and a half years in a concentration camp during the Second World War," he told Irina.

"Where?"

"At Topaz, in the middle of the Utah desert."

Irina had only heard of the German concentration camps in

Europe, but Seth explained what had happened, showing her a photograph from the Japanese American National Museum. The caption beneath the original stated that these were the Fukudas. He told her that his assistant was looking for the names and ages of each of them on the lists of the Topaz evacuees.

THE PRISONERS

*A*ll through their first year at Topaz, Ichimei often used to send Alma his drawings, but after that they became less frequent, because the censors couldn't keep up and had to restrict the evacuees' correspondence. Alma jealously kept those sketches, which provided the best glimpse into this stage of the Fukudas' lives: the family huddled in one of the barracks; children doing homework kneeling on the ground with benches for desks; lines of people outside the latrines; men playing cards; women washing clothes in huge tubs. The prisoners' cameras had been confiscated, and the few who managed to hide theirs were unable to develop the negatives. The only permitted photographs were optimistic ones that showed not only the humane treatment the prisoners received but the relaxed, cheerful atmosphere in the camp: kids playing baseball, adolescents dancing to the latest crazes, everybody singing the national anthem while the flag was raised every morning; on no account were the barbed-wire fences, the watchtowers, or the armed guards to be shown. One of the American soldiers eventually took a snapshot of the Fukuda family. His name was Boyd Anderson, and he had fallen in love with Megumi, whom he saw for the first time at the hospital, where she worked as a volunteer and where he had gone after cutting his hand opening a can of corned beef.

Boyd was twenty-three years old. He was tall and pale looking like his Swedish ancestors, with a straightforward, friendly character that made him one of the few whites to gain the evacuees' confidence. A girlfriend was waiting impatiently for him in Los Angeles, but when he saw Megumi in her white volunteer's uniform, his heart was taken. She cleaned the wound, the doctor inserted nine stitches, and she bandaged it with professional skill without once looking him in the face, while Boyd stared at her so bedazzled that he didn't feel the slightest pain. From that day on he hovered around her discreetly, partly because he did not want to abuse his position of authority, but above all because any mixing of the races was forbidden for the whites and was repugnant to the Japanese. Thanks to her moonlike face and the delicacy with which she moved through the world, Megumi could have had any of the most sought-after young men at Topaz, but she felt the same forbidden attraction for the guard, and also struggled with the monstrosity of racism, praying to the heavens that the war would come to an end and her family return to San Francisco so that she could tear this sinful temptation from her soul. For his part, Boyd prayed the war would never end.

On the Fourth of July there was an Independence Day celebration, just as there had been six months earlier for the New Year. On that occasion the event had been a failure, because the camp was still not properly finished, and the Japanese had not yet become resigned to the fact that they were prisoners. In July 1943, however, the evacuees tried their hardest to show their patriotism and the Americans their goodwill, despite the dust storms and the heat, which seemed to bother even the lizards. Everyone mingled cheerfully amidst the barbecues, bunting, cakes, and even beer for the men, who for once were able to avoid the dreadful liquor made clandestinely from fermented tinned peaches. Boyd was among those detailed to photograph the occasion in order to silence those ill-intentioned journalists who denounced what they saw as the inhumane treatment meted out to the Japanese-Americans. He took advantage of his assignment to ask the Fukudas to pose for him. Afterward, he gave a copy to Takao and surreptitiously passed another to Megumi, while he enlarged his own and cut out the figure of Megumi from the family group. This photo was with him for the rest of his life: he kept it protected in plastic inside his wallet and was buried with it fifty-two years later. In the family portrait, the Fukudas are standing in front of a squat black building: Takao has slumped shoulders and a dour expression, Heideko is small and defiant, James is in half profile and sullen looking, Megumi shows all the splendor of her eighteen years, and the skinny eleven-year-old Ichimei stands there with his mop of unruly hair and scabs on his knees.

In this photograph, the only one of the family at Topaz, Charles is missing. That year Takao and Heideko's eldest son had enlisted, because he considered it his duty, not in order to escape from confinement, an accusation some young men opposed to conscription made of these volunteers. He became part of the 442nd Infantry Regiment, made up exclusively of *nisei*. Ichimei sent Alma a drawing of his brother standing at attention before the flag, with a couple of lines of writing that weren't censored, explaining he had no room on the sheet of paper to show the other seventeen young men in uniform who were off to war. Ichimei was so talented that in just a few strokes he succeeded in capturing Charles's expression of extreme pride, a pride that went back to the distant past, to the earlier generations of *samurai* in his family who went into battle convinced they would not return, ready never to surrender and to die with honor, a conviction that gave them superhuman courage. When, as he always did, Isaac examined the drawing, he pointed out to Alma the irony that those young men were willing to risk their lives defending the interests of a country that was holding their families in concentration camps.

The day James Fukuda turned seventeen, he was led away between two armed soldiers. His family was given no explanation, but Takao and Heideko had anticipated this calamity, as their second son had been difficult since birth and a continual problem after their internment. Like the rest of the evacuees, the Fukuda family had accepted their situation with philosophical resignation, but James and some other *nisei* had protested constantly, first by breaking the rules at every opportunity and later by encouraging revolt. At first, Takao and Heideko put this down to the boy's explosive nature, then to the waywardness of adolescence, and finally to a poor choice of friends. The camp warden had warned them several times that he would not tolerate James's behavior. He put him in a cell for fighting, insubordination, and minor damage to federal property, but none of this justified his being taken away to prison. Apart from the dissent of some adolescent *nisei* like James, the atmosphere at Topaz was one of complete calm. There were never any serious disturbances, the worst being the strikes and protests that took place when a sentry killed one old man who had got too close to the fence and didn't hear the order to stop. The warden always took James's youth into consideration and allowed himself to be swayed by the discreet maneuvers Boyd Anderson undertook in the boy's defense.

The government had sent a questionnaire to which the only correct answers were yes. All evacuees aged seventeen and over had to answer them. Among the leading questions, they were asked to be loyal to the United States, fight wherever they were sent—in the army in the case of men, and in the auxiliary forces for women—and to renounce their allegiance to the emperor of Japan. For *issei* like Takao, this meant giving up their nationality without having the right to become American, but almost all of them complied. The only ones who refused to sign, because they were American and felt insulted, were a few young *nisei*. They were nicknamed the No-Nos, and were regarded as dangerous by the government and rejected by the Japanese community, who from time immemorial had detested scandal. James was one of these No-Nos. Deeply ashamed when his son was arrested, his father shut himself in the barracks room assigned to his family and only left it to use the communal latrine. Ichimei would take him his food and then stand in line a second time to get himself something to eat. Heideko and Megumi, who also suffered from the trouble James had caused, tried to continue their lives as normal, heads held high despite the nasty rumors or disapproving looks from their own people and harassment by the camp authorities. The Fukudas, Ichimei included, were interrogated on several occasions, but thanks to Boyd, who had been promoted and protected them as best he could, they were never really threatened.

"What's going to happen to my brother?" Megumi asked Anderson.

"I don't know, Megumi. They could have sent him to Tule Lake in California, or Fort Leavenworth in Kansas. The Federal Bureau of Prisons is in charge of that. I guess he won't be released until the war is over."

"People here say that the No-Nos are going to be shot as spies . . ."

"Don't believe everything you hear, Megumi."

Takao was completely changed by his son's arrest. During the first few months at Topaz he had taken part in the community and filled the empty hours growing vegetables and making furniture from the wooden crates they got from the camp kitchen. When there was no more space in their cramped barrack room, Heideko encouraged him to make things for other families. He asked permission to teach the children judo, but this was denied; the camp commander was afraid he might give his pupils subversive ideas and put his soldiers' security at risk. Takao continued practicing in secret with his own children. He lived in anticipation of their release: he counted the days, weeks, and months, crossing them off on the calendar. He thought constantly of his ill-fated dream of setting up a plant nursery with Isaac, of the money he had saved and lost, of the house he had been paying for over many years, which had now been repossessed. Decades of effort, hard work, and fulfilling his obligations, only to find himself imprisoned behind a barbed-wire fence like a criminal, he would say bitterly. He was not sociable. The crush of people, the inevitable lines, the noise, the lack of privacy all irritated him.

Heideko on the other hand blossomed at Topaz. Compared to other Japanese women, she was a disobedient wife who confronted her husband arms akimbo, and yet she had lived her life devoted to her family and to the laborious toil of agriculture, without the slightest suspicion that the spirit of activism lay dormant within her. In the concentration camp she had no time for despair or boredom; she spent her days resolving other people's problems and struggling with the authorities to obtain the apparently impossible. Her children were captive and secure behind the fence; she had no need to watch over them since eight thousand pairs of eyes and a detachment of the armed forces were doing that for her. Her chief worry was making sure that Takao didn't collapse completely; she was running out of ideas for what he could do to keep busy and not have time to think. Her husband had grown old: the ten years' age difference between them was very noticeable now. The forced proximity of life in the barracks had put a stop to the passion that had previously rubbed the rough edges off living together: for him, affection had turned into exasperation, and for her, into impatience. Out of a sense of shame toward the children, who shared the same room, they tried to avoid contact in the narrow bed, which meant that the easy relationship they'd once enjoyed gradually withered. Takao took refuge in rancor, whereas Heideko discovered her vocation for service and leadership.

Megumi had received three marriage proposals in less than two years, and no one understood why she had rejected them, except for Ichimei, who was the intermediary between his sister and Boyd. Megumi wanted two things in life: to become a doctor and to marry Boyd, in that order. She finished secondary school effortlessly at Topaz and graduated with honors, but higher education was beyond her reach. A few universities back east did accept a small number of students of Japanese origin, chosen from among the most brilliant in the concentration camps, and these lucky ones could get financial help from the government, but James's arrest was a black mark against the Fukudas, and so Megumi did not have that option. Nor could she leave her family; with Charles absent, she felt responsible for her younger brother and her parents. So she worked in the hospital alongside the doctors and nurses who had been recruited from among the prisoners. Her mentor was a white doctor by the name of Frank Delillo. He was in his fifties; stank of sweat, tobacco, and whisky; and was a complete failure in his private life but a competent and selfless doctor. He took Megumi under his wing from the very first day, when she appeared at the hospital in her pleated skirt and starched white blouse to offer her services as an apprentice. They were both recent arrivals at Topaz. Megumi began by emptying bedpans and cleaning up, but showed such willingness and ability that Delillo soon appointed her his assistant.

"Once this war is over, I'm going to study medicine," she told him.

"That could take longer than you think, Megumi. It's going to be hard for you to become a doctor: you are not only a woman, but a Japanese one."

"I'm an American, the same as you," she retorted.

"Have it your own way. Stick close to me and you'll learn something at least."

Megumi took him literally. She clung to Delillo and ended up sewing cuts, setting bones, treating burns, and helping at births— nothing more complicated than that, as the most serious cases were sent to the hospitals in Delta or Salt Lake City. Although her work kept her busy ten hours a day, some nights she managed to get together for a while with Boyd, thanks to the protection of Frank Delillo, who apart from Ichimei was the only one in on their secret. Despite the risks, the lovers enjoyed two years of clandestine meetings, with luck on their side. The desert was so barren there were no hiding places, but the young *nisei* found ingenious ways to avoid their parents' supervision and prying eyes. Megumi however could not hope to do so, because Boyd's helmet and rifle made it impossible for him to burrow like a rabbit among the sparse bushes available. The headquarters and living quarters of the whites, where they might have found a nest, were at some distance from the camp. She would never have gained access had it not been for Delillo's divine intervention. Not only did he obtain a pass for her to get through the checkpoints, he also conveniently absented himself from his room. There, in the midst of the disorder and dirt in which Delillo lived, with ashtrays full of cigarette butts and empty bottles scattered around, Megumi lost her virginity and Boyd found heaven.

Ichimei's passion for gardening, inculcated by his father, became even more intense at Topaz. From the outset, many of the evacuees who had earned a living in agriculture before the war set themselves to grow vegetables, undeterred by the desolate landscape and harsh climate. They watered by hand, counting each drop, and in summer protected the plants with paper tents, and with bonfires in the depths of winter. Thanks to their care, they managed to get the grudging desert to produce vegetables and fruit. There was never any lack of food in the canteens—the evacuees could fill their plates and come back for more—but without the determination of the gardeners they would have had only canned food to eat. Nothing healthy grows in a tin, they used to say. Ichimei attended the school classes and spent the rest of the time in the vegetable plots. He was soon known by the nickname "Green Fingers," because everything he touched germinated and grew. At night, after lining up twice for food, once for his father and a second time for himself, he would carefully bind the storybooks and school texts sent by distant teachers for the little *nisei*. He was a polite, thoughtful boy, who could spend hours in one spot, staring at the purple mountains against the clear blue sky, lost in his own thoughts and emotions. It was said of him that he had a monk's vocation, and that in Japan he would have been a novice in a Zen monastery. Although the Oomoto faith discouraged proselytizing, Takao surreptitiously preached his religion to Heideko and his children, but Ichimei was the only one who practiced it with fervor, because it fit in with his character and with the concept of life that he had had since childhood. He followed Oomoto with his father and an *issei* couple from another hut. There were Buddhist and several Christian services in the camp, but they were the only ones devoted to Oomoto. Heideko accompanied them occasionally, but without any great conviction; Charles and James had never been interested in their father's beliefs, while Megumi, to Takao's horror and Heideko's astonishment, converted to Christianity. She put this down to a premonitory dream she had in which Jesus appeared to her.

"How do you know it was Jesus?" a furious Takao demanded to know.

"Who else goes around wearing a crown of thorns?" she replied. She had to go to religion classes given by the Presbyterian pastor, followed by a short private confirmation ceremony attended only by Ichimei, out of curiosity, and Boyd, profoundly moved by this proof of her love. Naturally the pastor surmised that her conversion owed more to the guard than to Christianity, but he did not object. He gave them his blessing, wondering in which corner of the universe this couple would be able to find shelter.

ARIZONA

*I*n December 1944, a few days before the Supreme Court unan-
imously declared that no American citizens, whatever their
cultural background, could be detained without reason, the Topaz
military commander, escorted by two soldiers, handed Heideko
Fukuda a flag folded into a triangle and pinned a purple ribbon
with a medal on Takao's chest, while the funereal lament from a
trumpet tightened the throats of the hundreds of people gathered
around the family to honor Charles Fukuda, who had died in combat. Heideko, Megumi, and Ichimei wept, but Takao's expression
was indecipherable. Over the years spent in the concentration
camp his face had stiffened into an impassive, proud mask, but his
hunched-over bearing and stubborn silence bore witness to the
broken man he had become. At fifty-two, nothing was left of his
capacity for pleasure at the sight of a plant growing, of his gentle
sense of humor, his enthusiasm to create a future for his children,
the soft tenderness he had once shared with Heideko. The heroic
sacrifice made by Charles, the eldest son who was meant to support
the family when he no longer could, was the final blow. Charles
had perished in Italy, like hundreds of other Japanese-Americans

in the 442nd Infantry Regiment, which became known as the Purple Heart Battalion due to the extraordinary number of medals for valor it had been awarded. That regiment, made up entirely of *nisei*, was the most decorated in US military history, but this would never be any kind of consolation for the Fukudas.

After Japan surrendered on August 14, 1945, the process of closing the concentration camps began. The Fukuda family received twenty-five dollars and train tickets to a city in central Arizona. As with all the other evacuees, they would never publicly refer to those years of humiliation when their loyalty and patriotism had been called into question; life without honor was worth little. *Shikata ga nai.* They were not allowed to return to San Francisco, where they had nothing to go back to anyway. Takao had lost the right to rent the plots he used to cultivate, as well as his house; there was nothing left of his savings or of the money Isaac Belasco had given him when they were evacuated. He had a constant wheezing in his chest, coughed incessantly, and was wracked with back pains. He felt incapable of resuming work in the fields, the only job available to someone in his condition. To judge by his chilly attitude, his family's precarious position mattered little to him; sadness had frozen into indifference. Although the *issei* could finally acquire citizenship, not even that could lift Takao out of his despair. For thirty years he had wanted to have the same rights as an American, and now that he had the chance, all he wanted to do was to return to Japan, his vanquished homeland. When Heideko tried to get him to accompany her to register with the Immigration and Naturalization Service, she ended up going on her own, because her husband's only reply was to curse the United States.

Yet again, Megumi was forced to postpone her decision to

study medicine and her desire to get married, but Boyd, who was transferred to Los Angeles, did not forget her for a moment. The laws prohibiting marriage and cohabitation between races had been abolished in most states, but a relationship like theirs was still considered scandalous; neither of them would have dared tell their parents they had been together for more than three years. For Takao Fukuda it would have been a catastrophe; he would never have accepted that his daughter was with a white, especially not one who had patrolled the barbed-wire fences of his Utah prison. He would be forced to repudiate her and thus lose her as well. He had already lost Charles in the war and seen James deported to Japan, from where he did not expect any more news of him. Boyd Anderson's parents had earned their living with a dairy farm until they were ruined in the thirties and ended up managing a cemetery. They were scrupulously honest, very religious, and tolerant over racial matters, but their son was not going to mention Megumi to them until she had accepted a wedding ring.

Every Monday Boyd began a letter to her, and went on adding paragraphs each day, drawn from *The Art of Writing Love Letters*, a manual in fashion among soldiers who had come back from the war and had left girlfriends scattered around the world. On Friday, he would post the letter. Every second Saturday, this methodical man set himself the task of telephoning Megumi, although this did not always work out; on Sundays he went to the racetrack to bet. He lacked the real gambler's irresistible compulsion, and the vagaries of fortune made him nervous and affected his stomach ulcer, but soon he had discovered he was lucky with horses, and used his winnings to supplement the pittance he earned. In the evening he studied mechanics, as his plan was to leave the armed forces and open a garage in Hawaii. He thought that would be the best place to settle, because it had a large Japanese population, which had been spared the indignity of internment even though Japan's attack on Pearl Harbor had taken place there. In his letters, Boyd tried to convince Megumi of the advantages of Hawaii, where they would be able to raise children with less racial hatred, but children were the last thing on her mind. Megumi maintained a slow but tenacious correspondence with a couple of Chinese doctors to discover how she could study Oriental medicine, as the Western kind was denied her. She quickly learned that here too, the facts of being a woman and being of Japanese origin were insurmountable obstacles, just as her mentor Frank Delillo had warned her.

At the age of fourteen, Ichimei started going to secondary school. Since Takao was paralyzed by melancholy and Heideko could speak no more than a few words of English, Megumi had to be her brother's guardian. On the day she went to enroll him, she thought Ichimei was bound to feel at home, because the building was as ugly and the surroundings as barren as at Topaz. The school principal, Miss Brody, received them. She had spent the war years trying to convince politicians and public opinion that children from Japanese families had just as much right to education as all Americans. She had collected thousands of books to send to the concentration camps. Ichimei had bound several of them, and remembered them perfectly because each one had an inscription by Miss Brody on the title page. He imagined his benefactor as being like the fairy godmother in Cinderella but found himself confronted by a woman built like a tank, with a woodcutter's arms and the voice of a town crier.

"My brother is behind with his studies. He's not good at reading or writing, or arithmetic," an embarrassed Megumi told her.

"What are you good at then, Ichimei?" Miss Brody asked him directly.

"Drawing and planting," whispered Ichimei, without raising his eyes from the tips of his shoes.

"Perfect! That's exactly what we need here!" Miss Brody exclaimed.

For the first week, the other children bombarded Ichimei with the insults against his race that were common during the war but that he had never heard at Topaz. He did not know either that the Japanese were more hated than the Germans, and he had not seen the comics where they were portrayed as degenerate and ruthless. He accepted the jibes with his usual placidity, but the first time a bully laid a finger on him, he threw him through the air with a judo move he had learned from his father—the same one he had used years earlier to show Nathaniel what martial arts were capable of. He was sent to the principal's room to be punished. "Well done, Ichimei," was her only comment. After that crucial feat, he was able to go through the four years of schooling without ever being attacked again.

February 16, 2005

I went to Prescott, Arizona, to see Miss Brody. It was her ninety-fifth birthday, and many of her ex-pupils gathered to celebrate. She is doing very well for her age, and recognized me as soon as she saw me. Just imagine! How many children passed through her hands? How can she possibly remember them all? She recalled that I painted the posters for the school parties, and that on Sundays I worked in her garden. I was a dreadful student, but she always gave me good grades. Thanks to Miss Brody I'm not completely illiterate and can write to you now, my dear friend.

This week that we have not been able to meet has been an eternity. The rain and cold have made it especially sad. And I'm sorry, but I haven't been able to find any gardenias to send you. Please call me.

Ichi

BOSTON

*D*uring the first year of her separation from Ichimei, Alma lived in anticipation of his letters, but as time went by she grew accustomed to her friend's silence, just as she had done to that of her parents and brother. Her aunt and uncle did their best to protect her from the bad news from Europe, in particular about the fate of the Jews. Whenever Alma asked about her family, she was told such outlandish stories that the war sounded more like something out of the legends of King Arthur she had read with Ichimei in the garden pergola. According to her aunt Lillian, the lack of any correspondence was due to problems with the mail system in Poland, and in the case of her brother, Samuel, because of security measures in England. She told Alma he was carrying out vital missions for the Royal Air Force that were both dangerous and secret, and so had to remain in strict anonymity. Why should she tell her niece that her brother had been shot down with his plane in France? Isaac stuck pins in a map to show Alma how the Allied forces were advancing or retreating but did not have the heart to tell her the truth about her parents. Ever since the Mendels had been stripped of their possessions and forced into the terrible Warsaw ghetto, he had received no news of them. He sent large sums of money to organizations trying to help the people in the ghetto and knew that the number of Jews deported by the Nazis between July and September 1942 had reached more than two hundred and fifty thousand. He also knew about the thousands who died every day of starvation and illnesses. The wire-topped wall separating the ghetto from the rest of the city was not completely impermeable, for some food and medicine could be smuggled in, and the horrific photos of children dying of hunger could get out, so there were some means of communicating. If none of the methods he had employed to locate Alma's parents had met with any success, and if Samuel's plane had crashed, it was reasonable to assume that all three were dead, but until there was irrefutable proof, Isaac intended to spare his niece all that pain.

For a while Alma seemed to have adapted to her aunt and uncle, her cousins, and the Sea Cliff mansion, but at puberty she once again became the sullen child she had been when she reached California. She was an early developer, and the first hormonal onslaught coincided with Ichimei's indefinite absence. She was ten when they were separated, promising to stay together in their thoughts and by writing; eleven when his letters started drying up; and twelve when the distance between them became insuperable and she resigned herself to losing Ichimei. She fulfilled her obligations without protesting at a school she detested and behaved in the way her adopted family expected, trying to remain invisible so as to avoid questions about her feelings that would have unleashed the torment of rebellion and anguish she kept bottled up inside. Nathaniel was the only one she couldn't fool with her irreproachable behavior. He had a sixth sense for detecting when his cousin was shut in the wardrobe and tiptoed there often to persuade her to come out of her hiding place, speaking in whispers in order not to wake his father, who had sharp ears and was a light sleeper. He would tuck her up in bed and lie next to her until she fell asleep. He too was going through life walking on eggshells but with a storm raging inside him. He was counting the months he had left at school before going to Harvard to study law, because it had never occurred to him to go against his father's wishes. His mother wanted him to go to law school in San Francisco instead of vanishing to the other side of the continent, but Isaac insisted the boy needed to get far away, as he himself had done at that age. His son had to become a responsible, upstanding man, a mensch.

Alma took Nathaniel's decision to go to Harvard as a personal affront and added her cousin to the list of those who had abandoned her: first her brother and her parents, then Ichimei, and now him. She concluded it was her destiny to lose everyone she loved most. She was still as attached to Nathaniel as on that first day at the quayside in San Francisco.

"I'll write to you," Nathaniel assured her.

"That's what Ichimei said," she replied angrily.

"Ichimei is in an internment camp, Alma. I'll be in Harvard."

"That's even further away. Isn't it in Boston?"

"I'll come and spend all my vacations with you, I promise."

While he was preparing for his departure, Alma followed him around the house like a shadow, inventing excuses for him not to go, and when that didn't work, inventing reasons for loving him less. When she was eight she had fallen in love with Ichimei with all the

intensity of childhood passions; with Nathaniel it was the calm love
of later years. The two of them fulfilled different roles in her heart,
but they were equally indispensable: she was sure that without Ichimei and Nathaniel she wouldn't survive. She had loved the former
vehemently; she needed to see him all the time, to run off with him
to the Sea Cliff garden, which was full of tremendous hiding places
where they could discover the infallible language of caresses. After
Ichimei was sent to Topaz, Alma was nourished by her memories
of the garden and the pages of her diary, filled to the margins with
all her sighs and regrets written in tiny handwriting. Even at this
age she gave signs of her fanatical tenacity for love. With Nathaniel
on the other hand, it would never have occurred to her to go and
hide in the garden. She loved him devotedly and thought she knew
him better than anyone else. In the nights he had rescued her from
the wardrobe, they slept together holding hands; he was her confidant, her closest friend. The first time she discovered dark stains
in her underpants she waited trembling for Nathaniel to come back
from school so she could drag him off to the bathroom to show him
the evidence that she was bleeding down below. Nathaniel had a
vague idea of the reason, but not of the practical steps to take, and
so he was the one who had to ask his mother, as Alma didn't have
the courage to do so. He knew everything she was going through.
She had given him copies of the keys to her diaries but he had no
need to read them to know how she felt.

Alma finished secondary school a year before Ichimei. By then they
had lost all contact, but she regarded him as still being with her, because in the uninterrupted monologue of her diary she was writing

to him, more out of a habit of loyalty than any sense of nostalgia. She had resigned herself to never seeing him again, but as she had no other friends she fed a tragic heroine's love with the memory of their secret games in the garden. While he was working from sunup to sundown as a laborer in a beet field, she reluctantly consented to the debutante balls her aunt Lillian insisted she attend. There were dances at the Sea Cliff mansion, and others in the interior courtyard of the Palace Hotel, with its half century of history, its fabulous glass roof, enormous crystal chandeliers, and tropical palms in Portuguese ceramic pots. Lillian had assumed the responsibility of making sure she married well, convinced it would be easier than it had been to marry off her own rather plain daughters, yet she found that Alma sabotaged all her best-laid plans. Isaac did not like getting involved in the lives of the women of the family, but in this instance he could not remain silent.

"This hunt for a husband is not worthy of you, Lillian!"

"How innocent you are, Isaac! Do you think you'd be married to me if my mother hadn't lassoed you?"

"Alma is still a child. There ought to be a law against getting married before you are twenty-five."

"Twenty-five! At that age she'll never find a good match, Isaac. Everyone will be taken," said Lillian.

Her niece wanted to go and study far away, and Lillian eventually gave in. A couple of years' higher education won't do her any harm, she thought. They finally agreed that Alma should go to a girls' college in Boston, where Nathaniel was still studying. He could protect her from the city's dangers and temptations. So Lillian gave up presenting her with potential husbands and instead began to prepare her wardrobe with frilly skirts and outfits of fashionable pastel-colored angora tops and sweaters, even though they did little for a big-boned young woman with strong features like Alma.

Although her aunt was desperate to find someone she could trust to accompany her east, Alma insisted on going on her own. She flew to New York, intending to take the train from there to Boston. When she disembarked, she found Nathaniel waiting at the airport. His parents had sent him a telegram, and he had decided to come and meet her so that they could travel together by train. The two cousins embraced with all the pent-up emotion of the seven months since Nathaniel had last been in San Francisco, and hurriedly brought each other up to date with family news as a uniformed black porter loaded all her luggage onto a cart to follow them to the taxi. Nathaniel counted the suitcases and hatboxes and asked his cousin if she was bringing clothes to sell.

"You're not one to criticize, you've always been a dandy," she retorted.

"What are your plans, Alma?"

"What I told you in my letter, cousin. You know I adore your parents, but I'm suffocating in that house. I have to make myself independent."

"So I see. With my father's money?"

Alma had not noticed that particular detail. Her first step toward independence was to obtain a diploma of some kind or other. Her vocation was yet to be defined.

"Your mama is determined to find me a husband. I don't have the courage to tell her I'm going to marry Ichimei."

"Why don't you wake up, Alma? It's been ten years since Ichimei disappeared from your life."

"Eight, not ten."

"Get him out of your head. Even in the unlikely event that he should reappear and still be interested in you, you know very well you can't marry him."

"Why not?"

"Why not! Because he's from another race, another social class, another culture, another religion, another economic level. Do you need any more reasons?"

"Well then, I'll be an old maid. What about you, do you have a girlfriend, Nat?"

"No, but if I do, you'll be the first to know."

"That's good. We could pretend we're a couple."

"Why?"

"To put off any idiot who comes near me."

His cousin had changed a lot in recent months. She was no longer a schoolgirl in white socks, but although her new clothes made her look like an elegant grown-up woman, Nathaniel knew her too well to be taken in by the cigarettes, the navy-blue suit, or the hat, gloves, and cherry-colored shoes. Alma was still the spoiled little child who clung to him, frightened by the crowds and the noise in New York, and only let go once they had reached her hotel room. "Stay and sleep with me, Nat," she begged him, with that terrified look she used to have in the wardrobe of sorrows, but he had lost his innocence and sleeping with her now meant something different. The following day they caught the train to Boston, hauling her mound of luggage with them.

Alma imagined that the Boston college would be like a freer version of her secondary schooling, which she had completed with ease. She was eager to show off her new wardrobe, lead a bohemian existence in the city cafés and bars with Nathaniel, and attend a few classes in her spare time so as not to disappoint her aunt and uncle. She soon discovered that nobody looked at her, that there were hundreds of girls more sophisticated than she was, that her cousin always came up with an excuse not to meet, and that she was poorly prepared for her studies. She found herself sharing a room with a plump girl from Virginia, who whenever the occasion arose presented her proof from the Bible that the white race was superior. Blacks, Orientals, and redskins descended from monkeys; Adam and Eve were white; Jesus might have been American, although she wasn't sure about that. While she didn't approve of the way Hitler had behaved, she said, one had to admit he wasn't wrong when it came to the Jews: they were a condemned race, because they had killed Jesus. Alma asked to be moved. This took two weeks to arrange, and her new roommate turned out to suffer from a whole host of manias and phobias but at least wasn't anti-Semitic.

For the first three months, Alma felt lost, incapable of organizing even the simplest things in her life such as food, laundry, transportation, or her college schedule; previously it had been her governesses and then her selfless aunt Lillian who had seen to that kind of thing. She had never made her bed or ironed a blouse: that was what the domestic staff was for; nor had she ever had to keep within a budget, since in the Belasco home it was rude to talk about money. She was taken aback when Nathaniel explained her allowance did not include restaurants, tearooms, manicures, hairdressers, or masseuses. Once a week he appeared, notebook and pencil in hand, to teach her to keep a record of what she had spent. She always promised him she would improve, but the next week she was always in debt again. She felt foreign in this stuck-up, proud city; her fellow college students shunned her, and boys ignored her, but she never mentioned any of this in letters to her aunt and uncle, and whenever Nathaniel suggested she return home she would insist that anything was better than having to face the humiliation of returning to Sea Cliff with her tail between her legs. Just as she had once done in the wardrobe, she would shut herself in the bathroom and turn on the shower so that the noise would cover the swear words she shouted to curse her misfortune.

In November the whole weight of winter fell on Boston. Alma had spent the first seven years of her life in Warsaw but did not remember its climate; nothing had prepared her for what she had to endure over the following months. Lashed by hail, blizzards, and snow, the city lost all color; the light faded, and everything became gray and white. Life went on indoors, with people shivering as close as possible to the radiators. However many clothes Alma put on, the cold chapped her skin and got into her bones whenever she set foot outside. Her hands and feet swelled with chilblains; her coughs and colds seemed never ending. She had to summon all her willpower to get out of bed in the morning, wrap herself up like an Inuit, and face the freezing weather to cross from one college building to the next, hugging the walls so that the wind would not bowl her over, dragging her feet across the ice. The streets became impassable; most mornings the cars were covered with a mountain of snow that their owners had to attack with picks and shovels; everybody went around buried in wool and furs; and the children, pets, and birds all disappeared.

But then, just when Alma had finally accepted defeat and had admitted to Nathaniel that she was ready to call her aunt and uncle and beg them to rescue her from this freezer, she met Vera Neumann. Vera was an artist and businesswoman who had made her art accessible to ordinary people in the form of scarves, sheets, tablecloths, tableware, clothing—anything that could be painted or printed on. She had registered her brand name in 1942, and within a few years had created a market. Alma vaguely recalled that her aunt Lillian competed with her friends to be the first each season to show off Vera's new designs for scarves and dresses, but she knew nothing about the artist herself. She went to her talk on impulse, to escape the cold between two classes, and found herself at the back of a packed room whose walls were lined with painted fabrics. All the colors that had fled the Boston winter were captured there—bold, whimsical, fantastic.

The audience greeted the speaker with a standing ovation that reminded Alma yet again of how ignorant she was. She had no idea that the woman who designed her aunt Lillian's scarves was a celebrity. Vera Neumann was not an imposing figure—she was barely five feet tall, and very shy, hiding behind a pair of enormous glasses with dark frames that covered half her face—but as soon as she opened her mouth no one could doubt she was a giant. Alma could barely see her up on the platform, but she felt her stomach flutter when the artist spoke and knew with complete certainty that this was a decisive moment for her. In an hour and a quarter this eccentric, tiny woman roused her audience with stories from her tireless journeying to source her various collections: India, China, Guatemala, Iceland, Italy, and seemingly everywhere else on the planet. A feminist, she spoke of her philosophy, of the techniques she employed, of selling and marketing her products, of the obstacles she had encountered along the way.

That same night, Alma called Nathaniel to announce her future in great gusts of enthusiasm: she was going to follow in Vera's footsteps.

"Whose footsteps?"

"The woman who designed your parents' sheets and tablecloths, Nat. I've no intention of going on with classes that are of no use to me. I've decided to study design and painting at the university. I'm going to attend Vera's workshops and then travel the world the way she has."

A few months later, Nathaniel completed his law studies and returned to California. In spite of pressure from her aunt Lillian, Alma refused to go back to California with him. She endured four winters in Boston without complaining ever again about the climate, spending her whole time drawing and painting. Not having Ichimei's facility for sketching or Vera's boldness with color, she set herself to supplement talent with good taste. She already had a clear idea of the direction she wanted to take. Her designs would be more refined than Vera's, because she did not intend to satisfy popular taste and create a brand, but to create for pleasure. The possibility of earning a living never occurred to her. She wasn't interested in scarves for ten dollars, or sheets and napkins sold wholesale; she would only design and print certain items of clothing, all of them in top-quality silk, and would add her signature to each one. Her work would be so exclusive and expensive that her aunt Lillian's friends would kill to have it. During those four years she overcame the paralysis that this imposing city had produced in her; she learned to get around, to drink cocktails without completely losing her head, and to make friends. She came to feel like such a Bostonian that whenever she vacationed in California it seemed to her as if she were in a backward country on some other continent. She also won admirers on the dance floor, where the frantic practicing she had done with Ichimei in her childhood served her well. She had her first unceremonious sexual encounter, behind some bushes at a picnic, which served to satisfy her curiosity as well as her complex at still being a virgin over the age of twenty. Later on she had two or three similarly unremarkable experiences with different young men, which confirmed her decision to wait for Ichimei.

THE RESURRECTION

*T*wo weeks before she graduated, Alma called Nathaniel in San Francisco to organize the details of the Belascos' trip to Boston. She was the first woman in the family to obtain a university degree, and the fact that it was in the relatively obscure disciplines of design and art history did not detract from its merit. Even Martha and Sarah were planning to attend the ceremony, partly because they were counting on going on to New York on a shopping spree, but her uncle Isaac would be absent, as his cardiologist had forbidden him to fly. Isaac was ready to disobey him, as Alma was more deeply rooted in his affections than his own daughters, but Lillian would not hear of it. In her conversation with Nathaniel, Alma commented in passing that for several days she'd had the impression she was being spied on. She said she was sure it wasn't important, that it was merely her hyperactive imagination because she was nervous about her finals, but Nathaniel insisted on hearing the details. A couple of anonymous phone calls when somebody—a masculine voice with a foreign accent—asked if she was there and then hung up; the awkward feeling that she was being watched and followed; a man had been making inquiries about her among her friends, and from the description they gave, it seemed he was the same person she had seen several times in recent days in class, in corridors, in the street. With his suspicious legal mind, Nathaniel advised her to write to the college security office as a precaution: if anything happened, there would be evidence of her concern. He also told her not to go out alone at night. Alma paid him no attention.

It was the time of year when the students held wild farewell parties at the university. Thanks to the music, alcohol, and dancing, Alma forgot about the sinister shadow she had imagined, until the Friday before her graduation. She had spent most of the night in a mad whirl, drinking too much and keeping herself on her feet thanks to cocaine—neither of which did her much good. At three in the morning, a rowdy group of students in a convertible dropped her off outside her dorm. Stumbling, disheveled, and carrying her shoes in one hand, Alma rummaged for the key in her handbag but, before she could find it, fell to her knees and brought up the entire contents of her stomach. The dry retching went on for several minutes, while tears coursed down her cheeks. Eventually she tried to get to her feet, covered in sweat and with her stomach heaving. She was shivering and groaning in despair. All of a sudden a pair of rough hands clamped on her arms, and she could feel herself being lifted and held upright.

"Alma Mendel, you ought to be ashamed of yourself!"

She did not recognize the voice from the telephone. She doubled up as another wave of nausea hit her, but the claws only dug deeper.

"Let me go, let me go!" she moaned, kicking and screaming.

A slap to the face sobered her up momentarily, and she glimpsed the outline of a man, a dark face slashed with lines that looked like scars, a shaven head. For some strange reason she felt an enormous sense of relief. She closed her eyes and succumbed to the ghastliness of her drunken state and the danger of being in the iron grip of a stranger who had just slapped her.

At seven that Saturday morning, Alma awoke to find herself wrapped in a rough, scratchy blanket on the backseat of a car. She smelled of vomit, urine, cigarettes, and alcohol. She had no idea where she was and couldn't remember a thing about what had happened the night before. She sat up and tried to rearrange her clothes but discovered she had lost her dress and petticoat: she was in her bra, underpants, and garter belt. Her stockings were full of holes, and she had no shoes on. Merciless bells were ringing inside her head; she was cold, her mouth was parched, and she was very afraid. She lay down again and curled up in a ball, moaning and calling out to Nathaniel.

Moments later, she felt somebody shaking her. Opening her eyes with great difficulty, she tried to focus and eventually made out the silhouette of a man who had opened the car door and was leaning over her.

"Coffee and aspirin. That will help a bit," he said, handing her a paper cup and two pills.

"Leave me, I have to go," she said thickly, trying to sit up.

"You can't go anywhere like that. Your family will be here in a few hours. Your graduation ceremony is tomorrow. Drink the coffee. And in case you're wondering, I'm your brother, Samuel."

This was the resurrection of Samuel Mendel, eleven years after he had died in the north of France.

———

After the war, Isaac Belasco had received convincing proof of the fate that had befallen Alma's parents in a Nazi death camp near the town of Treblinka in northeastern Poland. Unlike the Americans elsewhere, the Russians did not document the camp's liberation, and officially little was known of what had happened in that hell, but the Jewish Agency calculated that 840,000 people had perished there between July 1942 and October 1943, 800,000 of whom were Jews. As for Samuel Mendel, Isaac established that his plane was shot down in the occupied zone of France, and according to the British war records, there were no survivors. By then Alma had heard nothing about her family for several years and assumed they were dead long before her uncle confirmed it. When she was told, Alma did not weep for them, as might have been expected, because during that time she had learned to control her feelings to such an extent she had lost the ability to express them. Isaac and Lillian thought it necessary to bring closure to this tragedy and took Alma with them to Europe. In the French village where Samuel's plane was shot down, they put up a memorial plaque with his name and the dates of his birth and death. They did not obtain permission to visit Poland, which was then under Soviet control; Alma was to make that pilgrimage many years later. The war had finished four years earlier, but Europe was still in ruins, and huge groups of people were still wandering around in search of a homeland. Alma concluded that her entire lifetime would not be enough to pay for the privilege of being her family's only survivor.

Shaken by this stranger's declaration that he was her brother, Samuel, Alma sat up in the car seat and gulped down the coffee and aspirins in three swallows. The man looked nothing like the brother she had seen off at the Danzig quayside, a youth with rosy cheeks and a playful expression. Her real brother was that blurred memory, not this person standing beside her, lean, dry, with hard eyes and a cruel mouth, sunburned skin, and a face lined with deep furrows and a couple of scars.

"How do I know you're my brother?"

"You don't. But I wouldn't be wasting my time with you if I weren't."

"Where are my clothes?"

"At the laundry. They'll be ready in an hour. That gives us time to talk."

Samuel told her that the last thing he saw was the earth from above, as his plane went into a tailspin. He had no time to parachute out, he was sure of that, otherwise the Germans would have found him, and he couldn't explain clearly how he managed not to be killed when his plane crashed and burst into flames. He guessed he must have been thrown out of his seat and ended up in the tops of some trees, dangling down. The enemy patrol found the body of his copilot and didn't search any further. He was rescued by a couple of members of the resistance, who, when they saw he was circumcised, handed him on to a Jewish group. For months they hid him in caves, stables, basements, abandoned factories, and the houses of kind people willing to help, often changing his hiding place until his broken bones were mended and he was no longer a burden but could join the group as a fighter. The mist in his brain took far longer to clear than his bones did to knit. From the uniform he was wearing when they found him, they knew he came from England. He understood English and French, but answered in Polish; it would be months before he recovered the other languages he spoke fluently. Since they did not know his name, his companions decided to call him Scarface, but he eventually chose to name himself Jean Valjean like the protagonist of Victor Hugo's novel, which he read during his convalescence. He fought with his colleagues in a guerrilla war that seemed to be doomed. The German forces were so efficient, their arrogance so immense, and their thirst for power and blood so insatiable that the acts of sabotage Samuel's group carried out did not even scratch the monster's armor plating. They lived in the shadows, moving about like desperate rats and with a constant sense of failure and pointlessness, and yet they carried on, because there was no choice. They greeted one another with a single word: victory. They said farewell with that same word: victory.

At the end of the war, after surviving Auschwitz, Jean Valjean succeeded in landing clandestinely in Palestine, where waves of Jewish refugees were arriving despite the best efforts of the British, who controlled the region and tried to stop the influx to avoid conflict with the Arabs. The war had turned him into a lone wolf who never dropped his guard. He made do with casual affairs until a female colleague in Mossad, a painstaking and daring agent, announced that he was going to be a father. Her name was Anat Rakosi; she had emigrated with her father from Hungary, the only survivors of a big family. Her relationship with Samuel was above all a friendship, devoid of romance or any thought of the future, which suited them and which they would not have changed were it not for the unexpected pregnancy. Anat had been sure she was sterile because of the hunger, beatings, rapes, and the pseudomedical experiments she had suffered. When she found that the swelling in her belly was not a tumor but a baby, she thought it must be God's joke. She said nothing to her lover until the sixth month.

"My goodness! I thought you were finally putting on a bit of weight," was his only commentary, but he could not hide his enthusiasm.

"The first thing we have to do is to find out who you are, so that this baby knows where it's coming from. The name Valjean is too melodramatic," she told him.

Year after year, Jean Valjean had been postponing the decision to discover his identity, but Anat set to work at once, with the same tenacity that had enabled her to uncover for Mossad the hiding places of those Nazi criminals who had escaped the Nuremberg trials. She started at Auschwitz, Samuel's last destination before the armistice, and followed the thread of the story step by step. With her pregnant belly swaying to and fro, she traveled to France to speak to one of the few members of the Jewish resistance still in the country. He helped her locate the fighters who had rescued the pilot from the British plane, although this wasn't easy because after the war it seemed as though every Frenchman was a resistance hero. Anat ended up in London searching through the RAF archives, where she found several photographs of young men who looked like her lover. There was nothing else she could cling to. She called him on the phone and read out the five names.

"Do any of them sound familiar?" she asked him.

"Mendel! I'm sure of it! My surname is Mendel," he replied, scarcely able to contain the sob choking him.

"My son is four now, and he's called Baruj, like our father, Baruj Mendel," Samuel told Alma, who was sitting beside him on the backseat of the car.

"Did you marry Anat?"

"No. We're trying to live together, but it's not easy."

"You've known about me for four years. Why did you only come and find me now?" Alma asked reproachfully.

"Why would I have? The brother you knew died in that plane. There's nothing left of the boy who enlisted as a pilot in England. I know the story because Anat insists on repeating it, but I don't feel it's mine. It's empty, it has no meaning. The truth is, I don't remember you, but I'm sure you are my sister, because Anat doesn't make mistakes about that kind of thing."

"Well, I remember having a brother who had fun with me and played the piano, but you're nothing like him."

"We haven't seen each other in years, and as I said, I'm not the same."

"Why did you decide to come now?"

"I'm not here because of you. I'm on a mission, but I can't tell you anything about that. I made the most of my journey by coming to see you in Boston, because Anat thinks Baruj needs an aunt. Anat's father died a couple of months ago. There's no one left in her family or mine apart from you. I'm not trying to force anything on you, Alma. I just want you to know I'm alive and that you have a nephew. Anat sent you this," he said.

He gave her a color photo of the boy and his parents. Anat was sitting down with her son on her lap. She was a very slender, pale-looking woman wearing round glasses. Samuel was sitting next to them, arms folded across his chest. The boy had strong features and his father's dark, curly hair. On the back of the photo, Samuel had written a Tel Aviv address.

"Come and visit us, Alma. That way you'll get to know Baruj," he said as he waved good-bye, after recovering her dress from the laundry and accompanying her back to her dorm.

THE SWORD OF THE FUKUDAS

*O*n his deathbed, his lungs eaten away with cancer, and gasping for breath like a fish out of water, Takao Fukuda was still clinging to life. He could barely speak and was so weak that his attempts to communicate through writing proved useless, as his swollen, trembling hands could not form the delicate Japanese characters. He refused to eat, and whenever his family or the nurses weren't looking, he pulled out the drip that was feeding him. He soon fell into a heavy doze, but Ichimei, who took turns with his mother and sister to be with him in the hospital, knew he was conscious and troubled. He would plump up the pillows so that he was half sitting up, dry off the perspiration, rub his scaly skin with lotion, put slivers of ice on his tongue, and talk to him about plants and gardens. In one of these intimate moments he saw his father's lips moving, repeatedly articulating what sounded like the name of a brand of cigarettes, but the idea that in circumstances like these he might still want to smoke was so ridiculous Ichimei dismissed it. He spent the evening trying to decipher what his father was trying to say.

"Kemi Morita? Is that what you're saying, Papa? Do you want to see her?" he asked finally.

Takao nodded with what little strength he had left.

Kemi Morita was the Oomoto spiritual leader. She was reputed to speak with the spirits, and Ichimei knew her well, because he often traveled to join the small communities who shared his religion.

"Papa wants us to call Kemi Morita," Ichimei told Megumi.

"She lives in Los Angeles, Ichimei."

"How much savings do we still have? We have to buy her ticket here."

On the day Kemi arrived, Takao was no longer moving. He didn't open his eyes, and the only sign of life was the purring of the respirator. He was suspended in limbo, waiting. Megumi had borrowed a car from a colleague at the factory and drove to the airport to pick up the priestess, who looked like a ten-year-old boy in her white pajamas. Her gray hair, her hunched shoulders, and the way she dragged her feet were in stark contrast to her smooth, wrinkle-free face, which was a serene bronze mask.

Kemi shuffled over to the bed and took Takao's hand. The patient half-opened his eyes. It took him awhile to recognize his spiritual guide, but then an almost imperceptible smile brought a flicker of life back to his haggard features. Ichimei, Megumi, and Heideko withdrew to the back of the room while Kemi murmured a long prayer or poem in archaic Japanese. Then she bent her head down close to the dying man's mouth. After several long minutes, Kemi kissed Takao's brow and turned to the family.

"Takao's mother, father, and grandparents are here. They have come from afar to guide him to the Other Side," she said in Japanese, pointing to the end of the bed. "Takao is ready to depart, but before he does he has a message for Ichimei: '*The Fukuda* katana *is buried in a garden overlooking the sea. It cannot remain there. Ichimei, you have to recover it and place it where it should be, on the altar of our family's ancestors.'"*

When he heard the message, Ichimei bowed deeply, folding his hands in front of his face. The memory of the night they had buried the sword of the Fukudas had become blurred with the years, but Heideko and Megumi knew which garden it was.

"Takao is also asking for one last cigarette," said Kemi before she left them.

On her return from Boston, Alma realized that during the years she had been away the Belasco family had changed more than was transmitted in their letters. For the first few days she felt superfluous, like a visitor passing through, and wondered not only what her place was in this family but what she was going to do with her life. San Francisco seemed provincial to her; to make a name for herself with her painting she would have to go to New York, where she could be among famous artists and closer to European influences.

Three Belasco grandchildren had been born: Martha had a three-month-old boy, and Sarah had twins, who by some flaw in the laws of genetics had come out looking like Scandinavians. Nathaniel headed the family law firm and lived alone in a penthouse with a view over the bay. A man of few words and few friends, he filled his leisure time sailing on his yacht. At twenty-seven he was still resisting his mother's insistent campaign to find him a suitable wife. There were more than enough candidates, because Nathaniel was from a good family, had money, and was extremely handsome. He had turned into the mensch his father had wanted, and all the matchmakers in the Jewish community had their eyes on him. Aunt Lillian had not changed much; she was the same generous and active woman as before. Her deafness had grown worse, and so she shouted all the time. Her hair had turned gray, but she refused to dye it because she had no wish to seem younger; quite the opposite. Her husband had suddenly been hit by the weight of two decades, so that the few years' age difference between them appeared to have tripled.

Isaac had suffered a heart attack, and although he had recovered, he was left weakened. He forced himself to go to the office for a couple of hours each day but had delegated all the work to Nathaniel. He had abandoned social life, which had never attracted him anyway. He read a lot, and above all enjoyed sitting in his garden pergola to enjoy the view of the sea and the bay. He grew seedlings in the greenhouse, and studied books about the law and plants. He had grown sentimental with the years, so that even the most trivial emotions brought tears to his eyes. Lillian would often feel a stab of fear in her guts. "Promise me you won't die before me, Isaac," she demanded whenever he was short of breath and crawled into bed and collapsed, his face as pale as the sheets, his bones aching. Lillian had always counted on a cook and knew nothing about food, but when her husband started to decline she took it upon herself to prepare magical soups from recipes her mother had written in a notebook for her. She had forced Isaac to see a dozen doctors, accompanying him to make sure he didn't hide his problems from her, and she herself gave him his medicines. She also employed more esoteric methods. She called on God, not only at dawn and dusk as required, but at all hours:

Shema Yisrael, Adonai Eloheinu, Adonai Echad. For Isaac's pro-tection he had a blue Turkish evil eye and a painted tin hand of Fatima hanging from the bedpost; a candle was always lit on his chest of drawers, next to Hebrew and Christian Bibles and a jar of holy water that one of the domestic staff had brought from the Shrine of Saint Jude.

"What on earth is this?" Isaac asked the day a skeleton wearing a top hat appeared on his bedside table.

"Baron Samedi. I had it sent here from New Orleans. He's the god of death and also of good health," Lillian told him.

Isaac's initial impulse was to sweep away all these fetishes that had invaded his room, but love for his wife won out. He could eas-ily overlook them if they prevented Lillian from sliding any further down the slope of fear. He had no other means of comforting her. He was aghast at his own physical collapse, since he had always been strong and healthy, and considered himself indestructible. He was bone-weary, and only his determination allowed him to fulfill the obligations he had imposed on himself. Among them was that of remaining alive so as not to betray his wife.

Alma's arrival gave him a burst of energy. He had never been one for displays of sentiment, but his poor health had made him vulnerable, and he had to be very careful to avoid the flood of feelings he felt inside from overflowing. It was only Lillian in their most intimate moments who glimpsed this side of her husband's character. Isaac turned to his son, Nathaniel, for support: he was his best friend, associate, and confidant, but he had never needed to make that explicit, because both of them took it for granted and would have been embarrassed to do so. He treated his daugh-ters, Martha and Sarah, with a benevolent patriarch's affection, and yet in secret he had confessed to Lillian that he didn't really like his daughters, because he found them mean-spirited. Although she would never have admitted it, Lillian did not much like them either. Isaac celebrated his grandchildren from a prudent distance. "Let's wait for them to grow a little, they're not human beings yet," he would say jokingly to excuse his behavior, but deep down this was what he really felt. However, he had always had a soft spot for Alma.

When, back in 1939, this niece arrived from Poland to live at Sea Cliff, Isaac was so smitten with her that he later came to feel a guilty pleasure that her parents never appeared, as this gave him the chance to replace them in the little girl's heart. He did not want to mold her as he did his own children, simply to protect her, and that allowed him the freedom to love her. He left it to Lillian to look after her female needs, and instead had fun challenging her intellectually and sharing with her his passion for botany and geography. It was when he was showing her his gardening books that the idea of creating the Belasco Foundation occurred to him. They spent months going through different possibilities together until the idea took shape, and it was Alma, who by then was thirteen, who thought of creating gardens in the city's poorest neighborhoods. Isaac admired her and watched fascinated as her mind developed; he understood her loneliness and was moved when she turned to him for company. She would sit beside him, one hand on his knee, to watch television or study gardening books, and the weight and warmth of that hand was a precious gift to him. He in turn would pat her on the head when he passed by and the others were not looking, and would buy her sweets that he left under her pillow.

However, the young woman who returned from Boston, with her geometrical hairstyle, red lips, and confident stride, was a far cry from the timid Alma of the past, the little girl who had slept clutching her cat because she was afraid of sleeping alone. Still, once they had overcome the initial awkwardness, they soon resumed the sensitive relationship they had enjoyed for more than a decade.

"Do you remember the Fukuda family?" Isaac asked his niece a few days after her arrival.

"Of course I do!" Alma replied, startled.

"One of the sons called me yesterday."

"Ichimei?"

"Yes, he's the youngest, isn't he? He asked if he could come to see me; he has something he needs to talk about. They are living in Arizona."

"Uncle, Ichimei is my friend, and I haven't seen him since his family was interned. Can I be there when he talks to you, please?"

"He gave me to understand it was a private matter."

"When is he coming?"

"I'll let you know."

A fortnight later, Ichimei appeared at Sea Cliff, dressed in a cheap dark suit and black tie. Alma had been waiting for him with a racing heart, and before he could even ring the bell she opened the door and flung herself into his arms. She was still taller than he was and almost knocked him to the ground. Ichimei, amazed at seeing her and taken aback because public demonstrations of affection were not made among the Japanese, did not know how to respond to such effusiveness. A moist-eyed Alma gave him no time to think about it. She grabbed his hand and dragged him inside, repeating his name over and over, and as soon as they had crossed the threshold she planted a kiss squarely on his mouth. Isaac Belasco was in the library in his favorite armchair, with Ichimei's cat, Neko, who by now was sixteen years old, sitting on his lap. Shocked at what he was witnessing, he hid behind his newspaper until Alma finally brought Ichimei to him. Then she left them together and closed the door.

Ichimei briefly outlined for Isaac Belasco the fate that had befallen his family: the old man was already aware of most of it, because following the telephone call he had investigated as much as he could about the Fukudas. He not only knew about the deaths of Takao and Charles, how James had been deported, and the poverty the widow and her two children found themselves in, but had done something about it. The only novelty Ichimei provided was Takao's message regarding the sword.

"I am truly sorry about Takao's passing, he was my friend and teacher. I'm also sorry about Charles and James. No one has touched the spot where your family *katana* is buried, Ichimei. You may take it whenever you wish, but it was buried ceremoniously, and I think your father would like it to be dug up with equal solemnity."

"That's true, sir. And at the moment, I have nowhere to put it. Could I leave it here? It won't be for much longer, I hope."

"That sword honors this house, Ichimei. What's the hurry to remove it?"

"Its place is on my ancestors' altar, but for now we have no house or altar. My mother, sister, and I live in lodgings."

"How old are you, Ichimei?"

"Twenty-two."

"Then you are an adult, and head of your family. It is for you to take on the business I started with your father."

So Isaac Belasco explained to the astonished Ichimei that in 1941 he had set up a partnership with Takao Fukuda for a flower and decorative plant nursery. The war had prevented the business from going ahead, but neither of them had ended their verbal agreement, and so it still existed. There was a suitable plot of land in Martinez, to the east of San Francisco Bay, which he had bought at a very good price. It was five acres of level, fertile, and well-watered soil, and there was a modest but decent house on the property that the Fukudas could live in until they found something better. Ichimei would have to work very hard to make the business a success, as had been the agreement with Takao.

"We already own the land, Ichimei. I'll put in the initial capital to prepare the soil and plant; the rest is up to you. As you make sales you can pay off your part as best you can, without having to hurry or pay interest. When the time is ripe, we'll put the business in your name. For now the land is in the name of Belasco, Fukuda, and Sons."

What he did not say was that this company and the land purchase had gone through less than a week earlier. Ichimei only discovered this four years later, when he went to transfer the business to his own name.

The Fukudas returned to California and established themselves in Martinez, forty-five minutes from San Francisco. By working side by side from dawn till dusk, Ichimei, Megumi, and Heideko succeeded in producing a first crop of flowers. They found that the soil and the climate were among the best they could have hoped for; all that was needed was to place their product on the market. Heideko had shown she had more guts and muscle than anyone else in the family. At Topaz she had developed her fighting spirit and her talent for organization; in Arizona she kept the family going when Takao could scarcely breathe for all his cigarettes and coughing fits. She had loved her husband with the fierce loyalty of someone who does not question her destiny as a wife, but becoming a widow was a liberation for her. When she returned to California and discovered five acres full of possibilities, she took charge of the business without hesitation. At first, Megumi had to obey her mother and wield the spade and rake on the land, but her mind was set on a future far from agriculture. Ichimei loved botany and had an iron will for heavy work, and yet he was not good at practicalities and had no eye for money. He was an idealist, a dreamer, with a taste for drawing and poetry, more inclined toward meditation than commerce. He did not go to sell his spectacular crop of flowers in San Francisco until his mother told him to go and wash the dirt from under his nails and put on a suit, a white shirt, and a colored tie (no hint of mourning); load up the van; and drive it into the city.

Megumi had made a list of all the most elegant florists, and Heideko visited them one by one, list in hand. However, she would wait in the van, because she realized she looked like a Japanese peasant and spoke dreadful English, while Ichimei, his ears red with embarrassment, went in to sell their wares. Anything that involved money made him uncomfortable. Megumi thought her brother was not made to live in America: he was discreet, austere, passive, and humble; if it were up to him, he would go around dressed in a loincloth begging for food with a bowl, just like the holy men and prophets in India.

That night, Heideko and Ichimei returned from San Francisco with an empty van. "That's the first and last time I'm going with you, son. You're responsible for this family. We can't eat flowers, you'll have to learn how to sell them," Heideko told him. Ichimei tried to delegate this role to his sister, but Megumi was already halfway out the door. They realized how easy it was to get a good price for their flowers and calculated they would be able to pay for the land in four or five years, providing they lived frugally and did not meet up with any disasters. In addition, when he saw what they had produced, Isaac promised he could get a contract with the Fairmont Hotel for them to maintain the spectacular floral arrangements in the reception hall and lounges that gave the place its fame.

After thirteen years of bad luck, the Fukuda family was finally taking off. It was then that Megumi announced that she was thirty years old and thought it was time she set off on her own. In the intervening years Boyd had married and divorced; he was the father of two children and had yet again asked Megumi to join him in Hawaii, where he was doing well with his garage and a fleet of trucks. "Forget Hawaii, if you want to be with me, it will have to be in San Francisco," she told him. She had decided to study nursing. At Topaz she had attended several births, and each time she held a newborn baby she experienced the same ecstatic feeling, the closest thing to a divine revelation she could imagine. This area of obstetrics, until then dominated by male doctors and surgeons, was just beginning to open up to midwives, and she wanted to be in the vanguard of the profession.

She was accepted in a nursing program specializing in female health, which had the advantage of being free. Over the following three years, Boyd went on wooing her discreetly from afar, convinced that once she had her diploma she would marry him and come to Hawaii.

November 27, 2005

It seems incredible, Alma: Megumi has decided to retire.
She had such a struggle to get her diploma, and loves her
profession so much that we thought she would never do so.
We've calculated that in forty-five years she has brought
some five thousand five hundred babies into the world. As
she says, it's her contribution to the population explosion.
She is eighty, a widow for ten years now, and has five
grandchildren. It is high time she took a rest, but she's got it
into her head to open a food business. No one in the family
can understand it, because my sister can't even fry an egg.
I have had a few free hours to paint in. This time I am not
going to re-create the Topaz landscape, as I have done so
often in the past. I'm painting a path in the mountains of
southern Japan, near a very ancient, isolated temple. You
should come with me to Japan, I'd love to show you that
temple.

Ichi

LOVE

That year, 1955, was not just one of effort and sweat for Ichimei. It was the year of his great love. Alma abandoned her project of going back to Boston, becoming a second Vera Neumann, and traveling around the world. Instead, her only aim in life was to be with Ichimei. They met almost every day at nightfall, once his work in the fields was done, at a motel six miles from Martinez. Alma always arrived first and paid for the room to a Pakistani clerk, who looked her up and down with deep disdain. Proud and haughty, she stared him in the eye until he was forced to lower his gaze and hand over the key. The same scene was repeated most every weekday.

At home, Alma had announced she was taking evening classes at the University of Berkeley. Isaac, who prided himself on having progressive ideas and who could do business with or be a friend to his gardener, would have been unable to accept the idea that someone from his family had intimate relations with one of the Fukudas. As for Lillian, she took it for granted that Alma would marry a mensch from the Jewish community, just as Martha and Sarah had done. The only one who knew Alma's secret was Nathaniel, and he did not approve either. Alma had not told him about the motel, and he had not asked, because he preferred not to know the details. He could no longer dismiss Ichimei as a childish whim of his cousin's that she would get over as soon as she saw him again, but he still hoped that at some point Alma would understand they had nothing in common. He no longer remembered his boyhood friendship with Ichimei, except for the martial arts classes at Pine Street. Once Nathaniel had gone to secondary school and the theatrical performances in the attic were over, he had seen little of Ichimei, even though Ichimei often came to Sea Cliff to play with Alma.

When the Fukuda family returned to San Francisco, Nathaniel met him briefly once or twice, sent by his father to give him money for the plant nursery. He could not understand what on earth his cousin saw in him: he was an insubstantial figure who floated by without leaving a trace, the opposite of the kind of strong, self-confident man needed to handle a woman as complex as Alma. Nathaniel was sure his opinion of Ichimei would be the same even if he weren't Japanese; it was a question of character, not of race. Ichimei was lacking that quota of ambition and aggression all men need, and which he himself had developed through sheer willpower. He recalled very clearly his years of fear, the torment at school, and the superhuman effort he had made to study a profession that required an evil streak completely missing in him. He was grateful to his father for making him follow in his footsteps, because working as a lawyer had toughened him; he had acquired an alligator's hide that allowed him to manage on his own and to succeed.

"That's what you think, Nat, but you don't know Ichimei, and you don't know yourself," Alma told him when he explained his theory of masculinity to her.

The memory of those blessed months when she and Ichimei met at the motel, where they couldn't switch off the light because of the cockroaches that emerged at night from the corners of the room, was able to sustain Alma in later years, when she sternly tried to drive out love and desire and replace them with the penance of fidelity. With Ichimei she discovered the multiple subtleties of love and pleasure, from frantic, urgent passion to those sacred moments when they were lifted by emotion and lay still in bed side by side, staring endlessly into each other's eyes, content and sated, abashed at having touched their souls' deepest levels, purified from having stripped away all pretense and lying together totally vulnerable, in such a state of ecstasy they could no longer distinguish between joy and sadness, the elation of life or the sweet temptation of dying there and then so that they would never be apart. Isolated from the world through the magic of love, Alma could ignore the voices inside her head calling her back, crying out for her to be careful, warning her of the consequences. They lived only for the day's encounter; there was no tomorrow or yesterday. All that mattered was the grimy room with its jammed window; the smell of damp, worn-out sheets; and the endless wheezing of the air-conditioning. Only the two of them existed, from the first longing kiss as they crossed the threshold and before they even locked the door; their caresses standing up; flinging off their clothing, which lay where it fell; their naked, quivering bodies; each drinking in the heat, savor, and smell of the other; the texture of skin and hair; the marvel of losing themselves in desire until they were exhausted, of dozing in one another's arms for a moment, only to renew their pleasure; the jokes, laughter, and whispered secrets; the wonderful universe of intimacy. Ichimei's fingers, capable of returning a dying plant to life or repairing a watch without looking, revealed to Alma her own rebellious, hungry nature. She enjoyed shocking him, challenging him, seeing him blush with embarrassment and delight. She was daring, he was restrained; she was noisy during her orgasms, he covered her mouth. She dreamed up a rosary of romantic, passionate, flattering, and filthy phrases to whisper in his ear or write to him in urgent missives; he maintained the reserve typical of his character and culture.

Alma gave herself to the unconscious joy of love. She wondered how nobody noticed the bloom on her skin, the bottomless dark of her eyes, the lightness of her footsteps, the languor in her voice, the burning energy she could not and would not control. She wrote in her diary that she was floating and felt bubbles of mineral water on her skin, making the down on her body bristle with pleasure; that her heart had blown up like a balloon and was sure to burst, although there was no room for anyone but Ichimei in that huge, inflated heart because the rest of the world had become distant and hazy; that she studied herself in the mirror, imagining it was Ichimei observing her from the far side of the glass, admiring her long legs, her strong hands, her firm breasts with their dark nipples, her flat stomach with its faint line of black hair from navel to pubis, her lipstick-red lips, and her bedouin skin; that she slept with her face buried in one of his T-shirts soaked with his gardener's smell of earth and sweat; that she covered her ears to imagine Ichimei's slow, gentle voice, his hesitant laugh that was the opposite of her own exaggerated guffaws, his warnings to take care, his explanations about plants, the words of love he whispered in Japanese because in English they seemed unreal, his astonished exclamations at the designs she showed him and at her plans to imitate Vera Neumann, without pausing even for an instant to bemoan the fact that he himself, who had real talent, had only been able to paint when he could find a couple of hours after his incessant work on the land, before she came into his life, took up all his free time, and sucked out all the air. The need for her to know she was loved was insatiable.

TRACES OF THE PAST

*A*t first, Alma Belasco and Lenny Beal, the friend who had recently arrived at Lark House, planned to enjoy San Francisco's cultural life: they went to the cinema, the theater, to concerts and exhibitions. They experimented with exotic restaurants and took the dog for walks. For the first time in three years, Alma returned to the family box at the opera, but her friend got confused by the complications of the first act and fell asleep in the second, before Tosca managed to plunge a kitchen knife into Scarpia's heart. They gave up on opera. Lenny had a more comfortable car than Alma, so they took to going to Napa to enjoy the bucolic landscape of vineyards and to taste wines, or to Bolinas to breathe in the salty air and eat oysters, but in the end they grew tired of making all these efforts to stay young and active, and gave in to the temptation of simply resting. Instead of going out on excursions, which involved traveling, looking for somewhere to park, and having to be on their feet, they watched films on television, listened to music in their apartments, or visited Cathy with a bottle of pink champagne to go with the gray caviar that Cathy's daughter, a Lufthansa flight attendant, brought back from her trips. Lenny helped in the pain clinic by teaching the patients to make masks for Alma's theater from papier-mâché and dental glue. They spent the afternoons reading in the library, the only shared area that was more or less silent: noise was one of the disadvantages of living in a community. If there was no alternative, they ate in the Lark House dining room, scrutinized by other women who were envious of Alma's luck. Irina felt neglected; she was no longer indispensable to Alma.

"You're imagining it, Irina. Lenny's not competing with you in any way," Seth consoled her. But he too was worried, because if his grandmother cut Irina's hours, he would have fewer opportunities to see her.

That afternoon Alma and Lenny were sitting in the garden recalling the past as they often did, while a short distance away Irina was washing Sophia with the garden hose. On the Internet a couple of years before, Lenny had seen an organization dedicated to rescuing dogs from Romania, where they roamed the streets in wretched-looking packs, and bringing them to San Francisco for adoption by sensitive souls prone to that kind of charity. He was immediately taken with Sophia's face, with its black patch over one eye, and without thinking filled out the online form, sent the required five dollars, and the following day went to fetch her. In the description they had omitted mentioning that the little dog had a leg missing. She managed a normal life on the other three; the only consequence of the accident seemed to be that she destroyed the tips of anything that had four legs, like chairs and tables. Lenny solved the problem by keeping an endless supply of plastic dolls; as soon as the dog left one of them without an arm or leg, Lenny threw her another, and that was that. Sophia's only weakness was her disloyalty to her master. She was smitten with Catherine Hope and at the slightest excuse shot after her and jumped on her lap. She adored traveling in a wheelchair.

Sophia remained motionless under the stream of water as Irina spoke to her in Romanian to conceal her intentions as she listened in on Alma and Lenny's conversation in order to convey it to Seth. She felt bad about spying on them, but investigating the mystery surrounding Alma had become an obsession for her and Seth. Alma had already told her that her friendship with Lenny began in 1984, the year Nathaniel Belasco died, and had lasted only a few months, but the circumstances had lent it such intensity that when they met up again at Lark House they could resume it again as if they had never been apart. At that moment, Alma was explaining to Lenny that at the age of seventy-eight she had renounced her role as matriarch of the Belascos, weary of fulfilling her obligations to people and keeping up appearances, as she had done ever since she was a child. She had been at Lark House for three years now, and was increasingly enjoying it. She said she had imposed the move on herself as a penance, a way of paying for her life of privilege, for her vanity and materialism. The ideal would have been to spend the rest of her days in a Zen monastery, but she was not a vegetarian, and meditation gave her a backache, so she settled for Lark House, to the horror of her son and daughter-in-law, who would have preferred to see her with a shaven head in Dharamsala. She was comfortable at Lark House; she had not given up anything essential and if need be she was only thirty minutes from Sea Cliff, although she had never yielded to the temptation of returning to the family home, which anyway she had never considered hers: first it belonged to her in-laws, and then to her son and daughter-in-law. At first she spoke to no one, and it was like being in a second-rate hotel, but as time went by she made a few friends, and since Lenny had arrived, she felt real companionship.

"You could have chosen something better than this, Alma."

"I don't need anything more. The only thing I miss is an open fire in winter. I love to watch a fire burning, it's like the endless swell of the sea."

"I know a widow who has spent the last six years on cruises. As soon as the ship docks at its final destination, her family presents her with the ticket for the next round-the-world trip."

"I wonder why my son and daughter-in-law have never thought of that?" laughed Alma.

"The advantage is that if you die at sea, the captain throws your body overboard and your family doesn't have to pay for the funeral," Lenny added.

"I'm fine here, Lenny. I'm discovering who I am without all my ornaments and accessories. It's quite a slow process, but a very useful one. Everybody ought to do the same at the end of their life. If I had any self-discipline I would beat my grandson to it and write my own memoirs. I have time, freedom, and silence, the three things I never had amidst all the noise of my earlier life. I'm preparing to die."

"That won't be for a long while yet, Alma. You look splendid."

"Thank you. It must be love."

"Love?"

"Let's just say there is someone. You know who I'm talking about: Ichimei."

"Incredible! How many years have you been together?"

"Let's see, I'll count it up . . . I've loved him since we were both about eight years old, but we've been lovers for fifty-eight years, since 1955, although there have been long gaps."

"Why did you marry Nathaniel?"

"Because he wanted to protect me, and at that moment I needed his protection. Remember how noble he was. Nat helped me accept the fact that there are some things that are more powerful than my own will, things that are even stronger than love."

"I'd like to meet Ichimei, Alma. Tell me when he comes to visit you."

"Our relationship is still a secret," she replied, blushing.

"Why? Your family would understand."

"It's not because of the Belascos, but Ichimei's family. Out of respect for his wife, children, and grandchildren."

"After so many years, his wife must know, Alma."

"She's never given any indication of it. I don't want to hurt her; Ichimei would never forgive me. Besides, it has its advantages."

"Which are?"

"For a start, we've never had to struggle with domestic problems like children, money, and all the other things couples have to deal with. We get together to make love. Besides, Lenny, a clandestine relationship has to be defended: it's fragile and precious. You should know that better than anyone."

"We were both born half a century too late, Alma. We're experts in forbidden love."

"Ichimei and I had a chance when we were young, but I didn't have the courage. I was unable to give up on my security, and so I was trapped in convention. That was back in the fifties, when the world was very different. Do you remember?"

"How could I forget? A relationship like yours was almost impossible; you would have regretted it, Alma. Prejudice would have destroyed you both in the end, and killed your love."

"Ichimei knew that, and never asked me to do it."

After a long pause while the pair sat contemplating the hummingbirds eagerly hovering over a fuchsia bush, and while Irina was deliberately taking her time over drying Sophia with a towel and then brushing her, Lenny told Alma how sorry he was they had not seen each other for almost three decades.

"I knew you were living at Lark House. It's a coincidence that forces me to believe in fate, Alma, because I put my name on the waiting list years ago, a long time before you arrived. I kept postponing the decision to come and visit you, because I didn't want to stir up dead memories," he said.

"They're not dead, Lenny. They're more alive now than ever. That's what happens with age: stories from the past come alive and stick to our skin. I'm so pleased we're going to spend the next few years together."

"It will only be six months, Alma. I have an inoperable brain tumor. I don't have much time left before the worst symptoms begin."

"My God, I'm so sorry, Lenny!"

"Why? I've lived enough, Alma. I could go on for a little longer with aggressive treatment, but there's no point putting myself through that. I'm a coward, pain scares me."

"I'm surprised they accepted you at Lark House."

"Nobody knows what I have, and there's no reason they should, because I won't take up a place for long. I'm going to put an end to myself when my condition starts to worsen."

"How will you know?"

"For now I have headaches, I feel weak and clumsy in my movements. I no longer dare ride a bicycle, which used to be my life's passion, because I've fallen off several times. Do you know I've crossed the United States on a bike from the Pacific to the Atlantic three times? I intend to enjoy the time I have left. Soon I'll be vomiting, find it hard to walk and speak, my eyesight will fail, the convulsions will start . . . But I won't wait that long. I have to act while my mind still functions."

"How quickly life passes us by, Lenny."

Lenny's declaration did not surprise Irina. Death by their own hand was discussed quite naturally among the most lucid of the Lark House residents. Alma's view was that there were too many old people on the planet, people who lived much longer than was necessary for biology and possible for the economy. It made no sense to oblige them to remain prisoner in a painful body or a despairing mind. "Very few old folk are happy, Irina. Most of them are poor, aren't healthy, and have no family. It's the most fragile and difficult stage of life, more so than childhood, because it grows worse day by day, and there is no future other than death." Irina had commented on this to Cathy, who maintained that before long euthanasia would be a right rather than a crime. Cathy knew that several people in Lark House had what they needed for a dignified suicide, and although she understood the reasons for making such a decision, she had no intention of bowing out like that. "I live in constant pain, Irina, but if I don't think about it, it's bearable. The worst was the rehabilitation after the operations. Not even the morphine dulled the pain; the only thing that helped was knowing it wasn't going to last forever. Everything is temporary." Irina suspected that thanks to his profession, Lenny could call on more expeditious drugs than those that came from Thailand wrapped in plain brown paper.

"I'm not worried, Alma," said Lenny. "I enjoy life, especially the time you and I have together. I've been getting myself ready for a long while; it isn't going to catch me unawares. I've learned to pay attention to my body. Our body tells us everything if we only listen to it. I knew about my illness before it was diagnosed, and I know any treatment would be useless."

"Are you afraid?" asked Alma.

"No. I suppose that what comes after death is the same as before birth. What about you?"

"A little . . . I imagine that after death there's no contact with this world, no suffering, personality, or memory; it's as though this Alma Belasco had never existed. Something may transcend it: the spirit, the essence of our being. But I confess I am afraid of giving up this body, and I hope that then Ichimei will be with me or that Nathaniel comes to search for me."

"If as you said the spirit isn't in contact with this world, I don't see how Nathaniel can come searching for you."

"Yes, it's true, it's a contradiction," Alma laughed. "We cling so tightly to life, Lenny! You say you're a coward, but it takes courage to say good-bye to everything and cross a threshold without any idea where it leads."

"That's why I came here. I don't think I can do it on my own, Alma. I think you are the only person who can help me, the only one I can ask to be with me when the time comes. Is that asking too much?"

October 22, 2002

Yesterday, Alma, when at last we could meet to celebrate
our birthdays, I could see you were in a bad mood. You
said that all of a sudden, without us realizing it, we have
turned seventy. You are afraid our bodies will fail us, and of
what you call the ugliness of age, even though you are more
beautiful now than you were at twenty-three. We're not old
because we are seventy. We start to grow old as soon as we
are born, we change every day, life is a continuous state of
flux. We evolve. The only difference is that now we are a
little closer to death. What's so bad about that? Love and
friendship do not age.

Ichi

LIGHT AND SHADOW

*I*t did Alma Belasco good to have to systematically remember things for her grandson's book, as at her age her mind was starting to fail her. Previously she would ramble on, and was unable to recall precise details, but now in order to provide Seth with satisfactory answers she tried hard to reconstruct the past in an orderly way, instead of jumping all over the place as she did with Lenny in the many idle hours they had at Lark House. She visualized different-colored boxes, one for each year of her life, and stored her experiences and feelings inside them. She piled the boxes up in the large armoire in which she used to take refuge as a child to weep floods of tears. These virtual boxes, overflowing with nostalgia and a few regrets, contained her deepest childish terrors and fantasies, as well as the wild extravagances of youth and the struggles, hard work, passions, and loves of her mature years. With a light heart, because she tried to forgive all her mistakes, except those that had made others suffer, she pieced together the fragments of her biography, spicing them with touches of fantasy, allowing herself some exaggeration and white lies, since Seth could hardly contradict her own memories. She did this as an exercise of the imagination rather than because she really wanted to create a false impression. The one thing she never talked about was Ichimei, unaware that behind her back Irina and Seth were investigating this most precious and secret aspect of her existence, the one thing she could not reveal, because if she did Ichimei would vanish, and with him her only reason to continue living.

Irina was her copilot on this flight into the past. Not only did the photographs and other documents pass through her hands, but she was the one who classified them and compiled the albums. Her questions helped guide Alma when she drifted into dead ends, which allowed her life gradually to become clearer, better defined. Irina plunged herself into Alma's existence as if they were in a Victorian novel: the aristocratic lady and her female companion trapped amidst the boredom of endless cups of tea in a country house. Alma claimed we all have an inner private garden where we can seek refuge, but Irina did not like to peer into hers, preferring to replace it with Alma's, which was far more pleasant than her own. She got to know the melancholy little girl disembarking from Poland, the youthful Alma in Boston, the artist and wife; she knew about her favorite dresses and hats; her first painting studio, where she worked alone experimenting with brushes and colors as she defined her own style; her old-fashioned worn leather suitcases, covered in labels, the sort nobody used anymore. These images and experiences were so clear and precise it was as if she herself had existed in those times and had accompanied Alma every step of the way. She found it marvelous that it took only the evocative power of words or a photograph for them to become real, and for her to make them her own.

Alma Belasco had been an active, energetic woman who was as

intolerant of her own failings as of those of others, but as she grew older she was softening, and had more patience with her fellows and with herself. "If nothing hurts, that means I woke up dead," she would tell herself as she opened her eyes and had to stretch her muscles to ward off cramps. Her body was starting to become frail: she needed to find ways to avoid stairs or to guess the meaning of a sentence she hadn't truly heard. Everything cost her more effort and time, and there were things she simply could no longer do, such as driving at night, putting gas in the car, opening a bottle of water, carrying bags of food. That was why she needed Irina. By contrast, her mind was sharp; she could remember the present just as well as the past, provided that she didn't fall into the temptation of jumbling things up; neither her memory nor her reasoning failed her. She could still draw and had the same intuition for color; she went to the workshop but did not paint much because it tired her; she preferred to delegate this to Kirsten and the assistants. She never mentioned her limitations, confronting them without fuss, but Irina was aware of them. Alma detested old people's obsession with their ailments, their aches and pains, a subject of no possible interest to others, not even doctors.

"There's a widespread belief no one dares mention in public that we old people are redundant, we take up space and use resources that productive people need," she used to say.

She did not recognize many of the people in the photographs, fleeting faces from the past who could be done without. In others, the ones Irina stuck in the albums, she could appreciate the stages of her life, the passing years with their birthdays, parties, holidays, graduations, and weddings. These were happy moments, as nobody took pictures of the unhappy ones. She herself hardly featured in them, but by early autumn Irina was better able to appreciate the woman Alma had once been. Nathaniel's photographic portraits of her, part of the Belasco Foundation's legacy, were discovered by San Francisco's small artistic world, and a newspaper dubbed Alma the best-photographed woman in the city.

At Christmas the previous year, an Italian publisher had brought out a selection of Nathaniel's photographs in a luxury edition. A few months later an astute American agent organized one exhibition in New York and another in the most prestigious gallery on San Francisco's Geary Street. Alma refused to take part in these projects or to speak to the press. She said she preferred to be seen as the model of those years and not as the old lady of today, but confessed to Irina that this was out of not vanity but caution. She didn't have the strength to reexamine that period in her past; she was afraid of what the camera might reveal that was invisible to the naked eye. Yet Seth's insistence finally overcame her resistance. Her grandson had visited the gallery several times and been impressed. There was no way he was going to let Alma miss the exhibition: to him it seemed like an insult to Nathaniel's memory.

"Do it for Grandfather, who'll be turning in his grave if you don't go. I'll come to fetch you tomorrow. Tell Irina to come with us. The pair of you will be surprised."

He was right. Irina had leafed through the Italian edition, but nothing prepared her for the impact of those enormous portraits. Seth drove the three of them there in the family's heavy Mercedes-Benz, since it was impossible for them to fit either in Alma's car or on his motorbike. They went at a dead hour of the afternoon, when they thought they would find the gallery empty. The only people they saw were a hobo stretched out on the sidewalk by the entrance, and a couple of Australian tourists to whom the Chinese porcelain doll of a gallery assistant was trying to sell something. She barely glanced at the new arrivals.

Nathaniel Belasco had photographed his wife between 1977 and 1983, using one of the first twenty-by-twenty-four Polaroids capable of capturing the tiniest details with the utmost precision. Nathaniel was not among the famous professional photographers of his generation, and he himself claimed to be only an amateur, but he was one of the few who could afford such a good camera. Besides, he had an exceptional model. Irina was touched by the trust Alma obviously had in her husband; she felt almost ashamed when she saw the portraits, as if she were profaning a starkly intimate ritual. There was no distance between artist and model; they were joined in a tight bond, and out of this symbiosis were born photographs that were sensual without having any sexual overtones. Alma was naked in several poses, and appeared lost in herself, unaware she was being observed. Some of the images had an ethereal, translucent quality, where the female figure disappeared into the dream of the man behind the camera; others were more realistic, and Alma faced Nathaniel with the calm curiosity of a woman alone in front of a mirror, at ease with herself, not holding back in any way, with veins visible in her legs, her Caesarean scar, and a face showing all her fifty years. Irina would not have been able to express the disquiet they aroused in her, but she understood Alma's reticence at being seen in public under her husband's clinical gaze. The two of them appeared united by a feeling that was much more complex and perverse than married love. On the gallery's white walls, Alma was displayed as a submissive giant.

That woman frightened Irina; she was a stranger to her. She felt a choking sensation, and Seth, who possibly shared her emotion, took her hand. For once she did not pull away.

The tourists left without buying anything, and the Chinese doll turned eagerly toward them. She introduced herself as Meili, and immediately overwhelmed them with a prepared spiel about the Polaroid camera, Nathaniel's technique and intention, light and shadow, the influence of Flemish painting. Alma listened to all this with great amusement, nodding her silent agreement. Meili did not make the connection between this white-haired old woman and the model on the walls.

The following Monday at the end of her Lark House shift, Irina went to find Alma to take her to the movies to see *Lincoln* a second time. Lenny had gone to spend a few days in Santa Barbara, and so Irina had briefly recovered her position as cultural attaché, as Alma had always called her before Larry arrived and usurped her position. A few days earlier they had seen only half of the film because Alma had felt such a stabbing pain in her chest that she had cried out and they had been forced to leave the theater. She had rejected the manager's offer of help, as the prospect of an ambulance followed by a hospital seemed worse than dropping dead on the spot. Irina drove her back to Lark House. For some time now, Alma had lent Irina the key to her ridiculous car so that she could drive, since Irina flatly refused to risk her life as a passenger. Alma's recklessness when driving in heavy traffic had grown in proportion to her failing sight and trembling hands. The chest pains eased along the way, but she arrived back exhausted, gray faced, and with blue-tinged fingernails. Irina helped her lie down and, without asking permission, called Catherine Hope, whom she trusted more than the official Lark House doctor. Cathy rushed to Alma's apartment in her wheelchair, examined Alma with the care and attention that she bestowed on everything, and declared that she should see a cardiologist as soon as possible. That night Irina stayed in the apartment on a bed she made up on the sofa, which turned out to be more comfortable than the mattress on the floor she had in Berkeley. Alma slept peacefully with Neko stretched out at her feet but woke up listless and, for the first time since Irina had known her, decided to spend the day in bed.

"But tomorrow you're going to force me to get up, do you hear, Irina? Don't leave me lying here with a cup of tea and a good book. I don't want to end up living in pajamas and slippers. Old people who take to their beds never get up again."

True to her word, the next day she made an effort to start the day as she always did. After that, Alma never referred to her weak state over those twenty-four hours, and soon Irina, who had other things on her mind, forgot about it too. Catherine Hope however was determined not to leave her in peace until she saw a specialist, but Alma somehow managed to keep postponing it.

This time they were able to see the whole film, and left the cinema highly taken with both Lincoln and the actor playing his part. Alma was weary and preferred to return to her apartment rather than go on to a restaurant as planned. When they arrived, Alma said with a sigh that she felt cold and went to bed, while Irina made her oatmeal with milk by way of supper. Leaning back against her pillows, with a granny shawl around her shoulders, Alma looked ten pounds lighter and ten years older than a few hours earlier. Irina had considered her indestructible, which was why it took her until that night to realize how much she had aged in recent months. Alma had lost weight, and the violet-ringed eyes in her haggard face made her look like a raccoon. She no longer walked upright or strode along but hesitated as she got up from her chair; out on the street she clung to Lenny's arm; and at times she woke up with an irrational fear of feeling lost, as if she were awakening in a strange country. She went to her studio less and less, then decided to lay off her assistants, and bought comics and sweets for Kirsten to comfort her in her absence. Kirsten's mental stability depended on her routines and affections; as long as nothing changed, she was happy. She lived in a room above her brother and sister-in-law's garage, fussed over by three nephews and nieces whom she had helped raise. On workdays she always took the same midday bus, which dropped her two blocks from the workshop. She would unlock the door, air out the room, tidy up, sit in the director's chair that her nephews had given her for her fortieth birthday, and eat the chicken or tuna sandwich she carried in her backpack. After that she prepared the canvases, brushes, and paints; put water on to boil for tea; and waited, her eyes fixed on the studio door. If Alma wasn't thinking of going, she would call her on her cell phone, they would chat for a while, and she would give her some task or other to keep her busy until five, when Kirsten bravely closed the workshop and walked to the stop to take her bus home.

A year earlier, Alma had calculated she was going to live in much the same way until she was ninety, but now she was no longer so sure: she suspected that death was drawing closer. Previously she could sense it in the neighborhood, then hear it whispering in the dark corners of Lark House, but now it was lurking around her apartment. At sixty she had thought of death in abstract terms as something that did not concern her; at seventy it was a distant relative who was easy to forget because it never arose in conversation, but would inevitably come to visit one day. After she turned eighty, however, she began to become acquainted with it, and to talk about it with Irina. She saw death here and there, in a fallen tree in the park, a person bald from cancer, her mother and father crossing the street: she recognized them because they looked just like they did in the Danzig photograph. Sometimes it was her brother, Samuel, who had died a second time, peacefully in his bed. Her uncle Isaac seemed full of life when he appeared to her, as he had been before his heart failure, but when Aunt Lillian came to greet her occasionally in the dreamy moments of dawn she was as she had been in her last days, an old woman dressed all in lilac, blind and deaf, but happy, because she believed her husband was holding her hand.

One day Alma said, "Look at that shadow on the wall, doesn't it look like a man's silhouette? It must be Nathaniel. Don't worry, Irina, I'm not crazy, I know I'm only imagining it."

She went on speaking about Nathaniel, of how good he was, of his ability to solve problems and confront difficulties, of how he had been and still was her guardian angel.

"It's only a figure of speech, Irina, personal angels do not exist!"

"Of course they do! If I didn't have a pair of guardian angels I'd be dead by now, or in jail."

"What strange ideas you have, Irina! In the Jewish tradition angels are God's messengers, not bodyguards for humans, but I do have one: Nathaniel. He always looked after me, first like a big brother, then as the ideal husband. I could never repay him for all he did for me."

"You were married for thirty years, Alma, and had a son and grandchildren. You worked together at the Belasco Foundation, and you nursed him through his final illness. I'm sure he felt just the same way, that he could never pay you back for all you did for him."

"Nathaniel deserved far more love than I gave him, Irina."

"Do you mean you loved him more as a brother than as a husband?"

"Friend, cousin, brother, husband . . . I don't know the difference. When we got married there was gossip because we were cousins, and it was considered incest; I think it still is. I suppose our love always was incestuous."

AGENT WILKINS

*O*n the second Friday in October, Ron Wilkins appeared at Lark House, looking for Irina Bazili. He was an African-American FBI agent, aged sixty-five, with a big belly, gray hair, and expressive hands. When Irina asked with surprise how he had found her, Wilkins reminded her that being well informed was an essential part of his job. They had not seen each other for three years but were in the habit of talking on the phone. Wilkins would call from time to time to hear how she was. "Don't worry, I'm fine. The past is behind me, I don't even remember all that stuff," was her invariable reply, although they both knew this wasn't true. When Irina first met him, Wilkins appeared to be about to burst out of his suit from his ripped muscles; eleven years later, those muscles had turned to flab, but he still gave the same impression of solidity and energy as in his earlier days. He told her he was a grandfather and showed her a photo of his grandson, a two-year-old with much lighter skin than his grandfather. "His father is Dutch," Wilkins explained, although Irina had not asked. He added that he had reached the age of retirement, which was almost compulsory in the Agency, but that he was still tied to his desk. He couldn't bring himself to hand in his badge; he wanted to pursue the particular crime to which he had dedicated most of his professional life.

Wilkins arrived at Lark House midmorning. The pair of them sat on a wooden bench in the garden to have a cup of the watery coffee that was always available in the library though nobody wanted it. Wisps of mist were rising from the ground, still damp from the night's dew, and the pale autumn sun was just beginning to warm the air. They were alone and could talk in peace. A few residents were already attending their morning classes, but most of them got up late. Only Victor Vikashev, the head gardener, a Russian with the looks of a Tartar warrior who had worked at Lark House for almost nineteen years, was singing softly to himself in the vegetable garden, and Cathy sped past in her electric wheelchair on her way to the pain clinic.

"I've got good news for you, Elisabeta," Wilkins told Irina.

"No one has called me Elisabeta for years."

"Of course. I'm sorry."

"Remember that I am Irina Bazili now. In fact, you helped me choose that name."

"Tell me, Irina, how are things going? Are you in therapy?"

"Let's be realistic, Agent Wilkins. Do you know how much I earn? Not enough to pay for a psychologist. The county only pays for three sessions, and I've had those, but as you can see, I haven't committed suicide. I lead a normal life; I work and am thinking of taking classes on the Internet. I want to study therapeutic massage; it's a good profession for anyone with strong hands like mine."

"Are you under medical supervision?"

"Yes, I'm taking an antidepressant."

"Where do you live?"

"In Berkeley, in a good-sized room that's cheap."

"This job here suits you, Irina. It's peaceful, no one bothers you, you're safe. I've heard very good things about you. I talked to the director and he said you're his best employee. Do you have a boyfriend?"

"I did have, but he died."

"What? My God, that's all you needed, I'm so sorry. What did he die of?"

"Old age, I think; he was over ninety. But there are other old men here who'd be happy to become my boyfriends."

Wilkins was not amused. They sat awhile in silence, blowing on and then sipping their coffees from paper cups. Irina suddenly felt overwhelmed by sadness and solitude, as if this good man's thoughts had penetrated her mind and mingled with her own, and a lump rose in her throat. As if responding to a telepathic signal from her, Wilkins put an arm around her shoulder and pulled her toward his broad chest. He smelled of a rather cloying cologne that seemed out of place on such a big man. She could feel the warmth coming from Wilkins like a stove, the rough texture of his jacket on her cheek, the comforting weight of his arm, and rested for a couple of minutes feeling protected, breathing in his cheap cologne, while he patted her back, as if he were comforting his grandson.

"What's the news you've brought?" asked Irina, once she had recovered a little.

"Compensation, Irina. There's an old law that's still in existence, though nobody remembers it, that gives victims like you the right to compensation. With that money you could pay for your therapy, which you really do need, and for your studies, and with a bit of luck, you could even put down a deposit on a small apartment."

"All that is in theory, Mr. Wilkins."

"Some people have already received compensation."

He explained that although her case was not a recent one, a good lawyer would be able to prove she had undergone serious damage as a result of what had happened, that she suffered from post-traumatic stress syndrome, and needed psychological help and medication. Irina reminded him that the person responsible had no possessions that could be confiscated to compensate her with.

"Other people in the ring have been arrested, Irina. Powerful people who have money."

"Those men didn't do anything to me. There's only one guilty man, Mr. Wilkins."

"Listen to me, Irina. You've had to change your identity and where you live. You lost your mother, your schoolmates, and all the other people you knew. You live practically hidden in another state. What happened is not something in the past; it could be said it's still going on, and that there are lots of guilty men."

"That's what I used to think, Mr. Wilkins, but I decided I am not going to be a victim forever. I've turned the page. Nowadays I am Irina Bazili and I have another life."

"I'm sorry to have to remind you, but you're still a victim. Some of the accused would be more than happy to pay you compensation if it meant they could avoid a scandal. Will you authorize me to give your name to a lawyer who specializes in this kind of thing?"

"No. Why stir all that up again?"

"Think it over, Irina. Think it over carefully and call me on this number," said the agent, handing her his card.

Irina accompanied Wilkins to the gate, and put his card away with no intention of using it. She had sorted things out herself, she didn't need that money—as far as she was concerned it was tainted and meant she would again have to face the same questions and sign statements that revealed the most disgusting details. She had no wish to fan the ashes of the past in the courts; she was an adult now and no judge would exempt her from having to face the accused. Not to mention the press. She was horrified at the thought that the people she cared about would then hear about it: her few friends, the old ladies at Lark House, Alma, and above all, Seth.

At six that afternoon Cathy called Irina on her cell phone and invited her to tea in the library. They installed themselves in an out-of-the-way corner close to the window and far from anyone passing through. Cathy didn't like tea in condoms, as she called the bags they used at Lark House, and had her own teapot, china cups, and an endless supply of a French brand of loose tea, together with butter cookies. Irina went to the kitchen to pour boiling water into the teapot but didn't try to help Cathy with the rest of the preparations, as that ritual was important to her, and she always managed it despite her jerky arms. Since she was unable to raise the delicate cup to her mouth, she had to use a plastic one and sip the tea through a straw, but seeing the cup she had inherited from her grandmother held by her guest gave her pleasure.

"Who was that black man who gave you a hug in the garden this morning?" Cathy asked her, once they had finished commenting on the final episode of a TV series about women in prison that they were both avid fans of.

"J-Just a friend I hadn't seen in a while . . . ," stammered Irina, pouring Cathy more tea to hide her shock.

"I don't believe you, Irina. I've been studying you for some time, and I know something is gnawing away at you."

"Me? It's your imagination, Cathy! As I told you, he's just a friend."

"Ron Wilkins. They told me his name at reception. I went to ask who your visitor was, because I thought you were upset after he left."

The years of being unable to move and the tremendous effort she had made to survive had shrunk Cathy, so that she looked like a child in her enormous powered wheelchair, but she still conveyed the impression of great strength, softened by the innate kindness that her accident had only served to emphasize. Her permanent smile and cropped haircut lent her a mischievous look that contrasted with her age-old monk's wisdom. Physical suffering had freed her from the inevitable bonds of personality and had polished her spirit like a diamond. The strokes she had suffered had not damaged her intellect but, as she said, had altered the wiring, and stimulated her intuition so that she could see the invisible.

"Come closer, Irina," she told her.

Cathy's cold arthritic hands clasped the younger woman's arm.

"Do you know what helps most in misfortune, Irina? To talk. Nobody can go around in this world all alone. Why do you think I set up the pain clinic? Because shared pain is more bearable. The clinic is useful for the patients but is even more useful to me. We all have demons in the dark recesses of our soul, but if we bring them out into the light, they grow smaller and weaker, they fall silent and eventually leave us in peace."

Irina tried to free herself from the tentacle-like fingers but failed. Cathy's gray eyes drilled into hers with such affection and compassion that she could not avoid them. She fell to her knees on the floor, resting her head on Cathy's rough knees, and allowed herself to be caressed by her stiff fingers. No one had touched her like that since she had left her grandparents behind.

Cathy told her that the most important thing in life was to clean up one's own mess, commit oneself a hundred percent to reality, place all one's energy in the present moment, and to do so right now, immediately. Since her accident, she had learned that there was no point waiting. Her condition gave her the time to think things through, to get to know herself better. To just be, to be in the moment, enjoying the light of the sun, people, birds. Pain came and went, nausea came and went, but for some blessed reason or other, they did not overwhelm her for long. By contrast, she was able to enjoy every drop of water during her shower, the sensation of a pair of friendly hands shampooing her hair, a deliciously cold lemonade on a summer's day. She did not think of the future, but took each day as it came.

"What I'm trying to say, Irina, is that you shouldn't stay trapped in the past or be frightened of the future. You only have one life, but if you live it well, that's enough. The only reality is now, today. What are you waiting for to be happy? Every day counts, I can tell you!"

"Happiness is not for everyone, Cathy."

"Of course it is. We are all born happy. Life gets us dirty along the way, but we can clean it up. Happiness is not exuberant or noisy, like pleasure or joy; it's silent, tranquil, and gentle; it's a feeling of satisfaction inside that begins with self-love. You need to love yourself as I do, as all those who know you do, especially Alma's grandson."

"Seth doesn't know me."

"That's not his fault. The poor devil has been trying to get close to you for years, anyone can see that. If he hasn't succeeded, it's because you hide yourself. So tell me who this man Wilkins is, Irina."

Irina Bazili had an official version of her past, one that she had constructed with Wilkins's help and that she used to satisfy other people's curiosity, if it was impossible to avoid it. Part of it was true, but it wasn't the whole truth, only the more bearable aspects. When she was fifteen, the courts had assigned her a psychologist, who treated her for several months until she refused to go on talking about what had happened and decided to adopt another name, move to another state, and change addresses as often as necessary to start over. The psychologist had insisted that traumas don't go away just by ignoring them, that they are an insidious Medusa waiting in the shadows who at the first opportunity attacks with her head of writhing snakes. Rather than face up to this, Irina had run away. Ever since, her existence had been one long flight, until she reached Lark House. She sought refuge in her work and the virtual worlds of video games and fantasy novels, where she no longer was Irina Bazili but a valiant heroine with magic powers.

Wilkins's arrival had shattered this fragile, illusory world yet again. The nightmares of the past were like dust that had settled along the way: the slightest gust sent them billowing up once more. Irina surrendered, realizing that only Catherine Hope and her golden shield could come to her aid.

In 1997, when Irina was ten years old, her grandparents received a letter from Radmila that would change her destiny once and for all. Her mother had seen a television program about sex trafficking, and learned that countries such as Moldova supplied fresh young flesh to the Arab Emirates and the brothels of Europe. With a shudder, she recalled the time she had spent in the hands of brutal Turkish pimps and, determined to prevent her daughter from suffering the same fate, convinced her husband (the American mechanic she had met in Italy and who took her to Texas) to sponsor the girl for immigration to the United States. Her letter promised that Irina would have everything she could dream of: the best possible education, hamburgers with French fries, ice cream, even a trip to Disneyland. Her grandparents ordered Irina not to tell anyone so as to avoid their envy and the evil eye, which has a habit of punishing those who boast, until all the hurdles needed to obtain a visa had been completed. The process dragged on for two years. When at long last the passport and ticket arrived Irina was twelve, with almost white-blond hair and an indomitable spirit, although she resembled a malnourished boy of eight as she was short and very thin. Her incessant dreams of America had made her aware of the poverty and ugliness around her, something she had never noticed before because she had not had anything to compare it with. Her village looked as if it had been hit by a bomb: half the shacks were boarded up or in ruins, packs of starving dogs roamed the unpaved streets, loose hens scratched in the garbage, and old people sat on their doorsteps smoking black tobacco in silence, since by now everything had been said. In the course of those two years Irina bade farewell one by one to the trees, to the hills, and to the land and sky, which, according to her grandparents, were the same under communist rule and would remain unchanged forever. Irina bade a silent good-bye to her neighbors and school friends, to the donkey and the goat, the cats and the dog who had been her childhood companions. Last of all she bade farewell to Costea and Petruta.

Her grandparents filled a cardboard box with Irina's clothes and a new image of Saint Parascheva that they bought in a holy icon market in the nearest town, and tied it up with string. Possibly all three of them suspected they would never see one another again. After her escape from Texas, Irina had wandered around for years, and the only fixed point in her tumbling life was the altar she set up wherever she landed, even if only for one night, with the saint's image and the single, carefully hand-tinted photograph she had of her grandparents. It was taken on their wedding day, and they were decked out in traditional costumes: Petruta in an embroidered skirt and wearing a lace veil; Costea in knee breeches and a short jacket, with a broad sash around his waist. They stood upright and were almost unrecognizable, since the years of hard toil had not yet crippled their backs. Not a day went by without Irina's praying to them, because they could achieve more miracles than Saint Parascheva; as she had told Alma, they were her guardian angels.

The girl somehow managed to get from Chisinau to Dallas all on her own. She had only traveled once before, when she went with her grandmother to visit Costea in the hospital in the nearest city, when he had his gallbladder removed. She had never seen an airplane close up, only in the sky, and knew no English apart from the latest pop songs, which she had learned by heart without understanding their meaning. The airline put a plastic envelope around her neck with her name, passport, and ticket in it. Irina had nothing to eat or drink on the eleven-hour flight, because she didn't know that the food on board was free, and the air hostess neglected to tell her, or in the four hours she was stranded and penniless at Dallas airport. The gateway to the American dream was that enormous, confusing place. When her mother and stepfather finally arrived, they said they had gotten the flight's arrival time wrong. Irina did not recognize them, but they saw a very blond little girl sitting on a bench with a cardboard box at her feet and were able to identify her from a photograph they had. All Irina could remember from that first meeting was that they both stank of alcohol; that sour smell was very familiar to her, as her grandparents and the other villagers often used to drown their sorrows in home-brewed wine.

Radmila and her husband, Jim Robyns, drove the new arrival to their home. To Irina this seemed the height of luxury, even though it was an ordinary-looking clapboard house in a working-class neighborhood in the south of the city, and was very run-down. Her mother had made an attempt to decorate one of the two bedrooms with heart-shaped cushions and a teddy bear with the string of a pink balloon tied to one of its paws. She advised Irina to sit in front of the television for as many hours as she could face: that was the best way to learn English, as she herself had done. In forty-eight hours Radmila had enrolled her in a public school where the students were mostly black or Hispanic, two races the girl had never seen before. It took Irina a month to learn a few phrases in English, but she had a good ear and could soon follow her lessons. Within a year she could speak English without any trace of an accent.

Robyns was an electrician. He belonged to a union, charged the maximum hourly rate, and was protected against accidents, but didn't always have work. Contracts were awarded according to a list of union members, the first job going to the first on the list, and so on. When one of them finished a contract, he was put at the end of the list, and sometimes had to wait months before being called again, unless he was well connected with any of the union bosses. Radmila worked in the children's clothing section of a department store; it took her an hour and a quarter to get there by bus, and the same to come home. When Robyns had work, they hardly ever saw him, because he made the most of it and worked all hours to the point of exhaustion; he was paid double or triple for overtime. During these periods he did not drink or take drugs, because any slip could mean he was electrocuted, but in the lengthy periods he was laid off he got wasted with alcohol and used so many drugs it was amazing he could still stand.

"My Jim is as strong as an ox," Radmila boasted, "nothing can knock him out." She joined him on his sprees as far as possible, but her body could not take as much as his, and she soon collapsed.

From Irina's very first days in America, her stepfather made her understand what he called his rules. Her mother knew nothing about it, or pretended not to, until two years later, when Wilkins knocked on her door and showed her his FBI badge.

SECRETS

After repeated pleas from Irina and much hesitation on her part, Alma agreed to become the leader of the Letting Go Group. This idea had occurred to Irina when she realized how anxious those Lark House residents who clung to their possessions were compared to those who had less. She had seen Alma get rid of so much she was even afraid she might have to lend her a toothbrush, which was why she thought that Alma would be ideal to help guide the group. The first meeting was due to take place in the library. Five people had signed up, among them Lenny, and they had all arrived punctually, but there was no sign of Alma. They waited for a quarter of an hour before Irina went to call her. She found the apartment empty, exept for a note saying she would be away for a few days and asking her to look after Neko. The cat had been ill and couldn't be left on its own. Irina was forbidden as a tenant from having animals, so she had to smuggle him into her room in a shopping bag.

That night Seth called on her cell phone to ask after his grandmother. He had passed by to see her at suppertime but was unable to find her, and was worried because he thought Alma had not completely recovered from the incident at the cinema. Irina told him Alma had vanished on another of her trysts, having completely forgotten about her prior commitment, and as a result she herself had been left embarrassed at the group meeting. Seth had met with a client in the Port of Oakland, and since he was close to Berkeley he invited Irina to go and eat sushi, which seemed to him the most appropriate cuisine while they discussed the Japanese lover. Irina was in bed with Neko, playing her favorite video game, *The Elder Scrolls V*, but got dressed and went out to meet him. The restaurant was an oasis of oriental peace, with light wood walls and booths separated by rice-paper partitions, lit by red lanterns whose warm glow induced a great sense of calm.

"Where do you think Alma goes when she disappears?" Seth asked after they ordered.

Irina filled his small ceramic bowl with *sake*. Alma had told her that in Japan the correct thing to do was to serve the other person first and then wait for someone to serve you.

"To a guesthouse in Point Reyes, about an hour and a quarter from San Francisco. It has rustic cabins on the coast and is a pretty out-of-the-way place, with good fish and seafood, a sauna, a great view, and romantic bedrooms. It's chilly at this time of year, but each room has a fireplace."

"How do you know all this?"

"From the receipts on Alma's credit card. I looked the guesthouse up on the Internet. I guess that's where she meets up with Ichimei. You're not going to bother her there, are you, Seth?"

"How could you think that? She'd never forgive me. But I could send one of my investigators to take a discreet look . . ."

"No!"

"Of course not. But you have to admit this is disturbing, Irina. My grandmother is frail; she could have another attack like the one in the cinema."

"But she's still in charge of her own life, Seth. Do you know anything else about the Fukudas?"

"Yes. I decided to ask my father, and he remembers Ichimei."

Larry Belasco was twelve years old in 1970, when his parents renovated the Sea Cliff mansion and bought an adjacent plot to add to their garden, which was already vast but had never completely recovered from the spring frost that had destroyed it when Isaac Belasco died, or its subsequent neglect. According to Larry, one day an Asian-looking man turned up, wearing work clothes and a baseball cap, and refused to enter the house because of his muddy boots. This was Ichimei Fukuda, the owner of the flower and plant nursery that he had once shared with Isaac Belasco but that now belonged to him alone. Larry sensed that his mother and this man knew each other. His father had told Fukuda that he didn't understand the first thing about gardens and so it would be Alma who made the decisions, which seemed odd at the time to Larry, since his father, Nathaniel, was the Belasco Foundation's director and, at least in theory, was very knowledgeable about gardens. Given the extent of the property and Alma's grandiose plans, the project took several months to complete. Ichimei measured the land, and tested the soil quality, the temperature, and the prevailing wind direction; he drew lines and wrote numbers on a sketch pad, closely pursued by an intrigued Larry. Soon afterward he returned with a team of six workmen, all of them of the same race as him, and the first truckload of materials. Ichimei was a calm man with restrained gestures who observed his surroundings carefully and never seemed to be in a hurry. He never spoke much, and when he did his voice was so low that Larry had to get close to hear him. He rarely initiated a conversation or answered questions about himself, but when he noticed the young boy's interest, he talked to him about nature.

"My father told me something very odd, Irina. He assured me that Ichimei has an aura," Seth added.

"A what?"

"An aura, an invisible halo. It's a circle of light around the head, like the saints have in religious pictures. But Ichimei's is visible. My father said you couldn't always see it, only occasionally, depending on the light."

"You're joking, Seth . . ."

"My father never jokes, Irina. Ah, and something else: he must be some kind of fakir, because he can control his pulse rate and his temperature. He can heat one hand as if he were burning with fever, and freeze the other one. Ichimei demonstrated this to my father more than once."

"Your father told you all this, or are you making it up?"

"I promise it's what he said. My father is a skeptic, Irina, he doesn't believe in anything he can't verify for himself."

Ichimei Fukuda finished the project and as a bonus added a small Japanese garden, which he designed as a gift for Alma, and then left the work to the other gardeners. Larry only saw him at the start of each season when he came to supervise. He noticed that he never talked to Nathaniel, only Alma, with whom he had a formal relationship, at least when Larry was present. Ichimei would arrive at the tradesmen's entrance carrying a bunch of flowers, take his shoes off, and enter with a slight bow of greeting.

Alma, who was always waiting for him in the kitchen, would respond in the same way. She would arrange the flowers in a vase, and he would accept a cup of tea. For a while they would share that slow, silent ritual, a pause in both their lives. A few years later, when Ichimei did not reappear at Sea Cliff, his mother explained to Larry he had gone on a trip to Japan.

"Do you think they were lovers back then?" asked Irina.

"I couldn't possibly ask my father that, Irina. Besides, he wouldn't know. We know very little about our own parents. But let's suppose they were lovers in 1955, as my grandmother told Lenny Beal; they separated when Alma married Nathaniel, met again in 1962, and have been together ever since."

"Why 1962?" asked Irina.

"I'm guessing, Irina, I can't be sure. That was the year my great-grandfather Isaac died."

He told her about Isaac's two funerals, and how it was only then that the family learned of all the good the patriarch had done in the course of his life, the people he had defended for nothing as a lawyer, the money he gave or lent to anyone having a hard time, the children he helped educate, and the good causes he supported. Seth had discovered that the Fukuda family owed him many favors, and respected and loved him. He deduced that they must have gone to one of the funerals. According to family legend, shortly before Isaac's death the Fukudas dug up an ancient sword they had buried at Sea Cliff. The plaque Isaac had placed to mark the spot was still there. It seemed most likely that this was when Alma and Ichimei met again.

"It's fiftysomething years from 1955 to 2013, more or less what Alma told Lenny," Irina calculated.

"If my grandfather Nathaniel suspected his wife had a lover, he pretended not to know. In my family, appearances are more important than the truth."

"For you too?"

"No, I'm the black sheep. Just look at me, I'm in love with a girl who's as pale as a Moldovan vampire."

"Vampires are from Transylvania, Seth."

March 3, 2004

Recently I've been thinking a lot about Isaac Belasco,
because my son Mike turned forty and I decided to hand
him the katana of the Fukudas; it is his responsibility to
look after it. Your uncle Isaac called me one day early in
1962 to tell me perhaps the moment had come to retrieve
the sword that had been buried for twenty years in the Sea
Cliff garden. Doubtless he already suspected he was very ill
and his end was near. All of those left in our family went:
my mother, my sister, and me. We were accompanied by
Kemi Morita, Oomoto's spiritual leader. On the day of the
ceremony in the garden you were away on a journey with
your husband. Perhaps your uncle chose that date to avoid
having you and I meet. What did he know about us? Very
little, I suppose, but he was very astute.

Ichi

⌒～⌒

Whereas Irina drank green tea with her sushi, Seth drank more hot *sake* than he could cope with. The contents of the tiny cup disappeared in a sip, while Irina, distracted by their conversation, kept refilling it. Neither of them noticed when the waiter, dressed in a blue kimono with a bandana around his forehead, brought them a second bottle. Over their dessert—caramel ice cream—Irina saw Seth's inebriated, pleading look and decided the moment had come to say good-bye before things became awkward, but realized she couldn't leave him in this state. The waiter offered to call a taxi, but Seth refused. He stumbled out, leaning heavily on Irina. In the street, the cold air revived the effects of the *sake*.

"I don't think I ought to ride my bike . . . C-Can I spend the night with you?" he stammered, tripping over his tongue.

"What will you do with your bike? It could get stolen here."

"To hell with it."

They walked the ten blocks to Irina's room. It took them almost an hour because Seth meandered like a crab. She had lived in worse places, but in Seth's company she felt ashamed of this run-down, dirty old house. She shared the house with fourteen other lodgers, crammed into rooms made from particleboard partitions, some of them with no window or ventilation. It was one of those rent-controlled buildings in Berkeley that the owners did not bother to maintain because they could not raise the rent. Only patches of the exterior paint had survived, the shutters had come off their hinges, and the yard was full of useless objects: split tires, bits of bikes, an avocado-colored toilet that had been there for years. Indoors the smell was a mixture of patchouli and rancid cauliflower soup. Nobody cleaned the hallways or the shared bathrooms. Irina took her showers at Lark House.

"Why do you live in this pigsty?" asked Seth, scandalized.

"Because it's cheap."

"Well you must be much poorer than I ever imagined, Irina."

"I don't know what you imagined, Seth. Almost everyone in the world is poorer than the Belascos."

She helped him remove his shoes and pushed him down onto the mattress on the floor that she used as a bed. Like everything else in the room, the sheets were clean, because her grandparents had taught Irina that poverty is no excuse for grime.

"What's that?" asked Seth, pointing to a small bell on the wall attached to a cord that went through the wall to the next room.

"Nothing, don't worry about it."

"What do you mean, nothing? Who lives on the other side?"

"Tim, my friend from the café, the one who washes dogs with me. I sometimes have nightmares, and if I start crying out, he pulls the cord, the bell rings, and I wake up. It's an arrangement we've made."

"Do you suffer from nightmares, Irina?"

"Of course. Don't you?"

"No, but I do have erotic dreams. Would you like me to tell you one?"

"Go to sleep, Seth."

In less than two minutes, Seth had obeyed her. Irina gave Neko his medicine, washed up with the pitcher of water and basin she kept in a corner of the room, took off her jeans and blouse, put on a worn T-shirt, and curled up by the wall, with the cat between her and Seth. It took her a long while to get to sleep, as she was too aware of the man's presence, the noises in the rest of the house, and the stink of cauliflower. The one tiny window onto the outside world was so high up that all that could be seen through it was a small rectangle of sky. Sometimes the moon would give a brief greeting as it crossed the sky, but this was not one of those blessed nights.

The faint light of day seeping into her room woke Irina the next morning. She discovered Seth was no longer there. It was nine o'clock and she ought to have left for work an hour and a half earlier. Her head and all her bones were aching, as if she were suffering from the *sake* hangover by osmosis.

THE CONFESSION

*A*lma had not yet returned to Lark House, nor had she called to ask how Neko was. The cat had not eaten in three days and was barely able to swallow the water Irina squirted into his mouth with a syringe. Since the medicine had not had any effect, she was about to ask Lenny to take her to the vet, when Seth turned up. He looked refreshed, and was wearing clean clothes and a contrite expression, evidently ashamed of his conduct the previous night.

"I've just found out that *sake* is seventeen percent alcohol," he said.

"Have you got your motorbike?" Irina interrupted him.

"Yes, I found it untouched where we left it in Berkeley."

"Well then, take me to the vet."

Neko was seen by Dr. Kallet, the same person who years earlier had amputated Sophia's leg. This was no coincidence: the vet worked as a volunteer in the organization that arranged adoptions for Romanian dogs, and Lenny had recommended him to Alma. Dr. Kallet diagnosed an intestinal blockage and said the cat needed an immediate operation, but Irina couldn't make a decision like that, and there was no answer on Alma's cell phone. Seth stepped in, paying the seven-hundred-dollar deposit the vet was insisting on, and handed the cat over to the nurse. Shortly afterward, he and Irina were sitting in the café where she had worked before Lark House and Alma employed her. They were greeted by Tim, one of her former coworkers, who after three years was still working there.

Although Seth's stomach was still queasy from the *sake*, his mind had cleared, and he had reached the conclusion that his duty to look after Irina could not be postponed any longer. He was not in love with her as he had been with other women, a possessive passion that left no room for tenderness. He desired her, and had waited for her to take the lead along the narrow path of eroticism, but his patience had gone unrewarded; it was time to turn to direct action or to give up on her once and for all. There was something in Irina's past that held her back; there could be no other explanation for her visceral fear of intimacy. He was often tempted to turn to his investigators but had decided such underhanded tactics were unworthy for Irina. He thought the mystery was bound to be cleared up at some point, and so he held back his questions, even though he was fed up with having to make so many allowances for her. What was most urgent was to get her out of that mice-ridden hole where she was living. He had rehearsed his arguments as though presenting them to a jury, but when she was sitting opposite him, with her sprite's face and her ludicrous cap, he completely forgot his speech and asked her point-blank to come live with him.

"My apartment is comfortable, I have more than enough space, you would have your own room and bathroom. For free."

"In return for what?" she asked him incredulously.

"For you working for me."

"Doing what, exactly?"

"Working on the Belasco book. A lot of research is needed, and I don't have time to do it."

"I work forty hours a week at Lark House, and twelve more for your grandmother. I also bathe dogs on the weekend and want to start studying at night. I've got much less time than you, Seth."

"You could drop all that, apart from my grandmother, and dedicate yourself to my book. You'd have somewhere to live and a good salary. I want to try living with a woman. I've never done it, so I'd better give it a go."

"I can see my room shocked you. I don't want you to feel sorry for me."

"I don't feel sorry for you. Right now I'm angry with you."

"You want me to give up my job and my steady income, the rent-stabilized room in Berkeley I had a hard time finding, to live in your apartment for a while, and then I'll be out in the street once you get bored with me. That's really helpful."

"You don't understand a thing, Irina!"

"Yes I do, Seth. You want a secretary with benefits."

"My God! I'm not going to beg you, Irina, but I should let you know that I'm not about to just give up and disappear from your life. You know how I feel about you, it's obvious even to my grandmother."

"Alma? What's she got to do with this?"

"It was her idea. I wanted to ask you from the start to marry me, but she said it would be better if we tried living together for a year or two. That would give you time to get used to me, and my parents time to get used to the idea that you're poor and not Jewish."

Irina made no attempt to hold back her tears. She hid her face in her arms folded on the table, befuddled by her headache, which had grown worse over the previous hours, and confused by an avalanche of conflicting emotions: affection and gratitude toward Seth, shame at her own limitations, despair over her future. This man was offering her romance straight out of a novel, but it wasn't for her. She could love the old people at Lark House; a few friends like her former associate Tim, who at that moment was staring at her with a worried look from the counter; her grandparents in the trunk of a sequoia; Neko, Sophia, and the other pets in the home; she could love Seth more than anyone in the world, but it wasn't enough.

"What's wrong, Irina?" asked Seth, taken aback.

"Nothing to do with you. Just things from the past."

"Tell me about it."

"Why? It's not important," she replied, blowing her nose with a paper napkin.

"It's extremely important, Irina. Last night when I tried to take your hand you almost hit me. You were right, of course, I was behaving like a pig. I'm sorry. It won't happen again, I promise. You know I've loved you for three years. What are you waiting for to love me in return? Watch out, because I can always find another girl from Moldova, there are hundreds of them willing to marry in order to get an American visa."

"Good idea, Seth."

"Seriously, you'd be happy with me, Irina. I'm a good guy, totally harmless."

"No American lawyer on a motorbike is harmless, Seth. But I admit you're a fantastic person."

"So you accept then?"

"I can't. If you knew my reasons, you'd be off like a shot."

"Let me guess: trafficking endangered species of exotic animals? I don't care. Come and see my apartment, then decide."

The apartment, in a modern building in the Embarcadero district, with a doorman and beveled mirrors in the elevators, was so spotless it appeared unlived in. There was no furniture in this desert of picture windows and dark parquet floors apart from a spinach-colored sofa, a giant TV screen, and a glass table covered with neatly stacked magazines and books. No carpets, pictures, ornaments, or plants. The kitchen was dominated by a large black granite island and a shiny collection of unused copper pots and pans hanging from hooks in the ceiling. Out of curiosity, Irina glanced in the fridge, and saw orange juice, white wine, and skim milk.

"Don't you ever eat anything solid, Seth?"

"Yes, at my parents' place or in restaurants. As my mother says, I need the female touch here. Can you cook, Irina?"

"Potatoes and cabbage."

The bedroom Seth claimed was waiting for her was as aseptic and masculine as the rest of the apartment. The only furniture was a wide bed with a raw linen bedspread and cushions in three shades of brown that did nothing to lighten the atmosphere, along with a bedside table and a metal chair. On the sand-colored wall hung one of the black-and-white photographs of Alma that Nathaniel had taken, but unlike the others, which to Irina had seemed so revealing, this one showed her in profile, asleep in a dreamy atmosphere. This was the only decoration Irina had seen in Seth's desert.

"How long have you lived here?" she asked.

"Five years. Do you like it?"

"The view is impressive."

"But you think the apartment looks bare," Seth concluded. "Well, if you want to make changes, we'll have to agree on the details. No fringes or pastel colors, they don't suit me, but I'm willing to make some concessions as far as the décor goes. Not right now, but in the future, when you beg me to marry you."

"Thanks, but for the moment just take me to the subway, I have to get back to my room. I think I've got the flu, my whole body aches."

"No way. We're going to order Chinese food, watch a film, and wait for Dr. Kallet to phone. I'll give you aspirin and tea; they help with a cold. I'm sorry I haven't got any chicken soup, it's an infallible remedy."

"Forgive me, but could I have a bath instead? I haven't had one in years; at Lark House I use the staff showers."

It was a luminous afternoon, and through the large window next to the bathtub there was a panorama of the bustling city, with its traffic, sailboats, streets crowded with people on foot, on bikes, or on skates; customers sitting at sidewalk tables under orange awnings; and the nearby Ferry Building with its gigantic clocks. Shivering, Irina sank down into the hot water up to her ears, and felt her tense muscles and aching bones slowly relax; yet again she blessed the wealth and generosity of the Belascos. Shortly afterward, Seth shouted from the far side of the door that the food had arrived, but she stayed soaking for another half hour. Eventually she dressed without much enthusiasm, feeling sleepy and with her head in a spin. The smell from the cartons of sweet-and-sour pork, chow mein, and Peking duck almost made her retch. She curled up on the spinach sofa and fell asleep, not awakening until several hours later when it was already dark outside. Seth had slipped a pillow under her head, covered her with a blanket, and was sitting on a corner of the sofa watching his second movie of the night— spies, international crimes, and Russian Mafia villains—with her feet on his lap.

"I didn't want to wake you. Kallet called and said the operation on Neko was successful, but he has a big tumor in his spleen and this is the beginning of the end," he told her.

"Poor thing, I hope he isn't suffering . . ."

"Kallet won't let him suffer, Irina. How's your headache?"

"I don't know. I'm very sleepy. You didn't spike the tea, did you, Seth?"

"Yes, I put ketamine in it. Why don't you get into bed and sleep properly? You've got a temperature."

He led her to the room with Alma's photo in it, took off her shoes, helped her get into bed, covered her, and then went to watch the end of his film. The next day, Irina woke up late, having sweated off the fever. She felt better, but her legs were still like jelly. She found a note from Seth on the black kitchen island: "The coffee is already measured, just turn on the machine. My grandmother is back at Lark House; I explained about Neko. She'll tell Voigt you're sick and are not going to work. Get some rest. I'll call later. Kisses. Your future husband." Together with the note were a carton of chicken soup with noodles, a small box of raspberries, and a paper bag with a muffin from a nearby bakery.

Seth was back before six that afternoon, after spending the day in court. He was anxious to see Irina. He had called her on the phone several times to check that she hadn't left, but he was afraid she might vanish at the last minute. When he thought of her, the first image that came to mind was of a hare ready to leap away; the second was her pale, attentive face with half-open mouth and eyes wide with astonishment as she listened to Alma's stories, believing every last one of them. As soon as he opened the door, he could feel Irina's presence. He knew she was there before he saw her: the apartment was lived-in, the sand-colored walls seemed warmer, the floor had a satin glow he had never noticed before, even the air seemed somehow friendlier. She came out to meet him on unsteady legs, her eyes puffy with sleep and her hair as disheveled as a whitish clown's wig. Seth opened his arms wide, and for the first time ever she took refuge in them. They held each other for what to her seemed like an eternity, and to him seemed to be over in a flash. Afterward she took his hand and led him over to the sofa.

"We need to talk," she told him.

She had decided to follow Catherine Hope's advice. When she had heard about Irina's past, Cathy had made her promise she would tell Seth, not merely to tear out the malignant growth poisoning her, but also because he deserved to know the truth.

At the end of 2000, Agent Wilkins had collaborated with two Canadian investigators to identify hundreds of images being trafficked on the Internet of a girl who looked about nine years old and had been subjected to such excesses of depravity and violence that she possibly had not survived. These were the favorite images of the perverts who specialized in child pornography and exchanged photos and videos privately through an international network. There was nothing new about the sexual exploitation of children, it had been going on for centuries with complete impunity, but the police could now count on a law passed in 1978 that made it illegal in the United States. From then on, the production and distribution of photographs and films diminished because the rewards did not justify the legal risks, but then came the Internet, and the market grew uncontrollably. It was calculated that there were hundreds of thousands of websites devoted to child pornography, and more than twenty million consumers, half of them in the United States. The challenge was not only to discover who the clients were, more important still was to catch the producers. The code name given to the case of the little ash-blond girl with pointy ears and a dimpled chin was Alice. The material was recent. The Canadians suspected Alice could be older than she looked, because the producers tried to make their victims appear as young as possible to satisfy their customers' demands. After fifteen months of close collaboration, Wilkins and the Canadians tracked down one of the clients, a plastic surgeon in Montreal. They raided his house and clinic, impounded his computers, and discovered more than six hundred images, among which were two photographs and a video of Alice. The surgeon was arrested and agreed to help the authorities in exchange for a reduced sentence. Thanks to the information and contacts provided, Wilkins went into action. The giant FBI man described himself as a bloodhound: once he was on the scent of a trail, nothing could put him off, and he would track it right to the end, not resting until he had succeeded. Pretending to be an enthusiast, he downloaded several photos of Alice; digitally modified them so that they looked original and her face could not be seen, although they were recognizable for those in the know; and thanks to them obtained access to the network used by the Montreal collector. He soon had several potential customers. That was his first clue; the rest was down to his hound's instinct.

One night in November 2002, Wilkins rang the bell at a house in a poor district in south Dallas. Alice opened the door. He recognized her at first sight: she was unmistakable. "I've come to talk to your parents," he told her, breathing a sigh of relief: he hadn't been sure if she was still alive. This was during one of those fortunate periods when Robyns was working in another city and the girl was alone with her mother. He flashed his FBI badge and didn't wait to be invited in: he pushed open the door and barged straight into the living room. Irina would always remember that moment as if it had just happened: the giant black man with his sweet-smelling cologne; deep, drawling voice; big, delicate hands and their pink palms.

"How old are you?" he asked Irina.

Radmila was already on her second vodka and third bottle of beer, but still thought she was lucid, and tried to intervene by saying that her daughter was a minor and that his questions should be addressed to her.

Wilkins silenced her with a gesture.

"I'm almost fifteen," Alice murmured in a faint voice, as though caught doing something wrong.

Wilkins shuddered, because his only daughter, the light of his life, was the same age. Alice had evidently suffered a deprived childhood lacking in protein; she was a late developer and her small size and delicate bone structure meant she could easily be taken for a much younger girl. Wilkins calculated that if at that moment she looked twelve, in the first images that had circulated on the Internet she could have looked nine or ten years old.

"Let me talk to your mother on her own," an embarrassed Wilkins told her.

But by then Radmila had entered the aggressive stage of drunkenness and shouted that her daughter had the right to hear whatever he had to say. "Isn't that so, Elisabeta?"

The girl nodded as if in a trance, her eyes fixed on the wall.

"I'm so sorry, child," said Wilkins, laying half a dozen photographs on the table. This was what brought Radmila face-to-face with what had been going on in her house for more than two years, although she had refused to see it, and this was how Alice learned that millions of men all over the world had viewed her in secret "games" with her stepfather. For years she had felt dirty, evil, and guilty; when she saw the photographs on the table she wanted to die. For her, no redemption seemed possible.

Robyns had assured her that this kind of game with a father or uncle was perfectly normal, and that many boys and girls who played it did so willingly and happily. Those children were special. But nobody talked about it, it was a well-kept secret, and she shouldn't ever mention it to anyone, not her girlfriends or teachers, above all not to the doctor, because people would say she was sinful, filthy, and she would be left all alone, with no friends. Even her own mother would reject her, because Radmila was very jealous. Why didn't she want to play? Did she want presents? No? Okay, so he would pay her as if she were a little grown-up woman: not directly to her, but to her grandparents. He would make sure he sent them money in Moldova on behalf of their granddaughter; she had to write a card to go with the money, but again, she shouldn't say anything to Radmila, this was their secret too. Sometimes the old couple needed a bit extra; they had to repair the roof or buy another goat. That was no problem; he was bighearted and understood life was hard in Moldova. Fortunately, Elisabeta had been lucky enough to come to America, but it wasn't good to establish a precedent that money came for free, she had to earn it, didn't she? She could at least smile, that cost nothing, she had to put on the clothes he told her to, to get used to the ropes and chains, to drink gin to relax, mixed with apple juice so it didn't burn her throat, she'd soon become accustomed to the taste, did she want more sugar? Despite the alcohol, the drugs, and her fear, at some point she realized there were cameras in the toolshed, the "little house" the two of them shared, where no one else, not even her mother, could enter. Robyns swore that the photos and videos were private, they belonged just to him, nobody would ever see them, he would keep them as a memento in the years to come, when she was away at college. How he was going to miss her!

The arrival of this unknown black stranger, with his big hands, sad eyes, and photographs, were proof that her stepfather had lied to her. Everything that had gone on in their little house was circulating on the Internet and would continue to do so. There was no way of recovering or destroying it; it would be there forever. At every moment, somewhere in the world somebody was violating her, somebody was masturbating over her suffering. For the rest of her life, wherever she was, somebody could recognize her. There was no way out. The horror would never end. The smell of alcohol and the taste of apple would always take her back to that little house; she would permanently be looking over her shoulder, escaping; she would always loathe being touched.

That night while Ron Wilkins had stepped outside to wait for Children's Services, the girl shut herself in her room, paralyzed with terror and disgust. She was sure that when her stepfather returned he would kill her, just as he had warned her he would do if she let slip a single word about the games. Her only way out was death, but not at his hand in the slow, dreadful way he often described to her, always adding fresh details.

Radmila meanwhile poured the rest of the bottle of vodka down her throat and fell unconscious. When she came to, she started to take it out on her daughter, the seductress, the whore who had perverted her husband. The beating didn't last long, because a patrol car arrived with two policemen and a social worker, alerted by Wilkins. Radmila was arrested and the girl taken to a children's psychiatric hospital while the juvenile court decided what to do with her. She never saw her mother or stepfather again.

Radmila managed to warn Robyns that the police were after him, and he fled the country, but he had not counted on Wilkins, who spent the next four years scouring the world until he found him in Jamaica and brought him back in handcuffs to the United States. His victim did not have to confront him during the trial, because the lawyers took her statements in private, and the female judge exempted her from being present in court. It was from her that Elisabeta learned not only that her grandparents had died but that the money remittances had never been sent. Jim Robyns was sentenced to ten years in jail with no prospect of parole.

"He has three years and two months left. When he gets out

he's going to come looking for me, and I'll have nowhere to hide," Irina concluded.

"You won't need to hide. He'll have a restraining order, and if he comes anywhere near you he'll go back to prison. I'll be with you, and I'll make sure the order is carried out," said Seth.

"Don't you see it's impossible, Seth? At any moment somebody in your circle, an associate, a friend, a client, even your own father, could recognize me. I'm on thousands and thousands of screens at this minute."

"No, Irina. You're a twenty-six-year-old woman and the person on the Internet is Alice, a little girl who no longer exists. The pedophiles aren't interested in you anymore."

"You're wrong. I've had to move on several times from places because some swine was after me. And it's no use my going to the police, they can't stop the guy circulating my photographs. I used to think that by dyeing my hair black or using makeup I could escape being recognized, but that didn't work: my face is easy to identify, it hasn't changed much over the years. I can never be at ease, Seth. If your family rejects me for being poor and not Jewish, imagine what it would be like if they found all this out?"

"We'll tell them, Irina. It'll be hard for them to accept at first, but I think they'll end up loving you all the more for everything you've been through. They're good people. You've suffered terribly in the past; now is a time for healing and forgiving."

"Forgiving, Seth?"

"If you don't, your rancor will destroy you. Almost all wounds heal with loving care, Irina. You have to love yourself and to love me. Agreed?"

"That's what Cathy said."

"Listen to her, she's very wise. Let me help you. I may not be so wise, but I'm a good companion and I've given you more than enough proof of my stubbornness. I never give up. You'll have to accept it, Irina, I'm not going to leave you in peace. Can you hear my heart? It's calling out to you," he said, taking her hand and placing it on his chest.

"There's something more, Seth."

"More?"

"Ever since Agent Wilkins saved me from my stepfather, no one has touched me . . . You know what I mean. I've been alone, and prefer it that way."

"Well, Irina, that's going to have to change, but let's take it slowly. What happened had nothing to do with love and will never happen to you again. It's got nothing to do with the two of us either. You once told me that old folk take their time making love. That's not a bad idea. We'll make love like a pair of grandparents, okay?"

"I don't think I can manage it, Seth."

"Then we'll have to go to therapy. Come on, stop crying. Are you hungry? Comb your hair and we'll go out for something to eat. We can talk about my grandmother's sinful life, that always cheers us up."

TIJUANA

*D*uring those heavenly months in 1955 when Alma and Ichimei were able to love each other freely at the sad motel in Martinez, she told him she was sterile. This was not so much a lie as a wish, a hope. She said this to preserve spontaneity between the sheets, because she trusted in a diaphragm to avoid surprises, and because her menstruation had always been so irregular that the gynecologist her aunt Lillian had taken her to see diagnosed ovarian cysts that would affect her fertility. As with so many other things, Alma postponed the operation, since motherhood was the last of her priorities. She thought that somehow magically she would not suffer the misfortune of falling pregnant at this young age: accidents like that happened to women from another class without education or resources. Because she did not follow her cycles, she did not realize she was pregnant until the tenth week, and when she did, she trusted to luck for a further two weeks. She thought she might have got the calculation wrong, but if the worst came to the worst, it could be resolved by violent exercise: she started biking everywhere, pedaling furiously. She regularly examined her underwear to see if there was any blood, her anxiety increasing with each passing day, and yet she continued meeting Ichimei and making love with the same frantic concern with which she pedaled up and down hills. Finally, when she could no longer ignore her swollen breasts, morning sickness, and sudden anxiety attacks, it was not Ichimei she turned to but Nathaniel, as she had done ever since they were children. To lessen the risk that her aunt and uncle would find out, she went to see him at the Belasco and Belasco Law Firm, opened in 1920, in the same office on Montgomery Street as during the days of the patriarch, with its solemn furniture and bookshelves filled with legal volumes bound in dark green leather, a mausoleum to the law, where Persian rugs muffled footsteps and everyone talked in confidential whispers.

Nathaniel was at his desk, in shirtsleeves, his tie loosened and hair a mess, surrounded by piles of open documents and legal tomes, but as soon as he saw her he came over to greet her. Alma buried her face in his chest, deeply relieved to be able to pour out her drama to this man who had never failed her.

"I'm pregnant," was all she managed to utter.

Still holding on to her, Nathaniel led her over to the sofa, where they sat side by side. Alma told him about her love, the motel, and how the pregnancy was not Ichimei's fault but hers, and that if Ichimei found out he would doubtless insist on marrying her and taking responsibility for the child, but that she had thought it through carefully and wasn't brave enough to give up all she had always enjoyed by becoming Ichimei's wife. She adored him but knew that the disadvantages of poverty drove out love, because faced with the choice between a life of economic hardship within a Japanese community she had nothing in common with, or of continuing to be protected in her own environment, her fear of the unknown won out; she was ashamed of her own weakness, Ichimei deserved unconditional love, he was a wonderful man, a sage, a saint, a pure soul, a delicate, considerate lover in whose arms she felt blessed.

She spoke in a rushing torrent of phrases, blowing her nose to avoid crying, trying to retain some dignity.

She went on to add that Ichimei lived on a spiritual plane and was always going to be a simple gardener rather than develop his enormous artistic talent or to try to turn his flower nursery into a proper business; nothing like that, he didn't want more, he was satisfied to earn just what he needed to get by and wasn't the slightest bit concerned about prosperity or success; his passions were meditation and calmness, but they didn't put food on the table and she wasn't going to start a family in a wooden shack with a tin roof and live among gardeners with spades in their hands.

"I know, Nathaniel, forgive me, you warned me a thousand times and I didn't listen, you were right, you're always right, I can see now I can't marry Ichimei, but I can't stop loving him either, without him I'd wither away like a plant in the desert, I'd die, and from now on I'll be more careful, we'll take precautions, this won't happen again, I promise you, Nathaniel, I swear." She went on talking and talking without pause, the excuses and sense of guilt welling up alternately, while Nathaniel listened without interrupting until she had run out of breath and her voice had died down to a murmur.

"Let's see if I understand you, Alma. You're pregnant but aren't thinking of telling Ichimei," Nathaniel concluded.

"I can't have a child outside of wedlock, Nat. You have to help me. You're the only person I can turn to."

"An abortion? That's illegal and dangerous. Don't count on me for that, Alma."

"Listen, Nat. I've looked into it and it's safe, there's no risk and it would only cost a hundred dollars—but you have to come with me, because it's in Tijuana."

"Tijuana? Abortion is illegal in Mexico too, Alma. This is crazy!"

"It's much more dangerous here, Nat. In Mexico there are doctors who perform the operation under the noses of the police, and nobody cares."

Alma showed him a scrap of paper with a phone number on it, and explained that she had already called up and spoken to someone named Ramón. A man had answered in terrible English, asking her who had sent her and if she knew the conditions. She gave him the name of her contact, assured him she would pay cash, and they agreed that in two days' time he would pick her up in his car at three in the afternoon on a specific corner in Tijuana.

"Did you tell this Ramón you'll be accompanied by a lawyer?" asked Nathaniel, tacitly accepting the role she had given him.

They left at six the next morning in the family's black Lincoln, which was better suited to a fifteen-hour journey than Nathaniel's sports car. Furious at being trapped in this way, Nathaniel initially kept a hostile silence, his mouth a tight line, brow furrowed, hands like talons on the wheel as he stared fixedly at the highway, but the first time Alma asked him to stop at a truck stop to go to the restroom, he softened. She was gone for half an hour, and just as he was thinking of going to look for her, she returned to the car in a bad state. "I feel sick in the mornings, Nat, but later on it passes," she explained. For the rest of the journey he tried to take her mind off things, and they ended up singing out of tune the most syrupy Pat Boone songs, the only ones they knew, until eventually, exhausted, she clung to him, laid her head on his shoulder, and dozed off.

In San Diego they stopped overnight at a hotel to eat and get some sleep. The receptionist presumed they were married and gave them a room with a double bed. They lay down together holding hands, just as they had done as children. For the first time in weeks Alma slept without having nightmares, while Nathaniel stayed wide awake until dawn, breathing in the shampoo scent on his cousin's hair, thinking of the risks they were running, feeling upset and nervous as though he were the child's father, imagining the repercussions, regretting having agreed to this sordid adventure rather than bribing a doctor in California, where everything was possible if the price was right, just as in Tijuana. As the first light filtered through the gap in the curtains he was finally overcome with fatigue and didn't wake up until nine in the morning, when he heard Alma retching in the bathroom. They took their time crossing the border, with the predictable delays, and drove on to keep their appointment with Ramón.

Mexico greeted them with its well-known clichés. They had never been in Tijuana before and were expecting a sleepy little town, but instead found themselves in a city that went on forever, brimming with color and noise, people and traffic, where dilapidated buses and modern cars sped alongside carts and donkeys. In the same store you could buy Mexican artifacts and American household appliances, shoes and musical instruments, spare parts and furniture, caged birds and tortillas. The air was filled with the smell of fried food and garbage, and the din of popular music, evangelical preachers, and football commentators on the radios in bars and taco joints. They had difficulty finding their way, because many of the streets had no names or numbers, and so had to ask every three or four blocks, but didn't understand the directions they were given in Spanish, which more often than not consisted of a vague wave of the arm and a "right here, just round the corner." In their frustration they parked the Lincoln near a gas station and walked until they came to the agreed corner, which turned out to be at the intersection of four busy streets. They waited arm in arm, stared at shamelessly by a lone dog and a group of ragged children begging for money. The only indication they had been given, apart from the name of one of the streets at the intersection, was a store for first communion dresses and images of holy virgins and Catholic saints, bizarrely named Viva Zapata.

After they had waited for twenty minutes, Nathaniel decided they had been tricked and ought to go back home, but Alma reminded him that punctuality was not exactly a Mexican characteristic and went into Viva Zapata. She gesticulated to use the telephone and dialed Ramón's number. It rang nine times before a woman's voice answered in Spanish, which she couldn't understand. At four in the afternoon, by which time Alma had accepted they might as well give up, a pea-colored 1949 Ford with tinted rear windows just as Ramón had described it pulled up at the corner. Two men sat in the front seats: a youngster with a pockmarked face, a pompadour, and bushy sideburns was in the driver's seat; the other one got out to let them in, because the car was two doored. He introduced himself as Ramón. He was thirtysomething, with a carefully groomed mustache, slicked-back hair, a white shirt, and pointed high-heeled boots. Both men were smoking. "The cash,"

Ramón demanded as soon as they were inside the car. Nathaniel handed it over; Ramón counted it and stuffed the bills in his pocket. Neither of the men spoke during the journey, which to Alma and Nathaniel seemed endless: they were certain they were being driven around and around to get them lost—an unnecessary precaution, as neither of them knew the city. Clinging to Nathaniel the whole time, Alma was thinking how much worse the situation would have been if she had come on her own, while Nathaniel calculated that the men had already got their money and so could quite easily put a bullet in their heads and throw them down a ravine. They hadn't told anyone where they were going, and weeks or months would go by before their family found out what had become of them.

Finally the car came to a halt, and they were told to wait while the driver went into the house and the other man kept watch. They were outside a cheap-looking house similar to others along the street, in a neighborhood that to Nathaniel looked poor and dirty, although he could not judge it by San Francisco standards. After a couple of minutes the youngster reappeared, and the pair told Nathaniel to get out of the car. They patted him down and made as if to lead him away, but he swatted them off and confronted them, cursing in English. Taken aback, Ramón raised his hands to mollify him.

"Slow down, man, everything's okay." He laughed, flashing a pair of gold teeth.

He offered Nathaniel a cigarette, which he accepted, while the other Mexican helped Alma out of the car. They all went into the house, which was not the gangsters' den that Nathaniel had feared, but a modest family home, with low ceilings and small windows.

Inside, it was hot and dark. In the living room, two children were sprawled on the floor playing with lead toy soldiers next to a table and chairs, a plastic-covered sofa, a showy lamp with a fringed shade, and a refrigerator as noisy as an outboard motor. A smell of fried onions came from the kitchen, and they caught sight of a woman in black stirring something in a pan. She showed as little interest in the newcomers as the children had. The younger of the two men pointed Nathaniel to a chair and disappeared into the kitchen, while Ramón led Alma down a short corridor to another room with a blanket over the entrance instead of a door.

"Wait!" shouted Nathaniel. "Who's going to perform the operation?"

"I am," said Ramón, who apparently was the only one who spoke English.

"What do you know about medicine?" asked Nathaniel, staring at the man's hands with their long, polished nails.

Once more came the friendly laugh and the golden smile, with fresh reassuring gestures and a couple of stilted phrases explaining that he had a lot of experience and that it would take less than fifteen minutes, no problem. Anesthetic? No, *mano*, we don't have any of that here, but this helps, he said, handing Alma a bottle of tequila. When she hesitated, glancing mistrustfully at the bottle, Ramón took a lengthy swig, wiped the neck on his sleeve, and offered it to her again. Seeing the look of panic on Alma's face, Nathaniel instantly made the most important decision in his life.

"We've changed our minds, Ramón. We're going to get married and have the baby. You can keep the money."

Alma had many years ahead of her in which to carefully consider the way she had behaved in 1955. That was the year she was pitchforked into reality, and her efforts to avoid her nagging sense of shame proved useless: the disgrace at becoming pregnant, loving Ichimei less than herself, her horror of poverty, yielding to social pressure and racial prejudices, accepting Nathaniel's sacrifice, not living up to the role of the modern Amazon she had imagined herself to be, shame at herself for being not only fearful and conventional but another half dozen adjectives as well that she punished herself with. She was aware that she had avoided the abortion more from fear of the pain and of dying from a hemorrhage or infection than out of respect for the being that was growing inside her. When she examined herself once more in her wardrobe's full-length mirror, she could not discover the Alma from before, the bold, sensual young girl Ichimei would see if he were there, but a cowardly, capricious, and selfish woman. There was no point making excuses; nothing could lessen her feeling that she had lost her dignity. Years later, when it had become the fashion to love someone from a different race or to have children without marrying, Alma admitted to herself that her greatest prejudice was that of social class, which she never managed to overcome. In spite of the nightmare trip to Tijuana, which destroyed the illusion of love and humiliated her to such an extent that she took refuge in a monumental pride, she never doubted her decision to keep the truth from Ichimei. To confess would have meant facing up to her own complete cowardice.

On her return from Tijuana she arranged to meet Ichimei several hours earlier than usual in the motel they always used. She arrived with her head held high and with her lies well rehearsed, yet she was weeping inside. For once, Ichimei had arrived first, and was waiting for her in one of those filthy rooms where the roaches ruled, but which they lit with the flame of love. It had been five days since they had met, and several weeks since something obscure had been spoiling the perfection of their meetings, something that Ichimei felt was enveloping them like a thick fog but that she dismissed lightly, accusing him of being jealous and talking nonsense. Ichimei could tell there was something different about her: she was anxious, she talked too much and too quickly; her mood changed every few minutes, from amorous and affectionate to a stubborn silence or inexplicable bad temper. He had no doubt she was distancing herself emotionally, although her sudden passion and insistence on reaching an orgasm over and over again seemed to indicate the opposite. Occasionally, while they were resting in each other's arms after making love, her cheeks were wet. "They're tears of love," she would say, but to Ichimei, who until now had never seen her cry, they seemed more like tears of frustration, in the same way that her sexual acrobatics were an attempt to distract him. With his ancestral discretion, he tried to discover what was going on, but she responded to his questions with mocking laughter or foul language, which, even if meant as a joke, greatly upset him. Alma slid away like a lizard. During the five days they had been apart, which she justified as a family trip to Los Angeles she could not get out of, Ichimei withdrew into himself. All that week he continued working the land and cultivating flowers in his usual selfless manner, but his movements were those of a man in a trance. His mother, who knew him better than anyone, refrained from asking him questions and took their stock to the San Francisco florists herself. As he bent over the plants with the sun on his back, silently and undemonstratively Ichimei surrendered to his forebodings, which rarely proved wrong.

When Alma saw him by the light filtering in through the torn curtains of their motel room, she once again felt guilt tearing at her innards. For a split second she hated this man forcing her to confront her most despicable side, only to be instantly overwhelmed by the huge wave of love and desire she always felt when he was with her. Ichimei, standing by the window waiting for her, with his unshakable inner strength, his lack of vanity, his tenderness and delicacy, his serene expression; Ichi, with his body like teak, stiff hair, green fingers, affectionate eyes, his belly laugh, his way of making love as if it were always the last time. She couldn't look him in the face and pretended she was having a coughing fit to conceal the anxiety burning her up.

"What's wrong, Alma?" asked Ichimei, without touching her.

It was then that she launched into the speech she had prepared with all the care of a legal clerk, about how she loved him and would do so for the rest of her life, but that their love had no future, was impossible, how family and friends were starting to become suspicious and ask questions, how they came from very different worlds and had to fulfill their own destinies, how she had decided to continue her art studies in London, and so they would have to part.

Ichimei received this battering with the resoluteness of someone prepared for an attack. After Alma's declaration there was a prolonged silence, during which she imagined they could make love desperately one last time, in an ardent farewell, a final gift of the senses before they finally cut the thread of hope they had been weaving since their first fumbled caresses as children in the

Sea Cliff garden. She began to unbutton her blouse, but Ichimei stopped her with a gesture.

"I understand, Alma," he said.

"Forgive me, Ichimei. I've had a thousand mad thoughts about how we could continue to be together, to have a hideaway where we could make love rather than this disgusting motel, but I know it's not possible. I can't keep this secret any longer, it's destroying me. We have to say good-bye forever."

"Forever is a long time, Alma. I think we'll meet again in happier circumstances, or other lives," said Ichimei. He tried hard to remain calm, but an icy sadness was filling his heart and strangled his voice.

They embraced desolately, the orphans of love. Alma's knees buckled, and she was on the verge of collapsing against her lover's strong chest and confessing everything, even the darkest corners of her shame, begging that they get married and live in a shack, bring up mixed-race children, promising him she would be a submissive wife and would give up her silk-screening and her comfortable life at Sea Cliff and the splendid future that was her birthright, abandon this and much more just for him and the extraordinary love that bound them together. Ichimei might have had an inkling of all this, and was considerate enough to prevent her humiliating herself in this way by closing her mouth with a chaste, fleeting kiss. Still holding her close, he led her to the door and from there to her car. Kissing her on the forehead one last time, he walked to his gardening van without so much as a backward glance.

July 11, 1969

Our love is inevitable, Alma. I always knew it, although for years I struggled against it and tried to tear you from my mind, knowing I could not do so from my heart. When you left me without giving any reason I could not understand it. I felt cheated, but during my first trip to Japan I had time to calm down and eventually accepted I had lost you in this life. I stopped making pointless conjectures as to what had happened between us. I had no hope that destiny would reunite us. Now, after fourteen years apart, every day of which I have thought of you, I understand we will never be husband and wife, but also that we cannot renounce everything we feel so intensely. I invite you to live our love in a bubble, protected from the thorns of life and preserved intact for the rest of our lives, and beyond death. It is up to us to preserve our love forever.

Ichi

BEST FRIENDS

A lma Mendel and Nathaniel Belasco were married in a private ceremony on the terrace at Sea Cliff, on a day that started out warm and sunny but that turned colder and darker, with unexpected storm clouds that reflected the bride and groom's state of mind. Alma had purple shadows under her eyes from spending a sleepless night tossing and turning on a sea of doubts. As soon as she saw the rabbi she ran to the bathroom, stomach heaving, but Nathaniel shut himself in with her, made her splash herself with cold water, and urged her to control herself and put a brave face on it.

"You're not alone in this, Alma. I'm with you, and always will be," he promised.

The rabbi, who had at first been against the marriage because they were cousins, had to accept the situation once Isaac Belasco, the most prominent member of his congregation, explained that in view of Alma's condition there was no choice but to marry them. Isaac told him that the young couple had loved each other since childhood, and their affection had turned to passion upon Alma's return from Boston; that these accidents happen; that it was the way of the world, and faced with the facts all that remained was to give them their blessing.

Martha and Sarah had the idea that they could spread a story to silence any gossip—for example, that Alma had been adopted in Poland by the Mendel family and therefore was not a blood relative—but Isaac was against it. There was no point adding such an obvious lie to a mistake already made. Deep down, he was happy to see the union of the two people he loved most in the world apart from his wife. He preferred a thousand times that Alma marry Nathaniel and stay closely tied to his family than for her to wed a stranger and leave him. Lillian reminded him that incestuous relations produced mentally deficient offspring, but he assured her this was nothing but a popular superstition that only had scientific grounding in enclosed communities, where the inbreeding had taken place over several generations. That was not the case for Nathaniel and Alma.

Following the ceremony, attended only by the immediate family, the law firm's accountant, and the household staff, a formal dinner was served for them all in the mansion's great dining room, reserved for grand occasions. The cook, her assistant, the maids, and the chauffeur took to the table shyly with their employers; they were served by two waiters from Ernie's, the city's most refined restaurant, which provided the food. This idea had occurred to Isaac in order to officially establish that from this day on Alma and Nathaniel were man and wife. The domestic staff, who knew them as members of the same family, would not find it easy to become accustomed to the change; in fact, one of the maids who had been working for the Belasco family for four years still thought they were brother and sister, because no one had ever told her before that they were cousins. The meal began in a funereal silence, with everyone staring down at their plates in embarrassment, but things livened up as the wine started to flow and Isaac obliged his guests to toast the couple. Happy, talkative, filling his own and everyone else's glasses, Isaac was like the healthy, youthful version of the old man he had turned into in recent years. Fearful he might have a heart attack, a worried Lillian kept tugging at his trousers under the table to calm him down. Finally, the bride and groom cut a marzipan and cream cake with the same silver knife Isaac had used at his own wedding many years before. They left the house in a taxi, as the family chauffeur had drunk so much he was sobbing tearfully in his seat while muttering in Gaelic, his mother tongue.

They spent their first night as a married couple in the bridal suite at the Palace Hotel, where Alma had once had to suffer the debutantes' balls, surrounded by champagne, sweets, and flowers. The next day they flew to New York, and from there to Europe for a two-week honeymoon that Isaac had insisted they take even though neither of them wanted it. Nathaniel was busy with several legal cases and did not want to leave the office, but his father bought the tickets, stuffed them in his pocket, and convinced him to go with the argument that a honeymoon was a traditional obligation; there were enough rumors going around already about this hasty marriage between cousins to want to avoid any further speculation. Alma undressed in the bathroom and returned wearing the silk and lace nightgown Lillian had bought hurriedly as part of an improvised trousseau. She twirled around in front of Nathaniel, who was waiting for her fully dressed, sitting on a stool at the foot of the bed.

"Take a good look, Nat, because you won't have another opportunity to admire me. The gown is already tight around my waist. I don't think I'll be able to wear it again."

Her husband noticed how her voice was trembling despite her attempt to charm him, and patted the seat beside him. Alma sat down.

"I don't have any illusions, Alma. I know you love Ichimei."

"I also love you, Nat. I don't know how to explain it. There must be a dozen women in your life; I don't know why you've never introduced me to any of them. You once told me that when you fell in love I'd be the first to know. As soon as the baby is born we can get divorced, and you'll be free."

"I haven't renounced any great love for you, Alma, and I think it's in very bad taste for you to talk about divorce on our wedding night."

"Don't laugh, Nat. Tell me the truth: do I attract you in any way? As a woman, I mean."

"Until now I've always regarded you as my younger sister, but that could change when we live together. Would you like that?"

"I don't know. I'm confused, sad, angry; I have a chaos in my head and a child in my belly. You got a dreadful deal marrying me."

"That remains to be seen, but I want you to know I'll be a good father to the child, boy or girl."

"He or she will have Asian features, Nat. How are we going to explain that?"

"We won't, and no one will dare ask, Alma. Heads held high and lips sealed is the best way. The only person with the right to ask is Ichimei Fukuda."

"I'll never see him again, Nat. Thank you a thousand times for what you're doing for me. You're the noblest person in the world, and I'll try to make you a worthy wife. A few days ago I thought I would die without Ichimei, but now I think that with your help, I'll survive. I won't fail you. I'll always be faithful, I swear."

"Sshh, Alma. Let's not make promises we might not be able to keep. We're going to travel this path together, step by step, day by day, with the best of intentions. That's all we can promise one another."

Isaac Belasco had rejected outright the idea that the newlyweds have their own home. There was more than enough room at Sea Cliff, and the intention behind building such an enormous house had always been that several generations of the family would live under the same roof. Besides, Alma had to look after herself, and would need Lillian and her female cousins' help and company; he declared that to set up and manage a new house would take far too much effort. As a clinching argument he used emotional black-mail: he wanted to spend what little time he had left with them, and they could then keep Lillian company when she was widowed. Nathaniel and Alma accepted the patriarch's decision; she continued to sleep in her blue room, where the only change was to replace her bed with two new ones, separated by a night table. Nathaniel put his penthouse up for sale and returned to the family home. In his former bedroom he installed a study, his books and music, and a sofa. Everybody was aware that the couple's daily routines did not exactly encourage intimacy: Alma got up at noon and went to bed early; he worked like a galley slave, came back home late from the office, shut himself away with his books and classical records, went to bed after midnight, slept very little, and left before she was awake. On the weekend he played tennis, jogged up Mount Tamalpais, went sailing around the bay in his boat, and came back sunburned, sweaty, and relaxed. It was also obvious that he usually slept on the sofa in his study, but this was put down to his wife's need to rest. Nathaniel was so attentive to Alma, she depended so much on him, and there was so much trust and good humor between them that only Lillian suspected anything was amiss.

"How are things between you and my son?" she asked Alma in the second week after they had returned from their honeymoon, when her daughter-in-law was four months pregnant.

"Why do you ask, Aunt Lillian?"

"Because you two love each other just as you always did; nothing has changed. Marriage without passion is like food without salt."

"You want us to be passionate in front of everyone?" laughed Alma.

"My love for Isaac is the most precious thing I have, Alma, far more than for my children or grandchildren. I want the same for you two: for you to live in love with each other, like Isaac and me."

"What makes you think we don't, Aunt Lillian?"

"You're at the best time in your pregnancy, Alma. Between the fourth and seventh months a woman feels strong, full of energy, and sexy. Nobody tells you this, the doctors don't mention it, but it's like being in heat. That was how it was when I was expecting all my three children: I chased Isaac everywhere. It was scandalous! But I can't see that same enthusiasm between Nathaniel and you."

"How can you know what goes on between us behind closed doors?"

"Don't answer me with more questions, Alma!"

On the far side of San Francisco Bay, Ichimei was silent and unapproachable, consumed by a bitter sense of betrayed love. He buried himself in his work, and his flowers grew more colorful and perfumed than ever to console him. He learned of Alma's marriage because Megumi had been leafing through a society gossip magazine at the hairdresser's and saw a photograph of Alma and Nathaniel Belasco in formal attire, presiding over the annual banquet of the family foundation. The caption stated that the couple had recently returned from their honeymoon in Italy and described the splendid reception as well as Alma's elegant dress, inspired by the flowing tunics of ancient Greece. According to the magazine, they were the most talked-about couple of the year. Not suspecting she was going to drive a stake through her brother's heart, Megumi had cut out the page and took it to show him. Ichimei studied it without showing the slightest emotion. He had been trying for several weeks to comprehend what had happened during those months with Alma in the motel and their intense lovemaking. He thought he had experienced something completely extraordinary, a passion worthy of literature, the meeting of two souls destined repeatedly to be together across time, but while he was embracing that magnificent certainty, she had been planning to marry someone else!

The betrayal was so immense there was not enough room for it in his chest: he could scarcely breathe. In Alma and Nathaniel Belasco's world, marriage was more than the union of two individuals: it was a social, economic, and family strategy. It was impossible that Alma could have been preparing for it without revealing the slightest hint of her intentions; the evidence must have been there, but he was too blind and deaf to spot it. Now though he could tie up loose ends and understand Alma's erratic behavior in their final days together, her hesitations, her subterfuges to avoid questions, her subtle devices for distracting him, her contortions to make love without looking him in the face. The falsehood was so complete, the web of lies so intricate and complex, the hurt done so irreparable, that he could only conclude he did not know Alma in the slightest, that she was a stranger to him. The woman he loved had never existed; he had built her out of his dreams.

Tired of seeing her son drained of spirit like a sleepwalker, Heideko Fukuda decided the time had come to take him back to Japan to discover his roots and, with a bit of luck, find him a bride. The journey would help relieve him of the despair whose origin neither she nor Megumi had been able to fathom. Ichimei was still young to start a family, but he was mature beyond his years; it was a good idea to step in as soon as possible and choose her future daughter-in-law, before her son became ensnared in the pernicious American custom of getting married out of amorous infatuation. Megumi was completely devoted to her studies, but she agreed to supervise a couple of their compatriots who were taken on to keep their flower business going. She thought of asking Boyd, as a definitive proof of his love, to give up everything he had in Hawaii and come to Martinez to grow flowers, but Heideko could still not bring herself to even pronounce the name of this stubborn lover, whom she continued to refer to as the concentration camp guard. It was to be another five years before Heideko's first grandchild, Charles, was born and she finally agreed to talk to the white devil.

Heideko organized the trip to Japan without asking Ichimei's opinion. She simply told him they had to fulfill the inescapable duty of honoring Takao's ancestors, as she had promised him on his deathbed so that he could pass away in peace. Takao had not been able to do so during his lifetime, so now the pilgrimage was up to the two of them. They would have to visit a hundred temples and scatter a pinch of Takao's ashes in each of them. Ichimei only protested feebly for the sake of it, because deep down he did not care where he was; the geographical location in no way affected the process of inner cleansing on which he was embarked.

In Japan, Heideko announced to her son that her own first duty was not toward her deceased husband, but to her aged parents, if they were still alive, and to her siblings, whom she had not seen since 1922. She had no hope of finding her son James, who disappeared completely after he was deported. She did not invite Ichimei to accompany her. She said good-bye casually, as if she were going to the corner store, without asking how her son was going to survive in the meantime. Ichimei had given his mother all the money they had brought with them. He saw her off on the train, left his suitcase at the station, and started walking with only the clothes he was wearing, a toothbrush, and the oilskin bag containing his father's ashes. He had no need of a map, because he had memorized his itinerary. He walked all the first day on an empty stomach until at nightfall he came to a tiny Shinto shrine, where he lay down by a wall. He was about to fall asleep when a mendicant monk came up and told him that inside the shrine there was always tea and rice cakes for any pilgrim. This was to be Ichimei's life for the next four months. He walked all day until he was overwhelmed with fatigue, went hungry until somebody offered him a bite to eat, and slept wherever night found him. He never had to beg and never needed money. He walked along with his mind blank, enjoying the landscapes and his own tiredness, while the effort of keeping going gradually wore away his sad memories of Alma. When he completed his mission of visiting a hundred temples, the oilskin bag was empty, and he had rid himself of the dark thoughts that had so oppressed him at the start of the journey.

August 2, 1994

To live with uncertainty, with nothing sure or safe, with no plans or goals, letting myself be carried along like a bird on the wind: that is what I learned on my pilgrimage. You are amazed that at the age of sixty-two I can still leave from one day to the next and set out with no itinerary or baggage, like a youngster hitchhiking, that I can go away for an undefined length of time without calling you or writing to you, and that on my return I can't tell you where I've been. There is no secret, Alma; I walk, and that's all. I need very little, almost nothing, to survive. Ah, freedom!

I go, but I always remember you.

Ichi

AUTUMN

When she had failed to turn up to meet him for two consecutive days on the park bench, Lenny went to look for Alma at her apartment at Lark House. The door was opened by Irina, who had gone there to help her dress before she began her day at the home.

"I was waiting for you, Alma. You're late," said Lenny.

"Life is too short to be punctual." Alma sighed.

For several days now, Irina had been coming early to give her breakfast, keep an eye on her in the shower, and help with her clothes, but neither of them mentioned it, as that would have been to admit Alma was starting no longer to be able to live on her own, and would have to move to the second level or return to Sea Cliff with her family. They both preferred to see this sudden weakness as a temporary setback. Seth had asked Irina to give up her job at Lark House and leave her room (which he called the mousetrap) to go and live with him permanently, but she kept one foot in Berkeley so as to avoid the snare of dependency, which she feared as much as the idea of moving to the second level at Lark House scared Alma. When she tried to explain this to Seth, he was offended by the comparison.

Neko's absence had hit Alma like the beginning of a heart attack: there was a constant pain in her chest. The cat frequently appeared to her in the shape of a cushion on the sofa, a crumpled corner of the rug, her badly hung coat, or the shadow of a tree at the window. Neko had been her confidant for eighteen years. In order not to talk to herself, she would talk to him, knowing he was not going to answer her but understood everything in his feline wisdom. They had similar temperaments: arrogant, lazy, solitary. She loved not only that he was an unprepossessing street cat, but that time had left its mark on him: bare patches on his skin, a twisted tail, rheumy eyes, and the big belly of a good eater. She missed him in bed; without Neko's weight at her side or feet she found it hard to sleep. Apart from Kirsten, that animal was the only being who stroked her. Irina would have liked to do so, to give her a massage, wash her hair, polish her nails, find some way to get physically close to Alma and make her feel she was not alone, but Alma did not encourage intimacy with anyone. Irina found this kind of contact with other old women at Lark House quite natural, and little by little she was starting to want it with Seth. She tried to make up for Neko's absence by putting a hot water bottle in Alma's bed, but when this absurd ruse only made things worse, Irina offered to go to the Society for the Prevention of Cruelty to Animals to find another cat. Alma explained there was no way she could adopt an animal that would outlive her. Neko had been her last cat.

Lenny's dog, Sophia, waited in the doorway, just as she did when Neko was alive and defended his territory, sweeping the floor with her tail at the prospect of going for a walk, but Alma had exhausted herself with the effort of dressing and could not get up from the sofa. "I'm leaving you in good hands, Alma," Irina said as she left. Lenny noted with concern how much both Alma and the apartment had changed: the room had not been aired and smelled musty and of rotting gardenias.

"What's happened, dear friend?"

"Nothing serious. I may have something wrong in my ears that's making me lose my balance. And sometimes it feels like an elephant is stamping on my chest."

"What does your doctor say?"

"I don't want any doctors, examinations, or hospitals. Once you get into their hands, you never get out. And forget the Belascos! They love drama and would only make a fuss."

"Don't you dare die before me! Remember what we agreed, Alma. I came here to die in your arms, not the other way around," joked Lenny.

"I haven't forgotten. But if I fail you, you can rely on Cathy."

That friendship, discovered late in the day and savored like a fine wine, added color to a reality that was inexorably losing its brilliance for both of them. Alma was so solitary a person that she had never realized how lonely she was. Protected by her aunt and uncle, she had lived as part of the Belasco family in the vast mansion at Sea Cliff that was looked after by other people—her mother-in-law, the butler, her daughter-in-law—but had always felt she was a visitor. She felt disconnected and different everywhere else too, but far from being a problem this gave her a sense of pride, as it added to her view of herself as a distant, mysterious artist vaguely superior to the rest of mortals. This meant she had no need to mix with humanity in general, whom she considered in the main stupid, cruel when it had the opportunity, and sentimental at best. She was careful never to express these opinions in public, but old age had only reinforced them.

Looking back from this vantage point in her eighties, she had loved very few people, but she had loved them intensely, idealizing them with a fierce romanticism that resisted any assault from reality. She had not suffered the devastating infatuations typical of childhood and adolescence; she had been on her own at college, and had traveled and worked alone, without associates or colleagues, only subordinates. She had replaced all that with her obsessive love for Ichimei Fukuda and her exclusive friendship with Nathaniel Belasco, whom she thought of not as a husband but as her closest friend. During this final stage of her life she could count on Ichimei, her legendary lover; her grandson, Seth; and Irina, Lenny, and Cathy, who were the closest thing to friends that she had known in many years. Thanks to them, she was saved from boredom, one of the scourges of old age. The rest of the Lark House community was like the view of the bay: something to be enjoyed from a distance, without getting her feet wet.

For half a century she had been part of the closed little world of San Francisco's upper class; she appeared at the opera, charity events, and social occasions she could not avoid, saved by the insuperable distance she established from the first introduction. She told Lenny how much she hated the noise, empty chatter, and eccentricities of the human race, and that it was only a vague empathy for others that prevented her from being a psychopath. It was easy to feel compassion for unfortunate people she didn't know. She didn't like humans; she preferred cats. She could only take the human race in small doses: more than three gave her indigestion. She had always shied away from groups, clubs, and political parties; she was never a militant for any cause, even if she supported it in principle, like feminism, civil rights, or peace.

"I am not into saving whales so I don't have to mix with ecologists."

She never sacrificed herself for another person or an ideal: self-denial was not one of her virtues. Apart from Nathaniel in his final illness, she had never had to look after anyone, not even her son. Motherhood was not the cataclysm of adoration and anxiety that all mothers are supposed to experience; instead it was tranquil, sustained affection. Larry was a solid, unconditional presence for her; she loved him with a combination of complete trust and long habit, a comfortable feeling that demanded little from her. Although she had admired and loved Isaac and Lillian Belasco, whom she went on calling Uncle and Aunt even after they had become her in-laws, none of their kindness and vocation to serve had rubbed off on her.

"Thank goodness the Belasco Foundation creates green areas rather than trying to help beggars or orphans. That means I've been able to do some good without having to get too close to those who have benefited," she told Lenny.

"Be quiet, will you? If I didn't know you, I'd think you were a narcissistic monster."

"If I'm not one, it's thanks to Ichimei and Nathaniel, who taught me to give and receive. Without them I'd have retreated into indifference long ago."

"Many artists are introverts, Alma. They have to absent themselves to create," Lenny said.

"Don't look for excuses. The truth is that the older I get, the more I like my defects. Old age is the best moment to be and do whatever you enjoy. Soon no one will be able to bear me. Tell me, Lenny, is there anything you feel sorry about?"

"Of course. All the crazy things I never did, having given up cigarettes and margaritas, becoming vegetarian, and killing myself doing exercise. I'm going to die anyway, but at least I'll be fit," laughed Lenny.

"I don't want you to die . . ."

"Nor do I, but it's not optional."

"When I first knew you, you used to drink like a Cossack."

"I've been sober for thirty years now. I think I drank so much to avoid thinking. I was hyperactive; it was all I could do to sit still to cut my toenails. As a young man I was gregarious, always surrounded by noise and people, but even so I felt alone. Fear of loneliness defined my character, Alma. I needed to be accepted and loved."

"You're talking in the past. Isn't it like that anymore?"

"I've changed. I spent my youth searching for approval and adventures, until I really fell in love. Afterward my heart was broken and I spent a decade trying to pick up the pieces."

"And did you succeed?"

"Let's say I did, thanks to a smorgasbord of psychology: individual, group, gestalt, biodynamic therapies. Anything I could lay my hands on, including primal scream therapy."

"What on earth is that?"

"I used to shut myself in with the woman psychologist to shout like a man possessed while I punched a cushion for fifty-five minutes."

"I don't believe you."

"It's true. And what was more, I paid to do it. I was in therapy for years. It was a rocky road, Alma, but I learned to know myself and to look my loneliness in the face. It doesn't frighten me anymore."

"Something like that would have helped Nathaniel and me a lot, but it never occurred to us. It wasn't something that was done in our circles. By the time psychology became fashionable it was too late for us."

All of a sudden the anonymous packages of gardenias Alma received on Mondays ceased to appear, just when she would have most enjoyed them, yet she gave no indication that she had noticed. Following her last escapade she hardly ever went out. If Irina, Seth, Lenny, and Cathy had not kept her active, she would have shut herself away like an anchorite. She lost all interest in reading, TV series, yoga, Victor Vikashev's garden, and the other activities that once filled the time for her. She had no appetite, and if Irina was not keeping a close watch, she could get by for days on apples and green tea. She did not tell a soul that sometimes her heart started racing, her vision clouded over, and she became confused over the simplest tasks. Her apartment, which until then had fitted her needs perfectly, now seemed to grow bigger and its layout to constantly change: when she thought she was standing outside the bathroom, she went out into the building's corridor, which had become so long and twisting she had difficulty finding her own door, as they all looked the same; the floor swayed so that she had to cling to the walls to stay on her feet; the light switches moved around so that she couldn't find them in the dark; new drawers and shelves appeared, where everyday objects got lost; photographs shifted around in their albums without anyone touching them. She couldn't find anything; the cleaner or Irina kept hiding things. She did however realize it was unlikely that the universe was playing all these tricks on her; it was probably a lack of oxygen in her brain. She went to the window to do the breathing exercises she had seen in a manual borrowed from the library, but kept postponing the visit to the cardiologist Cathy had recommended, still clinging to the belief that, given time, almost all ailments resolve themselves.

She would soon be eighty-two; she was old, but she refused to cross the threshold into decrepitude. She had no intention of sitting in the shade of the years staring into space, her mind on a hypothetical past. She had fallen a couple of times but suffered nothing worse than a few bruises. The time had come when she had to accept being gripped by the elbow to help her walk, but she fed the remains of her vanity on whatever scraps she could find and fought against the temptation to give in to an easy lethargy. She was horrified at the thought of having to go to the second level, where she would have no privacy and mercenary carers would assist her with her most personal needs.

"Good night, Death," she would say before she went to sleep, in the vague hope that she wouldn't wake up; that would be the most elegant way to go, comparable only to falling asleep forever in Ichimei's arms after they had made love. She didn't really believe she deserved such good luck: she had led a fortunate life, and there was no reason for her death to be the same.

She had lost her fear of death thirty years earlier, when it had arrived like a friend to carry off Nathaniel. She herself had summoned it, and handed him over without regret. She never talked about this with Seth, because he accused her of being morbid, but with Lenny it was a favorite topic: they spent long hours speculating on the possibilities of the other side, the eternity of the spirit and the harmless specters that accompany the dead. She could talk to Irina about everything, because she was a good listener, but at her age she still had the illusion of immortality and could not fully identify with the feelings of those whose race was almost run. Irina could not imagine the courage it took to grow old without becoming too frightened; her knowledge of age was theoretical.

Everything published about the third age was theoretical as well, those know-it-all tomes and self-help manuals in the library, written by people who were not themselves old. Even the two women psychologists at Lark House were young. What did they know, however many diplomas they had, of all that is lost? Faculties, energy, independence, places, people. Although if truth be told, Alma did not miss anyone except Nathaniel. She saw enough of her family and was glad they did not often come to visit her. Her daughter-in-law thought Lark House was a depository for decrepit communists and potheads. Alma preferred to speak to her family on the phone, to see them on the easier ground of Sea Cliff or on the outings they planned for her. She couldn't complain, since her small family, consisting only of Larry, Doris, Pauline, and Seth, had never failed her. Unlike many of those around her at Lark House, she could not consider herself abandoned in her old age.

She could not postpone any longer her decision to close the painting studio, which she had only kept going for Kirsten's sake. She explained to Seth that her assistant had some learning difficulties but had worked with her for many years—this was the only job that Kirsten had ever known, and she had always carried out her tasks scrupulously.

"I have to protect her, Seth, that's the least I can do, but I haven't the strength to deal with all the details. You're a lawyer, you can sort that out," she told him.

Kirsten had her legal allowances, a pension, and her savings; Alma had opened an account for her into which she had deposited funds every year in case of an emergency, but none had arisen, and the money had been invested well. Seth came to an agreement with Kirsten's brother to secure her economic future, and with Hans Voigt to take her on as Catherine Hope's assistant at the pain clinic. The director's doubts about employing someone with Down syndrome evaporated as soon as he was told he wouldn't have to pay her a cent; Kirsten would be supported at Lark House by the Belasco family.

GARDENIAS

On the second Monday without gardenias, Seth turned up with three of them in a box. They were in memory of Neko, he said. The cat's recent death added to the weary ache of Alma's bones, and the overpowering scent of the flowers did little to relieve her. Seth put them in water, made some tea for them both, and then settled down on the sofa with his grandmother.

"What happened to Ichimei Fukuda's flowers, Grandma?" he asked casually.

"What do you know about Ichimei, Seth?" Alma replied in alarm.

"Quite a lot. I suppose that friend of yours is behind the letters and gardenias you receive, as well as your little adventures. You can do as you wish, of course, but I don't think that at your age you should be going around alone or in bad company."

"You've been spying on me! How dare you poke your nose into my life!"

"I'm worried about you, Grandma. I must have grown to like you, however grouchy you are. You've got nothing to hide, you can trust me and Irina. We're your accomplices in whatever crazy things you may get up to."

"It's not crazy!"

"Of course not. I'm sorry. I know he's the love of your life. Irina happened to overhear a conversation between you and Lenny Beal."

By this time Alma and the rest of the Belasco clan knew Irina was living in Seth's apartment, if not permanently, then at least several days a week. Doris and Larry made no comment, in the hope that this pathetic immigrant from Moldova was nothing more than a passing fancy on their son's behalf. They received Irina with icy courtesy, and as a result she stopped going to the Sunday lunches at Sea Cliff that Alma and Seth had insisted on dragging her to. Pauline on the other hand, who had been against every single one of Seth's athletic girlfriends, told her brother, "Congratulations, she's refreshing, and she's got more backbone than you. She'll straighten you out."

She had welcomed Irina with open arms.

Seth continued pressing Alma.

"Why don't you tell me the whole story, Grandma? I'm not cut out to be a detective or a spy."

Alma's trembling hands risked spilling the tea, so her grandson took the cup from her and put it on the table. Her initial anger had subsided and given way to an immense weariness, a deep-seated desire to make a clean breast of everything, to confess all her mistakes to her grandson, to tell him she felt she was growing moldy inside, dying bit by bit, which was fine because she was so tired and would die happy and in love—what more could she wish for now that she was in her eighties and had lived a full life, had loved, and had always choked back her tears?

"Call Irina. I don't want to have to repeat myself," she told Seth.

Irina received the text message on her cell phone while she was in Hans Voigt's office with Catherine Hope, Lupita Farias, and the heads of health aides and nursing. They were discussing the right to elective death, a euphemism that had replaced the term suicide, which the director had prohibited. A fateful package from Thailand had been intercepted at reception, and it now lay on Voigt's desk as evidence. It was addressed to Helen Dempsey, a third-level resident without family, aged eighty-nine, who had cancer that had spread and could not bring herself to undergo another bout of chemotherapy. According to the instructions, the contents were to be taken with alcohol, and the end would arrive peacefully in the person's sleep.

"They must be barbiturates," said Cathy.

"Or rat poison," added Lupita.

The director wanted to know how on earth Helen Dempsey had ordered this without anybody's finding out. The staff were supposed to be on the lookout, since it wouldn't do for word to get around that people committed suicide at Lark House; it would be disastrous for its reputation. In the case of suspicious deaths such as Jacques Devine's they were careful not to carry out too thorough an investigation; it was better not to know the details. The staff blamed the ghosts of Emily and her son: they took the most desperate clients away with them, because whenever someone died, from natural or illegal causes, the Haitian aide Jean Daniel swore he saw the young woman in her pink veils and her unfortunate son. The sight made his hair stand on end. He had asked them to hire a compatriot of his, a woman who was a hairdresser out of necessity but by vocation a voodoo priestess, so that she could dispatch them to the kingdom of the other world, but Hans Voigt's budget did not stretch to that kind of thing; he had to juggle enough as it was to keep the community afloat.

The topic was particularly difficult for Irina, who was still upset because a few days earlier she had held Neko in her arms while he was given a merciful injection that put an end to the ailments of old age. Alma and Seth had not been with the cat for the event, the former because she was too sad, the latter out of cowardice. They left Irina on her own in the apartment to receive the vet. This was not Dr. Kallet, who at the last moment had a family problem, but a nearsighted and nervous young woman with the air of a recent graduate. However, she turned out to be competent and sympathetic; the cat passed away purring, unaware of what was happening. Seth was meant to take the body to the animal crematorium, but for the moment Neko was in a plastic bag in Alma's freezer. Lupita knew a Mexican taxidermist who could leave him looking alive, stuffed with burlap and adorned with glass eyes, or who could clean and polish his skull and mount it on a small pedestal for use as an ornament. She suggested to Irina and Seth that they give Alma this surprise, but they thought the gesture might not be appreciated.

"At Lark House we have to discourage any attempt at elective death, is that clear?" Hans Voigt stressed for the third or fourth time, glaring at Catherine Hope in particular, because it was to her that the most vulnerable patients, the ones in chronic pain, turned. He suspected quite rightly that these women knew more than they were prepared to tell him.

"I'm sorry, Mr. Voigt, it's an emergency," Irina interrupted him when she saw Seth's message on her phone.

That gave all five of them the chance to escape, leaving the director in midsentence.

She found Alma sitting with her shawl across her legs on her bed, where her grandson had installed her after seeing her trembling so badly. Pale and wearing no lipstick, she looked like a shrunken old woman.

"Open the window. This thin Bolivian air is killing me," she pleaded. Irina explained to Seth that his grandmother wasn't delirious, but was referring to the feeling of breathlessness, the buzzing in the ears and weakness in the body that was similar to the altitude sickness she had experienced many years earlier in La Paz at some thirteen thousand feet above sea level. Seth suspected the symptoms were not due to any Bolivian air but to the cat in the freezer.

Alma began by making the two of them promise they would keep her secrets until after her death and repeating what she had already told them, because she decided it was better to weave the tapestry of her life from the very beginning. She recalled saying farewell to her parents on the quayside at Danzig, her arrival at San Francisco and how she had clutched Nathaniel's hand, intuiting perhaps that she would never let it go; she went on to tell them about the precise moment she met Ichimei Fukuda, the most persistent of all the images stored in her memory, and then advanced along the path of her past with such clarity that it was as though she were reading aloud. Seth's worries about his grandmother's mental state evaporated. Over the previous three years when he had wormed material out of her for his novel, Alma had demonstrated her great skill as a narrator, her sense of rhythm and ability to keep up suspense, her way of contrasting luminous events with the most tragic ones, light and shade as in Nathaniel's photographs, but it wasn't until that afternoon that he had the chance to admire her in such a marathon of sustained effort. With a few pauses for tea and to nibble at some cookies, Alma talked for hours. Night fell without any of them realizing, as Seth's grandmother told them all about her life and they listened attentively. She told them about how she met Ichimei again at the age of twenty-two after twelve years without seeing him, and how the dormant love they had felt in childhood now knocked them both out with irresistible force, even though they knew it was doomed and it did in fact last less than a year.

Passion is universal and eternal throughout the centuries, she said, but circumstances and customs are constantly changing; sixty years on, it was hard to understand the insurmountable obstacles they had to face back then. If she could be young again, knowing what she now knew about herself, she would do what she did all over again, because she would never have dared reject convention and commit herself fully to Ichimei; she had never been courageous and had basically abided by the norms. Her only act of rebellion had been when she was seventy-eight and had abandoned the house at Sea Cliff to come and live at Lark House. At the age of twenty-two, suspecting their time was limited, Ichimei and she had gorged on love to enjoy it to the full, but the more they tried to exhaust it, the wilder their desire became, and whoever says that every flame must sooner or later be extinguished is wrong, because there are passions that blaze on until destiny destroys them with a swipe of its paw, and even then hot embers remain that need only a breath of oxygen to be rekindled. She told them about Tijuana and her marriage to Nathaniel, and of how it was to be another seven years before she saw Ichimei once more, at her father-in-law's funeral, years she spent thinking of him tranquilly since she never expected to meet him again, and another seven years before they could finally consummate the love they still felt for one another.

"So, Grandma, my father isn't Nathaniel's son? In that case I'm Ichimei's grandson! Tell me whether I'm a Fukuda or a Belasco!" exclaimed Seth.

"If you were a Fukuda, you'd have Japanese features, wouldn't you? You're a Belasco."

THE CHILD NEVER BORN

*D*uring the first months of married life, Alma was so caught up in her pregnancy that her anger at having renounced her love for Ichimei became a bearable inconvenience, like having a stone in her shoe. She settled into a placid, ruminant existence, secure in Nathaniel's tender care and the shelter the family provided. Although Martha and Sarah had already given them grandchildren, Lillian and Isaac were expecting this baby as if it were royalty, because it would bear the name Belasco. They set aside a sunny room decorated with children's furniture and Walt Disney characters painted on the walls by an artist brought specially from Los Angeles. They devoted themselves to looking after Alma and satisfied her every whim. By the sixth month she had put on too much weight; her blood pressure was high, her face blotchy, her legs swollen, and she lived with a perpetual headache; she could not fit into her shoes and was forced to wear beach slippers, and yet from the very first signs of life in her belly she fell in love with the creature she was bringing into the world. It was not Nathaniel or Ichimei's, but entirely hers. She wanted a boy, to call him Isaac and offer her father-in-law the grandson who would continue the name of Belasco. She had promised Nathaniel that nobody would ever know they did not share the same blood. She remembered, with stabs of guilt, that if Nathaniel had not prevented her, the child would have ended up in some Tijuana sewer.

As she became increasingly besotted with the baby, so she was more and more horrified at the changes to her body, even though Nathaniel assured her that she was radiant, more beautiful than ever, and increased her weight problems by bringing her orange-filled chocolates and other treats. Their happy relationship as brother and sister continued. Elegant and neat, he always used the bathroom near his study at the far end of the house and never undressed in front of her. Alma however lost all sense of shame with him and gave in to her misshapen state, sharing the prosaic details, her ailments, the nervous crises of maternity in a fulsome manner she had never demonstrated before. In these months she broke the fundamental rules her father had instilled in her of never complaining, never asking for favors, and never trusting anyone.

Nathaniel became the center of her existence; beneath his wing she felt happy, safe, and accepted. This created a lopsided intimacy between them that seemed natural as it fitted both their characters. If they ever spoke of this imbalance, it was to agree that once the baby was born and Alma had recovered they would try to live as a normal couple, although neither of them seemed in any great hurry to do so. Alma meanwhile had discovered the perfect place on his shoulder, just below the chin, where she could lay her head and doze.

"You're free to go with other women, Nat. All I ask is that you're discreet, I don't want to be humiliated," Alma often said.

He responded each time with a kiss and a joke. Even though

she found it impossible to free herself from the impression Ichimei had made on her mind and body, she was jealous of Nathaniel; half a dozen women were pursuing him, and she guessed that seeing him married might not be a drawback, but for several of them could even be an incentive.

They were at the family house on Lake Tahoe, where the Belasco family went to ski, drinking hot cider at eleven in the morning while they waited for a snowstorm to subside so that they could go outside, when Alma came stumbling barefoot into the living room in her nightgown. Lillian rushed over to steady her, but Alma pushed her away, trying to focus.

"Tell my brother, Samuel, my head is exploding," she murmured.

Isaac tried to lead her over to a sofa and called out to Nathaniel, but Alma seemed rooted to the spot, as heavy as a piece of furniture, clutching her head in her hands and muttering some nonsense about Samuel, Poland, and diamonds in the lining of a coat. Nathaniel arrived in time to see his wife collapse with convulsions.

This attack of eclampsia occurred in the twenty-second week of her pregnancy and lasted one minute fifteen seconds. None of the three other people in the room understood what it was: they all thought it was epilepsy. Nathaniel only managed to lay her on her side, hold her to stop her harming herself, and keep her mouth open with a spoon. The terrible shuddering soon calmed, leaving Alma exhausted and disoriented. She had no idea where she was or who was with her; she was groaning from her headache and the stomach spasms. They put her in the car wrapped in blankets and skidded along the icy track down to the local clinic, where the duty doctor, a specialist in skiers' broken bones and bruises, could do little more than bring her blood pressure down. The ambulance took seven hours to get from Tahoe to San Francisco, battling the storm and obstacles along the highway. When at last an obstetrician examined Alma, he warned the family of the imminent risk of fresh convulsions or a brain seizure. At five and a half months, the child had no hope of surviving; they would have to wait six weeks before inducing the birth, but during that period both mother and child ran the risk of dying. As if hearing this, a few minutes later the baby's heartbeat ceased in the womb, thus saving Nathaniel from a tragic decision. Alma was quickly wheeled to the surgical ward.

Nathaniel was the only one who saw the child. Shaking with exhaustion and sadness, he took him in his hands, pushed apart the folds of the toweling, and saw a tiny being, all shriveled and blue, the skin as fine and translucent as an onion, completely formed and with half-open eyes. He bent down and gave his head a long kiss. The cold shocked his lips, and he could feel the deep rumble of silent sobs rising from the soles of his feet, shaking his whole body and emerging as tears. He wept, thinking he was doing so for the dead child and for Alma, but in fact he was doing so for himself, for his constrained, conventional life, the weight of the responsibilities he could never free himself from, the loneliness that had oppressed him since birth, the love he longed for but would never know, the marked cards he had been dealt, all the underhanded tricks destiny had played on him.

Seven months after the miscarriage, Nathaniel took Alma on a trip to Europe to help her forget the overwhelming melancholy that was paralyzing her. She had started talking about her brother, Samuel, at the time they lived together in Poland; a governess who haunted her nightmares; a blue velvet coat; Vera Neumann and her owl spectacles; a pair of horrible classmates from school; books she had read whose titles she couldn't remember but whose characters she felt sorry for; and other nonsensical memories. Nathaniel thought that a cultural tour might reawaken Alma's inspiration and her enthusiasm for her silk screens, and if that happened, he intended to suggest she study for a while at the Royal Academy of Arts, the United Kingdom's oldest art school. He considered the best therapy for Alma would be to get away from San Francisco, from the Belascos in general and from him in particular. They had not mentioned Ichimei again, and Nathaniel assumed she had kept her word and was not in contact with him. He intended to spend more time with his wife, cut down on the hours he worked, and whenever possible took cases and studied his pleas at home. They continued to sleep in separate rooms but gave up the pretense that they spent the night together. Nathaniel's bed was installed once and for all in his former bedroom, surrounded by walls covered in hunting scenes, with horses, dogs, and foxes. Neither of them could sleep, but any sensual temptation had dried up between them. They stayed up reading until past midnight in one of the living rooms, both on the same sofa and covered in the same blanket. On those Sundays when the weather was too poor to go sailing, Nathaniel persuaded Alma to accompany him to the movies, or they took a nap side by side on their insomnia sofa, which took the place of the marriage bed they did not have.

The journey was to range from Denmark to Greece, including a cruise on the Danube and another in Turkey. It was to last two months and end in London, where they would separate. In the second week, strolling hand in hand through the narrow back streets of Rome after a memorable meal and two bottles of the best Chianti, Alma came to a halt beneath a streetlamp, grabbed Nathaniel by the shirt, pulled him toward her, and kissed him full on the lips. "I want you to sleep with me," she ordered. That night, in the decadent palace-cum-hotel where they were staying, they made love intoxicated by the wine and the Roman summer, discovering what they already knew of each other, feeling as though they were committing a forbidden act. All Alma's knowledge of carnal love and her own body was thanks to Ichimei, who compensated for his lack of experience with unfailing intuition, the same he used to revive any drooping plant. In the cockroach motel, Alma had been a musical instrument in Ichimei's loving hands. She experienced nothing of this with Nathaniel. They made love hastily, as awkward and anxious as two schoolkids playing hooky, not giving themselves time to explore each other or smell each other's skin, let alone to laugh or sigh together. Afterward they were overcome by an inexplicable unease that they tried to disguise by smoking in silence covered by the sheet, with the moon's yellow light spying on them from the window.

The next day they exhausted themselves visiting ruins, climbing ancient stone steps, peering inside cathedrals, losing themselves among marble statues and extravagant fountains. After nightfall they again drank too much, staggered back to the decadent hotel, and for a second time made love without any great desire but with the best will in the world. And so, day by day and night after night, they toured the cities and cruised the waters of the trip as planned, gradually establishing the married couple's routine they had so carefully avoided so far, until it became natural to share the bathroom and wake up on the same pillow.

Alma did not stay on in London. She returned to San Francisco with piles of museum leaflets and postcards, art books, and photos of picturesque corners taken by Nathaniel. She was keen to take up her painting again; her head was filled with colors and images from all she had seen: Turkish rugs, Greek urns, Flemish tapestries, paintings from every age, icons overlaid with precious stones, languid Madonnas and starving saints, but also fruit and vegetable markets, fishing boats, laundry hanging from balconies in narrow streets, men playing dominoes in taverns, children on beaches, packs of stray dogs, sad donkeys, and ancient roofs in villages dozing under the weight of centuries of routine and tradition. Everything came alive in broad brushstrokes of vibrant color on her silk screens. By then she occupied a workshop of eight thousand square feet in San Francisco's industrial district, a place that had remained unused for many months and that she aimed to bring back to life. As she submerged herself in work, weeks went by without her thinking of either Ichimei or the child she had lost. On their return from Europe, the intimacy with Nathaniel dwindled away to almost nothing; each of them was very busy, and so the sleepless nights reading together on the sofa came to an end, although they were still united by the tender friendship they had always enjoyed. Alma seldom dozed off with her head in the exact spot between her husband's shoulder and chin where she had once felt so secure. They no longer slept between the same sheets or shared the same bathroom. Nathaniel used the bed in his study, leaving Alma on her own in the blue room. If they occasionally made love it was by coincidence, and always with too much alcohol in their veins.

"I want to free you from your promise to be faithful to me, Alma. It's not fair to you," Nathaniel said to her one night when they were admiring a shower of shooting stars from the garden pergola, smoking marijuana. "You are young and full of life, you deserve more romance than I can give you."

"What about you? Is there someone out there who is offering you romance that you want to be free for? I've never stood in your way, Nat."

"It's not about me, Alma."

"You're freeing me from my promise at a bad moment, Nat. I'm pregnant, and this time you are the only possible father. I was going to tell you once I was sure."

Isaac and Lillian Belasco greeted the news of the pregnancy with the same enthusiasm as the first time. They refurbished the room they had ready for the other baby and prepared to pamper it. "If it's a boy and I'm dead by the time he is born, I suppose you'll give him my name; but if I'm still alive you can't do that, because it would bring bad luck. In that case I want him to be called Lawrence Franklin Belasco, after my father and the great president Roosevelt, may they rest in peace," the patriarch declared. He was fading steadily and was hanging on only because he couldn't leave Lillian; his wife had become his shadow. She was almost deaf, but she didn't need to hear. She had learned to decipher other people's silences with great accuracy: it was impossible to hide anything from her or fool her, and she had developed an incredible ability to guess what people were about to say, and to reply even before they spoke. She had two obsessions: improving her husband's health, and seeing that Nathaniel and Alma loved each other as they should. For both of these she turned to alternative therapies, which went from magnetized mattresses to healing elixirs and aphrodisiacs. At the forefront of naturalist witchcraft, California offered a wide variety of people selling hope and consolation. Isaac resigned himself to hanging crystals around his neck and drinking alfalfa juice and scorpion syrup, while Alma and Nathaniel put up with massages of ylang-ylang essential oil, Chinese shark-fin soups, and other alchemical remedies Lillian turned to in order to boost their lukewarm love.

Lawrence Franklin Belasco was born in the spring with none of the problems the doctors had been anticipating as a result of the eclampsia his mother had previously suffered. From his first day in this world his name seemed too big for him, and everyone called him Larry. He grew healthy, fat, and self-reliant, without any need for special attention. He was so placid and quiet that sometimes he would fall asleep under the furniture and no one would notice for hours. His parents handed him over to the grandparents and a succession of nannies, without worrying too much about him, because at Sea Cliff there were several adults who doted on him. He didn't sleep with his parents, but with Isaac and Lillian, whom he called Papa and Mama; he called his own parents by the more formal Mother and Father.

Nathaniel spent little time in the house; he had become the city's most prominent lawyer, earning a vast amount of money, and in his free time played sports or explored the art of photography. He was waiting for his son to grow a little before initiating him into the pleasures of sailing, without ever dreaming that day would never come. Since her in-laws had taken charge of their grandson, Alma began to travel in search of ideas for her work without feeling guilty about leaving him behind. In Larry's early years she planned more or less short trips in order not to be apart from him for any great length of time, but she soon learned that this didn't matter, as whenever she returned from either a prolonged or shorter absence, her son greeted her with the same polite handshake rather than the passionate embrace she had been longing for. She concluded with regret that Larry loved his cat more than her, and this gave her the freedom to travel to the Far East, South America, and other remote spots.

THE PATRIARCH

*L*arry Belasco spent the first four years of his life spoiled by his grandparents and the employees at Sea Cliff, cosseted like an orchid, his every whim satisfied. This system, which would have forever ruined the character of a less balanced child, instead made him friendly, helpful, and even-tempered. This did not change with the death in 1962 of his grandfather Isaac, one of the two pillars holding up the fantasy universe he had lived in until then.

Isaac's health had recovered when his favorite grandson was born.

"Inside I feel like a twenty-year-old, Lillian. What on earth happened to my body?"

He had enough energy to take Larry for a walk every day, showing him the garden's botanical secrets, and even crawled around the floor with him. Isaac bought him the pets he himself had wanted as a boy: a boisterous parrot, fish in an aquarium, a rabbit that disappeared forever under the furniture as soon as Larry opened its cage, and a long-eared dog, the first of several generations of cocker spaniels that the family had from then on. While the doctors were at a loss to explain the marked improvement in Isaac's health, Lillian put it down to the healing arts and esoteric sciences in which she had become an expert.

One day Isaac took little Larry to Golden Gate Park, where they spent the afternoon on a rented horse, with the grandfather in the saddle and Larry sitting in front of him, enfolded in his arms. They returned home sunburned, smelling of sweat, and enthused with the idea of buying a horse and a pony so that they could ride together. Lillian was waiting for them at the garden barbecue to cook sausages and marshmallows, the favorite dinner of both grandfather and grandson. Afterward she bathed Larry, put him to bed in her husband's room, and read him a story until he fell asleep. She drank her small glass of sherry with a tincture of opium and went to bed herself.

At seven o'clock the next morning she was awakened by Larry's little hand shaking her shoulder. "Mama, Mama, Papa's had a fall."

They found Isaac sprawled on the bathroom floor. It took the combined effort of Nathaniel and the chauffeur to move the freezing, stiff body, which had become as heavy as lead, and lay him out on his bed. They tried to keep Lillian from seeing him, but she pushed everyone out of the room, shut the door, and did not open it again until she had finished washing her husband's corpse slowly, rubbing it with lotion and cologne, closely examining every detail of this body that she knew better than her own and loved so much, surprised to see it had not grown old in any way but was exactly as she had always seen it, the same tall, strong young man who could lift her in his arms with a laugh, tanned from his work in the garden, the same shock of black hair as when he was twenty-five, and the fine hands of a good man. When she reopened the door she was serene. Although the family was afraid that without him Lillian would soon shrivel up with grief, she showed them that death is not an insurmountable obstacle to communication between those who truly love each other.

Years later, during his second therapy session after his wife had threatened to leave him, Larry evoked that image of his grandfather in a heap on the bathroom floor as the most significant moment in his childhood, and the image of his father in his funeral shroud as the end of his youth and his forced landing in adulthood. He was four years old on the first occasion, and twenty-six when the second occurred. The psychologist asked, with a hint of doubt in his voice, whether he had any other memories from when he was four, at which Larry proceeded to reel off the names of all the staff in the house and of his pets, the titles of the books his grandmother used to read to him, and even the color of the dressing gown she was wearing when she suddenly went blind only hours after her husband's death. Those first years protected by his grandparents were the happiest time of his life, and he had stored up all his memories of them.

Lillian was diagnosed as having a temporary hysterical blindness, but neither of these adjectives proved to be true. Larry acted as her guide until he entered kindergarten, and after that she managed on her own, because she didn't want to depend on anyone. She knew Sea Cliff and everything in it by heart; she got around without hesitation and even ventured into the kitchen to bake cookies for her grandson. Besides, Isaac was leading her by the hand, as she said half jokingly and half seriously. To please her invisible husband she began to dress all in lilac, because that was the color she was wearing when she met him in 1914, and because it solved the problem of being blind and having to choose what to wear every day. She did not allow them to treat her as an invalid or give any indication that she felt isolated due to her lack of hearing and sight. Nathaniel reckoned that his mother had a gun dog's sense of smell and a bat's radar to help her find her way and to recognize people. Until Lillian's death in 1973, Larry received her unconditional love, and according to the psychologist who saved his marriage, he could not expect the same from his wife; in marriage nothing is unconditional.

The Fukudas' flower and houseplant nursery was in the phone book, and every so often Alma would check that the address remained the same, but she never gave in to the temptation to call Ichimei. It had cost her a lot to recover from her frustrated love, and she was afraid that if she heard his voice even for an instant she would drown in the same blind passion as before. In the years since then, her senses had gone to sleep; together with overcoming her obsession with Ichimei, she had transferred to her paintbrushes the sensuality she had experienced with him and never had with Nathaniel. This changed at her father-in-law's second funeral, when among the huge crowd she made out Ichimei's unmistakable face. He looked just the same as the young man she remembered. Ichimei followed the cortege accompanied by three women, two of whom Alma vaguely recognized even though she had not seen them in many years, and a young woman who stood out because she was not dressed in strict mourning like everyone else. Their small group stayed apart from the others, but once the ceremony was over and people began to disperse, Alma slipped out of Nathaniel's arm and followed them to the avenue, where the cars were lined up. When she called out to Ichimei, all four of them came back toward her.

"Mrs. Belasco," Ichimei greeted her, bowing formally.

"Ichimei," she answered, paralyzed.

"This is my mother, Heideko Fukuda; my sister, Megumi Anderson; and my wife, Delphine," he said.

The three women bowed. Alma could feel her stomach churn and a choking sensation in her chest as she openly examined Delphine. Fortunately the other woman did not notice, as she kept her eyes fixed on the ground as a sign of respect. She was young, pretty, and fresh looking, not wearing fashionable heavy makeup, and dressed in a pearl-gray suit with a short skirt and round pill-box hat in Jackie Kennedy's style, and with the same hairstyle as the First Lady. Her outfit was so American that her Asian face seemed incongruous.

"Thank you for coming," Alma managed to blurt out when she was able to breathe once more.

"Isaac Belasco was our benefactor; we shall always be grateful to him. It was thanks to him we could return to California. He financed our nursery and helped us succeed," said Megumi sadly.

Alma had already been told as much by Nathaniel and Ichimei, but the Fukuda family's solemn gratitude reinforced her certainty that her father-in-law must have been an exceptional man. She loved him more than she would have loved her own father if the war had not robbed her of him. Isaac Belasco was the opposite of Baruj Mendel—he was kind, tolerant, and always ready to give. She was suddenly struck by the pain of losing him, something she had not truly felt until that moment as she had been going around stunned like the entire Belasco family. Tears welled in her eyes, but she choked them back as well as the sobs that had been fighting to find a way out for days now. She realized Delphine was now examining her as closely as she had done in reverse a few minutes earlier. Alma thought she saw in her clear eyes an expression of knowing curiosity, as if she knew exactly what role she had played in Ichimei's past. She felt exposed and slightly ridiculous.

"Our sincere condolences, Mrs. Belasco," said Ichimei as he took his mother's arm to move away.

"Alma. I'm still Alma," she murmured.

"Good-bye, Alma," he said.

She waited two weeks for Ichimei to get in touch with her. She scrutinized the mail carefully and jumped every time the telephone rang, imagining a thousand reasons for his silence apart from the obvious one: he was married. She refused to think about small, slender Delphine, who was younger and prettier than she was, with her inquisitive look and her gloved hand on Ichimei's arm. One Saturday she drove to Martinez, wearing a pair of big sunglasses and a head scarf, but although she passed by the Fukuda nursery three times, she did not have the courage to get out. On the second Monday she could not bear the torment of desire any longer, and so called the number that, from seeing it so often in the phone book, she had learned by heart.

"Fukuda Flowers and Houseplants, how may we help you?"

It was a woman's voice, and Alma had no doubt it belonged to Delphine, even though she had not said a word on the only occasion they had met. Alma hung up. She called again several times, praying that Ichimei would answer, but it was always Delphine's friendly voice that came on the line, and she hung up each time.

On one of these calls the two women remained silent on the line for almost a minute, until Delphine inquired gently: "How may I help you, Mrs. Belasco?" Horrified, Alma slammed down the telephone and swore she would never again try to get in touch with Ichimei. Three days later a letter arrived bearing Ichimei's handwriting in black ink. She shut herself in her room, clutching the envelope to her breast and trembling with anguish and hope.

In his letter, Ichimei once more expressed his condolences for Isaac Belasco, and spoke of his emotion at seeing her again after so many years, even though he was aware of her success in her work and her philanthropy and had often seen her photograph in the papers. He told her that Megumi was a wife and mother, married to Boyd Anderson with one son, Charles, and that Heideko had visited Japan a couple of times, where she had learned the art of *ikebana*. In the final paragraph he wrote that he had married Delphine Akimura, a second-generation Japanese-American like him. Delphine was a year old when her family was interned at Topaz, but he did not remember seeing her there, and they only got to know each other much later on. She was a primary school teacher, but had left her job to manage the nursery, which had prospered as a result; they were soon going to open a branch in San Francisco. He said farewell without raising the possibility that they might meet or that he was expecting her to reply. He made no reference to the past they had shared. It was a formal, informative letter, with none of the poetic turns of phrase or philosophical speculation of others she had received during the brief period of their love. It didn't even include one of the drawings he often used to send with his missives. The only relief Alma felt on reading it was that there was no mention of her phone calls, which Delphine must have told him about. She took the letter for what it was: a farewell and a tacit warning that Ichimei wanted no further contact.

The next seven years went by in a life of routine that contained no great highlights for Alma. Her interesting and frequent trips became fused in her memory as one single Marco Polo adventure, as Nathaniel called them without the slightest hint of resentment at his wife's absences. They felt as viscerally comfortable with one another as Siamese twins who have never been separated. They could intuit each other's thoughts, states of mind, and wishes, could each finish the sentence the other had begun. Their affection was beyond question; it was so much taken for granted that it did not even bear talking about, as was their extraordinary friendship. They shared the family's social commitments; a taste for art and music, the refinement of good restaurants, and the wine cellar they gradually built up; as well as the pleasure of family vacations with Larry.

The little boy had turned out so docile and affectionate that his parents sometimes wondered whether he was completely normal. When they were not in the presence of Lillian, who would not tolerate the slightest criticism of her grandson, they joked that one day Larry was going to give them a ghastly shock by joining a cult or murdering someone; it was impossible for him to glide through life without any turmoil at all, like a satisfied porpoise. As soon as Larry was old enough to appreciate it, they took him to see the world on unforgettable annual excursions. They went to the Galápagos Islands, the Amazon, on various African safaris; Larry was later to do the same with his own children. Among the most magical moments of his childhood was giving a giraffe something to eat from his hand in a Kenyan game reserve: its long, blue, rough tongue, its gentle eyes with their operatic eyelashes, its intense smell of newly mown grass.

Nathaniel and Alma had their own space in the Sea Cliff mansion, and lived there carefree as though in a luxury hotel, because Lillian took care to keep the domestic machinery well oiled. She continued to pry into their private lives, regularly asking them if they were in love by any chance, but they regarded this odd insistence as charming rather than annoying. If Alma was in San Francisco, they saw to it that they spent some of the evening together for drinks and to recount the day's events to one another. They celebrated their mutual successes, and neither of them asked any more questions than the strictly necessary, as if they sensed that an inappropriate comment could bring the delicate balance of their relationship crashing down in an instant. They willingly accepted that each of them had their own secret world and private times, which they were under no obligation to account for. Omissions were not lies.

Since lovemaking between them was so infrequent as to be almost nonexistent, Alma imagined her husband must have had other women, because the idea that he lived a life of chastity was absurd; Nathaniel however had respected the agreement to be discreet and avoid humiliating her. For her part, Alma had allowed herself a few flings on her travels, where opportunities always arose. It was a matter of giving a signal, and generally finding it was accepted, and yet these moments of release not only gave her less pleasure than she hoped but left her confused. She was of an age to enjoy an active sex life, she thought, and that was as important for her well-being and health as exercise and a balanced diet: she shouldn't let her body dry up. But considered like that, sexuality became just another chore rather than a gift for the senses. For her, eroticism needed time and trust, which were not easy to come by in a night of fake or stiffly awkward romance with someone she would never see again. In the midst of the sexual revolution, in the time of free love, when in California couples were swapped and half the world slept with the other half, Alma still could not get Ichimei out of her mind. She asked herself more than once if this was not simply an excuse to disguise her frigidity, but when at last she encountered Ichimei once more she no longer posed herself that question, nor sought comfort in the arms of strangers.

September 12, 1978

You explained to me that inspiration is born of stillness, and creativity comes from movement. Painting is movement, Alma: that's why I like your recent designs so much. They seem effortless, although I know how much stillness is needed to control the brush as you do. I especially like your autumn trees, gracefully letting their leaves fall. That is how I would like to shed my own leaves in this autumn of life, easily and elegantly. Why be so attached to what we are bound to lose anyway? I suppose I mean youth, which has been so present in our conversations. On Thursday I prepared a bath for you with the salts and seaweed I was sent from Japan.

Ichi

SAMUEL MENDEL

A lma and Samuel Mendel met up in Paris in spring 1967. For Alma it was the penultimate stage in a two-month journey to Kyoto, where she studied *sumi-e* painting, using obsidian ink on white paper, under the strict supervision of a master calligrapher who made her repeat the same line a thousand times over until she achieved the perfect combination of lightness and strength. Only then could she move on to the next stroke. She had been to Japan a number of times. The country fascinated her, above all Kyoto and some of the local mountain villages, where she found traces of Ichimei everywhere. The free, fluid lines of *sumi-e*, painted with the brush held vertically, allowed her to express herself with great economy and originality, omitting detail, focusing purely on the essential, a style Vera Neumann had already developed into birds, butterflies, flowers, and abstract drawings. By this time Vera had an international business, selling millions and employing hundreds of artists. Art galleries bore her name, and twenty thousand shops all around the world offered her clothing, as well as decorative and domestic objects. Such mass production was not Alma's intention; she remained faithful to her choice of exclusivity. After two months of black brushstrokes, she was preparing to return to San Francisco to experiment in color.

It was the first time her brother, Samuel, had returned to Paris since the war. In her voluminous baggage, Alma carried a trunk containing her scrolled drawings and hundreds of slides of calligraphy and painting to act as inspiration. Samuel's luggage was minimal. He arrived from Israel wearing camouflage pants, a leather jacket, and army boots, together with a small knapsack containing two changes of clothes. Even at the age of forty-five he went on living like a soldier, with his shaven head and a complexion so toughened by the sun it was as hard as leather. For both brother and sister this was an excursion into the past. They had cultivated their friendship over a period of time thanks to the frequent exchange of letters they found themselves inspired to write. Alma had practice from childhood, when she used to completely confide her thoughts to her diary. Samuel, however taciturn and suspicious in person, was often voluble and friendly on the page.

In Paris they rented a car and Samuel drove to the village where he had died for the first time, guided by Alma, who had never forgotten the route she had taken with her aunt and uncle in the 1950s. Since then Europe had risen from the ashes, and it was hard to recognize the place, once a mass of ruins and rubble, now completely rebuilt and surrounded by vineyards and lavender fields, glorious in this most beautifully radiant season of the year. Even the cemetery was enjoying a new prosperity, with marble angels and headstones, wrought-iron crucifixes and railings, shady trees and sparrows, doves, and silence. The caretaker, a friendly young woman, led them along narrow paths between the graves searching for the memorial plaque placed there by the Belascos many years before. It was still intact: *Samuel Mendel, 1922–1944, pilot in the Royal Air Force.* Below it was a smaller plaque, also made of bronze: *Died in combat for France and freedom.* Samuel removed his beret and scratched his head with amusement.

"The metal looks newly polished."

"My grandfather cleans and maintains the soldiers' graves," the caretaker said. "He put the second plaque there. You know, my grandfather was in the Resistance."

"I don't believe it! What's his name?"

"Clotaire Martineaux."

"I'm afraid I didn't know him," Samuel replied.

"Were you in the Resistance too?"

"Yes, for a time."

"Then you should come to our house and have a drink, my grandfather will be pleased to meet you, Mr. . . ."

"Samuel Mendel."

The young woman hesitated a moment before bending over the name on the plaque again and turning around in astonishment.

"Yes, it's me. Not altogether dead, as you can see," said Samuel.

All three of them ended up in the kitchen of a nearby house, drinking Pernod and eating baguettes and sausages. Clotaire Martineaux was short and stocky, with a resounding laugh and the smell of garlic. He embraced them both and was happy to answer Samuel's questions, calling him *mon frère* and refilling his glass time and again. As Samuel could confirm, he was not one of those heroes who appeared as if by magic after the end of the war, as he knew all about the plane brought down near the village, the rescue of a crew member, and knew two of the men who had hidden him, as well as the names of the rest. He listened to Samuel's story, drying his eyes and blowing his nose on the same kerchief he wore around his neck, also employed to wipe sweat from his brow and grease from his hands. "My grandfather has always been a cry-baby," his granddaughter said by way of explanation.

Samuel told his host that his nom de guerre in the Jewish Re-sistance was Jean Valjean, and that he'd spent months in a state of confusion from the brain trauma he suffered when the plane came down, but that little by little he had begun to recover at least part of his memory. He had sketchy recollections of a great house with maidservants in black aprons and white caps, but none of his family. He thought that if there was anything still standing at the war's end, he would seek out his Polish roots, because that was where the language in which he did sums, swore, and dreamed came from; somewhere in that country the house etched in his memory must exist.

"I had to wait until the war was over to discover my own name and my family's fate. By 1944 it was already possible to foresee the defeat of the Nazis, do you remember, Monsieur Martineaux? The situation started to turn around on the eastern front, where the British and the Americans least expected it. They thought the Red Army was made up of ill-disciplined peasant bands, poorly nour-ished and worse armed, incapable of confronting Hitler."

"I remember it all perfectly, *mon frère*," said Martineaux. "After the Battle of Stalingrad, the myth of Hitler's invincibility began to crumble, and we could start to have hope. It has to be said that the Russians broke the morale and the backbone of the Germans in 1943."

"The defeat at Stalingrad forced them to withdraw to Berlin," added Samuel.

"Then came the Allies' Normandy landings in June 1944, and the liberation of Paris only two months later. Ah, what an unforgettable day that was!"

"I was taken prisoner. My group was decimated by the SS, and my surviving comrades were executed with a shot to the back of the neck as soon as they surrendered. I escaped by chance, because I was away searching for food. To be more exact, I was scouring the nearby farms to see what I could lay my hands on. We even ate cats and dogs, whatever we could find."

Samuel told him what those months were like, the worst of the war for him. Alone, lost, and starving, lacking all contact with the Resistance, he lived by night, eating worm-ridden earth and stolen food, until he was captured at the end of September. He spent the next four months in forced labor, first at Monowitz and then at Auschwitz-Birkenau, where one million two hundred thousand men, women, and children had already perished. In January 1945, faced with the Russians' imminent advance, the Nazis received orders to destroy all evidence of what they had done in the camps. They evacuated their prisoners on a forced march through the snow, providing neither food nor shelter, back toward Germany. Those too weak to leave were left behind to be executed, but in the rush to flee the Russians, the SS did not manage to obliterate everything and left seven thousand prisoners still alive. Samuel was one of them.

"I don't think the Russians came with the intention of liberating us," Samuel explained. "The Ukrainian front was passing close by and opened the camp gates. Those of us still able to move dragged ourselves outside. Nobody stopped us. Nobody helped us. Nobody offered us even a crust of bread. We were turned away by everyone."

"I know, *mon frère*. Here in France no one came to the aid of the Jews, and I say that with a great sense of shame. But remember those were terrible times, we were all hungry, and in those circumstances all sense of humanity gets lost."

"Not even the Zionists in Palestine wanted to take in concentration camp survivors; we were the useless detritus of the war," said Samuel.

He explained how the Zionists only wanted young, strong, healthy people—brave warriors to confront the Arabs, and stubborn laborers to work the arid land. But one of the few things he recalled from his earlier life was how to fly a plane, and this helped facilitate the immigration process. He became a soldier, pilot, and spy. He was David Ben-Gurion's bodyguard during the creation of the State of Israel in 1948, and a year later he became one of the first Mossad agents, working for Israel's new intelligence agency.

Brother and sister spent the night in a village inn and the next day returned to Paris to fly to Warsaw. In Poland, they searched in vain for traces of their parents, but only found their names on a list of the victims of Treblinka they obtained from the Jewish Agency. Together they visited the remains of Auschwitz, where Samuel attempted to reconcile himself to the past, but it was a journey straight out of his worst nightmares that only served to confirm his certainty that human beings are the cruelest beasts on the planet.

"The Germans are not a race of psychopaths, Alma. They're normal people like you and me, but with fanaticism, power, and impunity, anyone can turn into a monster, like the SS at Auschwitz," he told his sister.

"Do you think that, given the opportunity, you'd also behave like a monster, Samuel?"

"I don't think it, Alma, I know it. I've been a soldier all my life. I've been to war. I've interrogated prisoners, a large number of them. But I assume you don't want details."

NATHANIEL

*T*he sly illness that was to end Nathaniel Belasco's life was prowling around him for years without anybody, himself included, realizing it. The first symptoms were easily confused with flu, which that winter was affecting nearly half the population of San Francisco, and disappeared again within a fortnight. They did not return for some years, this time leaving him with a sensation of enormous fatigue; some days he would walk about dragging his feet, his shoulders hunched as if he were lugging a sack of sand on his back. He went on working the same number of hours every day, but the time spent in his office brought little reward; documents piled up on his desk, seeming only to expand and multiply overnight. He became confused, lost the thread of the cases he was pursuing conscientiously, ones he could once have resolved with his eyes shut, and all of a sudden couldn't remember what he had just read. He had suffered from insomnia all his life, and this now grew worse, with bouts of fever and sweating.

"We're both suffering from menopausal hot flashes," he told Alma, laughing aloud, but she didn't find it so amusing.

He gave up sports, and the sailboat remained moored in the marina for gulls to nest in. He found it hard to swallow, began to lose weight, had no appetite. Alma prepared high-protein smoothies for him, which he drank with great difficulty, then took himself off to throw up as quietly as possible so as not to alarm her. When ulcers began to appear on his skin, the family doctor—a relic as ancient as some of the furniture bought by Isaac Belasco in 1914—successively treated his symptoms as those of anemia, intestinal infection, migraine, and depression, and finally referred him to an oncologist.

Terror-stricken, Alma realized how much she loved and needed Nathaniel, and threw herself into fighting the illness, destiny, the gods and the demons. She gave up everything else to focus on his care. She stopped painting, laid off the staff at the workshop, and only went there once a month to supervise the cleaning. Her vast studio, lit by the diffused light from the opaque windows, took on a cathedral calm. Work ceased from one day to the next, and the studio was left paused in time like a cinematographic trick, ready to resume a moment later, its long tables under wraps; rolled canvases standing upright like slender sentries, and others already painted hanging on their stretchers; sketches and color samples on the walls; pots and jars; paint rollers and brushes; and the faint whirr of the air conditioner endlessly spreading the acrid smell of paint and solvent. She stopped traveling, something that for years had brought her inspiration and freedom. Away from home, Alma shed her skin and was born anew, curious and ready for adventure, open to whatever the day might bring, without either plans or fears. This migratory new Alma was so real she was sometimes taken by surprise by her own reflection in hotel mirrors, as she somehow did not expect to find the same face she had in San Francisco. She also stopped seeing Ichimei.

They had met up by chance seven years after Isaac's funeral, and fourteen before Nathaniel's illness became fully apparent, at the annual show held by the Society of Orchid Growers, among thousands of other visitors. Ichimei saw her first and came over to greet her. He was on his own. They commented on the orchids— two specimens from his nursery were included in the show—and they went to eat at a nearby restaurant. They began talking of this and that, Alma of her recent travels, her new designs, and her son, Larry; Ichimei of his plants and his children, Mike, aged two, and Peter, an eight-month-old baby. No mention was made of either Nathaniel or Delphine.

The meal lasted over three hours without a pause. They had everything to tell each other, and they did so cautiously and un- certainly, without falling back into the past, as if skating on thin ice, constantly studying, noting the changes and trying to decipher each other's intentions, aware of the mutual attraction that was still burning. They were both now thirty-seven; she looked older, as her features had become more accentuated, and she had grown thinner, more angular and sure of herself, but Ichimei had not changed: he had the same serene adolescent appearance as before, the same quiet voice and considerate manners, the same capacity to penetrate her every last cell with the intensity of his presence. In him, Alma could see the eight-year-old child in the Sea Cliff greenhouse, the ten-year-old who handed her a cat before van- ishing, the tireless lover in the motel full of cockroaches, the man in mourning at her father-in-law's funeral. All these images were intact, like lines superimposed on sheets of tracing paper. Ichi- mei was unchanging, eternal. Love and desire for him scorched her skin; she wanted to stretch her hands out across the table and touch him, draw closer, bury her nose in his neck and confirm it still smelled of earth and herbs, tell him that without him she lived like a sleepwalker, that nothing and nobody could fill the terrible gap of his absence, that she would give anything to be naked in his arms once more, that nothing mattered apart from him. Ichimei accompanied her to her car. They walked slowly, almost in circles, to delay the moment of separation. They took the elevator up to the third floor of the parking garage; she found her key and offered to drive him to his car, less than a block away. He accepted. They kissed in the intimate twilight inside the car, rediscovering one another.

Over the years that followed they were obliged to keep their love in a separate compartment from the rest of their lives, and they lived it to the full without allowing it to affect Nathaniel and Delphine. When they were together, nothing else existed, and when they said good-bye at the hotel where they had just sated their love it was implicit they would not stay in contact until their next assignation, except by letter. Alma treasured those letters, although Ichimei always maintained the reserve typical of his people, in direct contrast to his delicate demonstrations of love and his flights of passion when they were together. He was deeply embarrassed by any kind of sentimentality; his way of showing his feelings was to prepare a picnic for her in beautiful lacquer boxes, to send her the gardenias whose fragrance she so loved (although she would never use it as a perfume), to perform a tea ceremony, or to dedicate poems and drawings to her. In private he sometimes called her "my little one," an expression he never put in writing. Alma had no need to explain anything to her husband, as they led independent lives, and she never asked Ichimei how he managed to keep Delphine in the dark when they lived and worked so closely together. She knew he loved his wife, that he was a good father and family man, that he held a special position within the Japanese community, where he was considered a master and was called on to give advice to anyone who went astray, to reconcile enemies and serve as a fair arbitrator in disputes. The man who was capable of burning desire, erotic invention; of laughter, jokes, and games between the sheets; of urgency, appetite, and joy; of whispered confidences in the interludes between embraces; of interminable kisses and delirious intimacies, was someone who existed for her alone.

The letters began after the chance encounter among the orchids, and intensified when Nathaniel fell ill. For a period that to them seemed endless, this correspondence replaced their clandestine meetings. Alma's letters were stark and anguished, those of a woman deeply affected by separation. Ichimei's were like cool, clear water, but their shared passion pulsed between the lines. To Alma, the letters revealed Ichimei's exquisite inner workings, his emotions, dreams, longings, and ideals; she could know and love and desire him even more through his missives than during their amorous skirmishes. They became so vital to her that, when widowhood brought her freedom and they could talk on the telephone, see each other more frequently, and even travel together, they continued to write to each other. Ichimei strictly complied with their agreement to destroy her letters, but Alma kept his to reread as often as possible.

July 18, 1984

I know how much you are suffering and it hurts me not to be able to help. Even as I write I know you are anxious, trying to cope with your husband's illness. You can't control it, Alma, you can only bravely keep him company.

Our separation is so painful. We have grown used to our sacred Thursdays, the private dinners, walks in the park, brief weekend escapes. Why does the world seem so colorless? Sounds reach me muffled as if from afar, food tastes of soap. So many months without seeing each other! I bought your cologne to smell your scent. I console myself by writing poetry, which I'll give you one day, since it is yours.

And you accuse me of not being romantic!

My years of spiritual practice have been of little use if I have been unable to free myself from desire. I wait for your letters and your voice on the telephone, I imagine you running to get here ... Sometimes love hurts.

Ichi

Nathaniel and Alma lived in the two bedrooms that had once belonged to Lillian and Isaac, with the interconnecting door that had been propped open so long it could no longer be closed. They went back to sharing their insomnia, as in the days of being newlyweds, huddled up close together on a sofa or bed, with her reading, the book in one hand and stroking Nathaniel with the other, while he rested, eyes closed, breathing heavily, his chest rattling. On one of those long nights they caught each other crying silently, trying to avoid disturbing one another. First Alma felt her husband's wet cheeks, and he immediately noticed her tears, which were such a rare sight that he sat up to check they were real. He couldn't remember having seen her cry before, even at the bitterest moments.

"You're dying, aren't you?" she murmured.

"Yes, Alma, but don't cry for me."

"I'm not crying for you, but for me. And for us, for everything I've never told you, the omissions and lies, the betrayals and the time I robbed you of."

"For God's sake, what are you talking about? There's no betrayal of me in your love for Ichimei, Alma. There are always some necessary lies and omissions, just as there are truths it's better to keep quiet about."

"You know about Ichimei? Since when?" said a startled Alma.

"I've always known. Hearts are big enough to contain love for more than one person."

"Tell me about you, Nat. I've never pried into your secrets—and I assume there are lots of them—so as not to have to reveal my own to you."

"We've loved each other so much, Alma! One should always marry one's best friend. I know you like no one else. What you haven't told me I can guess; but you don't know me. You have the right to know who I really am."

And then he told her about Lenny Beal. All the rest of that sleepless night they told each other everything with the urgency of knowing how little time together was left for them.

Ever since he could remember, Nathaniel had experienced a mixture of fascination, fear, and desire for those of his own sex, starting with his schoolmates, then for other men, and finally for Lenny, who had been his partner for eight years. He had fought against those feelings, torn between his heart's desires and the implacable voice of reason. At school, when he was as yet unable to identify what it was he felt, the other boys knew instinctively that he was different, and punished him with beatings, jokes, and ostracism. Those years, constantly menaced by thugs, were the worst of his life.

When he left school, torn between his scruples and the uncontrollable passions of youth, he noticed that his predicament was not as unusual as he had assumed; everywhere he went he met men who looked directly into his eyes, offering either an invitation or a plea. He was initiated by a fellow student at Harvard. He discovered that homosexuality was a parallel world that existed alongside accepted reality. He came to know men from many different backgrounds. At the university they were professors, intellectuals, students, a rabbi, and a football player; out on the street they were sailors, workmen, bureaucrats, politicians, businessmen, and criminals. It was an inclusive world, promiscuous yet still hidden as it came up against a categorical rejection by morality and the law. People who were openly gay were not allowed into hotels, clubs, or churches; often, they would not be served alcohol in bars and could be thrown out of public places, accused—rightly or wrongly—of unruly behavior; the gay clubs and bars belonged to the Mafia. Back in San Francisco, with his lawyer's diploma in his hand, Nathaniel encountered the first signs of a nascent gay culture, one that would not come out into the open until several years later. When the 1960s social movements came along, including the one for gay rights, Nathaniel was married to Alma and their son, Larry, was ten years old.

"I didn't marry you to disguise my homosexuality, but out of love and friendship," he told Alma that night.

Those had been schizophrenic years: an irreproachable and successful public life, and another that was hidden and illicit. He met Lenny Beal in 1976 at a men's Turkish bath, the ideal place for casual sex, but completely unsuited to the start of a love like theirs.

Nathaniel was about to celebrate his fiftieth birthday and Lenny was six years his junior, as beautiful as a statue of a Roman god. Irreverent, hotheaded, and promiscuous, he was the complete opposite of Nathaniel. The physical attraction was instantaneous. They locked themselves in a cubicle and spent until dawn immersed in pleasure, going at one another like wrestlers and wallowing in the entwined delirium of their bodies. They arranged to meet the next day at a hotel, each arriving separately. Lenny brought marijuana and cocaine, but Nathaniel begged him not to use them; he wanted to be fully aware of the experience. A week later they already knew that the blinding flash of desire had simply been the beginning of an immense love, and they gave in completely to the imperative of living it to the limit. They rented a studio in the city center, where they installed a minimum of furniture and the best sound system, each promising no one else would set foot there.

Nathaniel ended a search begun thirty-five years before, although outwardly nothing altered in his life: he continued to be the model of bourgeois male respectability, without a soul guessing what had happened, or noticing that his office hours and addiction to sports were drastically reduced. On his side, Lenny was transformed by his lover's influence. For the first time in his turbulent life he paused, and dared substitute the contemplation of his newfound happiness for all the previous noise and insane activity. If he wasn't with Nathaniel, he was thinking about him. He never went back to the gay baths or clubs, and his friends rarely succeeded in tempting him to parties, since he had lost interest in getting to meet new people. Nathaniel was more than enough; he was the sun around which his days revolved. He basked in the calm of this love with a puritan's devotion. He adopted Nathaniel's taste in music, food, and drink, then his cashmere sweaters, camel-hair coat, and aftershave lotion. Nathaniel had a private phone line installed in his office for Lenny's exclusive use, and they were constantly in touch; they went out sailing together, made trips, and met up in distant cities where no one knew them.

At first, Nathaniel's incomprehensible illness did not cloud his relationship with Lenny: the symptoms were so random and sporadic, they came and went apparently without cause or connection. But as Nathaniel began to fade, reduced to a specter of the man he once was, when he had to accept his limitations and ask for help, the fun came to an end. He lost his zest for life, felt that everything around him was pale and faint, and abandoned himself to nostalgia for the past like an old man, regretting some things he had done and the many more he had not managed to achieve. He knew his life would soon be over, and was scared. Lenny did not let him slump into depression; he kept him going with feigned good humor and the constancy of his love, which continued to grow even in such trying circumstances. They met in their little apartment to console one another. Nathaniel lacked the strength and desire to make love, and Lenny did not demand it; he was happy with the moments of intimacy when he could calm Nathaniel if he was shaking with fever, feed him teaspoonfuls of yogurt like a baby, lie by his side listening to music, rub his lesions with balm, hold him upright on the toilet. Toward the end, when Nathaniel could no longer leave home and Alma took over the role of nurse with the same tender persistence as Lenny, her role remained that of his friend and wife, while Lenny was the great love of his life. Or so Alma came to see it during their night of exchanged secrets.

At dawn, when at last Nathaniel fell asleep, she looked Lenny Beal's phone number up in the directory and called to beg him to come and help her. She told him they could better endure the agony of those days if they were shared. Lenny arrived in less than thirty minutes. Alma, still wearing pajamas and a dressing gown, opened the door. He found himself confronted by a woman exhausted from fatigue and suffering; she saw a handsome young man, hair still damp from the shower, with the bluest eyes in the world, now rimmed with red.

"I'm L-Lenny Beal," he stammered, clearly moved.

"Please call me Alma. This is your home," she responded.

He held out his hand but failed to complete the handshake before they fell into each other's arms.

Lenny began visiting the Sea Cliff mansion on a daily basis, after his working hours at the dental clinic. They told Larry and Doris and the household staff that Lenny was a nurse. Nobody asked anything further. Alma called a carpenter to fix the jammed door between the bedrooms and left the two men alone. She felt a huge sense of relief when her husband's face lit up at seeing Lenny come in. As dusk fell, the three of them took tea and English muffins and, if Nathaniel was up to it, played cards. By then they had a diagnosis, the worst possible: it was AIDS. The illness had only been given a name a couple of years earlier, but by now everyone knew it was a death sentence; sufferers died sooner or later, it was merely a matter of time. Alma did not want to know why Nathaniel and not Lenny was infected, but even if she had asked, no one could have given her a clear answer. Cases were multiplying at such a rate that there was already talk of a worldwide epidemic and of God's punishment on the infamy of homosexuality. AIDS was a word only mentioned in a whisper, not to be uttered in a family or community, as it was tantamount to declaring unforgivable perversions. The official explanation, even to the family, was that Nathaniel had cancer. As conventional medicine had nothing to offer, Lenny went to Mexico to look for mysterious drug treatments, which ended up having no effect, while Alma ran around seeking out whatever alternative therapies could offer, from oils, herbs, and acupuncture in Chinatown to mud baths with magical properties at Calistoga Spa. This led her to appreciate the crazy

The Japanese Lover

efforts Lillian had resorted to in her attempt to cure Isaac; she even regretted having thrown Baron Samedi's statuette into the garbage.

Nine months later, Nathaniel's body was wasted to a skeleton by the ravages of the illness, while air could scarcely enter the blocked labyrinths of his lungs. He suffered from insatiable thirst and skin ulcers, he had lost his voice, and his mind was wandering deliriously. And so one sleepy Sunday when they were alone in the house, Alma and Lenny took each other's hand in the dark, airless room and begged Nathaniel to give up the struggle and go peacefully. They could no longer bear to witness his torment. In a miraculous moment of lucidity, Nathaniel opened eyes clouded by pain and his lips formed a thank-you. They took this for what it actually was: a command. Lenny kissed him on the lips before injecting him with a massive dose of morphine via the intravenous drip bag. On her knees on the far side of the bed, Alma softly reminded her husband how much she and Lenny loved him and how much he had given them and many others, that he would always be remembered, that nothing could ever separate them.

Over a cup of mango tea and reminiscences at Lark House, Alma and Lenny wondered how they could have let three decades go by without making any attempt to contact each other again. After closing Nathaniel's eyes and helping Alma to lay out the body to present it to Larry and Doris, and to remove any telltale traces of what had happened, Lenny said good-bye to Alma and left. They had spent months in the total intimacy created by suffering and flickering hope. They had never seen each other in the light of day, only in a bedroom that smelled of menthol and of death well before it came to bear Nathaniel away. They had shared sleepless nights, drinking watered-down whisky or smoking marijuana to relieve the anguish, while they told each other the story of their lives, unearthed longings and secrets, and came to know each other intimately. In the face of such prolonged agony there was no room for any kind of pretense; they revealed what they truly were when they were alone with themselves, stripped naked. Despite or perhaps because of this, they had come to love one another with a transparent, desperate tenderness that called for a separation, as it would not have resisted the inevitable attrition of the everyday.

"We had a strange friendship," said Alma.

"Nathaniel was so grateful that the two of us were with him that he once asked me to marry you when you were widowed. He didn't want to leave you unprotected."

"What a wonderful idea! Why didn't you suggest it, Lenny? We'd have made a fine couple. We'd have been companions and watched each other's backs, like Nathaniel and I did!"

"I'm gay, Alma."

"So was Nathaniel. We would have had a sexless marriage, without a marital bed, you with your own love life, and me with Ichimei. Very convenient, given that we could neither of us show our love in public."

"There's still time. Will you marry me, Alma Belasco?"

"But didn't you tell me you were going to die soon? I don't want to be widowed a second time."

At this they burst out laughing, and their laughter spurred them to go to the dining room and see if there was anything tempting on the menu. Lenny offered Alma his arm, and they walked along the glassed-in corridor to the main house, the chocolate magnate's former mansion, feeling their age but contented, wondering why people talk so much about sadness and illness and not about happiness.

"What can we do with this happiness that appears for no obvious reason, the joy that needs no cause to exist?" asked Alma.

They took short, shaky steps, leaning on one another and feeling the late-autumn cold, dazed by the rush of stubborn memories that gripped them, memories of love, flooded by a mutual happiness. Alma pointed out to Lenny a fleeting glimpse of pink veils in the park, but it was growing dark, and possibly it wasn't Emily heralding disaster, but a mirage like so many others at Lark House.

THE JAPANESE LOVER

*O*n Friday Irina Bazili arrived early at Lark House to look in on Alma before starting her day. Alma no longer needed her assistance to get dressed, but she was grateful to the young woman for coming to her apartment to share the day's first cup of tea.

"Marry my grandson, Irina; you'd be doing all the Belascos a favor," she often said to her.

Irina ought to have explained that she hadn't yet succeeded in overcoming the terrors of the past, but could not mention it without dying of shame. How could she tell Seth's grandmother that the monsters of her memory poked their lizard heads out of their lairs whenever she thought of making love with him? He understood that she wasn't ready to talk and stopped pressing her to see a psychiatrist; for the time being it was enough for him to be her confidant. They could wait. Irina had proposed a drastic solution: to watch together the videos filmed by her stepfather, which were still circulating around the world and which would go on tormenting her to the end of her days. But Seth was afraid that once unleashed, these deformed creatures would become uncontrollable. His prescription consisted in taking things little by little, with love and good humor, advancing in a dance of two steps forward and one step back. They now slept in the same bed, and occasionally awoke in each other's arms.

On this particular morning, Irina did not find Alma in her apartment or see any trace of the overnight bag she took on her secret outings, or her silk nightgowns. For the first time, however, Ichimei's portrait had also gone. She already knew the car wasn't going to be in its parking place but Irina was not alarmed, because Alma had grown steadier on her legs and she assumed Ichimei would be waiting for her. She wasn't going to be alone.

Since it was Saturday, Irina did not have a shift at Lark House and had snoozed until nine, a luxury she could afford on weekends now that she was living with Seth and had given up washing dogs. He woke her with a big cup of milky coffee and sat beside her on the bed to plan their day. He had come in from the gym, freshly showered, his skin moist and still pumped up from the exercise, never imagining there would be no plans with Irina that day: it was to be a day for farewells. At that moment the phone rang. It was Larry Belasco calling to tell his son that his grandmother's car had slid off a rural track and rolled fifty feet down a ravine.

"She is in the intensive care unit at Marin General Hospital," he told him.

"Is it serious?" Seth asked, terrified.

"Yes. Her car was completely wrecked. I've no idea what my mother was doing driving out there."

"Was she on her own, Papa?"

"Yes."

At the hospital, they found Alma conscious and lucid, despite the drugs being dripped into her vein, which, according to the doctor, would have knocked out a horse. She had received the full impact of the accident. In a more solid car, the disaster would possibly not have been so great, but the tiny lime-green Smart car was smashed to pieces and Alma, strapped in by her safety belt, was crushed. While the rest of the Belasco family were grief stricken in the waiting room, Larry explained to Seth that one extreme course of action remained: to slit Alma open, reposition the displaced inner organs in their proper places, and keep her body split open for several days until the swelling subsided and they could intervene. After that they could consider operating on the broken bones. The risk, already huge for a young person, was much greater for someone in her eighties like Alma; the surgeon who saw her at the hospital did not dare attempt it. Catherine Hope, who came at once with Lenny Beal, maintained that such a major operation would be cruel and pointless; all they should do was to keep Alma as comfortable as possible and await her end, which would not be long in coming. Irina left the family discussing with Cathy the proposal to move her to San Francisco, where there would be better facilities, and slipped silently into Alma's room.

"Are you in pain?" she whispered. "Do you want me to call Ichimei?"

Alma was on oxygen but breathing independently and made a slight sign for her to approach. Irina didn't want to think about the wounded body under the sheet-covered frame; instead she focused on her face, which remained intact and looked more beautiful than ever.

"Kirsten," stammered Alma.

"You want me to find Kirsten?" Irina asked in surprise.

"And tell them not to touch me," added Alma in a clear voice, before closing her eyes in exhaustion.

Seth phoned Kirsten's brother and that afternoon he brought her to the hospital. She sat on the only chair in Alma's room, waiting patiently for instructions as she had done during the previous months in the workshop, before she began working with Catherine Hope at the pain clinic. At some point when the last rays of daylight were filtering in through the window, Alma came around from her drug-induced lethargy. She ran her eyes over those around her, trying to recognize them: her family, Irina, Lenny, Cathy; she seemed to revive when her gaze rested on Kirsten. Kirsten got up and approached the bed, took the hand not hooked up to the drip, and began placing wet kisses on it from fingers to elbow, asking Alma anxiously if she was ill, if she was going to get better, and repeating how much she loved her. Larry tried to pull her away, but Alma feebly signed that he should leave them alone.

Larry, Doris, and Seth took the first two nights of the vigil in turn, but by the third Irina understood that the family was at the end of their tether and offered to sit with Alma, who had not spoken since Kirsten's visit and lay dozing, panting lightly like a weary dog, freeing herself from life. It's not easy either to live or to die, thought Irina. The doctor assured her that Alma was not in pain; she was sedated to the hilt.

At a certain time of night, the sounds on the hospital floor died away. In Alma's room a peaceful twilight reigned, but the corridors were always lit with powerful lights, and there was the reflection from the blue computer screens in the nurses' hub. The murmur of the air-conditioning, Alma's painful breathing, and the occasional sound of footsteps or discreet voices on the far side of the door were the only noises reaching Irina. She had been given a blanket and a cushion to make herself as comfortable as possible, but it was stuffy and she found it impossible to sleep on the chair. She sat on the floor propped against the wall and thought of Alma, who three days earlier was still a passionate woman who had rushed to meet her lover and was now on her deathbed. During a brief moment awake before she once more lapsed into a drug-induced stupor of hallucinations, Alma asked her to put some lipstick on her because Ichimei would be coming. Irina felt a terrible sense of grief, a wave of love for this wonderful old woman, the tenderness of a granddaughter, daughter, sister, friend, while the tears poured down her cheeks, soaking her neck and blouse. She longed for Alma to be gone once and for all to put an end to her suffering, but also wanted her never to leave, wishing that thanks to divine intervention all her displaced organs and broken bones could be mended, that she would be restored to life and they could go back to Lark House and continue living as before. She would devote more time to her, be more at her side, entice her secrets from their hiding place, find a new cat just like Neko, and arrange things so that she could have fresh gardenias every week, without telling her who was sending them.

Images of those she had lost teemed forth, augmenting Irina's sorrow: her grandparents, now the color of earth; Jacques Devine and his topaz scarab; the old people who had died at Lark House over the three years she had worked there; Neko with the kink in his tail and his contented purr; even her mother, Radmila, whom she had forgiven but had heard nothing of for many years. She wished Seth were beside her at that moment, to present him to the characters he did not know in this cast and to be able to rest, clutching his hand. She fell asleep immersed in nostalgia and sadness, curled up in her corner. She didn't hear the nurse enter at regular intervals to check on Alma, adjust the drip and needle, take her temperature and blood pressure, administer sedatives.

In the darkest hour of the night, that mysterious hour when time thins and often the veil between this world and that of the spirits is drawn back, the guest Alma was waiting for arrived at long last. He came in noiselessly, on rubber-soled slippers, so slender that Irina would not have woken but for Alma's low moan when she sensed him near her. Ichi! He was by the bedside leaning over Alma, but Irina, who could only see him in profile, would have recognized him anywhere, anytime, for she too had been waiting for him. He was just as she had imagined him when she studied his portrait in its silver frame: of average height with strong shoulders, his hair thick and gray, skin almost greenish in the monitor light, his features noble and serene. Ichimei! It seemed as though Alma opened her eyes and repeated his name, but Irina wasn't sure, and understood they should be left alone for this final farewell. She rose quietly so as not to disturb them and slipped out of the room, closing the door behind her. She waited in the corridor, pacing up and down to bring the circulation back into her legs; drank two glasses of water from the drinking fountain by the elevator; then took up her post again outside Alma's door.

At four in the morning, the shift changed and a new nurse arrived and found Irina blocking the entrance. She was a large black woman who smelled of fresh bread.

"Please, leave them on their own a little longer," the young woman begged her, and went on to pour out the story of the lover who had come to keep Alma company on this final journey. They could not be interrupted.

"At this time of day there are no visitors," the bewildered nurse told Irina, pushing her aside and opening the door.

Ichimei had gone, and the air in the room was filled with his absence.

They kept a private vigil over Alma's body for a few hours in the Sea Cliff mansion, where she had spent almost all her life. Her simple pine box was placed in the dining room lit by eighteen tall candles in the same solid silver menorahs the family had always used for traditional celebrations. Although they were not observant, the Belascos arranged the funeral rites in accordance with the rabbi's instructions. Alma had frequently repeated that she wished to go from bed to cemetery, with no synagogue rite of passage between. Two pious women from the Chevra Kadisha washed the body and wrapped it in a white linen shroud without pockets, to signify equality in death and the abandonment of all worldly goods.

Like an invisible shadow, Irina joined in the mourning, remaining behind Seth. He seemed beside himself with grief, unable to believe his immortal grandmother had suddenly abandoned him. A family member had remained with Alma until the moment they took her to the cemetery, to give her spirit time to detach and bid good-bye. Flowers were considered frivolous and so there were none, but Irina carried a gardenia to the cemetery, where the rabbi recited a brief prayer: *Baruch dayan ha'emet*, "Blessed is the true judge." The coffin was lowered into the ground, alongside that of Nathaniel, and when the family members came to throw handfuls of earth to cover it, Irina let her gardenia drop onto her friend. That night saw the start of seven days of mourning in seclusion and shiva prayers. In an unexpected gesture, Larry and Doris asked Irina to stay with them, to console Seth. Like the rest of the family, Irina put a piece of torn fabric on her chest, as a symbol of mourning.

On the seventh day, after receiving the line of visitors who came to offer their condolences each afternoon, the Belascos resumed their everyday routines, returning to their own lives. A month after the funeral, they would light a candle in Alma's name, and at the end of a year there would be a simple ceremony when her name was engraved on the headstone. By that time, most of those who had known her would think of her only occasionally. Alma would live on in her silk screens, in her grandson Seth's obsessive memory, and in the hearts of Irina Bazili as well as Kirsten, who would never comprehend where she had gone. During shiva, Irina and Seth impatiently waited for Ichimei Fukuda to put in an appearance, but the seven days went by without a sign of him.

The first thing Irina did after the week of ritual mourning was to go to Lark House to collect Alma's belongings. She had obtained Hans Voigt's permission to take a few days off but soon had to return to work. The apartment was exactly as Alma had left it, since Lupita had decided not to clean until the family relinquished it. The scant pieces of furniture, bought to be of use rather than decorative in such a reduced space, were to be donated to the Shop of Forgotten Objects, except for the apricot-colored armchair where the cat had spent his last years. Irina decided to give this to Cathy, who had always liked it. As she put the clothes into suitcases—the pairs of baggy trousers, linen tunics, long vicuña wool jackets, silk scarves—she wondered who would inherit all this, wishing she herself was as tall and strong as Alma to be able to wear her clothes, to wear bright-red lipstick like her and use her masculine bergamot-and-orange-scented cologne. She put everything else into boxes, which the Belasco chauffeur would pick up later. In them were the albums that traced Alma's life, some documents, a few books, the gloomy oil painting of Topaz, and little else.

Irina realized that Alma had prepared her departure as thoroughly as she did everything: she had divested herself of all the superfluous and kept only the indispensable; she had sorted out both her belongings and her memories. During the week of shiva Irina had found time to mourn, but as she swept away Alma's presence at Lark House, she said good-bye again; it was like burying her a second time. Overcome with grief, she sat down amidst the boxes and cases and opened the bag Alma always took with her on her escapades, which the police had recovered from the ruins of the Smart car and which Irina had brought back from the hospital. Inside she found Alma's silk nightshirts, her lotions and creams, a couple of changes of clothes, and the portrait of Ichimei in its silver frame. The glass was splintered. She removed the pieces carefully and took out the photograph, to bid farewell to the mysterious lover. It was then that a letter that Alma must have kept behind the photograph fell into her lap.

At that moment somebody pushed the door half-open and timidly stuck their head in. It was Kirsten. Irina got to her feet, and Kirsten hugged her with her customary enthusiasm.

"Where is Alma?" she asked.

"In heaven," was the only answer that occurred to Irina.

"When will she return?"

"She won't be coming back, Kirsten."

"Never ever?"

"No."

A shadow of sorrow or concern flitted across Kirsten's innocent face. She took off her glasses, wiped them on the edge of her T-shirt, and put them back on before poking her face closer to Irina, to see her more clearly.

"Do you promise me she won't return?"

"I promise you. But you have a lot of friends here, Kirsten, and we all love you very much."

Kirsten signaled for her to wait and set off down the glassed-in corridor, her flat feet clumping, toward the chocolate magnate's mansion, where the pain clinic was housed. Fifteen minutes later she returned with her knapsack on her back, panting from her haste, which her big heart had difficulty coping with. She closed and then locked the apartment door, drew the curtains stealthily, and put her fingers to her lips to warn Irina to keep quiet. Finally she handed her the knapsack and waited, hands behind her back and a knowing smile on her face as she rocked back and forth on her heels. "It's for you," she said.

Undoing the backpack, Irina saw several packets tied with rubber bands and knew instantly they were the letters Alma had received so regularly and that she and Seth had sought for so long, the ones from Ichimei. They had not been lost forever in a bank vault as the two of them had feared, but had been stored in the safest place in the world, in Kirsten's backpack. Irina understood now that Alma, realizing death was drawing near, had given Kirsten the responsibility of looking after them and had told her who to give them to. But why to her? Why not to her son or grandson?

Irina took it as a posthumous message from Alma, her way of showing how much she loved and trusted her. At that moment, she could feel something in her chest shattering like a clay vessel, while her heart swelled with profound gratitude. Faced with such a proof of friendship, she realized how deeply cherished she was, as she had been during her early childhood. The monsters of her past were beginning to recede, and her stepfather's videos, which had exerted such frightening power over her, were somehow reduced to their true dimensions. They seemed like bleak carcasses fed on by anonymous scavengers without identity or soul, now powerless.

"My God, Kirsten. Just imagine, I've lived half my life fearing something that isn't real."

"For you," Kirsten repeated, pointing to the contents of her backpack strewn across the floor.

That afternoon, when Seth returned to his apartment, Irina threw her arms around his neck and kissed him with a newfound joy, scarcely appropriate to a time of mourning.

"I've got a surprise for you, Seth," she announced.

"Me too. But tell me yours first."

Irina steered him impatiently toward the granite kitchen island, where she had put the packets of letters from the backpack.

"These are Alma's letters. I was waiting for you to come to open them."

The packets were numbered from one to eleven, and con-

tained ten envelopes apiece, all except the first, which had six letters and a few drawings. They sat on the sofa and looked at them
in the order their owner had left them. A hundred and six missives
in total, some brief and others longer, some more informative than
others, all signed simply "Ichi." The ones in the first packet were
written on sheets torn from an exercise book in a childish hand,
from Tanforan and Topaz, and were so badly censored that their
meaning was lost. The drawings already hinted at the polished
style and firm brushstrokes that characterized the painting that
Alma had taken with her to Lark House. It would take them several days to read all the correspondence, but a swift glance at the
other packets showed they were dated from 1969 on. Forty years
of an irregular correspondence that had one thing in common:
they were all love letters.

"I also found a letter dated January 2010; it was behind Ichi-
mei's portrait. But all these letters are old and are addressed to the
Belascos' house at Sea Cliff. Where are those she received at Lark
House over the past three years?"

"I think these are the ones, Irina."

"I don't understand."

"My grandmother collected Ichimei's letters her whole life
through, all those that came to Sea Cliff, where she always lived.
Then, when she moved to Lark House, she began sending the letters to herself every so often, one by one, in the yellow envelopes
you and I saw. She received and read them, treasuring them as if
they were new."

"Why would she do such a thing, Seth? Alma was in her right
mind. She never showed any sign of senility."

"That's what is so extraordinary, Irina. She was well aware of what she was doing; she wanted to keep the great love of her life alive. That old woman, who seemed so armor plated, was at heart an incurable romantic. I'm sure she also sent herself the weekly gardenias, and that her escapades were not spent with her lover; she went alone to the cabin at Point Reyes to relive her past encounters there, to dream about what she could no longer share with Ichimei."

"But why not? She was on her way back from being with him when the accident occurred. Ichimei went to the hospital to say good-bye to her; I saw him kiss her, I know they loved each other, Seth."

"You couldn't have seen him, Irina. I was surprised he showed no reaction to my grandmother's death, given that the news came out in the press. If he loved her as much as we believe, he would have attended the funeral or have offered his condolences at shiva. Today I decided to look him up; I wanted to meet him and lay to rest the doubts I had about my grandmother. It was very easy: all I had to do was turn up at the Fukudas' nursery."

"It still exists?"

"Yes. It's run by Peter Fukuda, one of Ichimei's sons. When I told him my name, he received me very warmly, because he knew all about the Belasco family, and he went to call Delphine, his mother. She is very friendly and pretty; she has one of those Asian faces that seem never to age."

"She's Ichimei's wife. Alma said she met her at your great-grandfather's funeral."

"She's not Ichimei's wife, Irina. She's his widow. Ichimei died of a heart attack three years ago."

"That's impossible!" she exclaimed.

"He died around the same time my grandmother went to live at Lark House. Possibly the two things are connected in some way. I think that letter dated 2010, the last one Alma received, was his good-bye."

"But I saw Ichimei at the hospital!"

"You saw what you wanted to see, Irina."

"No, Seth. I'm sure it was him. That is what happened: Alma loved Ichimei so much that she succeeded in having him come to find her."

January 8, 2010

*How exuberant and boisterous the universe is, Alma!
It turns and turns, and the only constant is everything
changes. It is a mystery we can only appreciate out of
stillness. I'm living through a very interesting stage. My
spirit contemplates the changes in my body with fascination,
but this contemplation is not from a distance, but from
within. My spirit and my body are together in this process.
Yesterday you told me how you missed our youthful illusion
of immortality. Not me. I take pleasure in my reality of being
a mature man, or should I say an old one. If I were going to
die in the next three days, what would I do during that time?
Nothing! I would empty myself of everything but love.*

*We have often said that loving each other is our destiny,
that we have loved each other in past lives and will go
on meeting in lives to come. Or it may be there is no past
or future, and everything takes place simultaneously in
the universe's infinite dimensions. If that is so, we remain
together forever.*

*It's fantastic to be alive. We are still seventeen years old,
my Alma.*

Ichi

Turn the page for an exciting extract from
Isabel Allende's latest novel

In the Midst of Winter

Out now in hardback, eBook and eAudio,
out soon in paperback

Lucia

Brooklyn, New York, 2016

At the end of December 2015 winter had not yet reached Brooklyn. As Christmas approached with its jangle of bells, people were still in short sleeves and sandals, some of them celebrating nature's oversight and others fearing global warming, while to the confusion of squirrels and birds, artificial trees sprinkled with silver frost appeared in house windows. Three weeks after New Year's Day, when no one gave any further thought to how out of step the calendar was, nature suddenly awoke from its fall torpor and unleashed the worst snowstorm in living memory.

Lucia Maraz was cursing the cold in her Prospect Heights basement apartment, a cement-and-brick cave with a mountain of snow blocking the doorway. Blessed with the stoic character of her people, accustomed as they are to earthquakes, floods, occasional tsunamis, and political cataclysms, she grew worried if no disaster occurred within a given length of time. Yet she was unprepared for this Siberian winter that seemed to have struck Brooklyn in error.

Storms in Chile are limited to the Andes Mountains and the deep south of Tierra del Fuego, where the continent crumbles into islands torn to shreds by the austral wind, where ice splits bones and life is brutal. Lucia was from Santiago, undeservedly renowned for its benign climate, although its winters are damp and cold, its summers hot and dry. The capital lies nestled among purple mountains that at dawn are sometimes covered in snow, and then the purest light on earth is reflected from their dazzling peaks. On very rare occasions a sad, pale dusting falls over the city like ashes, never managing to turn the urban landscape white before melting into dirty slush. Snow is always pristine from a distance.

In Lucia's Brooklyn cave, largely below street level and with poor heating, snow was a nightmare. The frost-covered glass impeded light from entering through the small window, and the inside gloom was hardly dispelled by the naked bulbs dangling from the ceiling. The apartment contained only the essentials: a jumble of shabby second- or thirdhand furniture and a few kitchen utensils. Richard Bowmaster, the owner, was not interested in either decor or comfort.

The storm began on Friday with a heavy snowfall followed by a fierce squall that lashed the nearly deserted streets. The force of the wind caused trees to bend and the freezing weather killed many birds who had forgotten to migrate, fooled by the previous month's warmth. When the cleanup operation began, sanitation trucks carted away frozen sparrows along with the scattered debris. However, the mysterious parakeets in Green-Wood Cemetery survived the blizzard, as was confirmed three days later, when they reappeared intact, pecking for crumbs among the gravestones. On Thursday, television reporters with funereal expressions and the solemn tone usually reserved for news about terrorism in far-off countries had predicted the upcoming storm as well as dire consequences for the weekend. A state of emergency was declared in New York, and the dean at NYU, where Lucia worked, had heeded the warning, informing all faculty that Friday classes were canceled. It would have been an adventure to reach Manhattan in any case.

Lucia took advantage of that day's unexpected freedom to prepare a life-restoring *cazuela*, a Chilean soup that lifts downhearted spirits and sick bodies. By now she had been in the United States more than four months, eating mostly at the university cafeteria and with no reason to cook for herself except on a couple of occasions when she did so out of nostalgia or to celebrate a friendship. For this traditional dish she made a hearty, well-seasoned stock; she fried onion and meat, cooked vegetables, potatoes, and pumpkin separately, and finally added rice. Although she used all the pots in the kitchen and it looked as if a bomb had exploded there, the result was well worth it. For it dispelled the feeling of loneliness that had overwhelmed her since the storm began. That loneliness, which in the past used to arrive unannounced like an unwelcome visitor, had now been relegated to a distant corner of her mind.

That night, as the wind roared outside, whipping up the snow and filtering in impudently through the chinks, she felt a visceral childhood dread. She knew she was safe in her cave, that her fear of the elements was absurd, and that there was no cause to disturb Richard, apart from the fact that he was the only person she could turn to in circumstances like this, because he lived on the floor above. At nine in the evening she gave in to her need to hear a human voice and phoned him.

"What are you doing?" she asked, trying to conceal her apprehension.

"Playing the piano. Is the noise disturbing you?"

"I can't hear your piano. The only noise down here is the crash of the end of the world. Is this normal here in Brooklyn?"

"There's bad weather every so often in winter, Lucía."

"I'm scared."

"What of?"

"Just scared, nothing specific. I guess it would be stupid to ask you to come and keep me company for a while. I made a Chilean soup."

"Is it vegetarian?"

"No. Well, never mind, Richard. Good night."

"Good night."

She drank a shot of pisco and buried her head beneath her pillow. She slept badly, waking up every half hour with the same fragmented dream about being shipwrecked in a substance as thick and sour as yogurt.

By Saturday the storm had continued on its raging path toward the Atlantic, but the weather in Brooklyn remained cold and snowy. Lucía did not want to venture out as many streets were still blocked, although efforts to clear them had begun at first light. She would have plenty of time to read and prepare her classes for the coming week. On the news she saw that the storm continued wreaking havoc wherever it went. She was pleased at the prospect of some peace, a good novel, and a rest. Eventually someone would come and clear the snow from her door. That would be no problem, the neighborhood kids were already out offering to work for a few dollars. Lucia appreciated her good fortune, realizing she felt at ease living in this inhospitable Prospect Heights cave, which wasn't so bad after all.

As evening fell, she began to feel bored with being shut in. She shared some of the soup with Marcelo, the Chihuahua, and the two of them settled down together in the bed on the floor, on a lumpy mattress under a mountain of blankets, to watch several episodes of their favorite TV crime series. The apartment was freezing. Lucia put on her wool hat and gloves.

In the first weeks, when her decision to leave Chile had hung heavy on her—there at least she could employ her sense of humor in Spanish—she had consoled herself with the certainty that everything changes. By tomorrow, all of today's misfortunes will be ancient history. In fact, her doubts had been short-lived: she was enjoying her work; she had Marcelo; she'd made friends at the university and in her neighborhood; people were kind everywhere; after going three times to any coffee shop, she would be treated as one of the family. The idea Chileans had that Yankees were cold was a myth. The only person she had to deal with who was somewhat cold was Richard Bowmaster, her landlord. Well, the hell with him.

Richard had paid a pittance for this large Brooklyn brownstone, which was similar to dozens of other houses in the neighborhood. He bought it from his best friend, an Argentinian who suddenly inherited a fortune and returned to his own country to administer it. A few years later, the same house, but more run-down, was worth over three million dollars. He became the owner just before young professionals from Manhattan arrived en masse to buy and refurbish these picturesque dwellings, raising the prices to ridiculous levels. Before this, the neighborhood had been an area of crime, drugs, and gangs where no one dared to walk at night. But by the time Richard moved in, it had become one of the most sought-after areas in the country, despite the garbage cans, the skeletal trees, and all the junk in the yards. Lucia had joked to Richard that he should sell this relic with its rickety stairs and dilapidated doors and grow old living like royalty on a Caribbean island, but Richard was a gloomy man whose natural pessimism was reinforced by the demands and drawbacks of a house with five large empty rooms, three unused bathrooms, a closed-off attic, and a first floor with such high ceilings that you needed an extension ladder to change a lightbulb.

Richard Bowmaster was Lucia's boss at New York University, where she had a one-year contract as a visiting professor. Once the year was over, her life was a blank slate: she would need another job and somewhere else to live while she decided on her long-term future. Sooner or later she would return to end her days in Chile, but that was still quite a way off. And since her daughter, Daniela, had moved to Miami to study marine biology, and was possibly in love and planning to stay, there was nothing to draw Lucia back to her home country. She intended to enjoy her remaining years of good health before she was defeated by decrepitude. She wanted to live abroad, where the daily challenges kept her mind occupied and her heart in relative calm, because in Chile she was crushed by the weight of the familiar, its routines and limitations. Back there she felt she was condemned to be a lonely old woman besieged by pointless memories; in another country, there could be surprises and opportunities.

She had agreed to teach at NYU's Center for Latin American and Caribbean Studies in order to get away from Chile for a while and be closer to Daniela. Also, she had to admit, because Richard Bowmaster intrigued her. She was just emerging from a failed romance and thought Richard could be the cure, a way of definitively forgetting Julian, her last love, the only one to leave any kind of imprint on her since her divorce in 2010. In the years since then, Lucia had learned how few suitors were available for a woman her age. Before Julian appeared, she had had a few insignificant flings. She had known Richard for more than ten years, while she was still married, and had been attracted to him ever since she met him, although she could not have clearly said why. They had contrasting characters and little in common beyond academic matters. Although they had met here and there at conferences, spent hours talking about their work, and kept up a regular correspondence, he had never shown the slightest romantic interest in her. Uncharacteristically, as she lacked the boldness of flirtatious women, Lucia had even hinted at it on one occasion. Before she came to New York, Richard's thoughtful, shy demeanor had been a powerful attraction, for she imagined that a man like him must be deep and serious, noble spirited: a prize for whoever succeeded in overcoming the obstacles he placed in the way of any kind of intimacy.

Lucia still entertained the fantasies of a young girl despite the fact that she was almost sixty-two. She had a wrinkled neck, dry skin, and flabby arms; her knees were heavy; and she had become resigned to watching her waist disappear because she did not have the discipline to combat the process in the gym. Although she had youthful breasts, they were not hers. She avoided looking at herself naked, because she felt much better when she was dressed. Aware of which colors and styles favored her, she kept to them rigorously and was able to purchase a complete outfit in twenty minutes, without ever allowing curiosity to distract her. Like photographs, the mirror was an implacable enemy, because both showed her immobile, with her flaws mercilessly exposed. She thought that if she had any attraction, it lay in movement, for she was flexible and had a grace that was unearned, since she had done nothing to foster it. She was as sweet-toothed and lazy as an odalisque, and if there had been any justice in the world, she would have been obese. Her forebears, spirited and probably hungry people, had bequeathed her a fortunate metabolism. In her passport photograph, where she was staring straight ahead with a dour expression, she looked like a Soviet prison guard, as her daughter, Daniela, said to tease her, but nobody ever saw her looking that stiff. She had an expressive face and knew how to apply makeup.

In short, she was satisfied with her appearance and resigned to the inevitable damages of age. Her body was growing old, but inside she still kept intact the adolescent she once was. She could not imagine the old woman she would be. Her desire to get the most out of life grew greater as her future shrank, and part of that enthusiasm was the vague hope of having someone to cherish, even if this clashed with the reality of a lack of opportunities. She missed sex, romance, and love. The first of these she could obtain every so often, the second was a matter of luck, and the third was a gift from the gods that would probably never happen, as her daughter had told her more than once.

Although Lucia was somewhat sad that she had broken off her affair with Julian, she never regretted it. She wanted stability, but even though he was seventy years old he was still flitting from one relationship to another, like a hummingbird. Despite the advice of her daughter, who advocated the advantages of free love, for Lucia intimacy was impossible with a man distracted by other women. "What is it you're after, Mom? To get married?" Daniela had laughed when she learned her mother was finished with Julian. No, but Lucia wanted to make love in a loving way, for the pleasure of her body as well as the tranquility of her spirit. She wanted to make love with someone who felt as she did. She wanted to be accepted without concealing or pretending anything, to get to know the other person deeply and to accept him in the same way. She wanted somebody she could spend Sunday mornings in bed with reading the newspapers, somebody to hold hands with at movies, to laugh with at nonsense, to discuss ideas with. She had gotten beyond any enthusiasm for fleeting adventures.

However, now that Lucia had grown accustomed to her space, her silence, and her solitude, she had concluded it would be a high price to pay to share her bed, bathroom, and closet, and that no man would be able to satisfy all her needs. In her youth she had thought she was incomplete without being in a loving couple, that something essential was missing. In her maturity she was thankful for the cornucopia of her existence, although she had vaguely thought of turning to an Internet dating site simply out of curiosity. She gave this up at once, because Daniela was sure to find out from Miami. Besides, Lucia did not know how to describe herself so that she seemed more attractive without lying. She guessed that the same thing happened with others; everyone lied.

Men around her age wanted women who were twenty or thirty years younger, which was understandable since she herself would not want to get together with an ailing old man and preferred a younger Romeo. According to Daniela, it was a waste she was heterosexual. There were more than enough single women with rich inner lives and in good physical and emotional condition who were far more interesting than the widowed or divorced men of sixty or seventy out there. Lucia admitted her limitations in this respect but thought it was too late to change. Since her divorce she had had a few brief intimate encounters with one friend or another after a few drinks at a disco, or with strangers on her travels, or at a party. These were nothing to write home about, but they helped her overcome the embarrassment of taking her clothes off in front of a male witness. The scars on her chest were visible, and her virginal breasts belonged to a young bride. Having nothing to do with the rest of her body, they mocked her current anatomy.

Her fantasy of seducing Richard, which had seemed so enticing when she received his invitation to teach at the university, had evaporated barely a week after she moved into the basement apartment. Rather than bringing them closer, their relative proximity—meeting regularly at work, in the street, on the subway, or at the front door to the house—had quickly distanced them. The once warm camaraderie of international meetings and electronic communication had frozen when put to the test of physical closeness. No, there would definitely be no romance with Richard

Bowmaster, which was a shame because he was the kind of tranquil, reliable man she would not have minded being bored with. Lucia was only a year and eight months older than him. As she often told herself, this was a negligible difference, although in secret she admitted that she was at a disadvantage. She felt heavy and was shrinking steadily as her spine contracted, but she could no longer wear very high heels without falling flat on her face. Around her, everyone else seemed to be growing taller. Her students towered over her, as gangly and aloof as giraffes. She was fed up with seeing all the nose hairs of the rest of humanity from down below. Richard on the other hand wore his years with the awkward charm of a professor absorbed in his studies.

As Lucia described him to Daniela, Richard Bowmaster was of medium height, still with enough hair and good teeth, and with eyes somewhere between gray and green depending on the reflection of light on his glasses and the state of his ulcer. He seldom smiled without a real reason, but his permanent dimples and tousled hair gave him a youthful look, even though he walked along staring at the ground, loaded down with books and bent under the weight of all his concerns. Lucia could not imagine what they could be, because he looked healthy, had reached the pinnacle of his academic career, and would be able to retire with the means to ensure a comfortable old age. The only financial burden he had was his father, Joseph Bowmaster, who lived in a senior residence fifteen minutes away, and whom Richard phoned every day and visited a couple of times a week. Although Joseph was ninety-six and confined to a wheelchair, he had more fire in his belly and mental lucidity than many half his age. He spent his time writing letters of advice to Barack Obama.

Lucia suspected that Richard's taciturn appearance hid a store of kindness and a well-disguised wish to help without any fuss, from discreetly serving at a charity soup kitchen to volunteering to monitor the parakeets in the cemetery. Richard must surely have owed that side of his character to his father. Joseph would never allow a son of his to go through life without embracing some worthy cause. In the beginning, Lucia studied Richard to try to find any openings to secure his friendship, but as she was not drawn to the charity soup kitchen or any species of parrot, all they shared was their work, and she could not find a way to insinuate herself into his life. She was not offended by Richard's lack of interest, because he equally ignored the attentions of his female colleagues and the hordes of young girls at the university. His hermit's life was a mystery: Who knew what secrets it concealed? How could he have lived six decades without any unsettling challenges, protected by his armadillo's hide?

By contrast, she was proud of the dramas in her past and wished for an interesting existence in her future. She mistrusted happiness on principle; she found it rather kitschy. She was content to be more or less satisfied. Richard had spent a long period in Brazil, where, to judge by a photograph Lucia had seen, he had been married to a voluptuous young woman, yet neither the exuberance of that country nor that mysterious woman seemed to have rubbed off on him. Despite his odd behavior, Richard always made a good impression. In her description of him to her daughter, Lucia said that he was *liviano de sangre*—light blooded—a Chilean expression for someone who is good natured and makes himself loved without meaning to and for no obvious reason. "He's a strange sort, Daniela. He lives alone with four cats." She added,

"He doesn't know it yet, but when I leave he'll also have to look after Marcelo." She had thought this over carefully. It would be heart wrenching, but she couldn't drag an aged Chihuahua around the world with her.

Eva Luna
Isabel Allende

Meet the unforgettable Eva Luna: a lover, a writer, a revolutionary and above all, a storyteller

Eva Luna is the daughter of a professor›s assistant and a snake-bitten gardener – born poor, orphaned at an early age and working as a servant.

Eva is a naturally gifted and imaginative storyteller. Though she has no wealth, she trades her stories like currency with people who are kind to her. As she shares her stories, she introduces an eccentric cast of characters: the Lebanese émigré who takes her in, her Catholic godmother who believes in saints, a street urchin who grows up to be the leader of the guerrilla struggle, a celebrated trans cabaret star and a young refugee whose flight from post-war Europe will change Eva's life forever.

As Eva tells her story, Isabel Allende brings to life a complex South American country – the rich, the poor, the sophisticated – in a novel that celebrates the power of imagination and storytelling.

'Vibrant, colourful characters; the ordinary fused with the grotesque . . . vivid, elegant narrative. The narrator, Eva Luna, is herself a story-teller in the Allende tradition' *Guardian*

SCRIBNER

The Stories of Eva Luna
Isabel Allende

A captivating collection of short fiction by one of the most beloved writers of our time

Eva Luna is a young woman whose powers as a storyteller bring her friendship and love. Lying in bed with her lover, European refugee and journalist Rolf Carlé, Eva answers his request for a story 'you have never told anyone before' with these twenty-three samples of her vibrant artistry. Interweaving the real and the magical, she explores love, vengeance, compassion and female power, depicting worlds that are at once poignantly familiar and intriguingly new.

Rendered in her sumptuously imagined, uniquely lyrical style, *The Stories of Eva Luna* is a cornerstone of Isabel Allende's work, and in her character Eva Luna she creates a modern-day Scheherazade.

'Eva Luna's stories are delicate, their images akin to poetry ... Perfectly crafted and thematically rich' Barbara Kingsolver

AVAILABLE NOW IN PAPERBACK AND EBOOK

SCRIBNER

Of Love and Shadows
Isabel Allende

Irene Beltrán is a force to be reckoned with. As a magazine journalist – an unusual profession for a woman with her privileged upbringing – she is constantly challenging the oppressive regime. Her investigative partner is photographer Francisco Leal, the son of impoverished Spanish Marxist émigrés.

They are an inseparable team, and – despite Irene's engagement to an army captain – form a passionate connection. When an assignment leads them to uncover an unspeakable crime, they are determined to reveal the truth in a nation overrun by terror and violence. Together they will risk everything for justice – and ultimately to embrace the passion that binds them.

Of Love and Shadows is a moving tale of love, bravery and tragedy.

AVAILABLE NOW IN PAPERBACK AND EBOOK

SCRIBNER